Stained-Glass Curtain

Stained-Glass Curtain

Frank Wardlaw Wright

iUniverse, Inc.
Bloomington

Stained-Glass Curtain

Copyright © 2012 by Frank Wardlaw Wright

All rights reserved. No part of this book may be used or reproduced by any means, graphic, electronic, or mechanical, including photocopying, recording, taping or by any information storage retrieval system without the written permission of the publisher except in the case of brief quotations embodied in critical articles and reviews.

The scripture quotations contained herein are from the New Revised Standard Version Bible, copyright © 1989 by the Division of Christian Education of the National Council of the Churches of Christ in the USA, and are used by permission. All rights reserved.

iUniverse books may be ordered through booksellers or by contacting:

iUniverse
1663 Liberty Drive
Bloomington, IN 47403
www.iuniverse.com
1-800-Authors (1-800-288-4677)

Because of the dynamic nature of the Internet, any web addresses or links contained in this book may have changed since publication and may no longer be valid. The views expressed in this work are solely those of the author and do not necessarily reflect the views of the publisher, and the publisher hereby disclaims any responsibility for them.

Any people depicted in stock imagery provided by Thinkstock are models, and such images are being used for illustrative purposes only.

Certain stock imagery © Thinkstock.

ISBN: 978-1-4759-4439-6 (sc)
ISBN: 978-1-4759-4438-9 (hc)
ISBN: 978-1-4759-4437-2 (e)

Library of Congress Control Number: 2012914552

Printed in the United States of America

iUniverse rev. date: 10/25/2012

for Jeanne

and in memory of
Thomas Perrin Wright and Ella Gaines Wardlaw Wright

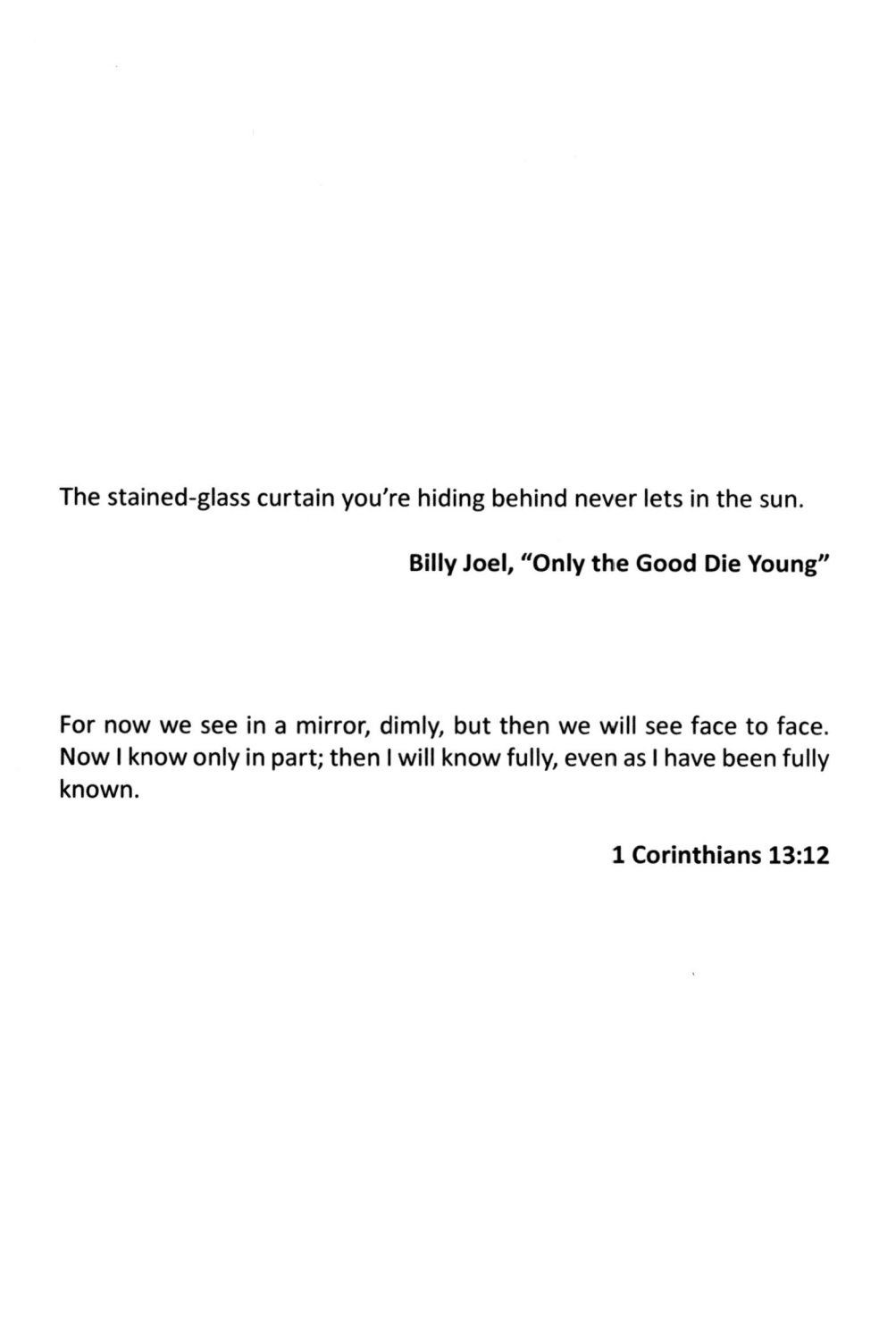

The stained-glass curtain you're hiding behind never lets in the sun.

> Billy Joel, "Only the Good Die Young"

For now we see in a mirror, dimly, but then we will see face to face. Now I know only in part; then I will know fully, even as I have been fully known.

> 1 Corinthians 13:12

Chapter 1

A ... An-gie, A ... An ... gie
The Rolling Stones

"You lied to me!"

"I didn't say it would be easy. I said I was sure you could do it."

"Why do I let you talk me into these things?"

"You're doin' great!"

Splicing epithets into heavy breathing, Angie struggled with her maiden voyage to Blood Mountain. She bitched in equal measure about the steep climb and his treachery.

Her complaints ceased when they reached the top. A huge granite boulder dwarfed the adjacent hiker shelter, and they climbed up to the top for the view. She connected to the magic he always felt on a summit. He knew where the treasures were, but he let her discover them for herself.

"Look at the trees!"

A palette of yellow, orange, rust, and crimson vaulted from the ridges far below. The crisp October sky magnified the colors, reducing miles to yards. Angie reached out to touch the chromatic branches. She drew back her hand, laughing. "My eyes are playing tricks on me."

She fixed her gaze on the southern horizon. The long-range view, free of haze and smog, extended seventy-five miles. Glass and concrete towers, lit by the sun, shimmered against the immense blue curtain.

"Bobby, that's Atlanta!" She was the only one who ever called him Bobby. His parents had insisted from birth that he be Robert.

"Babe, you can almost count the cars on Peachtree."

"And Stone Mountain!" The granite hulk, silhouetted against the azure expanse, rose to the east of the skyline. "Funny. It's not so big from here."

Robert pointed to an isolated, double-humped peak to the west of the city. "Know what that is?"

"Kennesaw!"

"With binoculars, you could spot the Confederate cannon on the ridge. Now, turn around and look to the north."

She pirouetted on the rock. "What's the high one over there? With the tower."

"Brasstown Bald. Highest point in Georgia at 4,784 feet."

"Looks 4,783 to me." She poked him in the stomach, further mocking his penchant for precision.

He reached over her shoulder and pulled a small microfiber towel out of her day pack. "You'll see better if you wipe the sarcasm off your glasses."

They sat on the rock and ate peanut butter and jelly sandwiches. He put his arm around her and squeezed her tightly. They kissed like teenagers on a first date.

Angie smiled. "I'm glad I came. But I won't make a habit of this."

—⁂—

A thick shroud leaked cold drizzle and completely obliterated the panorama. The fog rendered the shelter an occasional apparition. The wind whipped over the exposed rocks and peppered Robert's face with stinging droplets. The small thermometer attached to a zipper on his pack read thirty-seven degrees. He moved on to avoid hypothermia—and any more memories.

The wet, rocky trail descended steeply toward Neel Gap. Sodden laurel branches hung low into the trail, ready to douse any unwary hiker. Robert proceeded gingerly, poling his way with Old Hickory.

Ahead, two men negotiated the slippery slope with trekking poles. Their features were concealed under hooded rain jackets. However, a shock of carrot hair protruded under each bill, and a bushy red beard squirted from the cavern of the taller hiker.

"It's only a matter of time until you do a butt plant in a mud puddle."

"You'd love that," the shorter hiker responded. "You'd blab it to everyone around the campfire tonight."

Robert interrupted their conversation. "You guys enjoying this slop?"

The shorter redhead wheeled to look at him. "I've never had so much fun!" He skipped a few steps to prove his point and almost lost his balance. "Damn rocks are slick." He resumed a cautious gait. "Hey, what's your name?"

"Dances with Snakes."

"Ooh! Sounds interesting. Was it a slow dance?"

"More like a jitterbug."

At the risk of falling, he began to dance again. "I bet you were high-stepping."

"Only briefly. She didn't connect, and left me for another partner." Robert continued. "I see red. Double red. Clues to your trail names?"

"Very perceptive, Dances with Snakes. I'm Raggedy Anton."

Robert moaned.

"Don't insult my mother. She chose a perfectly good Austrian name. And he's Andy."

"That figures. Hello, Andy."

The beard nodded inside the nylon.

"We're getting wet here. Not good for old men and rag dolls. What say I lead down the hill? I'll knock the water off the branches with my stick."

"You're on!" Andy exclaimed with gratitude.

The three splashed down the steep northern slope of Blood Mountain. Robert thrust Old Hickory into the approaching laurel and dislodged beads of water.

"Shit, it's cold on this mountain." Anton shivered under his rainsuit. "Even in the shelter."

"Not surprising at this elevation."

"How high is it?"

"It's 4,470 on the top. Highest point on the AT in Georgia. The winter can resemble New England's."

"We're from Buffalo. It gets cold as hell there. But this Georgia wet and cold cuts right through me."

"The sunny South. Say, you ever been to Walasi-Yi?"

"What's that?"

"The store. Down in Neel Gap."

Andy responded. "We're headed there. First time. We hear they give good advice to northbounders about equipment and stuff."

Robert noticed their large, bulky packs. Years in the backcountry had taught him to keep pack weight down. "Yeah, they'll show you how to ditch the things you don't need."

"We want to be lighter, but we hate to give up creature comforts." Anton looked enviously at Robert's pack. "How much are you carrying?"

"Thirty pounds, with a full load of food. Less when it gets warm."

Andy sighed. "We aren't that streamlined. Hope they can help us."

The sound of a "semi" groaning up Highway 19 rose to meet them. Robert halted their choreography of dodging trees and mud puddles. "Hear that? We're getting close."

Anton perked up. "How far have we hiked from the start, at Springer?"

"About thirty miles."

"Jeez, we've only crossed one paved road. No other sign of humanity."

They hiked around an arm of the main ridge and spotted the highway and the store. They crossed the asphalt in a trot and clamored up the stone steps to the entrance.

Raggedy Anton shouted, "I'm so ready for some civilization!"

Andy reached for the knob. "I'm ready for a warm, dry place."

Robert completed the chorus. "I'm ready for a conversation with a clean person dressed in cotton."

They were greeted by racks of T-shirts, vests, and jackets. To the right were shelves of books, maps, and videos. A back room to the left housed an impressive selection of packs, boots, tents, and sleeping bags. A very clean lady, wearing a gray AT sweatshirt and jeans, sat behind the counter. "Good morning. I'm Lauren. How can I help you?"

Anton spoke in a rush. "We're too heavy! Please give our packs the once-over."

Robert watched patiently as Lauren inventoried the contents of their packs.

"Too many pots. The AT's not the place for gourmet cooking."

"But I'm a great cook!"

"Trust me. All you need to do out here is boil water. You can replace all this aluminum with one small titanium pot, and save at least a pound."

"Okay." Raggedy Anton nodded reluctantly.

She held up a large red fuel bottle. "You're carrying too much fuel. You can get by with one half this size."

"I guess so, if all I'll do is boil water."

Raggedy Anton shared another problem. "Last night, at the shelter up on Blood, we hung our food from the rafters."

"With a steel can baffle?" Lauren asked.

"Just like we were supposed to. Critter proof, we thought. We slept like babies. But I left a Snickers wrapper in the pocket of my pack, down on the floor." He held up his expensive Dana Designs pack and wiggled a finger through a hole gnawed in the pocket. "I'm guessing the mouse was freaked to find foil instead of candy. But not as pissed as I was when I found this damn hole."

"Hiking 101. Don't leave food or trash in your pack. You learned the hard way. But I think I can help." Lauren walked into the alcove where the new packs were on display. She returned with a ripstop nylon patch in cobalt blue. "Try this."

Raggedy Anton was effusive. "Cool! Same color as my pack. I'll sew it on from the inside. It won't even show."

They completed the inventory. The two paid for their purchases and arranged with Lauren to ship home their superfluous items.

She turned to Robert. "What about you?"

"Robert Martin. I have a mail drop."

"I'll check in the back." She left and returned with the box he had mailed before starting out. It contained enough food to get him to Hiawassee. "Here you go."

"And I'll take these." He placed a bottle of orange juice, two bananas, and a candy bar on the counter.

She rang up his purchases and made conversation. "You don't have a hole that needs patching, do you?"

The words caught him off guard. For months he had built labyrinths of distractions. Read a book. Watch a movie. Volunteer at the homeless shelter. Planning for the hike was the ultimate diversion. Just when he thought these dodges were succeeding, a simple little thing, like Lauren's harmless question, pierced his defenses. He heard his own voice answer, "Can you patch a hole in the heart?"

Lauren laughed nervously. She looked into his eyes and became serious. "No, you'll have to fix that hole yourself."

March 14. Bad news. The blister on my left heel popped yesterday. Oozed all over my sock. Turned fifteen bucks of merino into toxic medical waste. Good news. I bathed it in polysporin and zapped the infection. Wrapped it in duct tape this morning. Good as new. The ordeal has made me stronger. I can kick ass all the way to Maine.
The Pilgrim.

Robert closed the spiral notebook. The smudged lettering on the frayed label read, "Official register of Blue Mountain shelter." He laid the chronicle respectfully on the floor.

He took a swig from his Nalgene and set the bottle beside the book. From the edge of the shelter platform, he swung his right foot to and fro, ruffling leaves on the ground below. He dug into the blue foil pouch with his Lexan spork and spread bits of tuna on a piece of Melba toast.

Chit. Chit. Chit.

A red oak towered in front of the shelter. At its base, a junco foraged for morsels dropped by careless hikers. Four more juncos materialized in the dead leaves under the tree. The quintet began to stalk him like a pack of wolves. The arc of tiny predators closed around him as he ate the last of his tuna.

He dipped into the bag of gorp and extracted a fistful of peanuts, almonds, raisins, M&M's, and sunflower seeds. A stray peanut slipped through his fingers and bounced off the shelter floor onto the ground. Emboldened, an opportunistic squirrel scampered toward him along a rotting log.

Robert stood up and walked to the blackened fire ring near the shelter. He inverted the Ziploc that had encased the Melba and sprinkled the crumbs on the ground. The *chitting* grew urgent. He stuffed the empty bag into the pocket of his nylon shorts and moved away with his gorp to take in the view.

Twisted branches from skeletal oaks and poplars reached for the noonday sun. Below them, the ground fell away steeply. Legions of trunks marched down the mountain to the Hiwassee River, crossed the valley, and climbed to the distant ridge beyond. Their gray bark darkened into the trademark smoky blue of the southern Appalachians.

Hello, Blue Ridge.

The initial view of pinnacles to come was the icebreaker, and the thousands of steps to their summits were the discourse that cemented a lasting friendship. The more challenging their slopes, the stronger the bond he forged with them.

Two days of peaks beckoned. Blue Mountain loomed immediately in front. Over its shoulder, the more distant crag of Tray Mountain punctured the blue-and-white mottle.

I'll sleep well when I get to you tonight.

A gentle ridge extended from Tray several miles to the north.

Blue Ridge swag. You'll be easy on my tender knees tomorrow.

Abruptly, the mellow contours of the swag yielded to a heart-pounding ascent.

Kelly Knob. I'm ready for your punishment.

Beyond the Kelly massif, the ridge that cradled the trail was hidden from sight. He visualized its many undulations, and then its sudden plunge of fourteen hundred feet to Dicks Creek Gap, where it crossed the highway to Hiawassee. He retrieved another mouthful of gorp. The delectables conjured pleasurable thoughts of tomorrow night in town.

Real food. A real bed. Clean clothes. First shower in six days.

Chit. Chit.

Robert glanced over his shoulder. The juncos had made quick work of the crumbs. He walked back toward the shelter. The outline of a different mountain range stretched behind a phalanx of gray trunks to the right. He gestured with a thumbs-up.

Brasstown Bald.

He shivered with exhilaration.

I'm on the Appalachian Trail. I've waited twenty years for this.

A sunbeam sneaked through the tree limbs and sparkled on the ring on his outstretched hand. His arm froze in midair. He stared at the band for several seconds. The sunlight branded the inscription inside the ring onto the skin underneath.

Angie. 5-5-67.

The heat shot through his hand and arm to his shoulder. It seared his neck and face. The numbers reached his frontal lobe and transposed in an incandescent burst.

Angie. 10-10-01.

The nascent excitement of his grand adventure exploded like a pricked balloon. His arm dropped limply to his side. His sadness changed quickly to frustration.

Damn you!

He turned again and faced Tray Mountain. He looked at his watch. Twelve thirty. Seven miles to go.

As a parting tribute to the juncos and the squirrel, he scattered several sunflower seeds on the ground. He tucked the bag of gorp into the top pocket of his Newstar. He hoisted the pack onto his back, picked up Old Hickory, and turned toward the path leading from the shelter back to the AT. From the corner of his eye he spied the register, on the wooden floor where he had left it. He sat down and rested the bottom of his pack on the platform. He opened the book to the blank lines under The Pilgrim's entry, and scribbled a terse message.

3/14/02. What makes you stronger is to keep going north.
Dances with Snakes.

―ᴡ―

The ochre road slashed through the carpet of brown leaves. Murky water puddled in the potholes. Even though the sun peeked from behind the high cumuli, Indian Grave Gap was bleak. Robert inhaled a handful of gorp and chased it with two gulps of water. He chose not to remain in an ancient cemetery.

He stowed the bottle and the gorp in their respective pack pockets. A creature of habit, he had trained himself to assign each piece of equipment to a designated place in the pack while hiking, or in the tent while camping, and to return it to that place religiously after use. Rummaging for an item in the rain or the dark was not only inconvenient, but unsettling.

He was not mechanically inclined. Pitching a tent illustrated his limitations. It was not intuitive, but rather a job learned and relearned by constant repetition. He practiced until he was comfortable that in any adverse condition he could erect it quickly and unconsciously.

Soldiers in his army unit had been able to disassemble and reassemble their rifles while blindfolded. He craved that same reflexive precision. His brother Tom teased him about being so anal, but to Robert it was better to be the butt of jokes than to be caught unprepared in the woods.

He rested the pack on his right knee and slid his right arm under the shoulder strap. In a continuous pivot, he lifted the pack onto his right shoulder and slipped the left arm under the other strap. He buckled the hip and sternum clasps and cinched them to the desired tension. He double-checked the four load-leveling straps for optimum shoulder support and comfort. Satisfied with the rigging, he grasped Old Hickory and searched for a white blaze on the trees across the road. He found the "Star in the East" and zigzagged through the ruts in the muddy roadway.

A few yards into the forest, he encountered a rhododendron slick. It differed from the laurel thickets he and the Raggedies had penetrated on Blood Mountain. The ground beneath was covered with a dense growth of galax. The heart-shaped leaves carpeted both sides of the trail for over a hundred feet. No more than six inches tall, they stayed green in water for months after being picked. While hiking in North Carolina as a youth, he had met whole families camped on the ridges, picking bushels of leaves to sell to florists and decorators in the towns below. His mother often adorned their dining room table with a few leaves in a small crystal vase.

In the summer, the plant sent up a cone-shaped stalk with tiny white blooms. The flowers shed onto the dark green leaves, giving the plant a frightful case of dandruff. It had an unmistakable pungent, earthy smell. Like mountain laurel and rhododendron, galax proved the superiority of natural scenery. Its irregular profusion easily shamed any manicured suburban landscape.

In winter, galax naturally turned a dull red. The leafy expanse before him was divided into green and crimson. The reversion in progress was a harbinger of the coming spring. In a few more weeks all the leaves would again be a dark, waxy green. He marveled at this transformation. Only on the trail, isolated in the forest, could he truly appreciate the beauty inherent in the cycles of nature.

A thought discharged in his brain like a pistol shot.

Why weren't you like the galax? A superficial change, then back to normal. What switched on that oncogene?

He was meticulous. She was spontaneous. Yielding to her, he allowed the evening to unfold on her terms. They grilled salmon and corn on the cob in the charcoal smoker and splurged with a large dish of mint chocolate chip, her favorite flavor. After dinner they entwined on the couch with a bottle of white wine and watched *The Gods Must Be Crazy*. She never tired of the African misadventures. After the movie, they showered together, taking turns scrubbing each other's backs. He shampooed her hair, using her favorite herbal formula. They dried each other off and then brushed their teeth. After walking arm in arm to the bedroom, they curled up under the sheet.

He chided her about her frosty feet. Her response was to slide an icy toe up his thigh. "Whatcha gonna do about it?"

In mock anger, he rolled on top of her and pinned her arms in the pillows. For a moment she continued the pretense of a struggle and then lay still. He stared into her intoxicating hazel eyes. "I'm gonna love you warm."

He bent forward and lightly kissed her lashes. His lips found hers for a gentle caress, which ripened into a long, deep kiss. He released her arms and slid to her side. "The best way to get warm is to lose those pj's."

She removed them quickly, and his boxers also. She rolled on top of him and nestled into all the right places. He inhaled with pleasure as her warmth surrounded him. He lay under her, selfishly savoring her rhythm. She whispered in his ear, "You on top, lazy bones."

He slid his hand up her left side to guide her over. His fingers pressed against her breast, near the armpit. She let out a muted cry.

"What?"

"A twinge. Where you poked me."

Angie grasped his hand and led it to the spot. She pressed his fingers into her flesh. She winced again. He felt a lump.

Their eyes met. For the first time ever she was really scared. Her fear was a contagion. It jerked aside the curtain of his present happiness and revealed a dark and empty window.

His recollections fast-forwarded. The doctors' visits, the MRI, the diagnosis, the phone calls to Mandy, Rob, and her parents. Surgery, radiation, and chemo. The doctor's pessimism, his own growing despair. All the questions that began with *why*.

Why didn't it show up on the mammogram six months ago? *Why* did she miss it on her self-exam? *Why* isn't it responding to treatment?

Why is it so virulent? *Why* can't I do anything to help? *Why* her? *Why* her?

The doctors offered no answers. Preoccupied with his own fears and frustrations, he left Mandy and Rob to deal with their mother's deteriorating condition. He was also at a loss with Angie. Every word he spoke, every effort he made was pitifully unequal to the task. Nothing had ever come between them, but now she had a new mate. A deathly apparition stood beside her, and they were speeding away without him.

After the terminal diagnosis, Angie summoned strength from a previously untapped reservoir. She put forward her best spin on what lay ahead. "Concentrate on the good times, Bobby. Remember us at our best. And hike for me. Hike for us."

Then she was gone. What bravery there was left with her.

The shapes of hikers jarred him back to the present. Three ladies in their sixties, he guessed. They sat side by side on a huge log, bootless and sockless, checking intently for blisters. He could only see the crowns of their heads. Gray, brown, and blonde. Robert slowed down, gathering composure for a conversation that he could not avoid. The six pink feet under microscopic inspection ushered him from disconsolation to affected charm.

"Let's see. Six times five is thirty. Do we still have all thirty toes?"

The ladies raised their heads. The blonde offered a flat, midwestern retort. "With our aches and pains, it feels like sixty toes." She eyed his pack and stick. "Okay, wise guy, how far you hiking?"

"Maine." Robert's reply was guarded. It was presumptuous, after only fifty-five miles, to assume he would complete over twenty-one hundred more.

"So are we. That is, if our feets don't fail us."

He asked the stock question. "To whom am I speaking?"

"We're the Go-High-O trio. I'm from Akron. My cousins live in Toledo."

Trail names ran the gamut, from uninspired to ingenious to outrageous. Robert mentally graded "Go-High-O" as a C+. At this point the ladies should ask about his trail name. He did not want to talk about himself, so he rechanneled the conversation.

"How long have you been hiking?"

"About fifteen years, dear. Decided this winter it was now or never. For the big one."

"Need anything for blisters?"

The blonde replied, "You name it, we got it. Moleskin, duct tape, polysporin. And we have a great support group. Husbands, children, grandchildren. Up and down the trail."

The brunette interrupted. "My son's from Chattanooga. He's meeting us at Dicks Creek Gap tomorrow night to take us to Hiawassee."

"Looking forward to that shower?"

"You better believe it! Now I understand why cleanliness is next to godliness."

Robert sensed an opportunity to disengage. "I plan to go there tomorrow too. But I need to get to Tray tonight." He gripped his stick. "Nice meeting you. I'm heading up the trail."

"Be careful hiking alone," said Go-High-O blonde. "Until we see you again."

Robert proceeded up the path. Her words reverberated. He was *not* hiking alone. He was a trio, like the Ohio ladies. Dances with Snakes and his companions, Grief and Memories.

He tried to focus on the trail, but it worked against him. The AT climbed a ridge toward Tray Gap, and his despondency rose in concert with the path. He walked through a grove of giant poplars. Their large branches spread high above and pressed down on him. The height and girth of the trees made him feel small and insignificant.

God, You don't give a shit, do You? Where the hell were You when Angie needed You?

He bent over, gasping. His heart rate accelerated. He took several deep breaths to clear his head. All thoughts, recollections, and sensory perceptions reminded him that she was gone. He couldn't walk away from that aching hole.

He was traveling with two companions, but one was monopolizing the conversation. He was listening too much to Grief and wallowing in the puddles of anguish conjured up by his thoughts. Angie had charged him to remember their best times.

He recalled a night out with friends at a karaoke bar. A hopeless monotone, he quietly drank beer while others sang. Angie was in her element. The lead alto in the church choir, she loved to sing extemporaneously and relished any chance to perform. When her turn came, she bounded to the stage, grabbed the mike, and belted out her rendition of "Hit Me with Your Best Shot." Every time she repeated the refrain, she faced him down. She finished to great applause and returned to the table with a devilish grin. "Okay, lover, fire away."

He rose to the challenge. Feeding off her confidence and fortified with the recklessness of four beers, he performed. Rising above limited skills, he became Mick Jagger. His pouting, sneering lips devoured the microphone.

A ... Angie, I still love you, baby. Everywhere I look, I see your eyes.

―⁂―

At first light, he crawled out of the down mummy and dressed quickly in the brisk chill. He stuffed the sleeping bag into its sack and rolled up his Thermarest pad. He assembled cereal, powdered milk, cup, spork, and Nalgene and stepped out of the tent. Avoiding the taut ropes stretching the rainfly, he sliced through the lingering black to a large rock outcrop. He sat in a natural depression at the top of the cold rock and waited for his butt to warm it up.

A distant ridge in the east stood in relief against the gloom. To the west, and closer at hand, the silhouette of Tray Mountain also lay black on the black sky. A pale sliver of moon hung overhead. In the fading darkness, he mixed powdered milk and water in his cup and stirred with the spork until the clumps disappeared. He poured the milk into his bag of cereal and scooped out a mouthful.

He looked east again. The sky behind the ridge was a deep crimson. He watched it lighten into a rich lavender, burnt orange, fire pink, and finally bright yellow. He looked west to Tray. Morning came more slowly. The navy silhouette lingered against the midnight sky. He glanced once more to the east. The top of the sun broke over the ridge and forced him to look away.

The contrasting skies yanked him in two directions. Dawn, with its warmth and light, promised a new start.

I've waited twenty years to hike the AT.

The cold western darkness reanimated his forebodings.

Do I really think it will be any better out here?

The new moon was winning out over the sun. His sense of adventure was eroding. With great effort he forced himself to challenge his enduring malaise. He had put it in its place yesterday, but it was back this morning, sowing doubts about his hike (his hike!) in the same way a "super cell" spawns tornadoes. It was too persistent simply to wish it away. He needed a procedure to deal with it. He would have to practice and practice the directions for taking it down daily, just like his tent.

He realized he had to continue, at least for today. He was ten miles deep in the woods. Regardless of how he felt, he had to keep going to get out. Hiawassee, and not Tray Mountain, was the place of decision.

He finished his cereal, returned to camp, and collapsed his Light Year CD. In ten minutes he was packed and ready to leave. He walked to the spring to fill the two Nalgenes. In the mounting sunlight, he shouldered his pack and followed the side trail back to the AT. He adjusted his straps and hip belt, and also checked to make sure his two companions were riding securely on his shoulders.

While preparing for the thru-hike, Robert had composed a prayer. He had hoped it would be a way to ground himself. But given his state of mind, reciting it now seemed a fruitless exercise.

You didn't care yesterday. Why should I think You would today?

He turned left on the AT toward Hiawassee. Something inside urged him to resist doubt and sarcasm. He uttered the words with lackluster conviction.

God, I'm a thru-hiker. Today, I want to go from Tray campsite to Dicks Creek Gap. Please give me wisdom, patience, and perseverance. Thank You for letting me walk in Your world.

He strode to the northeast. The warmth from the rising sun permeated the skin on his face. His spirits lifted. At least for today, he was walking away from the darkness behind him, walking away from the siren of despair.

It occurred to him that he had never been a quitter. It also occurred to him that he might have found a procedure. He repeated his supplication.

Please give me wisdom, patience, and perseverance.

Chapter 2

Your rod and your staff, they comfort me ...
Psalm 23:4

A prolonged rumble woke Robert from a deep sleep. The spatter on the motel window was not as jarring as the drum roll on a shelter's tin roof, but it was just as ominous. Between bites of breakfast, he watched the merciless rain pelt the cars in the parking lot. On the shuttle ride from Hiawassee back to the AT, the mesmeric rhythm of the windshield wiper on the Chevy pickup lulled him into a false security. However, the full force of the deluge registered when he exited the cab at the gap. The drops beaded on his jacket like water on a freshly waxed car. He was thankful to be inside the Gore-Tex chrysalis, and thankful for the waterproof nylon that enveloped his pack. The truck splashed back to town. Alone with his thoughts, Robert chanted the favorite thru-hiker mantra.

No rain, no Maine! No rain, no Maine!

His personal standard for untimely rain had been established on a weekender in the Smokies several years earlier. He and his brother Tom had been thoroughly drenched fifteen minutes out of Newfound Gap on their way to Mount LeConte. He greeted the new record with resignation. He walked up the trail from the road and steeled his resolve by reciting his prayer.

God, I'm a thru-hiker. Today I want to go from Dicks Creek Gap to Muskrat Creek Shelter. Please give me wisdom, patience, and perseverance. Thank You for letting me walk in Your world. And thanks for Gore-Tex. I didn't wait twenty years just to get my butt soaked.

In one hour of steady rain, no outside moisture penetrated his suit. However, he perspired heavily in the thick humidity. He opened the pit-zips of his jacket, but not enough heat escaped to keep him cool. Sweat drenched his tee, and runoff from the shirt challenged the wicking properties of his polypro briefs. He had washed his clothes in Hiawassee and wished for sunny weather to keep them crisp. Instead, the clammy underwear he detested was a *fait accompli*. His hopes for keeping dry washed away in the rivulets flowing off the trail at the waterbars.

Each footstep spattered a circle of Georgia clay. The bottom three inches of his black rain pants were a mahogany cake, an unbroken continuation of the incrustation on his Sundowners. Underneath the mud on his boots, the Gore-Tex membrane kept his feet dry. It was small comfort.

The trail reached a ridge top and began to descend. Remembering earlier map reconnaissance, Robert concluded he was close to Cowart Gap. It would be a good place to take a break.

The rain subsided. He longed to get out of the suit, but he resisted any premature conclusion that the spring storm was over. His inclination to look for a silver lining often betrayed him.

He wished for May, when he could send the rain gear home. Higher temperatures meant less danger of hypothermia. The school solution for dealing with summer precipitation was to get wet. Rain felt good when hot and sweaty, particularly if he had dry clothes to change into at night.

He and Tom once had an animated discussion on the most significant advancements in backpacking gear in the last century. The finalists were Gore-Tex, Polartec, foam sleeping pads, and Ziplocs. Robert used the bags to protect everything from maps and matches to toilet paper. He "zippered" his camp clothes in the large one-gallon size.

He also took special precaution with the sleeping bag, to the point of anality. His light-weight down mummy was warmer than the synthetics, as long as it stayed dry. When wet, it lost its ability to insulate. He stuffed it first into a water-resistant sack and then inside a waterproof bag. The bag rode in his backpack under the nylon cover. In all his years of hiking, the down got damp only once, when his own sweat permeated the layers.

The trail flattened out when he reached the gap. To his surprise, large splotches of green poked through the mist. The first leaves on the hardwoods were weeks away. He had expected more brindled trunks with limbs devoid of foliage, but an impressive stand of pines towered above the forest floor. He moved underneath the arbor into a pristine grotto. The verdant boughs sheltered a thick mat of needles underfoot. The incessant pounding on nylon gave way to a gentle drip from the canopy. He stood motionless for several moments and enjoyed the stillness.

Robert leaned his pack against a tree, with Old Hickory beside. He took off the rain cover, shook it vigorously to shed water, and looped the drawstrings around a nub on the pine.

He pulled a Clif bar from the top pocket of the pack. Carrot Cake was his favorite flavor. He peeled back the foil wrapper and devoured it in large bites. The big breakfast at the motel clung to his ribs. With the snack to tide him over, he wouldn't need lunch until one o'clock.

He washed down the energy bar with several gulps of water. Given the humidity, he would need at least a gallon of water to stay hydrated throughout the day.

He looked around. A pair of blue rain pants, with ankle zippers open, hung from a dead limb of a nearby tree. A navy blue pack, flanked by a set of Leki trekking poles, rested against the trunk below. A blue-and-white patch, sewn onto one of the pack pockets, caught his eye. Even from a distance, he recognized the iconic Duke Blue Devil.

The leaves rustled behind him. Robert turned toward the sound. A young man emerged from the fog. He was in his early twenties, with long, thick black hair and a matching beard. His unzipped rain jacket revealed a slender, almost skinny torso. The legs below his nylon shorts were wiry sinews. In his right hand he held an orange plastic trowel, known on the AT as a "cat hole facilitator." In his left was a Ziploc, containing toilet paper and a small jar of hand sanitizer.

Robert grinned. "Heeding the call?"

"It's always good to lighten your load. Now I'm ready for Maine." His slight southern drawl belied his Mediterranean features. "You thru-hiking?"

Robert nodded. "I'm Dances with Snakes."

A smile creased the black beard. "I'm Socrates. You go first."

"I was hiking with my brother several years ago, near Damascus. Stepped on a copperhead."

"No shit! Whadja do?"

"I went straight up. All kinds of motion. Tom was behind me. He didn't think a man with a loaded pack could get that high off the ground. By the time I landed the snake had slid down the mountain."

"You're too old and too white for that kind of hang time."

"Hey, I was motivated."

"Did you kill it?"

"No. It never struck. It just wanted to get away."

"Good for you. Most of the idiots out here would have."

"Snakes are okay, as long as there's space between us. I don't need to seek revenge for Adam and Eve. Now, your turn. Tell me about Socrates."

"I'm not shy about sharing my opinions. And I have a high IQ."

"Genius?"

"They clocked me at 150."

"Wow! Mensa territory."

"And I'm Greek. The name settled on me in high school."

"You must come from southern Greece, with that accent."

"Charlotte, North Carolina. Lived there all my life."

"A Tarheel."

He hesitated. "Only if you refer to the state of my birth. If you mean the diploma mill in Chapel Hill, no way in hell."

Robert feigned surprise. "Dookie?"

"Graduated in December. Out here only 'cause I couldn't get tickets to the Final Four."

"Final Four? Typical Duke arrogance. C'mon, man. March Madness just started."

"When you're good, you go." Socrates beamed. "And we're goooood. Look at the record. And we have the best coach." He paused. "Speaking of accents, you're definitely not from Brooklyn."

"Atlanta. For thirty years. I'm a retired accountant."

"Retired? How old are you?"

"Fifty-seven."

"You don't look that old."

Robert's full head of brown hair had grayed only at the temples. Prehike conditioning had removed the paunch he acquired from sitting behind the desk before retirement. "Thanks for noticing. Must be the water in Georgia."

"Don't tell me you're a Georgia Tech guy?"

"No, but my son, Rob, is. A friend of mine has season tickets. I see Tech once or twice a year, usually a league game. Next to hiking, the purest thing around is Atlantic Coast Conference basketball."

"Damn straight."

"Actually, I graduated from Davidson. When Lefty Driesell was there."

"Cool! Just up the road from Charlotte. Say, were you at that East Regional final against Carolina?"

"In 1969? Couldn't make it. It was a bummer. Too much Charles Scott. But we got our revenge this year."

"Right on. Little Davidson beats mighty Carolina. It was sweet as honey. We absolutely loved it in Durham."

"You bet. Sweeter than Ulee's gold."

Socrates smiled at the movie reference. "You know, you're not so bad for an old guy."

Robert considered the backhanded compliment. Like his own generation, today's college youth must not trust anyone over thirty. "Thank you. And AARP thanks you."

"I mean, you're an old fart, but you know movies and college hoops. And you don't kill snakes."

"So my assets outweigh my liabilities?"

"Whoa! That accountant crap is a big liability."

"Okay, no more of that. But one thing. It sounds like you're testing me."

"Sorta."

"Do I pass?"

"One more question." There was a big gleam in his eye. "Can you spell Krzyzewski?"

Robert did not hesitate. "K-r-z-y-z-e-w-s-k-i."

A broad smile parted the thick mustache and the bristling chin whiskers. "Too much! Mr. Dances with Snakes, let's leave this Georgia rainforest and hike to the promised land."

"I'm ready for North Carolina. As soon as I get out of this sauna suit."

Robert peeled off the raingear and shook it forcefully. He gathered a handful of pine needles and used them to dislodge the mud from the hems of his pants. He stowed the suit and the pack cover in their designated places and hoisted the pack to his shoulders. He was cool and damp, but hiking would warm him fast enough. Socrates also loaded up, and then he led them north out of the Cowart bower.

—⚏—

Except for the day with the Raggedies, Robert had been a recluse. He had walked alone and kept to himself at campsites. His self-imposed isolation was difficult to maintain, given the gaggle of thru-hikers. When greeted by others, his replies were polite but short and never extended beyond initial pleasantries. Not searching for friends, he was satisfied with a sound bite of small talk.

Robert did not engage Socrates, but Socrates engaged him from the moment they began walking. He commanded a wealth of facts and figures on a wide variety of subjects, which he shared in a nonstop discourse. To Robert, he was the perfect *Jeopardy!* contestant.

"You're a southerner. You must have studied the Civil War."

"I took my share of history courses. And visited some battlefields."

"Really? Which ones?"

"Well, Appomattox. Although that wasn't much of a battle. We took the kids to see the McLean house, where Lee surrendered."

"You go to the jail? And the tavern?"

"Obviously, you've been there too."

"I've been to all of them. Kind of a hobby. What others did you visit?"

"Petersburg."

"Those earthen redoubts were something. I bet the engineers had a field day building them. And blowing them up."

"And Fredericksburg. When I was in college, I dated a girl who went to Mary Washington. We walked the battlefield one afternoon."

"Did you get any?"

"Made out a little. There were a lot of tourists there."

"The place was crawling when I was there too. But I didn't let it stop me. So what did you think?"

"About the girl, or the battlefield?"

"Not interested in your sex life."

"Then why did you ask if I got any?"

"The battle, you reptile! The battle."

"I wondered how Fighting Joe Hooker could be so stupid, crossing the river and then the open field while Lee rained artillery down from the hilltops."

"Good point. Lee had all his sharpshooters stationed behind that stone wall. Must have been like target practice. You'd think he would have remembered the carnage. But when he gets to Gettysburg, he has a brain fart and sends Pickett charging across an open field, just like Joe."

"A real disaster."

"Coach K should have been in charge. He's too smart for a frontal assault. He would have probed for weakness. Attacked the wings. His zone pressure would have disrupted Meade."

"You're insinuating that a basketball coach would have done a better job than a career army general?"

"All I'm saying is that there are winners in this world. The Yankees, Tiger Woods, Lance Armstrong. And Mike Krzyzewski. Like all winners, he would have figured out a way."

The miles and hours flew by. Socrates discoursed on the rise of the Republican Party in the South, and the concomitant demise of the Democrats. Before Robert realized, it was one o'clock. Socrates cut short a polemic about free trade in the twenty-first century to suggest they eat lunch. They picked a spot adjacent to a small spring that featured ottoman-sized boulders.

"What's for lunch, Snaky?" Dances with Snakes was a "reptilian mouthful," so he christened Robert with the shorter appellation. Robert was tempted to name him Windsock, but did not want to hurt his feelings. He called him "Soc."

Robert extracted a tin from his food bag. "Sardines."

"Ah, a fellow gourmand." Socrates held up his own rectangle and peeled back the top.

Robert glanced at the contents. "That really looks good. Other than sardines, what's in it?"

"Peppers in Louisiana hot sauce. Guaranteed to liven up the afternoons. Be alert hiking behind me."

"Mine are pedestrian by comparison. Where'd you find them?"

"Wal-Mart, I think. My mom picks them up for me."

"So your mom's your support system?"

"Absolutely. I put her in charge of the food so she can fuss over me. It channels her worrying."

"Better your mom than your girlfriend. I overheard this guy at Neel Gap. He'd asked his girl to send his mail drops. He got the first one with a note. She wasn't keen on his being gone so long. She was dating another guy and told him to find somebody else to support him."

"Ooh, that sucks. But you're right; my mom would never dump me."

Socrates rose from his rock to explore the little brook. He straddled the stream and bent over, his head no more than a foot above the water.

"Whatcha looking for?"

"Frogs, lizards, newts—oh, and these little salamanders," he said, holding up a tiny black creature with embryonic legs.

"Are you a herpetologist?"

Socrates walked toward Robert, cradling his specimen in his palm. "I study botany more than zoology, but all plants and animals interest me."

"Is there anything that doesn't interest you?"

"That interests me." Socrates noticed the carvings on Old Hickory, leaning against the rock next to Robert. He carefully deposited the salamander in the brook and hoisted the stick. "A fine piece of craftsmanship. Where'd you get this beauty?"

"From our backyard in Atlanta. My wife cut it down to make room for a bed of azaleas. She gave it to her dad. He's a big woodcarver. Next Christmas, this is under the tree. Warren knew I wanted to hike the trail, and his gift sorta sealed the deal. With this creation, there was no retreat from the dream. I *had* to hike the AT. Hickory is hard wood. Those faces were hell to work."

Socrates examined the carvings intently. "The one at the top has a flowing beard and everything. And the second one here is scary. The eyes stare right through you."

"He's a Blue Devil," Robert interjected.

"Cute, Snaky. The third one down looks out of the corner of his eye. Like someone's following him."

"There's a fourth, near the bottom. Yeah. That little one. Warren said they were wood sprites. Notice the third face. He got tired of digging in that hard hickory. He used a natural depression in the stick so he wouldn't have to carve the mouth."

"Cool. He signed it. 'To Robert from Warren, 1997.' I'd say you got yourself a keeper."

"It's coated with polyurethane and has a metal tip in the bottom, for durability. Old Hickory's a little nicked up, but otherwise okay. You get four points of support with your Lekis. He gives me three. I've crossed through mud and over slickrock, and I've rock-hopped streams without a slip. Uphill and down. Old Hickory's going all the way to Maine. And if I meet my copperhead in Virginia, I can keep him at pole's length."

"Your hiking stick has a better trail name than you do."

"It got me a ride."

"You're shitting me."

"I got to the gap yesterday and started hitching into Hiawassee. My pack's on the ground in front of me with the stick leaning on it. This guy drives up and stops. He gets out of the car and says, 'That's a fantastic pole you got there.' I don't think he even saw my thumb, but he sure drew a bead on Old Hickory. Turns out he carves sticks in his spare time and wanted to admire Warren's handiwork. For a while I thought he'd give the stick a ride into town and leave my ass by the side of the road."

"The stick can yogi! Old Hickory. Who came up with that name? Your wife or your father-in-law?"

"I'll take the credit. Hickory stick. Nickname of a mythic president. It wasn't brain surgery."

Socrates bit into a Snickers bar. There was a lull in the conversation while he chewed. He spoke again. "Say, Snaky. The thru-hike. How'd you convince your wife to let you do this?"

"She was all in favor of it." Robert plunged on. "But she won't get to enjoy it with me. Angie died last October."

Socrates looked uncomfortable for having broached the subject. "I'm sorry, man. How long were you guys married?"

"Thirty-four years. Not enough time. I had just retired, and she was getting ready to. We were going places."

"Like where?"

"Out west, after I finished the AT. Yellowstone, the Tetons, Glacier, the Sierras. Then to the Scottish Highlands and to New Zealand." Robert's throat tightened. "But it didn't happen."

Socrates was uncharacteristically silent. Finally he spoke. "A lot of dreams there. Doing the AT is the first one. And doing the trail means getting our butts to Muskrat Creek tonight." He handed Old Hickory back to Robert. "Let's get to North Carolina. Can't be much further."

Talking had been therapeutic, but now walking was a better prescription. Robert gathered the trash from lunch, and Socrates did likewise. Robert loaded the pack, rested it on a rock, and hunched it up and over his shoulders. Looking at Socrates, he mustered a smile. "Let's go north."

They reached Bly Gap and North Carolina. One state was behind them. Resting for a moment beneath a gnarled oak, they celebrated with a high five and a handful of trail mix. They soon discovered it was wise not to be too exuberant. North Carolina's first mile went straight up to a nondescript but punishing peak called Courthouse Bald.

Socrates curtailed his machine-gun delivery. At the top, they ripped off their packs and bent over at the waist, hands on knees, gasping for air. Their duet of heavy breathing serenaded several daddy-long-legs, who scurried along the ground.

"The promised land? Be careful what you wish for."

Socrates responded in intermittent bursts. "There's no stinking courthouse … and this is no damn bald … but we're at the top."

"Welcome to North Carolina. We're sorry the elevator's not in service." Robert inhaled deeply. "Don't know about you, but I'm in the sack early tonight." He pulled out the map and pinpointed their location. "Good news. The shelter's only a mile away."

They started again. Robert marveled at his recuperation. At the point of exhaustion minutes before, he now breathed normally. His heart had returned from his throat to its customary seat in his chest.

Socrates was back in stride also. His social commentary had moved to welfare reform. He applauded the reductions in the rolls achieved in the late 1990's but bemoaned the fact the country had reached a plateau. "Any future savings will be tied to improved education and training," he droned, "but even that may not be the total solution. There's an irreducible core that will need assistance. As Shakespeare said, 'You'll always have the poor with you.'"

Robert had been half-listening. Socrates's pronouncement brought back his focus. For the first time, he caught his companion in an error. "Actually, Soc, that pearl of wisdom isn't Shakespeare's. It's from the Bible."

Socrates turned sideways to confront him. His tone indicated how unaccustomed he was to being wrong. "You sure about that?"

"Yup. In three places. Matthew, Mark, and John. I have a New Testament in my pack, if you'd like to check."

Socrates was incredulous. "You're packing a Bible?"

"Just a New Testament. A lightweight miniature. You want to see the passages?"

"No. For some reason I believe you." He resumed walking. "How does an accountant know so much about the Bible?"

"My mother was a devout Presbyterian. To her, the original sin was Biblical illiteracy. I grew up in Sunday school and Bible study. I took some courses at Davidson. It's evolved into an ongoing interest in theology."

"Are you a seminary don or something?"

"I've taught Sunday school at my church for over twenty years. Junior highs and senior highs. The kids keep me honest. You simply cannot bullshit a teenager. I learn a lot more than they do. And I try to read the Bible every evening. Before bedtime."

"Then you can be our expert on the Good Book. Wear the official AT clerical collar."

Robert laughed sarcastically. "Yeah, right. A little Biblical learning is dangerous. Quoting it is one thing. Understanding it is a whole other ball game."

"Like the difference between hiking in Georgia and North Carolina?"

"For a motor mouth, you occasionally say something truly profound."

Socrates laughed. "It's nice to know how you really feel." He took several more steps and spoke over his shoulder. "So you believe in God?"

Robert was momentarily taken aback by the direct question. He did not immediately answer.

"Maybe I awarded that collar prematurely."

"God and I haven't been on good terms since Angie died. He really pissed me off. She was an intelligent, vibrant, caring, loving person. He took her much too soon. I'll never forgive Him for that."

"Your anger is at least an acknowledgment of His existence. By the way, that's an interesting spin on the Cartesian theorem. 'I piss you off, therefore I AM.' But I'll ask one more time. Do you believe in God?"

"You're full of questions today, aren't you?"

"Are you full of answers?"

"I don't know if I have the right answer, but I have my answer."

"Let's hear it."

"The perfectibility of man. The idea we keep getting better as history runs its course. Otherwise, there's no reason to hope. I couldn't live without hope."

"Life's a bitch, and then you die. That's not you?"

"No way."

"I'm not a nihilist either. But where does God fit in?"

"I believe in perfectibility, but I don't believe man is capable of bringing it off."

"Why not?"

"There's an underlying order to the universe ..."

"Natural laws, like in physics and mathematics."

"... and also in the life sciences. Genetics. And biology. The order of the universe is there, but we constantly screw it up. Out of pride, greed, arrogance, ignorance, whatever. Look at history. War, crime, DDT, strip mining, Three Mile Island. Hitler, Pol Pot, Idi Amin, Al Qaeda. Left to our own devices, we can never get right with nature. Or each other."

"You believe in original sin?"

"Yeah. I do."

"Gee, I never met a real Calvinist before. Can I touch you?"

"Cut the crap."

"Okay. What's it like? Original sin?"

"The book of Romans describes human failure. Doesn't matter what we do, how hard we try. We fall short. Abjectly. God has to show us how things are supposed to work."

"I thought Newton and Darwin and Freud did that."

"God works through guys like that to improve human knowledge. And through people like Mother Teresa and Francis of Assisi to show us how to care for each other. But in the final analysis, God, and not man, is the moral force."

"You believe in Jesus?"

"I may wax and wane, but yes."

"Why?"

"Because Newton, Freud, and Mother Teresa, all together, can't get us over the hump. We are so hopeless we have to have outside help."

"John 3:16?"

Stained-Glass Curtain

"Yeah. I believe that God interceded in human history."

The shelter appeared ahead and to the right. Several hikers milled around the platform, preparing dinner. A chorus of camp stoves roared like jets idling on the taxiway. Socrates stopped again and faced him.

"I think you've sold us short. For every Hitler there's a Jefferson, and for every DDT there's an MRI. I'd like to talk more about this, but it's time to eat. The smell of mac and cheese beckons like a whore on a street corner."

Robert was reluctant to end the discussion, but his empty stomach grumbled, as if on cue. "Okay. Let's eat."

Socrates smiled. "I get the final word."

"What?"

"You may doubt, but it's not permanent. It's obvious you're a lifer."

—ᴡ—

Robert was inside the mummy at seven. The bag had stayed dry in the rainstorm. His system was vindicated.

He was physically tired, but mentally refreshed. It was a moral victory to finish one state. Completing Georgia was a sign of progress, and he needed positives. It was nothing to get overly excited about, just the first of many milestones. What did excite him was Socrates. He had found a companion whose company he thoroughly enjoyed.

He had hung around after supper in hopes of resuming their conversation. However, his new buddy dropped hints that he wanted to be alone.

"Snaky, I need to write in the register. And catch up on my reading."

Robert backed off. "Sure. While you're at it, make an entry for me. Cuss and swear about Courthouse."

"Okay. And don't wait for me tomorrow. I'll catch you."

Comfortable and content in the waning light of the tent, Robert saw Old Hickory, lying parallel to him on the floor. Its faces stared back at him.

Your rod and your staff ...

He had not yet read from the Bible. That procedure seemed to be working also. He had endured a rainy day with no thoughts about quitting. He reached toward his pack for the book but lay back down on the Thermarest. He began to recite the twenty-third psalm from memory.

He spoke the familiar words slowly and audibly. When he finished, the image of his mother occupied his thoughts. Felled by a severe stroke at age eighty, she could scarcely string three words together. The aphasia was cruel punishment for such a literate and well-spoken woman. Yet at his father's funeral, she sat in her wheelchair at the graveside and repeated the entire psalm in unison with the minister and the rest of the family. She did not miss a single word.

There was a medical reason why she overcame the aphasia, something about using a different part of the brain for recalling what had been spoken a thousand times before and committed to memory. But something else was at work also. Eighty faithful years.

A second image took hold. Angie lay in bed, fighting pain with equal doses of guts and morphine. She asked him to read to her. He picked the twenty-third psalm. The words comforted her, and she fell asleep as he finished. He listened to her breathing and thanked God she found respite.

The psalm resounded in the chilly Carolina air. Perhaps goodness and mercy, like grief and memories, could also follow him. He pondered what being a "lifer" entailed and fell asleep.

Chapter 3

Get your motor running, get out on the highway ...
Steppenwolf

Robert woke at dawn. He had always been an early riser. His parents rarely had to roust him out for school. In college, he was the object of derision from his dorm mates, who cherished every precious second under the covers. Why get up early? And voluntarily? His wakefulness served him well in the army and during working years, but to his great chagrin it persisted into retirement. It was impossible for him to sleep in.

He glanced frequently at Socrates's tent. There was no sign of life. He sat at the table in front of the shelter and dawdled with breakfast, waiting for the familiar report of a zipper opening a rainfly. There was no sound. He recalled Socrates's final words the night before. "Don't wait for me. I'll catch you." In the cold light of morning, that seemed a tenuous commitment, but he had no other option but to trust him.

He hit the trail. The first full day in North Carolina brought crispness in the air. The average elevation in Georgia had been three thousand to thirty-five hundred feet. Muskrat Creek was over forty-five, surpassing Blood Mountain. North Carolina was poised to reward him with a succession of five-thousand-foot peaks. The first was Standing Indian. Robert targeted it for lunch.

He fell into a steady rhythm. There were no steep ascents like Courthouse. He maintained his desired pace of two miles an hour. The final approach to Standing Indian was gradual, but strenuous enough to solidify their friendship.

The view from the summit was jaw-dropping. From fifty-five hundred feet, he gazed down on Courthouse Bald and the Blue Ridge backbone, extending southwest into Georgia. The ridgeline formed the Tennessee Valley Divide. To its east, he located the Tallulah River valley, which drained into the Savannah River and the Atlantic Ocean. On the west side, Lake Chatuge glimmered in the sun. From its pool, the Hiwassee flowed into the Tennessee and on to the Mississippi.

The click-clicking of trekking poles punctured the silence. Socrates hurtled into the clearing on the summit. In spite of the cool air, beads of sweat covered his forehead. He deposited his pack abruptly next to Robert's and hastened to the edge of the clearing. He yanked up the left side of his shorts, extracted his penis, and with a sigh of relief began to urinate.

"What's out there, Snaky?"

"The Tennessee Valley Divide. When I was a teenager, I discovered that if I peed off the side where you are, it would flow to the Atlantic. But if I walked just a few feet over there, I could pee to the Gulf of Mexico."

Socrates stopped in midstream. He walked to where Robert had pointed and finished his business. "That covers all the bases." He struck an imperial pose. "I came, I saw, I peed."

"Caesar? No way. You're just a whiz kid. But come look at this view."

Socrates studied the expanse. "You're right. It's easy to make out the two watersheds."

"I'm really into this divide thing. I've tracked it on the topos. It winds through Georgia and North Carolina like a snake. It's hooked me on mountain geography and history. Say, d'you ever read Bartram's *Travels?*"

"Bartram? I grew up on him! Snaky, you amaze me."

"I've hiked the Bartram Trail. In his footsteps."

"Wouldn't it be great to come across that same Indian village he found? See how they lived two hundred years ago? Meet those luscious Cherokee maidens picking luscious strawberries?"

"Better Bartram than you. You'd have lost your scientific objectivity. I can only imagine what the Cherokee maidens would have lost."

"Bartram was lucky. He had a 'Dances with Wolves' experience. Know what I mean?"

"Kevin Costner's Lieutenant Dunbar. The first and last man to see the land in its pristine state. He found the Indians to be way more civilized than the white man."

"Damn. You do know your movies. But I would have loved to have been one of those explorers."

"Speaking of explorers, you ever hear of Arnold Guyot?"

"There's a Mount Guyot in the Smokies."

"Right. It's named for him. Several years ago, I stumbled on a copy of his treatise on the Carolina mountains. In a bookstore in Asheville."

"There's a Mount Guyot in the Whites too."

"Same guy. Swiss geographer. Taught at Princeton in the mid-nineteenth century. He explored in New England first. Then came south. He wrote this piece called *Notes on the Geography of the Mountain District of Western North Carolina*."

Socrates snored loudly. "A gripping title."

"Yeah, but it's full of priceless information. He spent four years down here. Systematically laid out all the peaks, ridges, and river valleys. You know how confusing these transverse ranges are."

Socrates waved at the mountains extending randomly in all directions. "Like right here."

"Guyot was the first to chart them in a way that made sense. He also calculated the elevation of all the major mountains. His degree of accuracy wasn't really improved upon until GPS came along."

"How'd he do the calculations?"

"Barometric readings. And levels. Anyway, Guyot submitted his paper to the Library of Congress in 1863. Being good bureaucrats, they pigeonholed it so deep in the archives they didn't find it again until 1929." Robert took pleasure that for once he was the source of information, even if it was pedantic and obscure.

Socrates pondered his story. "The Catholic Church got it wrong."

"What are you talking about?"

"When Martin Luther posted his theses on the door in Wittenburg. They should have told him he was right and had the pope give him a medal. Then they turn his paper over to a committee and lose it forever in the Vatican bureaucracy."

They feasted on beef jerky, wheat crackers, and banana chips. Socrates capped lunch with a Snickers, while Robert polished off a Clif bar.

"When did you get up this morning?"

"I dunno. Eight thirty, maybe. Why?"
"You must have been the last one out."
"The way I like it. Hey, at Duke I never had a class before ten."
Robert looked at his watch. "You hauled ass coming over here."
"Once I get going, I really move."
"Three miles an hour?"
"At least."
Robert chuckled. "Like high school math."
"Whattaya mean?"
"Snaky Tortoise starts at point x on vector AT. He hikes two miles per hour. Two hours later, Socrates Hare begins at the same point, racing at three miles an hour. How long does it take 'Speedy' to overtake 'The Tortoise'?"
"I'll run your scaly ass down in four hours."
After lunch, they hiked together. Socrates preferred discourse to the continuance of a mad dash to Maine. That suited Robert, who coasted along as the captive audience. Without fanfare they became hiking partners. There was no formal contract or handshake, but an unspoken understanding that accommodated their respective idiosyncracies. Robert settled in as Dr. Watson to Socrates's Holmes.

The climb to the summit of Albert Mountain was steep and slick, requiring all fours to reach the top. Rain and mist blotted out all objects more than ten feet away. They stood under the steel legs of an old fire tower. The observation platform above was obliterated by the dense soup.

Socrates held up his hands. Brown grit had collected between his fingers and under his nails. He tried to wipe his hands on his rain suit and succeeded only in smearing mud into the folds and ripples. With mock fastidiousness, he flicked away a daub of mud on Robert's cheek.

"You need to be more careful with your makeup."
"This is like army mud. Sticks to everything. The NCOs in my unit called it 'shit brindle brown.'"
The rain continued all night. It stopped the next day, when they reached the side trail to Siler Bald. The clouds lifted just enough to tempt them.
"How far to the top?"

"About a half mile."

"Want to try it?"

"The way the clouds are, whatever view there is will be fleeting."

"What the hell. Let's go for it." They shed their packs and scurried through the wet grass to the exposed summit.

"There's Standing Indian over there. And Albert Mountain, closer in."

"Shit, we can see more of it from here than we could standing on it yesterday." Socrates looked north. "How 'bout those high ones, poking through the clouds?"

"The Balsams. Some are over six thousand feet."

"We're starting to play with real money. And over there. Those twins?"

"That's Wayah Bald and Wine Spring Bald. My son Rob and I camped on Wine Spring. Guess what? It rained all night."

"He's not still in school, is he?"

"Air force. But not a pilot. He inherited my eyes."

"What does he do?"

"Information technology officer. Stationed in Alaska. His unit has a classified mission. He says if he told me what he does he'd have to kill me."

"Then I wouldn't ask. You got any other kids?"

"Mandy. She's older. Married. Lives in Jacksonville. Teaches Spanish at a junior college. Her husband's finishing dental school."

"Any grandkids?"

"Not yet. But hey, my turn to ask some questions. You got a girlfriend?"

"I grew up with four sisters. I'm in no hurry for a long-term commitment. But I would like some female companionship."

"Maybe you'll find her out here. Someone to sit at your feet and hang on your every word."

"Perhaps in your era, Snaky. That girl doesn't exist anymore. Besides, I'm not looking for adoration. Or love, for that matter. Common ordinary sex will do just fine. A solid basis for a great trail relationship. Would you be offended?"

"Personally, I hope you find her. And I hope she's neither common nor ordinary."

"I hope she shows up before semen starts pouring out my ears."

"Oh! The lad's a bit horny?"

"A slight understatement, asshole."

A jet emerged from a high cloud and streaked across a narrow window of open sky, the only break in the mounting bank of gray. After a few moments the plane disappeared. Its contrail lingered briefly and then was expunged.

Socrates broke the silence. "You mentioned Angie worked. What did she do?"

"Thanks for the chance to brag on her. Angie and her best friend, Louise, opened a florist shop fifteen years ago. They specialized in weddings, banquets, and funerals. Small family events. Then the word got around. Several Atlanta hotels contracted with them to do table decorations for large meetings and conventions. They were creative, and damn good businesswomen. It became a highly profitable operation. I did their books. The bottom line grew every year." Robert paused and let the good memories pass in review. "That's part of the reason I could retire early."

"What's happened to the business?"

"Louise is trying to make a go with a new partner. It's been difficult. She and Angie had a synergy that's hard to replicate."

Dark billows rolled in from the west, shuttering the view. "Ready to get wet again?"

"No shit. Let's get the hell off this bald and into the rain suits. At least it's not cold enough to snow."

The rain resumed. They plodded up Wine Spring Bald and camped near the summit, where Robert and Rob had stayed years earlier. Robert pitched his tent quickly and was proud that only a few drops dampened the nylon floor before he secured the fly. The rain relented long enough to fire up the Whisperlites for supper, but it returned soon after to drive them inside.

Robert read the first chapter of John. Afterward, he allowed the metronomic rhythm of the rain lull him to sleep. His last recollection was a diffuse glow emanating through the wall of Socrates's tent.

—⚭—

There was no pitter-patter on the rainfly. Robert sat up in his sleeping bag. In the half light, his breath was a heavy plume. He unzipped the tent and peered out. The first inkling of morning was reflected in the pale dust on the ground.

Not cold enough to snow?

He dressed quickly and crawled outside. The accumulation was less than an inch. Unlike wet snow, the fine granular powder was less apt to ice the trail.

Robert reentered the tent and ate breakfast. His mind began to race. It was thirteen miles to the Wesser shelter. The snow could get worse or even turn into a blizzard. He put away his gear and took down the tent, struggling with a sobering apprehension. There was usually greater snowfall at higher elevations. The AT was above four thousand feet all the way to the shelter. On Wayah and Copper Ridge, it was over five.

The wind was not strong, so he packed the knit cap and donned his Polartec ear band. If necessary, he could pull up the hood of his rain jacket to keep his head warm and dry. In deference to his "senior" circulation, he put on warm gloves.

He thought about Socrates. He would pitch a fit at an early wakeup, but it would be good to be together in a snow storm. He walked to the front of his tent.

"Hey, Soc."

Nothing. Robert turned up the volume. "Soc!"

"Mmmmm."

"Hate to wake you, but it's snowing. Not hard, but it could get worse. I'm heading to Wesser Bald. You might want to start earlier."

There was a long pause. "You want me to leave this warm sack?"

Robert's first thought had been right. Let the sleeping Blue Devil lie. "No. Come along when you're good and ready. See ya at the shelter."

"Catch you by noon, Snaky."

Robert headed north.

God, I'm a thru-hiker. Today I want to go from Wine Spring Bald to Wesser Shelter. Please give me wisdom, patience, and perseverance. Thank You for letting me walk in Your world. Just don't bury it.

The fine powder fell through the morning. By noon three inches had accumulated. The snow crunched underfoot and caked in the grid of his soles. At times he lost traction, but the suddenness of his slips and slides dislodged what had collected in the tread. Then another buildup, followed by another displacement.

The cold weather kept him from overheating. The trail rose and fell, but the inclines were not steep. He shortened his stride, particularly on the downhill, and leaned on Old Hickory. He hiked with greater purpose and awareness. He made good time, almost as fast as on dry trail.

When he reached Copper Ridge, he had come almost nine miles. He ate his lunch of canned salmon and crackers like a robot, devoid of any enjoyment. He stood the entire time, not wanting to sit in snow.

Robert shivered from lack of movement. The thermometer read twenty-six degrees. He needed to hike to keep warm, and he needed to negotiate the thousand-foot drop to Tellico Gap before the trail got nastier. Socrates never appeared out of the white, as promised.

He started again. In fifteen minutes he had warmed enough to lose "the shakes." He noted with pride that he should make it to the Wesser shelter with plenty of time to spare.

His left foot slid on a loose rock hidden in the snow. He tried to brake with his right, but it lost traction as well. He landed on his buttocks with an unceremonious thud. He rolled over twice, off the trail and downhill.

Robert lay in the snow and let the shock subside. His respiration was all that interrupted the silence. Consciousness and breathing were good signs. He wiggled his toes and fingers. Sensation in his extremities was another good indicator. He pressed his hands and knees into the snow and slowly brought himself to a kneeling position. There was no pain in his neck or back. He brushed snow off his cheek and discovered that his glasses were missing.

He squinted over the expanse of disturbed snow, twigs, and leaf litter. Halfway up the bank he spied Old Hickory. Its shiny polyurethane coat stood out from the duller sticks and branches. He began to comb the hillside visually, working back toward the trail in one-foot swaths. Three feet up, a sliver of chrome glinted from under a snow-capped wad of decayed leaves. He pushed off on one knee and retrieved the glasses and the pole.

Robert scrambled up the bank to the trail. He brushed more snow off his jacket. He swiped at his rump. A dull pain throbbed in both cheeks. His buttocks hurt, but not as much as his wounded dignity.

Robert remolded his pack to its familiar contours. Leaning even more on Old Hickory, he pigeon-toed deliberately to Tellico Gap. Without stopping, he began the mile-long climb to Wesser Bald. He felt safer going uphill. If he slipped, he'd fall into the hill and would not become a rolling stone.

Stained-Glass Curtain

He crested Wesser. Surrounded by falling snow, he bemoaned the loss of another great view. The task at hand was to navigate one mile to the shelter and to get under roof and out of the storm. The rate of fall had ratcheted upward. At least four inches underfoot. He told himself to relax and be positive.

Silence and solitude surrounded him. Except for the mumbled crunch of his steps on the snow, he heard nothing but the wind. The birds, squirrels, and chipmunks had retreated to their sanctuaries. The bears and raccoons were in their dens. The presence of other hikers had been obliterated. The snow blanched the limbs and branches of the trees so that they blended into the white canvas. Wesser Ridge was a vast sensory deprivation tank.

In the army, he had gone on temporary duty one summer to Fort Drum, New York. He was struck by the color of the barracks. At other army posts, buildings were painted white or a nondescript dull yellow. But Fort Drum sported lime-green, cobalt-blue, and burnt-orange hues. He asked one of the sergeants about the decidedly nonregulation paint.

"Lieutenant, you ever heard of a whiteout?" The sergeant explained how "lake effect" snow off Ontario fell so thick that visibility was limited to a few feet in any direction. In a blizzard, a brightly painted building was a safety feature.

Could he be the victim of a Nantahala whiteout? Could he walk by the shelter and not see it? Maybe the trail maintainer had painted it a glossy cerise. He chastised himself for such ludicrous thinking. If his imagination was vivid enough to conjure up cherry shelters, his visual acuity should be sharp enough to find the building in the falling snow.

A signpost rose out of the white beside the trail. He brushed the granules off its face. A shelter icon appeared with an arrow pointing left. He plowed in that direction for fifty yards and made out a black cave under an overhanging white roof. His looked at his watch. Ten after three. Thirteen miles through the snow in eight and a half hours.

He passed under the overhang. His eyes adjusted to the gloom. Two taffeta lumps materialized in the right corner. A red-and-white stocking cap protruded from one of the sleeping bags. Scrunched under the hat were a mouth, nose, eyes, and cheekbones.

"Welcome to the asylum." It was a female voice. He dropped his pack and sat down on the platform. The face was that of a twenty-five-year-old. He didn't recognize her.

"Hi. I'm Dances with Snakes."

She laughed. "All right! Another movie! I'm Thelma." She nodded toward the other sleeping bag. "That's Louise. Our powder-blue convertible's parked behind the shelter. And you better not try anything. I got my pistol right here in the mummy."

"Well, I wasn't planning a move, and I damn sure won't now. How long you been here?"

"Since one. We decided to quit fighting Mother Nature and ride it out inside. It's a lot easier this way."

"And prettier." The unseen Louise acknowledged her consciousness from inside the bag.

"Sounds like a plan," Robert added. Suddenly he felt the burning in his penis. Bundled up in his rain suit against the cold and snow, he had not gone for some time. "Excuse me. I have to go outside."

He hustled several yards behind the shelter for relief. His penis had withered in the cold, and his testicles had retreated almost out of sight, far back into his scrotum. With effort he positioned his shriveled member so that he would not pee on himself. He remembered George Costanza's complaint in his favorite *Seinfeld* episode. "Shrinkage" had taken its toll. He finished without accident and returned to the shelter.

"You didn't pee on my tires, did you?"

"No, Miss Thelma."

"Good for you."

The register lay nearby on the platform. He decided to make an entry before he changed into dry clothes. He took off his glove for a better grip on the pen.

> March 21. If a tree falls in the forest and no one hears it, does it make a sound? If a hiker falls in the snow, and no one was there to see, did he really fall?

"Writing a novel?" Robert looked up to see the familiar blue silhouette outlined against the snow.

"Where the hell you been? I waited for you at lunch. Froze my ass off."

"Slept longer this morning. I had an early interruption. Some inconsiderate thru-hiker. It was hard to get going in the cold, but it sure was beautiful coming over."

"The snow slow you down?"

"Not really. I'm light on my feet. How about you?"

"I fell. Hard. Aside from a sore butt, I'm all right."

"Snaky, I've been thinking. Got your map handy?"

He noticed Socrates's expression. Wheels were turning. "Yeah, just a sec." Robert signed the register and laid it on the floor. He reached into his pack and retrieved the map. "Here you go."

Socrates studied the elevation profile from Wesser Bald to the Nantahala Outdoor Center, down in the gorge. "You know, the snow's not getting any better. We could be stranded. We're both low on food. I don't want to spend a day or two starving on this mountain."

"What are you getting at?"

"It's five miles to the NOC. It's three thirty. We have about three and a half hours of light. We should go down now rather than risk being snowed in."

"Are you crazy? That's two thousand feet! Steep and slick!"

"Calm down, Snaky. Hear me out. Look at the profile. For a mile, it's mostly flat, then a mile of steep descent. Beyond that it's still down, but probably sidehill. And the lower we get, it'll be warmer, with less snow. We should be past the worst by five o'clock and in town by seven. I did some winter hiking in the Whites two years ago with friends from Duke. This couldn't be any tougher."

Robert started to protest but bit his tongue. His earlier fall might have closed his mind to Socrates's proposal. It was risky, but there were also risks in staying at the shelter, with only one dinner and one breakfast. If he balked, Socrates might go ahead without him. He might disappear for good into the clouds as quickly as he had appeared in Georgia.

Robert exhaled deeply. "Okay. But go easy on me."

Socrates handed him the map. "You're a scholar and a gentleman."

"You're a riverboat gambler."

"You're both idiots," moaned Thelma from deep inside her sleeping bag.

"By the way, Soc, meet Thelma and Louise. Thelma's the talkative one. By the sound of things, they aren't ready to drive off the cliff just yet."

"Nice meeting you, ladies. See you at the NOC."

They crept off the Wesser plateau and began the precipitous descent into the gorge. Socrates telescoped the Lekis and asked Robert to strap them securely to his pack.

"We're gonna need our hands."

Socrates made a point of being cautious. He attended to every detail, systematically picking the spot for the next step down. "Snaky, there are two keys to going down this hill. First, don't be in a hurry. We have plenty of time. Second, anticipate trouble before it happens. Always have a tree or bush picked out to grab on to, to break your fall. Drop Old Hickory if you have to. As neat as he is, he's not worth a broken neck."

The narrow trail was lined with scrub hardwood, rhododendron, and laurel. Rocks jutted out of the snow at random. There were many prospective footholds and handholds. Robert learned quickly how to use them.

At one point Socrates slid ten feet down the slope. He grabbed a boulder with his left hand and a laurel with his right. He stayed in a spread position for several seconds until he collected his feet under him.

Robert intoned in his best Jim McKay voice, "That's an impressive iron cross, Bob. The judges will give him a high score for this exercise."

Robert's time came. He dislodged some rocks hidden under the snow. In a flash he was hurtling down the steep descent with increasing momentum. He planted his left foot and lunged to the right. He wrapped both hands around a sturdy rhododendron and held on for dear life. The limb cracked but did not break. His feet swung back and forth in midair, until they finally found a boulder below.

He was surprised his weight and momentum had not uprooted the bush. Fortunately, it was large and healthy. Its long, green leaves curled inward tightly to preserve warmth, its natural defense in frigid weather. They reminded him of cigar wrappers. He thought of smoking one to celebrate his good fortune.

Socrates commentated, in a presentable Bob Costas. "That dismount looked like a disaster, Jim. But he stuck with it and salvaged the exercise."

"How do I get off this rock?"

"Grab that root close to your left leg, and let yourself down easy. Don't worry about Old Hickory. He's down here with me."

The mountain continued to demand, and receive, their undivided attention. They took no chances and avoided any more harrowing incidents. Robert's apprehension turned to grudging respect for Socrates. His partner had more technical knowledge about traversing snow than he expected, and he had shared it freely with Robert. He made it sound like a lark, but it was clear that this was serious business. By five fifteen they finished the steepest descent and welcomed the sidehill trail.

"Snaky, keep Old Hickory on the downhill side. If you slip, push back into the hill. If you hold it uphill, you'll propel your ass over the edge."

Robert recalled his fall near Tellico. At that time he was holding Old Hickory on the uphill. He had to admit that Socrates was right.

The snow slackened at three thousand feet but did not stop. Had they stayed at Wesser shelter, they would have faced eight inches to a foot in the morning. He hoped the girls had enough food to ride it out.

He reviewed their decision. He had tripled his respect for Socrates. He knew how to hike in the elements. His risk-taking was calculated; he was not a foolhardy college kid who did things on a whim.

But what about himself? Today he showed perseverance and certainly patience coming down the hill. But wisdom? He never thought the three would be in conflict. The key was realizing which attribute took precedence in any given situation. He wasn't sure he had done the right thing.

They passed a shelter about a mile from the Nantahala Outdoor Center, but there was no reason to stop. At seven fifteen the AT dumped them onto a darkened Highway 19 in the tiny village of Wesser.

In his best McKay, Robert underscored their accomplishment. "Bob, we've just witnessed an amazing feat. Eighteen miles and thirteen hours through a snowstorm, over some of the most rugged trail in North Carolina."

"A tale they'll tell and retell to their grandchildren, Jim," Socrates intoned in a stentorian Costas.

The NOC complex lay shrouded in front of them across the highway. In summer it would be packed with kayakers and rafters taking the measure of the Nantahala whitewater. For now it was virtually deserted. They walked up the road, found a motel, and stumbled into the warmth of the office.

Behind the counter a middle-aged lady looked up from a thick paperback. "What can I do for you boys?"

"A room with two beds, please," Socrates asked. "Nonsmoking."

"I can do that."

"You do have cable, don't you?"

"Yes, dear."

He smiled at Robert. "The Duke-Indiana game starts in thirty minutes."

"You sneaky son of a bitch!"

Chapter 4

Consider the lilies of the field ...
Matthew 6:28

The "burn" in his calves accelerated to conflagration. Robert stopped at a commanding prospect to catch his breath and rest his legs. He steadied himself with Old Hickory and wiped the sweat from his forehead with his free hand.

The stark splendor of the Nantahala Gorge lay below. Across the chasm, the eastern face had shed its blanket. All that remained from the snowstorm were random splotches of white. On his side, down below, the pattern was reversed. Yesterday's sun did not punch through the clouds until afternoon, too late to thaw the snow on the precipitous western slope.

The Nantahala tumbled and twisted down into Wesser. At intervals, the dark water roiled into the white rapids that lured the legions of rafters and kayakers. Beside the river, the rails curled in a more regular path, occasionally winking in the sunlight. The landscape resembled a model train layout, but without the essential ingredient. The freights had stopped running long ago, and the scenic passenger train operated only in the summer. He squinted at the N-scale buildings crammed along the riverbank to find the motel, yesterday's home. The blinding glare reflected from metal rooftops thwarted his search.

Across the river from the tracks, a "semi" began the long ascent on Highway 19 from Wesser to Topton. At that distance, the cab and trailer mimicked the segmented body of an ant, crawling on eighteen wheels instead of six legs.

The snow had stopped late on the night of their arrival. The following morning the temperature rose to its springtime norm. However, several inches of slush remained on the trail. There was no reason to attack the snowbank they had hiked down to avoid. They "took a zero," a day of rest.

Socrates survived the spring storm but fell victim to a more devastating maelstrom. The unthinkable had happened. His Blue Devils had gone down to Indiana by one point in the region semifinals. He shouted a painful string of profanities at the TV and questioned loud and long the meaning of existence. Robert placed the game off limits. It was not the moment to bring up the consequences of arrogance. The "Dookie" needed time to agonize over the missed layups and free throws, and time to heal his gravely wounded self-esteem.

They slept late, a luxury for Robert if not for Socrates. They found a restaurant for a huge breakfast of ham, eggs, and pancakes, proof that Socrates's appetite was not affected by his suffering. Robert volunteered to do laundry and to buy the provisions needed to get to Fontana. Socrates nodded silently and moped back to the room for one more look at the carnage on SportsCenter.

In succession, Robert found the coin-op washateria and a small grocery. The most bothersome privation on the trail was the lack of fresh fruit and vegetables. At every town stop, he gorged on whatever was available; apples, peaches, grapes, grapefruit, and always bananas and oranges. He loved carrots, tomatoes, squash, broccoli, yams, peas, and all varieties of beans. He particularly savored okra. Mandy had balked at that southern tradition, referring to it contemptuously as "BBs in mucus." To satisfy them both, Angie had camouflaged okra among the many ingredients in her delicious gumbo.

Robert returned to the motel with food for the trail, and bananas, oranges, and carrots for munching. He dropped the clean clothes and food on his motel bed and carefully placed some fruit on the night table beside Socrates. He looked up from his book and managed a barely audible "thank you." Robert accepted the attempted gratitude as a first sign of recovery.

Munching on carrots, Robert left to find a pay phone. He called Rob first. Given the time difference in Alaska, he hoped to reach him before he reported for duty. The phone rang several times until the answering machine kicked in. Rob was the apparent victim of another traumatic predawn wakeup. He loved to sleep in and would be practicing the

Socratic lifestyle had he not been in the air force. Robert remembered how difficult it had been to roust him from bed as an adolescent. He once slept for eighteen consecutive hours after finishing freshman exams at Georgia Tech.

He was disappointed they had failed to connect. Rob had bottled up his feelings after Angie's death, just as he had. Their subsequent phone calls had been textbook cases of dancing around an unpleasant subject. The conversation they needed to have would be awkward, but it was time to have it. He left a short message that he would phone again from Gatlinburg.

He checked the time. Mandy should be through with morning classes. He rang her cell phone.

"Hi, Dad!"

"Hello, sweetheart."

"Where are you?"

"Wesser. North Carolina. At the NOC."

"Where the white-water rafting is?"

"Today it's a ski resort."

"Really? How much snow?"

"Six plus. Coming down the mountain yesterday was a sporty course."

"I hope you didn't do anything risky."

Robert lied. "No, dear. Your dad doesn't do stupid."

He counseled himself silently. Even though Mandy was a big fan of basketball, it was best not to reveal Socrates's ulterior motive for getting down the hill.

"How're you doing? And the budding dentist?"

"We're just fine. Steven has exams coming up soon."

"Orals?"

"Nggghh!" Mandy recoiled at his pun. "You're still full of groaners." She became serious. "Dad, I may have news."

"News?"

"All the signs point to it. I see the doctor Tuesday. I think I'm pregnant."

A bittersweet rush engulfed him. Angie's approaching retirement had excited her, but thoughts of grandmothering made her spew like a geyser. He was not as vocal, but just as eager. Like all parents wishing to be grandparents, they dropped thinly disguised hints, which were met with curt responses. They bit their tongues while Mandy and Steven talked about their careers and the need to wait another year because of this or that. But now the future had arrived. The joy and sadness of the moment welled up inside him.

"Mandy, that's wonderful! Is this by accident or design?"

"Makes a lot of difference now, doesn't it? But for the record, it was planned. A recent decision. With almost instantaneous results."

Robert visualized Angie holding a smiling infant, rubbing noses amid coos and gurgles. "Your mother would have loved this."

There was a strained silence on the other end of the phone. "Don't you dare lay that on me. I know you and Mom wanted this, but we just weren't ready. And when she got sick …"

He rushed to repair the damage. "No, honey! No! I meant that at face value. Your mom would have loved that you're pregnant. Just that. I'm not accusing you of anything. Do you understand that? Please! Please understand."

He endured another taut silence. "I do. I just miss her so much."

"I know how you feel. I'm trying to deal with losing her, too. And doing a crappy job. Mandy, I'm sorry. I should have talked to you earlier. I just couldn't bring myself around to it."

"Don't blame yourself, Dad."

"But I do. I couldn't do anything to help her." He paused. "I hate to admit it, but I even blamed her for leaving me. Is that pitiful or what?"

"I got mad at Mom too, for going so soon. They say it's a natural part of grieving. But like you, I'm not proud of it."

"And I blame God, Mandy. He sat up there and didn't do a damn thing. Except piss me off."

"Should I worry about you, hiking in thunderstorms?"

"No. He can't zap me more than He already has. But back to the subject. Don't ever think I'm disappointed in you."

"Okay."

"And whatever you do, never think your mom was disappointed either. I haven't told you this, but she and I talked one night, shortly after her diagnosis. She sorta took stock of her life. She had regrets. Some things she wished she'd done better, and some things she wished she hadn't done at all. But when it came to you and Rob, she was perfectly content. She said, 'I did something right when I raised those two. They are great kids.'"

Mandy sobbed. "You don't know how good that makes me feel."

"She was awfully proud of you. And so am I. And now this! You have made my day. No, my year! Is it a boy or a girl?"

"Don't be in a rush. Let the doctor confirm it. And as to the sex, Steven and I don't care. We just want a healthy baby."

"You said Tuesday?"

"At two thirty."

"Okay, I'll call again from Gatlinburg. That'll give me a few days to work on what kind of grandfather I'll be."

"Be just like you are as a father."

Tears leaked from the corners of his eyes. "Angela Amanda, I love you. My best to Steven."

"I love you, too, Dad. Bye-bye."

He wiped away more sweat. It was eight miles from Wesser to the summit of Cheoah Bald, his goal for lunch. And thirty-three hundred feet, the most sustained climb yet. The slush underfoot did not determine his pace as much as the sheer aerobics of the ascent. Cheoah was several Courthouse Balds, laid end to end.

The view at the top was one of the best in the southern Appalachians, and that spurred him on. Robert also wanted to get there before Socrates overtook him. He didn't need the grouch carping that he was old and slow. To his satisfaction, he made steady progress up the daunting mountain. He passed several other hikers, and no one passed him.

He was surprised when he caught up to Raggedy Anton and Andy. He thought they were behind.

"I'll be damned! Didn't that blizzard slow you down?"

Anton huffed. "Blizzard? We're from Buffalo, remember? This was just a flurry. We reached the Wesser shelter just a few hours after you left. Came down yesterday afternoon with those two girls."

"Thelma and Louise."

"Yeah. They said you were crazy as hell to hike down in that storm."

"Maybe. But it was either that or go hungry."

Andy intervened. "We read your entry in the register. Did you fall?"

"Flat on my ass. It was sore for a day. But I'm better."

Raggedy Anton grinned impishly. "Know what you should have written?"

"Dare I ask?"

"If a man farts in the forest, and there is no woman there to hear it, is it still wrong?"

Robert laughed. "My wife had very sensitive hearing. And a very sensitive sense of smell. I couldn't get away with anything."

Andy added, "Neither could Anton. His mom was all over him."

"Say, the two of you want company?"

"Thanks for asking," Anton replied, "but I don't think we can keep up with you. We left at dawn to take our time climbing this bitch."

"Okay. By the way, look out for a guy with a black beard. Almost as bushy as yours, Andy. He'll come flying by. Tell him I'll see him on the mountain for lunch."

Robert moved on. He marveled that the AT was like a small-town grocery store, a sociable place where friends who hadn't met for a while could catch up on all the news.

No one passed him en route to the summit. The R&R from the "zero" day had renewed him physically, and the news from Mandy was an invigorating elixir. But something else had also happened. In one hundred and forty miles, he had hiked himself into shape. He had his legs. He was scooting up Cheoah. If he could climb it, he could climb anything.

This confidence was hard won. In his high school basketball days, at the season's first practice, he would die in the wind sprints. For days he fretted he would never reach the elusive mind-body harmony achieved by constant conditioning. The ultimate zone arrived only when he accomplished a really demanding feat, like playing hard-nosed "man" defense for thirty minutes in three-on-three drills. Or filling the lanes on the fast break time after time in full-court scrimmages. And now, forty years later, taming a mile-high monster with a pack on his back. The exhilaration had returned.

He topped the intermediate crest of Swim Bald. A short stretch of downhill pampered his calves and thighs before the final assault on Cheoah. The last mile was a fitting and brutal climax, like the drills at the end of practice. Run to the basket at the other end and touch the wall behind. Then run back to touch the wall at this end. Ten times.

Cheoah was "the eleventh time" and the ultimate reward. It was Blood Mountain and Standing Indian taken to a new level. The early spring skies were free of the summertime haze and smog that fouled long-range visibility. He stood in the cool wind and gaped at the 360° panorama.

Robert wondered how Guyot reacted when he saw this view. Did he maintain his scientific decorum and systematically identify the peaks and ranges? Did he allow himself to be taken in by the surpassing beauty? For Arnold's sake Robert hoped he did both. While filling up his notebook with azimuths and elevations, he needed to fill up his soul with the glory of creation. Perhaps he hollered "Gooollleee!" like Gomer Pyle. Robert laughed out loud at the thought.

Did Arnold read *Travels?* William Bartram stood on Cheoah and wrote of "a sublimely awful scene of power and magnificence, a world of mountains piled upon mountains." Robert saw the same scene two hundred years later.

A hawk rose on the thermals. The same brisk wind that lifted it chilled Robert's perspiration. He shivered involuntarily. He dug into the pack for his Polartec pullover and quickly pushed his head through the neckhole and his arms through the sleeves. Protected from the gusts, he looked eastward to renew friendships.

Wesser. Copper Ridge. And Wayah. You look so much better in sunshine.

He rotated to the south and found the high one in the distance.

Standing Indian! Seems like a year since I stood on the divide with you.

Turning west, he followed the Stecoah ridge below, rising and falling in rugged profile to the dam at Fontana Lake.

You'll kick my ass. That climb from Sweetwater Gap is a beast.

Saving the best for last, he turned north. The Smokies ran southwest to northeast, for what seemed like forever. To Arnold, they were "the master chain."

One road crossing in seventy miles. Thirty-five consecutive miles above five thousand feet. Fraser firs. Red spruce. Bears!

The range rose higher and whiter until it peaked at Clingman's Dome, the highest point on the AT.

Smoky Dome! I'll see you in four days. No blizzards, okay?

"Whatcha gawking at, Snaky?"

Socrates's face was streaked in sweat. His T-shirt, also drenched, shouted in defiance, "Duke Blue Devils – NCAA Champs – 2001." Robert accepted the boast as stage two of his recovery.

"That big, beautiful range over there. The Great Smoky. We'll be climbing her soon."

"Can't be worse than this ass kicker."

"You're sweating like a pig. And hot enough to melt the last of the snow. Did you run up from Wesser?"

"Just my usual. Passed two friends of yours."

"Raggedy Anton and Andy?"

"That's about the sweetest trail name I've run into."

"Blips on the gaydar?"

"You got it. Hey, I've worked up a hellacious appetite. You hungry?"

"Ravenous. But get a jacket on. You're gonna cool off quick."

They broke out two tuna pouches and a bag of onion bagels. They each devoured two albacore sandwiches and chased them with the leftover oranges and bananas from the motel. Socrates embraced a Snickers, and Robert closed with his daily Clif bar.

"You really put it away, Snaky. Like a growing boy."

"For the first time in twenty-five years I can eat with impunity." He accentuated his statement with a large bite of soy chocolate. "Anything I want." Robert slapped his svelte stomach. "No guilt. No shame. No spare tire."

"You're not supposed to eat like this until New England. Whatcha gonna do then? Rent a yak to carry your food?"

"I don't see you pushing it away," Robert retorted. "How many pancakes back in Wesser? Eight?"

Socrates gobbled down the last banana. "The difference is I *am* a growing boy." He shivered in the wind. "It's getting cold. Let's hike ourselves warm."

Descending was a welcome change. The stress shifted to ankles and knees, and away from calves and thighs. They hiked off the bald and into the trees, some of which were in bud. Socrates was unusually quiet, channeling his energy to digest his colossal lunch.

Robert broke the silence. "I'm glad we had this view before the leaves come out. In a few more weeks we'll be hiking through the green tunnel."

Socrates stopped abruptly, obviously annoyed. "What did you say?"

"I meant—"

Socrates cut him off. "The green tunnel is crap." His face reddened beneath the black beard. "Unscientific thinking. I thought better of you."

"What are you getting at, Professor?"

"You imply there'll be a boring monotony of green from here to Maine."

"It's just an expression. Green tunnel. The character of the trail changes when the trees leaf out."

"You don't get off that easy." Socrates lectured over his shoulder as he walked. "Hundreds of different species out here contain chlorophyll. That doesn't make them all the same."

"Soc, I know—"

"But it seems that to you they are. You're hung up on their greenness. To the exclusion of all other traits. To you a forest of incredible diversity is a numbing monochrome."

"I didn't mean—"

"You know the difference between a red spruce and a Fraser fir?"

Robert thought for a moment. "As I recall, the needles on the fir shoot out around the branch, like a bottle brush. The spruce is like the hemlock. Needles are flat, two dimensional. And the cones on the fir grow up from the branch. The cones on the spruce grow down."

"Good. Needles and cones. There may be hope for you. But the jury's still out. What about mountain laurel and rhododendron?"

"My favorites."

"How do you tell them apart?"

"By their flowers."

"And if they aren't in bloom?"

"The leaves. Rhodies are U-shaped, longer than they are wide. Laurels are smaller. The leaves come to a point."

"Shape of the leaves. Rhododendron are obovate. Laurel are lanceolate."

"Yeah!" The terms were distant echoes from freshman biology at Davidson, forty years removed. "That's exactly what I said."

"Can you identify poison ivy?"

"Your lecture is growing tiresome."

Socrates prodded. "Describe it."

Robert felt patronized. "A vine with dark green leaves." He had a cerebral spurt. "Clusters of three, either lobed or serrated."

"Good! That's almost a scientific description."

Robert continued. "Wraps around tree trunks. Yellows in the fall. The active ingredient is urushiol, which is highly toxic to human skin."

"Urushiol? Snaky, I'm impressed!"

"I'm sensitive. It takes only one exposure to learn that lesson."

"You know, blueberry bushes and poison ivy are both green," Socrates smirked. "Why don't you eat a big handful of poison ivy?"

"Uncle! *Uncle!*" Robert protested. "Jeez, Soc, when you're on a rant, you're worse than Dennis Miller."

"Just making a point. You overgeneralized. And you aren't alone. There's an astounding diversity of flora in the world. Most people are either too lazy or too indifferent to learn about it. They conveniently lump everything into simplistic categories they can deal with. Like 'the green tunnel.'"

"I may not be a botanist. But I understand and appreciate diversity."

"It's not just botany. Take politics. There are infinite nuances of opinion. It's hard to understand or keep track of all of them. Most people throw up their hands. There are a thousand shades of liberal and a thousand degrees of conservative. But turn on the news and all you hear is the one 'l' word. Or the one 'c' word."

"So we shoehorn everybody's ideas into categories. Whether they fit or not?"

"Right. At some point the artificial replaces the reality on which it's supposedly based."

"The label takes on a life of its own."

"Yeah. Instead of analysis, guys wear their anti-intellectualism as a badge of honor. There really are only two categories. There's 'us,' who are the good guys, and 'them,' who are the bad. Being an expert means you get to pop off about the people you don't like. Nobody uses the scientific method anymore. Take the talk shows. What passes for knowledge is a thousand feet wide and one inch deep."

"I know what you mean. There can be only one kind of Christian anymore. The born-again fundamentalists on TV, like Jerry Falwell or Pat Robertson. If I say I'm a Christian, people automatically lump me with them. It really frosts me."

"Why? You're all green."

"Enough already! But I like your point about a thousand feet wide and one inch deep. You've been watching Fox News."

"Bare and phalanxed."

Robert cackled. "You are bad, man!"

"Fox, CNN, Al Jazeera, whatever. They all know better, but they perpetuate the labels. And the myths and prejudices."

Robert framed his next remark carefully. "Soc, this conversation tells me that somewhere, sometime, somebody gave you a hard time."

Socrates stopped on a dime. Robert reined in his stride to avoid a collision. "More than once, Snaky. When you'd rather look for salamanders than play football, and your complexion's darker than the other white kids in school, and you're smarter than they are, and have a funny-sounding last name, you attract teasers and bullies. Anything out of the ordinary sets them off. "

Robert's curiosity overruled trail etiquette. "What is your name, Soc?"

"I don't like where this is going. But I'll tell you. Gregor Antoniades. And yours?"

"Robert Martin."

"Well, Robert Martin, let's make a deal. This is the last time we use those names. *Tabula rasa.* I am Socrates, and you are Dances with Snakes. This is the Appalachian Trail. Out here we're known by our trail names. We walk by the white blazes with a clean slate. What goes on outside the AT universe doesn't matter."

"Okay." Robert wanted to pursue the conversation, but the window to Socrates's past had closed. Changing the subject, he gestured at the prized T-shirt. "I'm confused about one thing. Does that mean Duke doesn't matter out here?"

"You're a real shit."

Robert regretted bringing up Duke. Fortunately the "green tunnel" came to his rescue. Something caught his friend's eye. Socrates walked to the base of a large tree and gently spread apart some dead leaves.

"Come here, Snaky."

Robert walked over and peered into the leaves. "What are we looking for?"

"I'm finishing the botany lesson. And also explaining to the smart-mouthed asshole why Duke matters. See this little plant?"

"Here?"

"No, this one." He pointed to a tiny sprig of slender dark green leaves. Each leaf had a pale green vein running down its length. The entire plant was only three inches across by two inches high.

Robert attempted to reclaim a seat in the pantheon. "Pipsissewa?"

"Close. You may redeem your sorry ass yet. This is spotted wintergreen, *Chimaphila maculata*. Pipsissewa is *Chimaphila umbellata*."

"Lanceolate leaves." Robert beamed.

"Excellent. You see these huge dead leaves matted around it?" Robert pointed to one with the foot of Old Hickory. "Yeah, that one. Even when it's desiccated, it's quite large. That leaf fell from this tree." Socrates rested his hand on the large trunk beside him. "Fraser magnolia. *Magnolia fraseri*. Not the magnolia you're used to, the *grandiflora*. This one is deciduous, not evergreen. The leaves on this sucker are about one foot long and a half-foot wide. They dwarf the little *Chimaphila*."

"I get it. Two green plants. One at each end of the size spectrum. Very large. Very small. Illustrates the diversity of the forest. But how does Duke fit in?"

"*Fraseri* is Duke. *Maculata* is Winthrop."

"Ah! March Madness. Number-one seed versus number sixteen. Number one wins by forty points."

"You're not quite with me, Snaky. Rank and size aren't the point. The point is both of them are in the big dance."

Robert was taken aback. "This is the first time you ever talked basketball without insisting that winning is paramount. Has losing made you philosophical?"

"No, losing sucks. What I'm saying is there are all different kinds of teams in the competitive mix. And all different kinds of plants. There is beauty in that. We ought to prize that diversity. *Maculata* and Winthrop are players, just like *fraseri* and Duke. Natural selection determines survival, but it doesn't diminish the efforts of all the species giving it their best shot."

"So when Coach K holds his postgame press conference and praises the opponent, he's engaging in a kind of neo-Darwinism."

"You could say that. In addition to the score, he recognizes their efforts to survive and thrive. He would call that the quintessential element in all things."

"Even if the opponent is Carolina?"

"Everybody knows Tarholes ain't got no quintessence."

"Science meets sports. Science loses. So much for your damn botany lesson."

"Some things are beyond your reptilian understanding." Socrates resumed walking. They were quiet for several minutes.

Robert broached the question that had been on his mind since their first day. "Soc?"

"Yeah?"

"You asked me once if I believed in God."

"You answered, sort of. We never finished the conversation."

"Let's do it now." He pressed on. "Do you believe in God?"

Socrates was silent for several steps. "No, Snaky, I don't. Are you surprised?"

"I guess not. I just thought that maybe when you examined the wintergreen and the magnolia, or the laurel and the rhody, and umpteen different varieties of salamanders, that you might acknowledge a force behind the complexities of creation."

"I don't see it that way. The complexities of creation just are. It's up to us to understand them. But I will agree with two things you said."

"And they are?"

"You said you couldn't live without hope."

"Yeah. I believe that."

"I can't either. I see hope in the pattern of our evolution. Like any other organism, if we don't adapt, we perish. We're smart enough to distinguish between what will destroy us and what will help us survive. That intelligence has improved the species over time, and it's what will continue to improve us in the future. It's our quintessence."

"And to you this quintessence is innate. I mean, it doesn't come from some other power. Something called God."

"Innate is a good word. We have the capability to make ourselves better. I believe that." He was silent for a few steps and then added, "Does this disappoint you?"

"No. You're entitled to believe what you want. And don't worry. I won't try to change your mind. I've got too much stuff of my own to deal with." They were silent for several more steps. "What was the second thing?"

"Second thing?"

"Yeah, you said you agreed with me on two things."

"Oh. You talked about examples of man's failures. Even though I believe we will eventually get there, mankind has made some spectacular messes along the way. Two steps forward, one back. You said the Bible had a good description of this."

"The book of Romans. But you can find it in literature. Have you ever read *All the King's Men*? Robert Penn Warren's novel?"

"No. Why?"

"The main character is a Louisiana politician. He has a great take on original sin: 'Man is conceived in sin and born in corruption, and he passeth from the stink of the didie to the stench of the shroud.'"

"Interesting. My own research has uncovered a prime example of man's fetid condition."

"Really? What?"

"I smell it every time I drive through Chapel Hill."

Chapter 5

Every picture tells a story ... don't it
Rod Stewart

They scaled a short hill and reached a junction on the top of the ridge. The white blazes steered them along the path to the right. The gentle crest curved like a stuffed pillow, a marked departure from the Stecoah sawteeth.

"Hold up, Soc. This is it."

"What?"

"The Smokies. We're on the main ridge. For the next sixty miles."

"Big deal."

Robert ignored the denigration. "This is Doe Knob, one of my favorites. Let's take a break and celebrate. We have plenty of time to get to Mollie's Ridge by nightfall."

Socrates unbuckled his pack and dropped it on the ground. "Don't know why we're celebrating, but it's a good excuse to eat a candy bar. If you produce a cold beer, I'll really make some noise."

"We're celebrating the beginning of the highest stretch on the whole AT. And also a fond memory. When Rob was still in high school, we hiked the AT through the Smokies."

"Another father-son thing?"

"Yeah. We stopped here for lunch. This doe comes right up to us, no more than six feet away. She wasn't the least bit spooked. We kept on eating, and she kept on staring, like she might come up and lick peanut butter right out of our hands. Finally she got bored and wandered off."

"Doe Knob. Appropriate name for the mountain."

"You got that right."

"That's a good omen. If you met your doe here, maybe I can meet my Mollie when we get to the shelter."

"So Mollie's her name. What's she look like?"

"A nice rack and a firm ass. I haven't thought about her face."

"For a Duke man, I'd expect at least a minimum standard. You must really be horny."

"Jeez, Snaky, we've been out here for weeks. You old guys can't remember how it feels."

"We old guys never get *that* old."

They hiked for another hour through a thickening mist. The trail plunged down the ridge and then rose steeply. Over their labored breaths they heard the babble of conversation. The fog grudgingly dissolved and revealed a three-sided hut. A dispersed group of males and females patrolled the woods around the shelter, scouring for firewood.

Robert stated the obvious. "Looks and sounds like a full house."

"Good. My odds are improving."

Robert did not see a familiar face. He assumed they were section hikers, going south. Their lively conversation rose and fell in an alien melody. He didn't understand a word they were saying.

"Not to insult you, but it sounds like Greek to me. What the hell are they speaking?"

"Not sure. It's not German."

"Not French or Spanish either. Scandinavian?"

"Don't think so. Hey, there's you answer. And mine!"

"Where?"

"The blonde in the T-shirt. With the really big ones."

Robert spotted the young lady. Across her buxom chest, "Polska" was emblazoned in red script. The lettering reminded him of the hand-painted signs waving on the TV newscasts from fifteen years ago. "Solidarity. Lech Walesa."

"You got it. With a slogan board like that, it's no wonder he could run off the Communists. You don't happen to know Polish for 'nice tits,' do you?"

"No, and I don't know Polish for 'chauvinist pig' either. But I think you've found your Mollie, judging from the ridge inside that T." He looked again in admiration. "That *is* a nice set."

"It is! It is! Firm ass, too. And hey, she's not bad looking."

"I didn't think you'd notice."

"I wonder if anybody speaks English."

They walked toward the group. The Poles stopped searching for wood as the duo approached. Socrates offered a friendly "Hello." The Poles rendered a foreign greeting.

"That answers your question."

Undeterred, Socrates pointed to the two vacant wire-mesh pads on the left side of the upper platform in the shelter. "Okay if we sleep there tonight?"

His question was met with ten blank faces. Still undaunted, he walked to the platform and slapped his hand on the wood frame of the empty bunks. He pointed to himself and to Robert and brought his two hands together under the side of his head in the universal sleep sign.

The Poles rewarded his charade with grunts of understanding. "*Tak. Tak.*"

He turned to Robert triumphantly. "Get your stuff inside."

"My God, the boy can act," Robert proclaimed. "Is there anything he doesn't do?"

"I don't do windows."

Robert hoisted his pack over one shoulder and walked to the vacant slots. He thrust his bag onto the second pad from the end.

"No, Snaky. Take the one by the wall. I'm betting Mollie is sleeping here." Socrates pointed at the bedroll in the third slot from the left.

"You wish! You're so horny, you're delusional."

"She's been eyeing me since I talked to them."

"You're dreaming. You can't see the forest for the breasts. I bet that bedroll belongs to the big guy over there. For all you know he's married to her."

They fired up their Whisperlites on a huge flat rock outside the shelter. As befits hosts with international guests, they ceded the prime cooking spots on the lower wooden platform to the Poles, who also busied themselves with dinner. With thru-hiker efficiency, the Americans finished long before the Poles, who prolonged their meal with laughter and socializing.

Robert and Socrates collected their food and trash and strolled to the food-hoist cable strung between two large oaks in front of the shelter. They looped the strings of their sacks over a large S-hook attached to the cable. Using the pulley, they lifted the bags twenty feet off the ground, out of harm's way. The Poles maintained their animated conversation and paid them no attention.

Biding his time until the Poles finished dinner, Socrates donned his headlamp and read from a paperback. Robert put away his stove and cookware. He stared at Mollie from the protective gloom inside the shelter. Was she checking Socrates out, as he had claimed? As far as Robert could tell, she was completely absorbed with her friends and not at all interested in his companion.

Robert opted for a sponge bath. He looked forward each evening to washing away the day's sweat and grime, a necessary prelude to climbing into the sleeping bag. Down was hard to wash, and he took pains to keep the bag as clean as possible. More than just a toasty cocoon, the mummy had taken on greater significance. It was the last vestige of civilization, a fantasy retreat from the unpleasant realities of dirt and odor.

He disappeared behind the shelter, carrying his biodegradable soap, water bottle, and microtowel. He stripped to the waist and lathered his arms and chest. He was well into his backcountry ablution when he heard a Socratic shout above the indecipherable Polish chatter.

"No! Don't do that!"

Robert stepped around the corner of the shelter. Socrates had jumped from the upper-level bunk and rushed to the clearing in front of the shelter. One of the Polish men stood in front of him. He held a bag of garbage in one hand and a shovel in the other. Robert had seen the shovel earlier, leaning against the outside wall of the shelter. He surmised the maintainers left it for hikers, a giant-sized "cat hole facilitator."

"Soc, I bet they bury trash in Poland."

"But if they do it here, the bears or the raccoons will dig it up and scatter it all over the place. How do I explain 'leave no trace' to this guy?"

Robert remembered the poster, tacked to the inside shelter wall. It outlined the dos and don'ts of dealing with bears. The words were useless, but there was a picture of a bear at the top. He trotted inside, unfastened the sign, and brought it to the clearing.

Socrates gleamed. "This'll work."

He turned to the quizzical Pole. Smiling politely, he took the trash and shovel away from him. The rest of his comrades were drawn to the ongoing production and gathered around the two protagonists. Mollie stood at the front, engrossed and engrossing.

Socrates dug a shallow hole in the ground. He laid the bag in the depression and covered it partially with dirt and leaves, to simulate a burial.

The Pole thought he understood. *"Tak, tak,"* he nodded. The friendly American was burying his trash.

"No, no!" Socrates implored.

"Nie?" His face screwed up.

Socrates pointed to the picture. "Bear."

"Czarny niedzwiedz."

Socrates pointed to the picture of the bear again and then to himself. Suddenly, he dropped on his hands and knees, grunting loudly. He tossed the dirt and leaves off the bag of garbage and tore it to shreds. With brutish noises, he pretended to gorge on banana and orange peels. Robert wondered if he'd go so far as to eat the garbage. He tossed the trash in all directions, making a considerable mess.

His audience understood. This is what a bear does with buried garbage. The Poles seemed to appreciate the medium even more than the message. Mollie, in particular, clapped enthusiastically.

Socrates acknowledged the acclaim with gracious bows and gave his friendliest smile to the goddess in the taut T-shirt. He held up his finger to indicate he wasn't finished. "Snaky, bring me my pack."

Robert made his way through the appreciative Poles and did as ordered. "Will that be all, sahib?"

"Yes. You're dismissed." Socrates pulled out a plastic bag he had saved from the Fontana grocery. He carefully picked up the trash he had strewn over the ground. Motioning the Pole to accompany him, he led him to the cables and demonstrated how to hoist the bags beyond a bear's reach. The Pole issued a short command to the others. They brought their food bags and ran them up the cables to safety.

Each one approached Socrates and shook his hand. To his consuming delight, Mollie gave him a generous, full-frontal hug. Socrates beamed the smile heretofore reserved for the day when Duke would repeat as NCAA champions.

The Poles retreated to the shelter. Robert rejoined the radiant thespian. "The lengths some of us will go to just to get a cheap feel."

"Some of us don't appreciate the intricacies of international discourse. The United States and Poland are cleaner and safer because of my enlightened statesmanship. And I ask that you not make disparaging remarks about my girlfriend."

"Your little acting triumph deludes you even more than your hormones."

"How so?"

"Well, once she saw me without my shirt, she couldn't take her eyes off me. I expect she'll crawl into my sleeping bag later."

"You are so full of it. Why would she want anything to do with a wrinkled old reptile?"

Robert tilted his head in the direction of the shelter. "Actually, there's your real problem. She's sleeping on the lower deck, between two healthy hunks."

Socrates glanced into the shelter to confirm the sleeping configuration. Mollie was surrounded by the fawning male members of her troupe. He bashed his fist into his palm. "Damn! The odds aren't good. And I have so many more things I want to show her."

"What could you possibly show her that's better than the bear?"

"Snaky, I have all sorts of animals inside me."

"No doubt. But you'll have to keep them in your shorts tonight."

Socrates grimaced. "I thought I had something going." He perked up slightly. "Tomorrow, I'll show Mollie how we pack out the trash. Maybe I can get some morning action."

"Right. Like you said, man cannot live without hope."

—m—

Robert steered around a mud puddle. Ahead, a blue rain suit and pack cover bobbed in and out of the fog. The depressingly familiar image was the only sight available.

Since Mollie's Ridge, they had endured relentless rain. The annual precipitation in the Smokies exceeded eighty inches. It seemed that all of it was falling in the few days they traversed the park.

The Cheoah panorama was gone. Visibility was reduced to a tight, fifty-foot diameter. His hopes for more views likewise imploded. The wraparound vista on Rocky Top had been obliterated. Immortalized in song by the Tennessee Volunteers, the mountain was murk and gloom and nothing to sing about.

Clingman's Dome, the high point, had also been a washout. Robert had asked his mountain "friend" for no blizzards. He should have wished for no rain and fog.

In deference to Socrates, they ascended the observation tower. He fulfilled an obligation to the folks back home, who would ask, "You went up that tower on Clingman's, didn't you?" The view was no better than standing in a steam room.

They met two tourists from Boston who had walked up a trail from the parking lot near the access road. Deprived of the expansive panorama, they groused about the rave reviews that had lured them there. Robert attempted to describe what was out beyond the pale, but the Bostonians left in disgust. He and Socrates continued north.

Bartram's "world of mountains piled upon mountains" had shrunk to the naked blueberry bushes beside the trail and the green shoots of new Fraser firs that lined the fallen carcasses of their once magnificent forebears. The other constants in this constricted world were rain on his cheeks and the fuzzy blue hulk in front of him.

At Newfound Gap, an elderly couple from Michigan driving a Winnebago gave them a ride to a motel in Gatlinburg. The shower came first, and then laundry and resupply. Rehabilitated, Socrates left to explore the sights and sounds of Dollywood.

Robert called Mandy. She was indeed pregnant, and the doctor said that everything was normal. He hung up the phone and danced a jig. In his little world, the rain clouds evaporated and the sun shone brightly.

His spirits lifted, Robert placed a second call.

"Rob?"

"Hi, Dad."

"You doing okay?"

"Yep. Where are you?"

"Gatlinburg."

"In the Smokies already?"

"Yeah. Hike's going great. I've hit my stride. Was at Doe Knob the other day, but we didn't see our friend."

"There are moose up here as tame as she was. So you're not hiking alone?"

"I've been with a kid from Charlotte since I left Georgia. He just graduated from Duke. Bleeds blue and white."

"You need to see a shrink."

"Spoken like a Tech grad. He's a nice kid, Rob, in spite of where he went to school. You'd like him. He's only a few years younger than you. Say, you been on an exercise or something?"

"Got back two days ago."

"I tried calling at Wesser and again at Fontana. Figured you were in the field. What did you do, besides freeze your ass?"

"That, mostly. Can't tell you much. Let's just say we completed our mandatory training."

"I'll rest easy then. Heard from your sister?"

"E-mail waiting when I got back."

"What do you think, Uncle Rob?"

"I think it's great. You'll have someone new to take on hikes. I've put in my time."

"Cut me to the quick! Aren't you forgetting about soccer? Me standing on the sidelines in the rain, cheering you on? Let's call it a draw. Speaking of soccer, are you playing?"

"I'm on the base team, but with work I miss some matches."

"Keep at it. You know how I feel about competitive sports. I just talked to Mandy. She's gonna keep swimming, to keep her weight down during pregnancy."

"Don't worry. I'm not about to give up soccer."

The small talk was not what Robert wanted. He felt awkward broaching the subject. Angie had always been the one to engage the kids, particularly Rob, for whom reticence was a virtue. There had been no entrée in the conversation, and he didn't see one coming. He resigned himself to blunder on.

"Rob, I wonder how you're feeling. You know, about your mom." The dead time on the phone seemed endless.

"How do you feel, Dad?"

Robert admired how Rob adeptly deflected the question. It was a stratagem he had learned from his mother. Robert blurted out his feelings. "Lonely. Devastated. Angry that I couldn't do anything to help her. Upset for being selfish and for not asking before now how you're dealing with it."

"I knew you wouldn't be able to talk about her for a while. The two of you were so close."

"She was my sun. I revolved around her. But you. How are you coping?"

There was more dead air. "I've never not had a mom before."

Robert appreciated his succinctness. He searched for ways to keep Rob talking. "When you think about her, what comes to mind?"

The silence was not as long. "I miss the radar."

Robert laughed. A long-standing family joke was that Angie could always sense when Rob was up to something. She would catch him red-handed when he least expected it. After she frustrated one of his machinations, he accused her of concealing a radar in the house. Her nose for trouble was legend. When it came time for stories at family gatherings, someone always brought up "the radar." Her unmaskings of Rob were reverently recounted.

"You're not still throwing ninja stars into the bedroom ceiling, are you?"

"Not what I mean. Over the years, as I grew up, the radar changed."

Robert's voice rose with interest. "How?"

"Mom's intuition was still uncanny. But different. She didn't worry I would trash the house. Or dig up the yard. She was more concerned about how I was doing. What I was thinking. She knew when I wanted her to talk to me."

"Your mom was a great listener."

A cavalcade of images from Rob's childhood and adolescence paraded before him. He grimaced at the lost opportunities when the two of them might have drawn closer. Angie had been able to connect with him in more meaningful ways.

"Remember when I came home on leave? About a month before Mom died?"

"Labor Day weekend."

"Yeah. The three of us were in the bedroom. She sent you off for something. She wanted to be alone with me. She realized it was our last chance to talk."

"What did she say?"

"She was proud of me. College grad, air force officer. She was sure I'd find the right girl, and she was sorry she wouldn't get to meet her. She wanted to leave this girl her radar." Rob paused momentarily. "I didn't know what to say. Finally, I asked if there was anything I could do. She was pleased that I asked. She said, 'Talk to your father. It'll help him.'"

Robert could not speak. There was a catch in his throat and tears in his eyes.

"Until now, I didn't know how to do that. I was there only that short time and back again three days for the funeral. Way up here, it's hard to figure out how to help. And you've been in a daze. I've never seen you so out of it."

"I was shell-shocked, Rob. I didn't speak to anyone."

"Mom said there'd come a time when we'd talk. She said that we would prop each other up."

"She's still the heart of this family, isn't she?"

"Like she was still here. But she's not."

"Son, I'm a lot better now than when she died. I've had a running dialogue with myself since I started the hike. I know I can't bring her back, but I have better control of my thoughts. It helps to concentrate on positive memories. I recommend you do something similar. It helps to talk about it. You have anybody to talk to up there? The chaplain?"

Rob snickered with disdain. Robert realized little had changed since he was in the service. Nobody would admit he needed the chaplain. "Okay, forget the chaplain. You got a friend?"

"As a matter of fact, yes."

"Good. What's his name?"

"Jennifer."

"Excuse me! That kind of friend. How long you been seeing her?"

"A couple of months. We're not serious or anything."

"She in the air force?"

"A nurse at the base hospital. First lieutenant."

"Outranks you?"

"Remember what you told me. Rank among lieutenants is like virtue among whores."

"Right! Where's she from?"

"Seattle. She plays soccer."

"She any good?"

"Better than I am." Robert noted the admission. Rob was even more competitive than he.

"But you didn't tell her that, did you?"

"No way. What do you take me for?"

"Just checking. It sounds like things are getting better for you."

"Yeah. They are."

Robert was relieved. The call was going much better than expected. "Rob, I'm glad we finally talked. As always, your mom was right. I'm propped up. What about you?"

"Yeah. So am I."

"And Rob ..." Robert paused for emphasis. "Most of the time it must seem like I'm navigating in a London fog. Without any instruments. But radar or no, I'm your friend. And I am also very proud of you."

"Thanks, Dad."

"You're not going back to the field anytime soon, are you?"

"No more exercises for a while."

"We'll talk more frequently. I'll call next week, when I get to Hot Springs or Erwin. Good luck with Jennifer. I love you, Rob."

"Okay, Dad. Bye."

Socrates returned to the motel. His face was glum.

"How was Dollywood?"

"Glorified tourist trap. Searched all over, but I couldn't find her."

"Who?"

"Dolly, you idiot."

"Well, excuse me!" Robert dragged out the *u* in mock apology.

"I was sure if we met, she'd like me. I mean, I really go for her."

"The logic's flawed. I understand how she turns you on, but I'm struggling to see how you ring her bell. But speaking of well-endowed women, whatever happened to your girlfriend Mollie?"

"Star-crossed. She went south with her guardian goons. I'm going north."

"And you and Dolly are going nowhere."

"No need to be cruel. Say, what's the news? Are we pregnant?"

Robert raised both arms over his head and clapped his hands. "I'm gonna be a grandpa!"

"Too much! Is everything okay?"

"Mandy's doin' fine. The doc's happy."

"So will the baby be named for you?"

"It's a bit early for that."

"I don't know. They can call him Fang. Or Serpentina, if it's a girl."

"Low on the list. But there are worse names."

"Like what?"

"Like Aristotle, or some other Greek philosopher."

They ate a massive spaghetti dinner at a local Italian restaurant and washed it down with a bottle of Chianti. Not wanting to waste the smallest dollop of meat sauce, they wiped their plates clean with the second helping of garlic bread. The feast culminated with large servings of spumoni and cheesecake. Stomachs swelled, they walked contentedly through the spattering rain to the motel.

Later that evening, Robert found a Gideon Bible in the nightstand by his bed. Daily meditations, like the morning prayer, had become part of the framework that kept him positive. He took advantage of the opportunity to read from the Old Testament. He turned to the familiar third chapter of Ecclesiastes. The words seemed to be written expressly for him.

For everything there is a season, and a time for every matter under heaven: a time to be born, and a time to die; ... a time to weep, and a time to laugh, a time to mourn, and a time to dance.

The poignant juxtapositions broke over him like waves at high tide. Would the joy growing in his heart shrink the memories of Angie? Would the proud grandfather crowd out the grieving widower? Was it really a time to laugh, a time to dance? Why would he get to hold that baby, when Angie could not?

The old doubts challenged his newfound contentment. He struggled to integrate his thoughts. The tears streaked his face like the raindrops on the motel window.

"Snaky, you all right?" From his bed, Socrates looked at him over the top of a paperback.

Robert took a moment to compose himself. "My minister said I would have episodes of sadness that would surprise me. Sometimes just reading something familiar sets it off."

"Whatcha got there?"

"The Bible. Ecclesiastes. Can I read you something?"

Socrates nodded unenthusiastically.

Robert read the passage aloud and put the Bible down on the table. "I'm having a hard time making this work. I'm ecstatic about becoming a grandparent. But I feel guilty, because Angie's not here to share in it. I'm enjoying the hell out of this hike. I let myself laugh at things, like you and the Poles. Then I worry that when I'm happy, I'm forgetting about her. When she sees me having fun, does she think I don't care anymore?"

Socrates put his book down on the bed and sat up. "How ironic that you ask me to interpret a Bible verse." He chose his words carefully. "Snaky, you ought to home in on the word 'season.' The writer said for everything there is a season, but he doesn't say these seasons are mutually exclusive. You're a sports fan. There's basketball season, which overlaps with baseball season, which overlaps with football, which ... you get the idea. Shit, hockey overlaps with them all. But the overlap doesn't cause you a problem. In Atlanta, you can follow the Braves and the Falcons in September, or the Hawks and Thrashers in December. That is, if you're a masochist."

Robert smiled weakly. "Winter has been a time to weep in Atlanta."

"It's okay for you to be happy about a grandchild and happy about hiking the AT, while being sad about losing your wife. The 'time to weep and the time to laugh' can be the same. If Angie looks down and sees you dancing, she knows a time will come when you'll mourn. Not only that, she wants you to dance. She'd think you were a jerk if you weren't ecstatic about this baby. And by all means enjoy this hike. She won't begrudge you."

"You think so?"

"Hell yes, you dummy. This hike is your big dance! You are Duke, and this is March Madness."

"I'll excuse that ghastly inappropriate example, because you have a point. By hiking, I'm being quintessential."

"Damn straight. And you should think of mourning as another way to dance. Dancing can be an expression of sadness."

"Angie used to say when it came to singing and dancing, I was just sad—period."

"Hey, you're laughing at yourself. And keeping your perspective. You're smart enough to figure this out."

Robert sat for a few moments, taking it all in. He wiped his eyes and smiled. "I was wrong."

"Whaddaya mean?"

"Maybe Mandy names the baby for a Greek philosopher after all."

Socrates smiled broadly.

"Thanks, Soc. You pulled me out of the bear wallow. I'm walking down the trail again. Breakfast is on me tomorrow."

"Good. There's a Waffle House right up the street."

Chapter 6

And I wonder, still I wonder ... who'll stop the rain?
Creedence Clearwater Revival

The blue pack cover bobbed in and out of the fog. It alternated with random vacuous images that fleeted for an instant through Robert's brain and then vanished without imprinting on his consciousness. Only when a low-hanging branch grazed the hood of his rain jacket did he snap out of the trance.

The rear end of the Blue Devil was a poor substitute for Appalachian expanse. The obdurate dreariness demanded an attitude reassessment. Staying positive in the rain required continuous effort.

Like his miserable surroundings, the episode of melancholy in Gatlinburg gnawed at him. Why did it suddenly occur after so many days of sanguinity? His emotional pendulum still swung too widely, with too many depressive outliers. The elaborate computer security at his accounting firm had been frequently reprogrammed to block new viruses and malware. Similarly, he needed to update his emotional firewall.

Socrates had suggested that he keep things in perspective. Before falling asleep in the motel, he had read more from the Old Testament, and bookmarked Psalm 118.

This is the day that the Lord has made ...

What happens, happens. He could have done nothing to keep Angie from dying. He had to accept his own limitations. A man of fifty-seven should not find this difficult, but it went against his point-guard mentality to concede anything.

Implicit in this concession was a positive. He would stop reliving what had happened. Instead, he would react to it. He would focus on what he could control. The best place to start was his attitude.

... *Let us rejoice and be glad in it.*

This was the new firewall. Grief would cripple him only if he allowed it. There were enough real hills to climb on the trail without conjuring up additional obstacles.

He had uttered the verse as a preamble to his prayer the morning they left Gatlinburg. He continued to do so each day afterward.

Chasing the blue apparition, he tested his freshly minted optimism on the disheartening weather. In the army they had called rain "infantry sunshine." And if the biblical flood ended after forty days, it couldn't rain in the Smokies forever.

Rejoice. Be glad.

Others could not. There were fewer and fewer northbound hikers. The shelters had been packed in Georgia, but on the previous evening in the Smokies, there were only five people, less than half of capacity. The horde had thinned for various reasons. A retired couple from Florida, Orlando Tony and Dawn, had yellow-blazed out of the Stecoahs to seek medical attention, he for throbbing knees and she for a pinched sciatic nerve. Socrates talked to some college students in Gatlinburg who had run out of money and were forced to go home. Many others simply lost their zest for hiking.

Ten years earlier, Robert had attended a hiking symposium featuring Bill Irwin, the blind man who thru-hiked the AT with his guide dog, Orient. His story was spellbinding. Bill emphasized the most difficult part of the AT is *the distance between one's ears*. Out there every day for hours on end, an irresolute mind can easily go down its own trail. Without purpose, a hiker will not be able to tough it out.

Loss of resilience was the principal cause of the "Virginia blues." This malaise struck six weeks or so into the hike, about the time hikers finished Tennessee. Those afflicted concluded, either from desperation or boredom, that they would not survive 550 miles of the Old Dominion.

Had the blues struck earlier this year? Rain was a big contributor. Consecutive days of wet feet and clammy clothes were palpable reasons to reevaluate the decision to hike. It was natural to question one's sanity while continuously plodding through slosh. But it had not been cold in the Smokies. He was able to dry off and warm up each night in the shelter. The long-sought adventure had withstood its tenuous beginnings. He was still finding positives, particularly when compared to the alternatives. A rainy day on the AT was better than staying home feeling sorry for himself, and much better than sitting at a desk filing tax returns.

The blue blob grew larger. Socrates had stopped. Robert halted and pushed up the brim of his hood for a better view. The root ball of a colossal Fraser fir had fallen beside the path. The tree was a victim of the balsam woolly adelgid. The insect had burrowed under the bark and disrupted the flow of sap, causing the tree to die.

Once a towering, majestic specimen, the Fraser was reduced to a grotesque nexus of roots, rocks, and dirt that stretched ten feet across and eight feet high. Cement-colored rainwater had collected in the hole vacated by the roots. It resembled a prop from the set of *The Legend of Sleepy Hollow.*

"Hard to believe a tiny insect did that," Robert lamented.

"That little adelgid had plenty of help," Socrates countered. "The Ph on the rain in the Smokies can read in the fives."

"Isn't that toxic?"

"Like sulfuric acid. It stresses the trees. The insect delivers the *coup de grace*. We couldn't see Mount Guyot for the fog, but it's covered with dead trunks. It looks like an old man's salt-and-pepper beard. Like yours."

Robert pondered what Arnold would think of deforestation on his mountain. Would he classify it as part of the cycle of nature? Or poor stewardship of the environment?

"You know, if Guyot were here, he'd kick our butts."

"He'd bust us for killing off the catamounts and the elk also. They roamed the Smokies when he was here."

"When I was young, I often went to Mount Mitchell, over in the Black Mountains. The balsam forest was a thing to behold. Tall trees in thickets. Dark green, almost black. The Smokies and the Roan Highlands were the same. I'm sorry you didn't get to see that."

Socrates pointed to the root ball. Several feet off the ground, a growth protruded from a clump of dirt trapped in the roots. Deer grass and moss grew suspended in midair, as if they did not need the earth below for sustenance.

"I'm always amazed how life reasserts itself after something dies."

Robert bristled. "But it's never the same."

"Sorry. I was into science. I didn't mean to—"

"Go ahead. I'll try to be objective."

Socrates continued. "The Fraser's dead. Other species will take its place. A century ago, there was a magnificent forest of chestnuts in the Appalachians. Then a blight killed them all. Now we have other hardwoods. Oaks, maple, beech, birch, ash, and poplar. Natural selection at work. Mother Nature is resilient. But I hate to lose the Frasers. They're the signature species at high elevation. Seeing them die is like ... well, it's like ..."

"Coach K leaving Duke?" Robert finished his sentence.

"Not quite." Socrates smiled. "That would be Armageddon. I thought you were being objective."

"I was. Apparently you have a different threshold. But say good-bye to the Frasers. At least until Roan Mountain. We're descending out of their range."

Socrates looked at the root ball. "I'd rather not see them at all than see them ass-end up."

"Just the way I feel after following your butt through the rain for three days."

"Then you lead. I'll bitch about your fat ass."

—⁂—

He woke to rain. Before he could mutter "Same old, same old," he felt the chill, the gift of a passing front. His pack thermometer, at thirty-four degrees, confirmed the drop. Fortunately, he would lose altitude today. At the highest elevations there would be sleet or freezing rain. He left Cosby Shelter and the snoring Socrates.

Hard to rejoice today, but what the hell.

The trail did not descend uniformly. It dropped sharply in the first mile to Low Gap, only to climb back eight hundred feet to Sunup Knob and Mount Cammerer. Jaded by the discomfort of the rain, he found irony in the place names. There were more "Low Gaps" on the AT than Peachtree Streets in Atlanta. And Sunup Knob, at least for today, was a derisive misnomer.

There was an old stone fire tower just off the AT, on Mount Cammerer. On most days, it offered marvelous views of the Pigeon River valley, but not today. The rain was steady and driven by gusts. The wind-propelled dampness was much more chilling than snow. Robert moved on, hoping to generate heat.

The muddy trail fell three thousand feet to Davenport Gap and the northern boundary of the Smokies. Going downhill, he wasn't expending enough energy to maintain warmth in his extremities. In spite of Polartec gloves and Gore-Tex rain mittens, his fingers were cold. Angie had always called him a hot box, but today his circulation failed to deliver.

He rubbed his hands together and on his thighs. At breaks, he removed the gloves, massaged his hands vigorously, blew on his fingers, and stuck them inside the jacket pockets next to his abdomen. The tingling persisted.

He arrived at the shelter near Davenport Gap and waited for Socrates. His buddy would come in to write in the register and to leave his mark for posterity. Shivering, Robert read the entries. Some hikers had scribbled poetry, mostly doggerel. Others meditated on the works of Far Eastern philosophers. Still others created stick-figure art and scatological graffiti.

Predictably, recent entries dealt with the weather. The Keystone Cop had written a few lines from "Raindrops Keep Fallin' on My Head." Robert sang aloud, "I'm never gonna stop the rain by complaining." The shivers returned and mercifully silenced his a cappella monotone.

The next comment was by Raggedy Anton. Robert guessed they got ahead while he and Socrates were in Gatlinburg. Anton quoted from the Sermon on the Mount:

> For he makes his sun rise on the evil and
> on the good and sends rain
> on the righteous and on the unrighteous.

Robert debated in which category he belonged. He decided he was cold, and wanted to be with the uncold.

The next entry was by Preacher.

> Complain all you want about weather, but the Lord could have rained down fire and brimstone, like at Sodom and Gomorrah.

Robert thanked God for small favors.

His fingers were so numb he could hardly grasp the pencil. He scrawled a nearly illegible entry, consisting only of his name and the date. He massaged his hands continuously, but the numbness did not improve. The pack thermometer hovered in the midthirties. To stoke what little fire he had left, he wolfed down some gorp. If Socrates did not arrive soon he would have to crawl into his sleeping bag.

R-r-rejoice and b-b-be g-glad in it.

Socrates did not disappoint him. He marched in five minutes later. "You don't look very happy."

"I can't get my h-hands warm. They weren't this bad in the snow, in the N-Nantahalas. Been numb since I s-started down Cammerer."

"You're not Snaky. You're Shaky. Hey, let's get out of this crap and head to Mountain Mama's. You like celebrations, so we'll celebrate completing the Smokies in a nice warm place. Lemme sign the register and we're outta here."

"I'd s-shake your hand but I'm afraid it w-would break my fingers."

—⁕—

At Davenport Gap, they left the AT and followed a winding gravel road down to a cluster of buildings. The main structure, formerly a stone school, housed a store and restaurant. The front was decorated in old license plates, conversation pieces for visitors from across the country. The rest of the building was adorned in advertisements for Winston, Camel, Salem, Doral, and Skoal. Strategically located just inside North Carolina, Mountain Mama's did a thriving business with Tennesseeans, who drove over on nearby Interstate 40 to take advantage of lower tobacco taxes.

They went inside and registered. The manager directed them to an outlying rustic cottage. The building was no bigger than an aluminum yard shed sold at a home improvement store and crammed with three stacks of bunks. They squeezed through the narrow door into the confined hut. Socrates cut on the light and took off his pack. Robert tried to follow suit, but his stiffened hands could not work the pack buckles.

"I've lost my grip."

"I've known that for weeks. What else is new?"

"No, asshole, I really have." He shrugged his shoulders, and the straps slid down his arms to the crook of his elbows. He lowered the pack clumsily to the floor. "I've never been this close to frostbite." Robert rubbed his hands forcefully. "I've lost the strength in my fingers."

Socrates noted the lack of color. "Your hands aren't exactly pink, but there's no permanent damage. It's just a condition of your advancing age."

"Call me an old fart, why don't you!"

Taking the cue, Socrates farted. "How about a hot shower?" The proprietor had indicated that the bathhouse was in an adjacent outbuilding.

"I don't think I can hold the soap."

"We don't want you dropping the soap in a community shower." Smiling, he continued. "We'll clean up later. Let's go to the grill and get you something hot to hold in your hands."

"I'll drink to that." Robert reached for the top pocket on his pack. With great difficulty he grasped the zipper and opened it just enough to slip his hand inside. He fished around and located the ziploc with his wallet. He tried again to pinch open the nylon buckles on the main compartment to retrieve his Polartec cap. His brain waves could not leap across the frozen synapses in his fingers.

"Jeez, can you help? I can't open these clasps."

Socrates snapped them open. "You *are* in a bad way, Old Fart. Get your stuff. Let's go get warm."

The diner was simple and functional. Square wooden tables, each attended by four straight chairs, lined the right side of the restaurant by the windows. A high counter in the middle separated the grill from the tables and also served as a pedestal for an ancient cash register and the guest reservation book. The day's menu was printed in multicolored chalk on a blackboard above the grill. Near the menu board was a picture of Dale Earnhardt, Sr. Photos of other NASCAR drivers were scattered throughout the restaurant and also the convenience store in the left side of the building. In the dining area, on the wall of honor, were several autographed photos of Dolly Parton.

"Local girl makes good," Socrates acknowledged. "But she doesn't know what she missed."

Several paintings of Cherokee braves and maidens, in stylized poses, completed the gallery. Beneath the pictures were shelves filled with cigarette cartons, accompanied by another menu board that listed tobacco prices.

Four hikers, engrossed in cheeseburgers and conversation, occupied the most distant table. Two locals, in Carhartt jackets and pants, sat at another. Socrates steered Robert to an empty table near the pair. Robert sat down, facing the other customers. The room was stuffy, like a laundromat with all dryers tumbling on high heat. Under normal circumstances he would be uncomfortable, but today he cherished the stifling blanket.

Socrates caught the eye of the waitress. She grabbed her pad and came toward them. Dressed for the warmth, she wore a short-sleeved tee, jeans, and tennis shoes. She was pleasingly plump, with long, curly, brown hair extending well below her shoulders. Her homemade nametag sported a green "MM" logo. Each M represented two adjoining mountains. "Brenda" was printed underneath in red.

"Hi, boys. What can I get you?"

"How are you, Brenda?" Her eyes brightened when Socrates called her by name. "For starters, I want a cup of black coffee. The hotter the better. What about you, Snaky?"

"I'll take hot chocolate. What's good on the menu?"

"Hon, our specialty's the jumbo cheeseburger. Comes with lettuce, tomato, mustard and mayo, pickle, onion, and a large helping of fries."

"Sounds like a winner."

"Make it two."

"Coming right up." She walked toward the grill.

Robert turned to Socrates. "I can't believe I ordered a burger and fries. My doctor put me on Lipitor last year to reduce my cholesterol. I'll go into shock from this."

"Snaky, this is exactly what you need. You've been eating too much healthy food. You suffer from chronic organic lipid deprivation, or C-O-L-D. That's why your fingers are so rigid. A good dose of sat fat'll lubricate you all the way to Hot Springs. You can glide on the triglycerides."

"I don't know who chokes first. Me on the burger or you on that line of bullshit. But right now I just want to circle my hands around a hot cup."

As soon as it arrived, Robert began first aid. The chocolate tasted good and felt good. To maximize its therapeutic value, he held the cup with both hands and bent directly over it. He alternated between inhaling hot fumes and sipping small slurps. His goal was to revive his fingers just as he took the last sweet swallow, the perfect confluence of warmth and appetite. He continued to medicate with small doses while Socrates made noisy love to his coffee.

Robert took in the room. He moved from Dale Earnhardt and the faces of other drivers to the nearby table. One of the locals sported a green John Deere baseball cap, like the one George Clooney wore in *The Perfect Storm*. His partner wore a black cap with the number "3" embroidered in white above the bill and outlined in red thread. Their conversation was audible, particularly the words Charlotte, Bristol, and Talladega. They were comparing the relative merits of NASCAR tracks.

"Soc, you ever been to the speedway at Charlotte?"

"Nope. Stock car racing's not my cup of coffee. But lemme tell you, it's big. *Big!*" He waved at the photographs on the wall. "Seems to be *numero uno* in this neck of the woods too." He corrected himself. "*Numero dos*, after Dolly."

Robert looked at the far table. The four hikers had finished their burgers and were eating huge slices of pie. One of the two facing him waved. It was Raggedy Anton, seated next to Andy. Robert returned the salute. Socrates pivoted in his chair and acknowledged the redheads.

One of the other hikers at the table turned to look at him. His face was familiar. Robert initially discounted the resemblance. Every stranger could remind him of someone he knew. He looked again. There was no mistaking the cherubic features under the whitewall haircut.

"I'll be damned."

"What?"

"One of those hikers with the Raggedies. We worked together on the Konnarock crew a few years ago."

"Konnarock? The volunteers who build new trail?"

"Yup."

"I didn't know you did that. Good for you. Where'd you do this?"

"Just north of the Roan Highlands. Tennessee side, near Doll Flats. We relocated the AT onto land the forest service had just acquired. Built a mile of sidehill through rugged terrain. The whole project took six weeks, but I only signed on for one. Hard work, but fun. I'd do it again."

"What about this guy?"

"Brian's a college kid. From out west somewhere. Don't remember his last name."

"Judging from your tone, he's not exactly a long-lost friend. I'm waiting for a shoe to fall."

"Yeah. Brian's a born-again Christian."

"A different shade of green."

"Yeah, and he's over the top with evangelism. Would not leave me alone. I'm out there swinging a Pulaski, sweating like a pig, digging a new trail on the side of a mountain. He's all over me, asking if I've been saved. I told him I was baptized and a Presbyterian all my life. That wasn't good enough."

"He wanted you to walk up the aisle again?"

"Right. I'm not demonstrative about my faith. I mean, I talk about it with you, but not to the exclusion of other stuff. And you bring up the subject half the time. But Brian's very vocal. And very persistent."

"Why didn't you tell him to buzz off?"

"The crew chief asked us to get along. You know, to rely on each other to get the job done. And Brian told me he got the call when he was eleven years old."

"To shit in the woods?"

"No, Turdface. The call to be a minister. He said from then on he knew saving souls was his life's work."

"I'm skeptical of such certainty."

"It was too pat for me also. But I couldn't hold it against him. I mean, this is who he is. Don't laugh, but this is his quintessence."

"More like your gullibility. You have way more patience and tolerance than I do."

"Funny. I always pictured scientists as patient and tolerant. Anyway, I was his conversion goal that week. I moved hundred-pound rocks with him, but I wasn't reborn. Looking back, I don't think he cared about me personally. I was a statistic; another soul to be added to his ledger."

"Did he try to convert anybody else?"

"The crew was happy for me to be the soul *de jour*. He stayed on for another week, so some other sinner probably took my place. I never got a report. But we're gonna get it now. He's finished dessert and is coming over. Rejoice and be glad in it."

"What?"

"I'll explain later."

Brian approached. Robert had forgotten how big and strong he was. He was well over six feet and two hundred pounds. A singular incongruity, cheeks with baby fat, marred his sculpted physique. At twenty-three or twenty-four, he retained a choir boy's visage.

Robert pushed back his chair and stood up.

"Robert?" He extended his hand. "Brian Thompson. From Konnarock."

Brian's strong grip pained his brittle fingers. "Sure. How you doing, Brian? Call me by my trail name, Dances with Snakes. This is my buddy Socrates."

Brian exchanged perfunctory nods with Socrates. "You guys thru-hiking?"

"That's the plan."

"When did you start?"

"March 11. How 'bout you? And your friends?"

"March 8 for me." He sensed a need to explain the disparity in the dates. "I took a few zeroes. I'm not sure about those guys. We hooked up two days ago. Say, you staying here tonight?"

"Yeah. We quit early. Hoping the weather breaks."

"Good choice. Starting tomorrow, God's bringing us several days of sunshine. It's rained steady since the day I passed those Polacks. You guys run into them?"

"No," Socrates shot back. "But we did spend an evening with some nice visitors from Poland."

Brian looked at him quizzically.

Robert broke in. "Say, Brian, you have a trail name?"

"Some guys gave it to me back in Georgia. 'Preacher.'"

"Preacher! I saw your entry back at the shelter. Fire and brimstone!"

"I got tired of all those people complaining to God about a little rain."

"You have to admit He's done an excellent job submersing all of us."

"Speaking of baptism, you never did tell me on Konnarock when you'd been saved."

The segue came too soon for Robert. He was in no mood to rehash the Tennessee dialogues. "Two thousand years ago, Preacher. Christ on the cross was sufficient. I don't need periodic booster shots."

"It never hurts to profess what you believe."

"He knows how I feel." Brenda stood at the counter with two large plates. "Our cheeseburgers are almost ready. We're starving. Maybe we can talk some later."

"Yeah. Rehash trail building. And you can tell me about Dancing Snakes."

"Will do, Preacher. And it's Dances with Snakes."

In spite of Robert's hints, Preacher did not leave. "I'm anxious to hear how Jesus Christ is working in your life. I want to share the personal witness of AT hikers with my students."

"You still in college?"

"No. I'm an organizer for 'Christ on Campus.' At colleges in the South and East. I'm doing this for two years before starting seminary." Preacher turned to Socrates. "Plato, are you a student?"

"It's Socrates." His response was as icy as the chocolate was hot. "I just graduated."

Preacher was quick to apologize, but his effort lacked sincerity. "Sorry. I'm bad with names." He added, "Where?"

"Duke."

"Really? I want to open a chapter there this fall after I finish the AT. I'd like to sit down some time and pick your brain."

"Here you go, sugah." Brenda arrived with two large platters.

"Thanks, Brenda." Robert waited with apprehension for Socrates's next move.

"Sure, Preacher. I'll be glad to help you with the 'Blue Devils for Christ.'"

Preacher laughed nervously. "No, it's Christ on Campus."

Socrates smiled impishly. "Sorry, I'm bad with names."

Preacher turned red with agitation. Before he could reply, Socrates cut him off. "We'll talk later, Preacher. Man does not live by bread alone, but right now it's a high priority. See ya." He reached for the catsup and drowned his fries in a sea of red. He picked up several and sucked them noisily into his mouth, licking the catsup off his thumb and index finger. He fixed his gaze on Robert.

Preacher strained against the curt dismissal. It was all he could do to stifle a retort. "Okay. See you later." He walked away.

Socrates took a big bite out of the greasy burger. He leaned toward Robert and whispered, "Is he gone?"

Robert glanced over Socrates's shoulder. "Yeah. Hey, you were pretty hard on him."

"Think you'll feel okay tomorrow?"

"I'm back to normal. The hot chocolate worked." Robert wiggled his hands. "Sensation."

"Well, get a good night's sleep. I'm thinking we do our first twenty tomorrow."

"No problem, if the weather's better. But why?"

"I want distance between me and that sanctimonious sonofabitch."

—⚏—

Robert stood on Max Patch. From the imposing grassy bald, he relished his first view in over a week. The midafternoon sun blanched countless freshly scrubbed mountains, visible in all directions.

Thank you, God, for letting me walk in your world.

Guideposts marched northward in the grass beside the trail to the treeline below. Atop each was the familiar white blaze. With no trees on the mountaintop, the maintainers had erected posts to mark the route. On a clear day, they weren't necessary, but in the clouds and fog they were indispensable. Years before, on Hump Mountain in the Roan Highlands, it had rained so hard he couldn't see from one post to the next. He followed the depression in the grass, stumbling like a drunkard from marker to marker.

The trail he had just climbed was etched into the verdant grass on the southern slope of Max Patch. Silhouetted against the lush greenery, the familiar jet-black hair and beard moved rapidly. Robert had taken eight hours to cover the sixteen miles. He guessed Socrates had done it in six. He dug out a carrot cake bar from the pack. He was enjoying the second bite when Socrates crested the exposed hill.

"Welcome to Max Patch. And sunshine. Remember what that is?"

"The funny yellow ball that revolves around the earth."

"Say what?"

"That's what Preacher told me. To think I always believed Copernicus."

Robert changed the subject. "Nice hiking?"

"That was a good pull up from the Pigeon River to Snowbird. And it's almost too warm for a change. Bet you like that."

"Right. I put my bandanna on." Years earlier, after days in the blistering sun, Robert returned home with more than a usual "redneck."

Angie took one look at his peeling skin and went to work. She sewed snap grippers onto his bandanna and the back of his baseball cap. The rag draped from the cap and covered his ears and neck. When he modeled it, she laughed and called him "Florence of Arabia." He didn't mind the name or the quirky appearance. The hanky kept the sun at bay.

"This is beautiful." Socrates did a pirouette. "We can see clear back to the Smokies. How far have we come?"

"Sixteen miles. Seventeen, if you count coming up the road from Mountain Mama's."

"That leaves five to the shelter, right?"

"You sound like an accountant. Did you take the CPA exam?"

"What do you think?"

"I think I can handle rejection. But the trail is mellow from here on."

"We ought to do twenty every day, Snaky." He tore the wrapper off the Snickers and took a huge bite. "Tell me something. Yesterday at Mountain Mama's, right before Preacher came over, you mumbled something about rejoicing. What the hell was that?"

Robert laughed. "I'm working on my attitude. Trying to stay positive. That's a verse from Psalms. 'This is the day that the Lord has made; rejoice, and be glad in it.'"

"You rejoiced about seeing Preacher?"

"Tongue firmly in cheek. Preacher's okay, until he comes on like a televangelist. I don't wanna be his project again."

"Well, I don't like that pious prick. Rubbed me wrong from the get-go. Polacks and such. But, as you say, rejoice. After this twenty, maybe we won't see him again. We'll be in Hot Springs tomorrow. We're rolling."

"Keep going north."

Chapter 7

Well, just-a look at that girl with the lights comin' up in her eyes ...
Jackson Browne

Robert crossed the paved road and shucked his pack. He drank greedily. The ascent from the Nolichucky had been long, and the April sun was hot, even at thirty-five hundred feet. The sunshine he craved in the Smokies had been abundant for several days, long enough to become the weather he now lamented. He reminded himself to stay positive. Heat was preferable to cold rain. Blue sky was better than the soup.

He swallowed a fistful of gorp, a new batch he had mixed the night before at the Erwin hostel. The aroma of fresh nuts and raisins was intoxicating.

Indian Grave Gap, like its Georgia namesake, held no attractions. He reshouldered his pack and began the thousand-foot climb to the Beauty Spot. As usual, he was determined to get there ahead of Socrates.

The ascent was steady and unbroken. His mind shifted into autopilot, somewhere between sentience and slumber. Thoughts paraded through his brain in kaleidoscopic patterns. They formed quickly from different combinations of the bits and pieces in his memory and just as quickly vanished as new ones fell into place.

He entered a rhododendron slick. The sight of the ubiquitous shrub would not normally jerk him out of his practiced subconsciousness. However, an anomaly revived his absentee senses. The bushes weren't green.

The bark on the hardwoods that sheltered the understory was charred. Blackened limbs lay on the ground. The thick leaf cover was burned in irregular swatches, exposing powdery soil. The intense heat from the fire had devastated the rhododendron. The twisted branches were scorched. The long green leaves (oblong? obovate?) had shriveled and fallen in wholesale numbers.

The unexpected change in color stunned him. He flashed back to an evening in college, playing bridge. His dorm mates had substituted a deck of cards in which the spades and clubs were red and the hearts and diamonds were black. He sorted his hand and realized something was amiss, but it took several seconds to comprehend how the mold was broken. His buddies had a big laugh at his confusion.

With each stride, Robert crackled brittle leaves underfoot. He was thankful that no fire had weakened the stout rhododendron that broke his fall in the Wesser snowstorm.

He wondered if lightning caused the blaze. Probably it was human carelessness. Or worse, human intent. A forest service road paralleled the trail to the Beauty Spot. Perhaps someone tossed a lighted cigarette from a car window.

Arnold, we've failed you again.

A denuded rhododendron stood beside the trail. Its former leaves were the new litter on the forest floor. At the end of one toasted branch he saw a solitary bud, closed tightly like a green pinecone. Miraculously, it was still alive. Its hermetic coat had protected the germinal core from the ravages of the fire. He looked at neighboring bushes. Several more buds had endured and were on course to flower in June.

He walked through the burn, tallying the conical survivors. The census preoccupied him, like a child counting cows in the back seat of a car. He stumbled onto the gravel mountain road. The foliage on the other side was green. The road had been a natural firebreak. He surveyed the destruction behind him one last time and crossed into the undamaged woods.

The ridgeline rose more steeply. As he walked, he identified with the durable buds. Like them, he had been scorched. Angie's death had burned away all the trappings, leaving a primal cone. When the blossoms of the rhododendron flowered again, they would look as they always had. Would the same hold true for him? Would his future resemble his past? Or would it be different? For the first time, he seriously considered his life without her.

He had told Rob he was taking control of his life. This self-assurance was premature. There were many unknowns and many decisions. He analyzed his choices.

What were the knowns? He was first and foremost a parent, and soon a grandparent. His family was still the center of his life. His relationships with his children had never been better. Last evening, in Erwin, he enjoyed two more affirming phone calls.

He would always be a hiker. He had many more "friends" in the mountains than back in Atlanta. The trail put him in peaceful places he never found anywhere else.

He would continue to teach Sunday school. He liked Bible study with youth. The systematic examination of scripture was a source of enlightenment. It gave him satisfaction to see the junior high kids exercise their curiosity, particularly when it led to greater understanding. And their questions kept his heart young and his mind fresh.

From time to time, he thought about going back to work. But he had never defined himself by his job, and he really enjoyed the freedom to come and go as he pleased. His pension and 401k were ample, particularly now that he was alone. He had resisted the rush to invest in the dot-coms, and his conservative approach had limited losses during the recent market meltdown. The choice was a no-brainer. He'd have to be penniless before reentering the work force.

Louise Patterson's new partner had brought a late-model van into the florist business. Angie's old Econoline sat in his garage, collecting dust. He had no use for it. What he needed was a four-wheel-drive vehicle that could take abuse, one he could leave at a trailhead for days while he hiked and not worry about. This decision was also easy. He would trade for a used pickup.

He thought of their house, Angie's belongings, and the furnishings they had painstakingly collected over thirty-five years. The keepsakes constantly reminded him of her absence, but at the same time their familiarity brought comfort. Mandy and Rob might want some of the pieces. He made a note to ask in the next phone call. There was no reason to rush. He left the decision to sell in the too-hard box. After the hike was over, he might be ready to burn that very long bridge.

Would he date other women? The thought seemed absurd. Why go through that contrived ritual again after thirty-five years? He could not help but compare any other woman to Angie, and that would jeopardize, if not doom, a relationship. But he did not dismiss it out of hand. He would welcome the companionship.

Since the onset of her cancer, Robert had not thought much about sex. Under the pall of illness and death he lost touch with his libido. Planning the hike, and the subsequent rigors of the AT experience, had also distracted him. His virility had not diminished; frequently he would wake in the middle of the night with an erection, the result of a truncated dream. Once, the dream was wet. He considered this to be evidence, not of a carnal need, but of the absence of Angie. Sex was not a front-burner issue, or back burner, either. The stove simply wasn't turned on. He had perked up when he saw Mollie. Perhaps the drive would return.

A twig snapped under his boot, and the sound ended his reflections. The cooler, drier air foretold the top of the mountain. The woods parted, and he entered an open meadow. The deep-blue sky intensified, no longer fragmented by overhead branches. He tugged on the bill of his cap to shade his eyes while they adjusted to the brightness.

The trail skirted patches of tall grass, rediscovering their verdure in the April sun. Brown wrens darted between the clumps, looking for the first seeds of spring. The dazzling sun highlighted a small butterfly searching for nectar in a patch of bluets. A colony of ladybugs scurried after aphids. Bees and flies buzzed around him. The field teemed with life. Had it been dawn or dusk, deer would be browsing in the sedge. He had never been artistically inclined, but at that moment he wished he were a painter, creating on canvas a replica of the emerging spring.

The pastoral tranquility disappeared abruptly. The gently sculpted summit of the Beauty Spot hosted a dozen Boy Scouts. An energetic trio chased each other in a game of tag. Another threesome threw a Frisbee across piles of rain flies and tents, drying in the sun after last night's thunderstorm. Others ate, or just lay about. The troop generated more noise than he had heard on his entire trip up from the Nolichucky.

Two adults stood apart from the fray, leaning against the fence that separated the meadow from the road he had crossed on his ascent. They pored over a notebook, oblivious to the cacophony created by their charges. Robert figured they tuned out the kids in order to keep their sanity. He approached the fence and took off his pack.

"Hi. How are you?"

They looked up from the notepad. The man on the left projected a belly above the belt in his Scoutmaster shorts. His body language intimated he was the leader. Robert guessed he was in his late forties. He gave Robert the once-over. "You a thru-hiker?"

Robert straightened up from his pack. "Yup."

"Lots of your kind out today," he replied gruffly.

The assistant, younger and thinner than his partner, was more curious. "How long you been hiking?"

"March 11."

"Man, I envy you. I really want to do the trail. This thing called a job keeps getting in the way."

The older man countered, "But it puts food on your table."

Robert empathized with the yearnings of the younger man. "I know exactly how you feel. I waited twenty years. But your time'll come. And when it does, jump at it. You'll never regret it." He paused for a long drink. "Say, where you guys from?"

"Kingsport." The leader reasserted control of the conversation.

"Scouts?"

"Troop 234. Counting us, there are fourteen. We started yesterday at Iron Mountain Gap. We'll finish this afternoon down at Indian Grave."

Good. You're going south.

"We got wet last night," the younger man added. "We're letting the boys dry their stuff in the sun."

"I was lucky. Indoors in Erwin in that storm."

"You came up from Erwin? That's ten miles uphill. It's only one o'clock!"

His admiration surprised Robert, who modestly downplayed any achievement. "Got an early start. And hiking's what I do. Hey, if you'll excuse me, I'll have lunch and check out the view. It must be the Beauty Spot for a reason."

The assistant pointed to his right. "You can see where you came from. Down there in the valley is Erwin. The big mountain across the gorge is No Business Knob. The higher one behind is Big Bald."

"That's cool. I can retrace where I've been for several days," Robert replied. "Where's the view of Roan Mountain?"

"It's right ..." The leader stopped in midsentence. Pointing northward on the trail, he continued brusquely. "Right over there."

The assistant smiled broadly. "The view is *very* good today."

Robert grabbed a bagel, jerky, water, and gorp. He headed in the indicated direction, dodging the Scouts and the equipment strewn in the sun. Unaka Mountain, framed by the cerulean sky, lay ahead. A dark rug of spruce covered its long, rounded summit.

See you this afternoon.

He looked to the northeast with anticipation. There would not be a mountain higher than Roan until Mount Washington in New Hampshire.

Robert did a double take. Thoughts of tall mountains evaporated. A young woman wearing a floral bikini lay on a beige rainfly, spread on the grass in the hollow. Her long, sandy-blonde hair partially obscured her face, but her legs and torso were in plain sight. There was not an extra ounce anywhere on her slender figure. His gaze froze on the concavity between her breasts and pelvic girdle.

Her abdomen reminded him of Angie's figure before their marriage. She had often bemoaned that while Robert remained enthralled by the hourglass over the years, hers had never fully recovered from two pregnancies.

One evening years ago, they had dined with Louise and Roger Patterson. Roger, now in charge of his mail drops, played softball with him on the church league team. The conversation got around to men eyeing good-looking women in public.

Robert offered, "It's natural. And harmless. Just part of our biological imperative to propagate the species."

"It's harmless only if you learn to control it," Louise shot back.

"I think I do a pretty good job," Robert offered innocently.

Angie snorted. "Sweetie, I'll give you a D minus. If a good-looking babe in a low-cut dress walks through that door, you might be able to hold it together. But if she comes through with a bare midriff, you'll totally lose it!"

Robert waited for the laughter to subside. "Okay. Guilty as charged. I like a flat stomach. Some of my friends are breast men—"

"Like Roger," Louise interrupted.

"—and some go for a nice firm butt. But if a bare midriff did come through that door, I think I could keep my tongue in my mouth."

"Yeah, right," Angie hooted. "You have spit on your chin just thinking about it."

Robert checked his face for drool. It was dry, and he felt vindicated. He looked again at the bikinied blonde. She was not alone. Another woman sat nearby. She wore nylon shorts, a polyester tee, heavy socks, boots, and a baseball cap. She was older than her companion, with cropped brown hair that gave her a mannish profile. She was short and blocky, but also with no excess fat on her frame. Behind her were two loaded packs and two sets of hiking poles. Beside one pack was a pair of boots, shorts, and a tee, shed for the sunbath.

Robert descended into the draw to a flat rock near the second woman. She looked up on his footfall. The younger woman also craned her neck in his direction.

"Good afternoon." Robert eased onto the rock with his food and water. "How you doing?" To his dismay it was a Yankee cap.

"Fine." She smiled tightly beneath the nested "NY" monogram. She seemed disappointed that he had interrupted their solitude. Her friend rolled back to worship the sun, saying nothing. She was even more exquisite at close range. Twenty-something, she had a strong nose, but with high cheekbones and full lips, it was not outsized to the rest of her face. Like most female hikers she wore no makeup. Unlike many, she didn't need to.

Where's Socrates? He'd be going crazy.

"Care for some gorp?" He extended his bag toward the older lady.

"No, thanks. We have snacks in the pack."

Robert opened the pouch of jerky and placed beef on the bagel. "Where you headed?"

"Maine." She stretched her short legs and rippled her well-toned muscles.

"Great," Robert responded. "So am I."

She looked at his Nalgene and food. "Traveling light, aren't you?"

Robert laughed. "I left my pack over by the Scoutmasters. They said the view of Roan was over here."

"That bastard."

"He vasn't friendly." The blonde opened her eyes as she spoke, but otherwise lay still. "He asked us to moof. I vas joost tekking a sunbath."

Robert drank in the European accent, which increased her considerable charm. "He did seem perturbed about something."

Her friend added indignantly, "Just because he's a dirty old man doesn't mean his boys are too. Are they peeking down here?"

"Last I saw they were playing Frisbee."

"That proves my point. He shouldn't worry about them."

Robert changed the subject. "Where'd you stay last night?"

"Curley Maple Shelter. We went into Erwin yesterday for a mail drop but decided not to stay. We're loafing here a little before heading to Cherry Gap."

Robert made a quick calculation. "Twelve miles is not exactly loafing."

"We're trying to increase mileage. To finish on schedule."

"Ve haf to be back by Labor Day."

He had an urge to pinpoint her accent. "Where are you from?"

"Baltimoor."

Robert was disappointed. No Marylander he had ever known talked as she did. "What do you have to get back to?"

"Ve are nurses. I go back to vork, und Mother vill teach a new class."

"Mother? You can't be—"

"I'm not," she said curtly. "That's my trail name. Mother Superior."

"Und don't you forget it," the blonde admonished, shaking her finger.

"And yours?" Robert asked.

"Czechmate. Dat's vith a 'z.'"

"With a 'z'? Ah. The Czech Republic. That's why I asked. I noticed your accent."

"*Ja.* Prague. My mother, she vas German. My father, he is Czech."

"How long have you been in the States?"

"Two yeers. I study nursing from Mother at St. Catherine's in Baltimoor. I graduated in February. I start vork in September. Meantime, I hike. Und you? Vat is your name?"

"Dances with Snakes."

Mother Superior needled him. "So you think you're Kevin Costner?"

Between bites of jerky bagel, Robert recounted the story behind his trail name.

"You didn't kill that snake, did you?" Mother Superior, like Socrates, checked his environmental credentials.

"Lord, no!" Robert replied. "After all, I initiated the contact. I stepped on it."

"Good for you." Mother Superior nodded approvingly.

"Dances vith Snecks." Czechmate sat upright and wiped away the beads of perspiration on her arms and legs. "Dat's too long. I vill call you 'Snecks.'" She stood up and shook out her rainfly.

With one gigantic bite, Robert finished his bagel. As he chewed, he marveled that her stomach was just as flat when she stood as when she reclined. She could call him anything she wanted.

Mother Superior rose. "Ready to go?"

"*Ja.* Let me get dressed." She walked to her pack and stuffed the fly inside. She slipped her shorts over the bikini bottoms and pulled the tee over her bikini top. In one efficient motion she reached under her shirt, undid the clasp behind her, and pulled out the bra. She gathered her long hair into a ponytail, rolled it, and pinned it up away from her neck and shoulders. Robert caught himself staring. He rechecked his chin.

Angie, just being a man. That's all.

He collected his stuff. His watch read 1:45. Socrates must still be in bed in Erwin. "Say, I'm heading to Cherry Gap Shelter, too. My partner's late. Mind if I hike over with you?"

"It's a free country," Mother Superior spoke with a hint of irritation.

"I'll get my pack and catch up." He added with a smile, "Any parting words for the Scoutmaster?"

"Tell that son-of-a-bitch the Serpent has left the Garden."

—☽—

Compared to Socrates, hiking with the nurses was tranquil. They spoke only intermittently and maintained a pace more tortoise than hare. Czechmate led the trio up Unaka. Robert brought up the rear.

He suspected that Mother Superior was determined to stay between him and her partner. He gleaned evidence from furtive eye contact and hostile body language. Halfway up Unaka, Mother Superior paused to adjust her pack straps. Not wanting to lose momentum going uphill, he kept walking as if to pass. He was halfway around when she lurched forward to keep her spot in the middle. From then on, he made a point to stay to the rear.

Each woman carried a hydration bladder and sipped from the tube on the go. They climbed the three miles and one thousand feet to the top of Unaka Mountain without stopping. Fortunately for Robert, he had drunk almost a liter of water at the Beauty Spot.

He admired their discipline. They would have no problem reaching Mount Katahdin by Labor Day.

Czechmate finally stopped on the long, flat summit of Unaka. Robert ripped off his pack and drained one of the Nalgenes. Czechmate and Mother Superior took in the surroundings. A thick grove of red spruce extended in all directions. The dense canopy blocked the growth of the understory bushes and shrubs common to the southern forest. The trail twisted through hundreds of spruce trunks on a thick carpet of needles.

"Like European forest," Czechmate said wistfully. "So green. Und clean."

"Wait till we get further north," Mother Superior replied encouragingly. "The boreal forest is even better than this."

The next three miles were downhill. They did not stop. Robert fared better. The descent did not dehydrate him like the climb. He dropped back once to sneak a drink and take a pee, but caught the pair ten minutes later. They reached Cherry Gap a few minutes after five.

Three male hikers were ensconced in the shelter. Robert had no preferences as to tenting or staying indoors, particularly with the nice weather. "You want to stay in here?" he asked Mother Superior.

"Oh, no. We always sleep in our tent. Take it if you want it." She and Czechmate scouted for a flat spot with good drainage and erected their Eureka a short distance away. Robert opted for the shelter. He emptied his pack and donned camp shorts and sandals. He unwound a nylon cord and tied it tautly between two trees. He hung up his sweaty Coolmax, shorts, and socks, hoping they would dry by dusk. He turned toward the tent and caught Mother Superior's eye. "There's plenty of room on this line if you guys want to hang up your stuff."

"Thanks, Snakes. We'll put up our own line if we need to."

He felt she was rebuffing his efforts to be friendly but cautioned himself against reading too much into her actions. He had stayed to himself before he met Socrates. Perhaps they wanted to be alone as he had. The best way to ingratiate himself was to do nothing.

"You slithering reptile! We finally caught you."

Socrates stood by the shelter. To his left was a large chocolate Labrador retriever, panting contentedly. He wore a harness with two pouches, each stuffed with sacks of dog food. Next to the dog was a long, lithe young lady, wearing short shorts and a sports bra. She was almost as tall as Socrates and disproportionately long in her calves and thighs. She stood erect, unaffected by the weight of her pack or the distance she had hiked. Her brown hair was woven into pigtails, which kept her tresses from matting against the back of her neck. The braids perfectly framed her guileless face, which was dotted with appealing freckles and creased with an infectious smile. Her "girl next door" countenance was matched by a pleasing if not spectacular figure, accentuated by the brevity of her outfit. Robert dwelled momentarily on her midriff. It was nice, but not in Czechmate's league.

Socrates was brimming. "Snaky, meet Southern Bell."

She spoke in a delightful drawl. "That's Bayull, with no 'e' on the end. My reayull name is Holly Bayull, and Ah'm from Alabamah." She squatted with hands outstretched toward the Lab. "Come heah, boy. Come to momma." Eager for affection, he placed his head between her knees, licking the inside of her long thighs. Southern Bell steadied herself and gave him a big hug. "That's mah boy!" Between strokes and caresses she announced, "This is War Eagle."

"Hello, Southern Bell. Hi, War Eagle. I'm Dances with Snakes. You can call me Snaky. Or whatever you like." While he spoke, War Eagle licked her wrists and, emboldened, lathered the point of her chin.

"What part of Alabama are you from?"

"Oh, yew've nevah hurd of it."

"Try me. I've been through your state many times."

"Greenville."

"Between Mobile and Montgomery. Where they raise turkeys."

"Yew do know! Well, Ah declayah!"

"Drove through on I-65. On my way to Texas. Stopped for lunch at Bates's House of Turkey."

"Ah'll be! Ah waited tables theyah when Ah wuz in high school."

"Small world. Hope I gave you a decent tip. What are you doing now? That is, when you're not hiking?"

"Ah'm at Auburn. Gonnah start vet'rinary school in the fall."

"With a dog named War Eagle, I assumed you were going to Alabama."

"Honey, yew said he was nice. Don't let him be mean to me."

Honey? Robert noted the train was moving fast.

"She knows more about animals than I do, Snaky. Been talking about them ever since we hooked up this morning at the hostel. Hey, she even assisted in an operation on a bull last year. And that's no bull."

"You didn't make him a steer, I hope?"

"That's all yew men evah think about. For yower informashun, it wuz a lacerated livah."

Robert looked at the beaming Socrates. Mollie went south. He couldn't find Dolly. But now he had Holly.

Socrates winked. "If you'll excuse us, we'll pitch our tents. Need to set up in a hurry. I'm starving. C'mon, Bell."

"Okay, Socks."

"There's flat ground over by that other tent. While you're there, introduce yourself to Mother Superior and Czechmate. That's with a 'z.' I met them at the Beauty Spot."

"Which is which?"

"You'll know."

Robert sighed. His days as a hiking partner were over.

He collected a bottle of water, soap, and the microtowel. He walked behind the structure, and in semiprivacy gave himself a thorough sponge bath. His stomach growled. The small picnic table in front of the shelter was ideal for cooking. He returned to his pack to retrieve his stove and food. He wasn't alone in the idea. Czechmate had brought her stove, also a Whisperlite, and set up at one end of the table. Mother Superior followed with a food sack. He thought about joining them, but not wanting to be labeled a pest, he left them alone.

He set up on the shelter platform. He cooked and ate chicken and rice by himself. The three hikers in the shelter were playing a spirited game of hearts. Thankfully he didn't have to make small talk. From time to time he looked at the table. The two women, absorbed in making and eating dinner, ignored him. Socrates and Southern Bell, more fascinated by each other with every passing minute, ate on the ground next to their tents. Their peals of laughter punctuated the evening air.

The warmth of the day lingered. The three men in the shelter turned in early. After reading from Luke, Robert lay on top of his Thermarest. He rested his head on his rolled-up sleeping bag and looked out in front of the shelter.

Mother Superior and Czechmate returned to the table from their tent. Czechmate sat down on the bench and placed a comb and brush set on top of the table. Mother Superior undid Czechmate's french twist and released her golden locks. She placed the pins on the table. With slow, gentle strokes she untangled Czechmate's tresses.

As she brushed, Mother Superior chatted softly to Czechmate, so softly that Robert could not hear the conversation. She placed her free hand on Czechmate's left shoulder. From time to time Czechmate raised her hand and touched her fingers. Mother Superior brushed until the tangles were gone. In the approaching darkness the sheen from the blonde hair mimicked the muted glow of a firefly, just bright enough to reveal the contentment on Mother Superior's face.

Mother Superior tapped Czechmate on the shoulder. Czechmate bent her head backward, and Mother Superior leaned over and kissed her sweetly on the lips. Czechmate stood up and collected her pins, brush, and comb. The two retreated arm in arm to the tent. They opened the flap and disappeared for the night.

Darkness descended. Two of his shelter mates snored. Muted laughter escaped from Southern Bell's tent. Those vibrations were not what kept Robert awake. A pulsating loneliness reverberated inside his skull. Love abounded in the sights and sounds of Cherry Gap, but there was none for him.

He retrieved a pinch light from inside one of his boots. He had placed it there next to the toilet paper in case of nighttime emergencies. He stood up and reached for the pack, hanging from an overhead peg. He pulled out his wallet and felt the single plastic sleeve inside. With his other hand he pressed on the bulb. Looking back in the halogen glow were Angie, Mandy, Rob, and himself. It was his favorite photo, taken for the church directory ten years ago, when Mandy was a high school senior. He stared for many seconds, touching each face lightly with the tip of his finger. A loud snore startled him. He relaxed his grip on the bulb, and the picture went dark. He put the wallet and the light back into their places and crawled into his sleeping bag.

Chapter 8

Be kind to one another ...
Ephesians 4:32

"Glad that sonofabitch is over." Hugging an armful of bladders and water bottles, Socrates skipped like a schoolgirl along the faint path beneath the evergreen canopy. "My pappy would call that hill a pure-T ball-buster."

The climb had left Robert tight and creaky, and he strained to keep pace. "You Greeks have really gone southern. I don't recall Plato talking about 'pure-T' universal truth. But what do I know?"

"I hope you know not to go up Roan High Knob ever again. How much was that?"

"Twenty-two hundred feet in two miles. Thought I'd have to crawl the last two hundred yards."

"But you didn't. You couldn't let three women show you up."

"No way! But God, they went up like mountain goats."

"Masculine pride has a helluva payback."

They reached the spring. Robert went first. He filled a bladder and the Nalgenes and sat on the top of the bank to measure iodine for each bottle. Socrates knelt by the shallow pool. He dropped the intake hose of the filter into the icy water. He placed the outlet into the mouth of one of Southern Bell's bottles. Still crouching, he pumped with a reciprocating motion, sucking water from the pool, through the filter and into the container.

It was Day Two of the post-Socrates era. Robert cautioned himself not to be melodramatic. He still saw his friend for brief interludes, such as now. However, there was no doubt about Socrates's priorities. The joke of the morning at Cherry Gap had been how early he rose to heat a pot of water, so that Southern Bell could have coffee when she woke. The daybreak attentiveness indicated how smitten he was. After the brutal climb from Hughes Gap to the top of Roan, he volunteered to get water, another sign of doting. He had asked Robert to come along, and Robert was flattered to be the secondary recipient of Socrates's newfound solicitousness.

Socrates capped the first bottle and started the second. His words did not flow in their usual torrents. "Snaky. How do you feel, you know, about me and Bell?"

The trace of guilt in his voice surprised Robert. Their pairing, like so many on the trail, was one of mutual convenience and subject to dissolution at the call of either partner. Given Socrates's stated objective to find a female companion, it would have been stupid not to expect this eventuality.

Socrates had buoyed his steps for many miles. Robert felt no ill will but sensed an opportunity to inflict pain before letting him off the hook. "Don't worry, man, it's cool. You're in luck. She's smart, charming, and good looking. I mean, those legs go on forever."

"You noticed them too, huh?"

"Yeah, and for some inscrutable reason, she's attracted to you. 'Socks.' 'Honey.' That's just precious."

"Spare me the sarcasm. But you're not upset?"

"Upset? Nah. It's not like we'll never see each other. We're hiking the same direction on the same trail. I'd be upset if you didn't do what you want. You've been looking for love for weeks. Maybe you've found it."

"Hope so. We seem to click." He finished the second bottle and transferred the outlet hose to the bladder. He rested momentarily before filtering more water.

"There's only one thing, Soc."

"What?" His eyes showed concern.

"The dog."

"You don't like War Eagle?"

"He doesn't fit."

"Whaddaya mean?"

"Dolly and Mollie were folly, but golly, Holly would be jolly with a collie named Polly."

Socrates groaned. In quick retaliation, he splashed water into Robert's face. "Worst piece of shit I ever heard! If I had a gun I'd take you out!"

Robert grabbed his chest. "A volley! Through the heart!"

Socrates threw two more handfuls. Robert scrambled to his feet, yelping as icy water rolled down the back of his neck. Out of range, he became penitent, bowing meekly in an Oriental curtsy. "Solly, so solly."

Socrates futilely shoveled more water in his direction. Laughing, Robert backpedaled several more steps. "I'm leaving. It's too dangerous to lollygag around here."

"Enough. One more oll and I'll slice off your bollies with my Swiss Army knife."

Halfway back to the shelter they passed Mother Superior, carrying several containers. Robert had debated volunteering to get water for them. But today's conversations on the trail from Cherry Gap had mirrored yesterday's pattern. They were civil but led nowhere. He wasn't ready to be told "no, thanks" again, so he demurred.

When she was out of earshot, Socrates asked, "You like them?"

"Yeah. Don't you?"

"I think they're lesbians."

"So?"

"I'm cool with it." His eyes twinkled. "But you Christians frown on that."

"Now you're the one in the green tunnel. Overgeneralizing. Not every Christian thinks that way."

"The ones I know do."

"I don't. And neither did the first Christian."

"Who?"

"Christ himself, dummy. He never once talked about homosexuals. Totally silent on the subject. He never condemned them. He never condoned them. He had more important things on His mind than human sexuality."

"Like what?"

"Feeding the poor. Healing the sick. Cleansing the temple."

"Then what's the big ruckus with Christians and gays? It's there when I turn on the TV. Or read the paper."

"I said Christ wasn't concerned. But there are a few passages in the Bible that, on the surface, condemn it. Some Christians blow them all out of proportion."

Socrates smirked. "Blow. Nice choice of words, Sigmund. But be honest. Isn't this some neat rationalization on your part because you like Czechmate?"

"Where'd you get that idea?"

"You're sending more messages than Marconi."

"Okay. I admit it. She's hot. But my little fantasies don't affect one whit what I believe about homosexuals. They're sinners. But everyone else is, too."

"I admire you, Snaky. A man of principle. You don't sacrifice your beliefs, even when you're horny." Robert started to protest, but Socrates brushed him off. "And don't tell me you're not. I'm the expert on that subject."

At the shelter, Socrates scurried to rejoin Southern Bell. Robert scaled the crude wooden ladder to the loft, his spot for the evening. He cleaned up and changed into camp clothes. The exertion of the day left him voracious. With anticipation he gathered pasta, stove, and utensils, and descended to the main floor to fix dinner.

Mother Superior had returned from the spring, and she and Czechmate also set up on the platform. He stayed to one side and gave them wide berth. Czechmate began to assemble her stove. She snapped the three supporting legs in place and seated the aluminum heat reflector between the fuel line and the burner. She connected her red MSR bottle to the fuel line. The pump was already screwed into the top of the fuel bottle. The manufacturer recommended that it be removed between uses. As a matter of convenience most hikers did not.

She pushed the plunger several times to put the fuel inside the bottle under pressure. Nothing happened. After a short pause, she tried again. She stopped after a few strokes. She turned to Mother Superior. "Domm stofe! I pump, but there iss no pressure."

Mother Superior took the bottle from Czechmate. She tried her hand with the pump. After several strokes, she quit. "It was okay last night, wasn't it?"

"*Ja*! Hass always vorked before."

Robert had forced himself to learn the operation and maintenance of the Whisperlite, backward and forward. He had a similar problem several years before. Dirt had accumulated inside the pump and broke the seal around the cup, allowing air to escape. He was confident he could fix it, but he hesitated. If Mother Superior already thought he was crowding them, it would get worse if he came on as the big, strong man condescending to assist two helpless females.

Mother Superior continued to examine the pump. Turning to Czechmate, she asked, "Does it have an instruction booklet?"

"He lost it."

"That dumb ass. I guess we're flying blind."

Robert saw an entrée. "How old is the stove?"

Czechmate looked at him, her brow knit tightly. "Ve don't know. It iss borrowed from Randy. A friend."

"Ex-friend," Mother Superior added.

"It won't pressurize?"

"Na!"

"Same thing happened with mine a few years ago. It took some messing with, but I finally got it working."

"Vat you do?"

"If you like, I'll talk you through it."

"Vould you?"

Robert looked at her friend. Mother Superior nodded grudgingly. "Yeah, we could use a hand."

"First thing is unscrew the pump. Take it out of the fuel bottle."

Czechmate took the pump out.

"Do you have the stopper cap for the bottle?"

"It comes mitt cap?"

"You're right, Mother. Randy's a great friend. He should have given it to you. But never mind. Just set the bottle out of the way, where it won't get knocked over." Robert joined the two women, huddled over the pump. He pointed to the plunger. "See those little black pegs on either side? Twist the plunger counterclockwise until they line up in those two gray slots on the pump. Yeah, just like that. Now pull it out."

Czechmate gave a gentle tug. The plunger separated from the pump. She held onto the plunger and passed the body of the pump to Mother Superior.

Robert turned to her. "Is the cavity dirty?"

"My God, it's gross."

"My guess is it's never been cleaned. Do you have a rag? Something to swoosh around in there?"

"In my pack."

"No need to walk back there to get it. I have one in my stove kit." He stepped over to his sack in the corner, and pulled out a tiny plastic box and a cotton cloth. He gave her the rag.

Mother Superior rolled it into a swab and packed it into the circular pump cavity. She twirled it several times and yanked it out. The rag was streaked with soot. "Randy's just as careless camping as he is around the hospital. I'm always after him to clean up."

Czechmate agreed. "He iss mess."

Mother Superior turned the rag to its clean side and swabbed again. She held up the pump body and eyeballed it, like a rifle barrel. "There. That ought to do it."

Robert looked at Czechmate. "Any dirt on that plunger?"

Seeing telltale signs, Czechmate reached for the rag.

"Before you clean it, check the leather cup on the end. It should be soft and pliable. If it's dry and hard, it won't make full contact with the walls of the pump cylinder. Air will escape around the cup and up the sides of the tube. When that happens, you can't pressurize the bottle."

Czechmate felt the cup between her thumb and forefinger. "It iss hard. Und dirty."

"That's the problem. Wipe it off. It's brittle, so be careful not to tear it. I'll get you something to oil it." Robert reached into his kit and pulled out a tiny eyedropper. He had told Angie he needed small, light containers. After considerable searching she'd found one at a kitchen store.

Czechmate stared inquisitively at the micro dropper. "Vat you have in dere?"

"Vegetable oil. If we have any left over, we can do french fries."

"Goot!" She laughed. "Do you haf also a bottle of schnapps?"

"Sorry. Take this and squeeze a couple of drops onto the cup. Work it into the fabric until it softens up. The leather should swell as it moistens."

Czechmate applied the lubricant and kneaded the leather. Robert put the dropper back into his bag.

Mother Superior admired the kit. "Where'd you find that?"

"My wife came up with the pieces over the years. That eyedropper was her pride and joy."

Mother Superior seemed to relax at the mention of a wife, particularly in a loving reference.

"What's her name?"

"Angie."

"Well, Angie should be out here. To see how great her stuff works. Does she hike?"

"Her great adventure is to go somewhere in an RV." He moved the conversation along. "Czechmate, is that cup flexible now?"

"*Ja*, I think so."

"Okay. Here's what you do. Put the plunger back into the pump and lock it with a clockwise turn." She joined the two pieces.

"Yeah, that's good. Now pump several times to check it. You should feel resistance and hear air exit out the hose at the bottom."

She did as he said. "It vorks! It vorks! Dank you, Snecks! *Danke!*"

"Put it back in the fuel bottle. Pump up and fire up. If you like, I'll show you how to clean the burner and the fuel line. They rarely need maintenance, but on a long trip like this, they might. Particularly if Randy never did it."

"I vill let you some other time. Ve are hungry!"

Czechmate assembled the stove and primed the burner. Robert moved to his corner of the platform and knelt to do the same. He pumped with his plunger and then lit his stove. Mother Superior stood beside him.

"Snakes, thanks for helping." Her tone had lost its bristle. "And thank your wife, too. She really set you up for success."

He adjusted the fuel control knob. The yellow primer flame contracted into blue heat. Czechmate's stove hummed in concert. This might be his last night in their company, or he might walk with them all the way to Maine. There was no way to know.

"Yeah, it's like she's out here, even though she isn't. Angie died last October."

The hissing of the Whisperlites was all that broke the awkward quiet. Robert added softly, "I'll get through it."

The sun set in the west behind Unaka Mountain. Shadows advanced over Roan High Knob. Like the darkness, the cold made inroads across the six-thousand-foot landscape. Perched by the loft window, Robert shivered and zipped up the neck of his Polartec pullover. Soon he would have to burrow into the down to fend off the chill.

A light bobbed below, under the spruce. A figure approached the shelter. It was Mother Superior.

He spoke softly. "Everything all right?"

She looked up in his direction. "Yeah, Snakes. Everything's fine. Czechmate's asleep, but I'm not quite ready to turn in. I wanted to write in the register."

Robert sensed an opportunity. "Care for a cup of cider?"

Surprised by his offer, she took a moment to respond. "Yeah. A nightcap. That sounds nice."

He went to his food sack, suspended from the rafter, and dug out several cider packets. He climbed down the ladder to his stove, still assembled on the lower floor. In a few minutes it hummed under the titanium pot. He dumped the packets into cups and waited for the water to boil.

Mother Superior chuckled.

"What are you laughing at?"

"Your entry."

"I was tired and hungry when I got up the hill. That's the only thing that came to mind. It wasn't very original."

"'Ain't no mountain high enough to keep me from spaghetti and meat sauce.' I'm a big fan of the Supremes. A nice touch. Not nearly as tiring as what Socrates wrote."

"He has to be the scientist. Me, I'm focusing more and more on food, to the exclusion of all other things. It didn't occur to me that getting here was a big milestone or anything. It was just another chance to chow down."

"In my book, all that mental stuff is overrated." She wrote a few more lines in the register. She closed it and put away her pen. The water boiled. Robert readied two cups of cider, one of which he handed to Mother Superior.

"Thanks." She took a sip. "This hits the spot. It's really cooling off up here." She settled back comfortably against the inside wall of the shelter and stretched her legs along the floorboards.

"Where you from, Mother?"

"We told you. Baltimore."

"No, I mean originally."

"The Bronx."

Robert chuckled. "A Noo Yawkah."

"I grew up in the shadow of Yankee Stadium. One of my first recollections is going to a game with my family. Been hooked on baseball and the Yankees ever since."

"I noticed your hat. I'm a Braves fan, so I didn't bring up the subject."

"Painful, huh?" She smirked. "Remember the argument about the team of the nineties? We settled that one."

"I concede. I just wish you Yankee fans weren't so damned arrogant."

"We're not arrogant. We tell it like it is. We're the best."

"Howard Cosell and George Steinbrenner. Two reasons I could never warm up to New York."

"You outlanders are just envious. You haven't learned how to play with the big boys."

"Sooner or later, arrogance gets its comeuppance. Soc found that out when Duke went down in the NCAA. And the Yanks got theirs last fall."

"That was an aberration. Mariano Rivera blowing a save? I guarantee you, order will be restored this year." She toasted her team with a draught of cider.

"You sound so sure."

"George opened his wallet. You know, he's the only person around who hates losing more than I do."

"Money's good, but it can't win pennants. The guys still have to play."

"And whose guys would you rather have? Yours? Or mine? Mark it down. We'll take the Series this year."

She spoke with finality. He took a drink and changed the subject. "Did you plan on being a nurse while you were growing up?"

"No. I was going to be the first female to make the majors. I saw myself in pinstripes."

"What position?"

"Catcher. None of the boys wanted to play there, so I went for it."

"You played with boys?"

Stained-Glass Curtain

"Look, Snakes. Title IX never made it to the sandlots of the Bronx. There were no girls' teams. Not even in softball. My only option was the boys' parish team."

"Were you any good?" He immediately regretted the way the question sounded.

"Plus .300 hitter. Line drives, no power. But I could really field my position."

"They give you a hard time?"

"They tried. You ever play ball?"

"I played some catcher. In fast-pitch softball."

"Then you know. They thought they could intimidate me. Run over me at the plate. But I wasn't scared. I stood up to everybody."

"There are ways to make the tag without getting killed."

"I learned that fast. For survival."

Robert recalled his home-plate collisions. Like the matador, he would stand in until the last possible moment, make the sweep tag, and avoid the horns of the charging bulls. "The only problem is when the ball and the runner get there at the same time."

"Yeah, make the tag. Then hold on for dear life. Fortunately, I never got hurt."

"Me either. How long did you play?"

"I was fourteen when they made me stop. This jerk pitcher from a parish in Yonkers didn't like playing against a girl. He threw at my head. I couldn't get out of the way. It hit my helmet. I was okay, but the coaches and the league commissioner were looking for an excuse to get rid of me. They said I had to quit for my own safety. They screwed me over. For all I know, they put the kid up to it."

"You couldn't appeal?"

"My dad asked the priest to intervene. He promised he would. But the powers that be got to him. He waffled. Suggested it was time I went out for field hockey. Short plaid skirts and all that crap."

"I take it you didn't play field hockey."

"No. I had it up to here with organized sports. And organized religion. I went for racquetball, in-line skating, mountaineering. You name it. As long as it was an individual effort and not a team game. So nobody could mess with me."

Robert recalled her virulent reaction to the Scoutmaster at the Beauty Spot. He was just another in a long line of meddlers. "Did you go into nursing right after you finished school?"

"Sort of. I got in to ROTC. My dad didn't have enough money to send me to college. I signed this contract with them and got a scholarship. The army paid for most of my schooling in exchange for a four-year commitment." She added, "I stayed longer."

"I was in the army, too. For three years, but way before your time. I should have guessed you were, also."

"How come?"

"There's a discipline, you know, a mindset that says 'army.' It's as tell-tale as the uniform. And you have it. Where were you stationed?"

"Stateside, at Letterman in San Francisco. Then Korea, Germany, and Iraq."

"You were in the desert?"

"My hospital unit deployed from Germany. Fortunately, we didn't see much action."

"Yeah. The expected casualties never materialized."

"No, but we still trained like hell. One day it was rehearsal for triage. The next we prepared for a Scud attack. Then we'd run through all the OR SOP's. It got kind of boring after a while. But all in all, I enjoyed the training. I was good at what I did." Her statement was matter-of-fact, rather than New York braggadocio.

"What rank were you?"

"I came back to the states as a major."

"Wow! You were moving up fast. Why'd you get out?"

"The handwriting was on the wall. The men had all the advantages. Officers in the combat branches get the plum assignments. Combat was off limits because I was female. All I could get were second-tier jobs. I was on the medical track. The best I could hope for was lieutenant colonel. Outside shot at full bird." She reflected for a few seconds. "Then the flap over 'don't ask, don't tell' came along. It was time to send out resumes."

"Is that how you got to Baltimore?"

"I had a variety of offers. The position at St. Catherine's appealed the most. I had some unique skills they were willing to pay for. And they promised the chance to continue my education."

"Does the hike qualify as continuing education?"

Mother Superior smiled. "No. My contract allows for a sabbatical every ten years. This is my first extended vacation."

"And you talked Czechmate into coming with you?"

"The other way around. She got into volksmarches in Germany a few years ago. Then into hiking. The Carpathians, the Alps. I think she even went into the Pyrenees. She had some money saved up after completing her schooling, so she delayed her nursing job for the opportunity to hike the AT."

"I've watched you both for two days. If I had to bet on anyone making it to Katahdin, barring injury, my money'd be riding on you. You have the determination."

"Thank you, Snakes. You look like a sure bet, too."

"Really? How's that?"

Mother Superior saluted. "You have the army discipline also. The way you kept coming up the mountain today."

Robert laughed. "What got me up that mountain was fear. I was afraid you and Czechmate would show me up."

She chuckled at his self-deprecation and turned her cup bottoms up. Robert broke open a new envelope and mixed her another cup.

"You'll have me peeing all night."

"You go south and I go north. With my prostate, I'm out there all the time."

"Benign prostatic hyperplasia?"

"There's nothing benign about it. I've been behind every tree on this trail."

She sipped more cider. "Were you ever in Vietnam?"

"No. Luck of the draw. I was at Fort Hood with the Second Armored Division. I met Angie. She lived in Austin. A student at UT. We got engaged three months later."

"You moved fast."

"I knew a good thing when I saw it. I got orders to Fort Bliss to command a basic training company. No problem, I thought. It's still in Texas. Turns out it was six hundred miles away. We spent a ton of dough on phone calls, gas, and plane tickets. Got married to save money. But the separation could have been worse. Right after I got orders to Bliss, they came down with another levy, and all the remaining junior officers went to 'Nam."

"What happened then?"

"I finished my tour at Bliss. I'm not a warrior. Never considered making the army a career. When my time was up, we moved to Atlanta. I had a job waiting in an accounting firm."

"Damn, you're a bean counter?"

"Yup. Over thirty years as a CPA."

"I had you figured as a teacher."

"I do teach Sunday school."

"Well, my instincts aren't entirely wrong. You must have liked Atlanta if you stayed that long."

"Good job, good friends, great weather. And best of all, the mountains are close by."

"I certainly understand that draw. You have family?"

"A daughter and a son."

"Are they still in Atlanta?"

"No. Our daughter's the teacher in the family. Lives in Florida. She's married to a dentist. And pregnant. My first grandchild."

"Great. When?"

"November."

"Right after the hike. And your son?"

"In the air force. In Alaska."

"Is he a pilot?"

"No, his eyesight's not good enough. He's a computer guy."

"Good. I don't like pilots. The Tailhook mentality. So you never moved?"

"No reason to. After the kids grew up, Angie became a florist. Loved what she was doing. We were very content. Thought it would go on forever. Then out of the blue she gets breast cancer. The doc called it one of the most invasive cases he'd ever seen. Six months later she's gone."

Mother Superior fingered a silver cross that dangled from a chain around her neck. She swallowed the last of her cider. "So you're out here with the rest of us. Trying to find your way to Katahdin."

"I don't think about Katahdin. I'm just trying to find my way to Damascus."

She laughed. "It's wise not to look too far ahead."

Robert looked at her necklace. "That's a nice cross. Pardon me for asking, but I thought you'd had it with religion."

"I said I gave up on the church. I didn't say I gave up on the cross."

"I haven't given up on it either."

She looked at her watch. "It's late. I need to go to bed. Or rather pee and go to bed. Thanks for the cider, and the companionship." She stood up. "See you tomorrow."

"One more question. The trail name. Mother Superior. How so?"

"You mean have I wanted to be a nun all my life? No. My mother harbored some ideas. She gave them up when I went cold on the church. Actually, Czechmate's responsible. She says it's the students' pet name for me. When I'm not around. Good night, Snakes. I really need to pee."

"Good night, Mother Superior." She disappeared into the darkness. The power of suggestion worked with a vengeance. He sped behind the shelter and relieved himself. He would have to go again during the night, but he was not sorry for sharing cider with her.

He came back to the shelter. The bright circle from his pinch light illuminated the register, lying on the floor. Curious, he bent over and picked it up. It opened automatically to the last page with writing. Socrates's dissertation was on the left-hand side, a reprise of their conversation in the Smokies about why the Fraser firs were dying. On the top right was his own paraphrase of the Supremes.

Underneath he found what he was looking for. It was written in a very even, legible script.

> Today Czechmate and I survived the hardest climb we've had so far on the AT. We're damn proud of how we charged up that hill. Nurses rule! And we have a new friend, Dances with Snakes, who helped us fix a balky stove. It was a good day.
> Mother Superior.

Robert closed the register and climbed to the loft. She was right. It was a good day.

Chapter 9

And them good old boys were drinking whiskey in Rye ...
Don McLean

I guess you look like an old man.
The imposing profile of Grandfather Mountain dominated the eastern sky. Discerning its features was an easy task when one looked at the peak straight on, but from his oblique vantage in the grass on Hump Mountain, Robert struggled to make out the visage. The face did not jump out readily from the conformation of the mountain. He turned loose his imagination and tried to define the forehead, nose, chin, and beard. The physiognomy never crystallized.

He had never hiked Grandfather Mountain. It was privately owned, and visitors had to register and pay a fee for the privilege. The summit could be reached by car, also for the price of admission. He wasn't a cheapskate, but there were scores of other interesting mountains nearby which were free. When deciding what to climb, he always relegated it to second or third place. Grandfather remained the celebrity across the room at the cocktail party. He never made the effort to fight through the crowd to introduce himself. He was having too good a time with other companions.

One of these days.

By comparison, Hump Mountain was a lifelong friend. He had climbed it as a Boy Scout. Its view was spectacular, like scores of other southern summits, but its baldness set it apart. The expansive meadow, like Max Patch, was a refreshing departure from the preponderant Appalachian forest. A farmer's field from the valley below had been miraculously transported to the state-line ridge. An alpine pasture at fifty-four hundred feet might be common in Switzerland, but not in North Carolina or Tennessee. Amid frolicking butterflies, he cupped his ear, awaiting a *yodel - o - aaaeeeoooh* from a goatherd named Hans. Had Arnold heard his Swiss comrade when he stood here?

There were no yodels, only the peaceful twitter from a flock of small birds. He lay back against the pack, closing his eyes to the brightness of the sun. Its warmth lubricated his aching joints. Fatigue evaporated through his pores. He settled into the grass mattress and relaxed his tensed muscles, fiber by fiber. The serendipity of the moment was mesmerizing.

He woke, startled by a vivid likeness of a beet-red Guyot, his skin peeling from ultraviolet exposure. Squinting in the bright sun, he checked his arms and legs for blisters. He touched the skin on his face with his fingertips. It was warm, but did not sting. The third-degree burns were a figment of his dreams.

Robert stood up and reshouldered his pack. The bald ridge fell off the summit to the northeast. Metal signposts with white rectangles, like wickets on a giant cricket field, were planted at regular intervals. The meandering rut of the trail extended for at least a half mile beside the shrinking sentinels.

The ground looked flat, but the terrain across the balds created an optical illusion. He had been fooled into thinking the climb to Max Patch would be gentle, and fooled again by Hump Mountain. Looking down, he fought the inclination that he would walk across a tableland. The trail lost altitude steadily through the meadow to the point where it switched back sharply into the trees. The foliage hid the continuing plunge to Doll Flats. Somewhere along that passage Mother Superior and Czechmate continued their northern pilgrimage. He walked off the summit after them, a lone silhouette in the mile-high meadow.

The two monopolized his thoughts. He was physically attracted to Czechmate. While embarrassed not to have concealed his preoccupation from Socrates, it pleased him to be roused from a prolonged sexual slumber. He harbored no illusions. She was half his age. She had shown no interest in him. But when she bent over to tend to her pack, her tank top drooped and revealed the white curvature of her well-toned breasts. He could not help but entertain fantasies. He had sat on the bench for a long time and wanted back in the starting lineup.

His attraction was complemented by an equally strong curiosity. She did not talk much on the trail, letting Mother Superior be her mouthpiece. When she did speak, it often was a rush of childlike exuberance, such as on Roan Mountain, when the contrary stove functioned properly. Why did she bottle up this delightful enthusiasm? There was an air of mystery about Czechmate, equally as alluring as the sculpted midriff. He hoped for an opportunity to sit and talk with her, as he had with Mother Superior, to unravel the intrigue.

He reached the tree line, marking the end of the concourse on the bald ridge. He paused for a drink. The treated water made him long for the sweetness of the cider from the night before. He tried to conjure the apple flavor but tasted only iodine.

He replayed the conversation with Mother Superior. Like Czechmate, she fascinated him, but for totally different reasons. Their dialogue had explained her standoffishness. So many men had treated her unfairly that she automatically assumed the next one she met would dump on her also. He respected her for what she had achieved. She had taken her hits. She had not rolled over in bitterness but rebounded to seek better opportunities. Her determination and fortitude guided her to a position of leadership. As Czechmate intimated, she was well respected by her students.

She brought up the subject of "don't ask, don't tell." The evidence pointed to the fact she was a lesbian, and by extension, Czechmate also. Socrates certainly thought so. But was she? She could have left the army for other reasons. Perhaps she suspected other officers would jump to conclusions about a single woman competing in a man's world. It would have been another fight against a male-dominated bureaucracy, something she didn't need or want. Her current job was devoid of these pressures. He cautioned himself about reading too much into her statement.

What about the kiss at Cherry Gap? And did they not walk arm in arm to the tent they shared? What one does is more telling than what one says. But he and Roger had once camped in the same tent for a week in the Smokies, and both of them were as straight as they come. One night many years ago, on a church retreat in the Shining Rock wilderness, he had shared his tent with a female member of the congregation. Hers had been ripped to pieces by the wind in a heavy storm. Angie teased him when he returned home. "You spent the night with Patsy? Well, how was it? How was the sex?" Preexisting notions often corrupted sensual impressions. Should he believe what he thought in his mind or what he saw in his eye?

The kiss could have been a sign of friendly affection. It was not particularly passionate, just a peck on the lips. He remembered the famous TV kiss between Ed Sullivan and Pearl Bailey. Kisses take on a whole portfolio of meanings in the eyes of different beholders.

What if he considered all the pieces together? Weren't the totality of facts more conclusive than when examined separately? Didn't they create the "smoking gun"?

He caught himself. He was too much an accountant, in search of the bottom line. Why did this matter so much? Why should he care if they were or if they weren't? Maybe, as Socrates suggested, it was because Czechmate had turned him on. It was the first time a beautiful woman had affected him for at least a year. He told himself for the nth time that fulfilling that desire was unlikely, by any stretch of the imagination. It was so far removed from reality only a fantasizing man could entertain it. He chuckled at the redundancy of "fantasizing man." When it came to sex, all men fantasized.

If she were a lesbian, it would shut the door on his imagination. With so few subjects available for his reemerging libido, he was unwilling to accept that outcome. He opted to keep the door ajar.

A protruding root grasped his boot. He staggered a few steps and fell to his knees. He stood up slowly and brushed away the dirt. A matched set of strawberries decorated his skinned kneecaps. He was disgusted that he let prurient thoughts sidetrack his trail awareness.

He needed to make a judgment about Mother Superior and Czechmate that was divorced from sexual impulses. Are they straight? Are they lesbian? It doesn't matter. What matters is that they are hikers, and damn good ones. And they called him a friend.

He reached Doll Flats, another milestone. The trail ended its hopscotch between Tennessee and North Carolina, and left the latter for good. Two states down, twelve to go. With Czechmate and Mother Superior ahead, and Socrates and Southern Bell behind, he conducted a solitary ceremony atop one of the large rocks in the flats. He gorged on a huge handful of gorp, and with both arms stretched above his head, he high-fived himself.

He reminded himself to keep this achievement in perspective. It was difficult, given Mother Superior's comment about his trailworthiness. He had been unaware he gave off indications of success. He pledged to fight off creeping overconfidence. He could break a leg in the next mile.

The next part of the trail passed the point where he had worked with Preacher and the Konnarock crew. He looked forward to critiquing the finished product, a small part of which was attributable to his labor. As he walked away from the flats, he remembered he was leaving not only North Carolina, but the Roan balds as well. He pivoted for one final look at the exposed ridge of Hump Mountain towering above and for one long view of Grandfather Mountain against the eastern horizon.

Thank You for letting me walk in Your world.

The trail changed its character in eastern Tennessee. Heretofore, it had followed remote ridges, far above the civilization in distant valleys. Atop the Blue Ridge, the Nantahalas, the Smokies, and the Roan Highlands, hikers were isolated from local farmers and landowners. Only when they descended from these insular ridges into "trail towns," like Hot Springs and Erwin, did hikers meet residents along the streets, at the hardware store, or in restaurants and supermarkets.

The pathway before Robert shifted from wilderness to grange and meandered upward through a grassy field. Fresh cow patties lay squarely in the middle of the tread, demanding a new set of motor skills. Robert concocted a syncopated dance, which he dubbed the "patty straddle," to avoid the malodorous hazards.

Unsullied, he topped the hill. The trail reentered the woods through a swinging gate and a zigzag chute in the barbed wire fence. The narrow passage, too confining for a bull or a cow, barely accommodated a human with a pack. Once through, he paused to survey the scene. An old barn stood at the other end of the field several hundred yards away. Behind it was a small farmhouse. Cattle were bunched near the barn, chewing placidly on newly greened grass.

A flock of goldfinches streaked across the meadow. They foraged in the scrub oaks near the fence. The striking transformation of the males to their brilliant spring plumage was complete. They were feisty, constantly bickering for supremacy, just like their Atlanta "cousins." Angie had filled several cylindrical feeders with thistle seed to attract them. In spite of the largesse, they fought interminably to secure one of the perches.

A low sound behind captured his attention. He cocked his head for the repeat.

Gobble, gobble.

He tried to spot the turkey, but it was hidden in the forest.

He crossed a gravel road. A white clapboard church stood on the right, another thread of civilization woven into the trail tapestry. About one hundred gravestones rose from the green grass in a clearing next to the church.

Back in North Carolina, north of Hot Springs, the AT passed by the headstones of two soldiers killed in the Civil War. Like many mountain men, these two were Union sympathizers. When war broke out, they enlisted in the Union army. They returned for a secret rendezvous with their families and were ambushed by the Confederates. Much later, in the twentieth century, the stones were erected to mark the solitary gravesite along the state line ridge. Socrates called them "Carolina Yankees." In a corollary to the "green tunnel," he concluded that people will not necessarily act in a certain way based solely on where they live.

Robert plunged back into the forest. The terrain rippled with successive hills and valleys. Each up and down mimicked the pair just completed. The roller coaster rose to yet another top. A male voice emanated from the other side. Something in its cadence troubled him, a haunting familiarity that he could not immediately pin down. He proceeded to a large oak and looked down into the swale. Facing him were two men dressed in camouflage suits and baseball caps. Each cradled a hunting rifle in the crook of his left elbow. They talked to two hikers, whose backs were to him. He recognized the legs. One pair was long and slender, the other short and stocky.

The hunter with the sinister inflection spoke again. "Know whut?"

"No. Tell me whut."

"Ah'm thinkin' these here are sweet on one another."

"You mean ..."

"Ah mean they's in love."

"Lezbee-yuns."

"Thass whut I mean."

Robert's circuits switched on. Twenty years ago his Atlanta church had hosted a choir from Mexico City. They treated their guests to a picnic in a public park. Robert set up a volleyball court. The Mexicans began a friendly but competitive struggle. The game was self-officiated, and the staccato of Spanish echoed across the field.

Three "good old boys" sat on a knoll behind Robert, drinking beer. In the eighties, Hispanics were rare in Georgia. These Mexicans may have been the first the locals had encountered. Through the spirited chatter of the game he caught fragments of the native conversation.

"Who let them in our park?"

"Ain't there a law you gotta speak English in public? I hate this shit, man."

"If Ronnie and them had showed up, we could run them wetbacks off."

Robert hoped that the beer wouldn't embolden them to do something stupid. Their epithets became more personal and profane.

"Chili con cocksucker."

"If Ah wuz Zorro, I'd slice their balls off."

A player spiked the ball at the net. It caromed off the hand of a defender and rolled up the knoll. One of the men corralled the ball, holding it firmly between his legs.

A cry came from the court. *"Por favor, señor."*

The man staggered to his feet, weaving from side to side. "If yew want the damn ball, yew have to ask fer it in English."

One of the Mexicans replied, "Sir, would you please give us the ball?"

The man took two unsteady steps forward and attempted to punt. He slipped on the corner of a towel and twisted his ankle. He missed the ball entirely and landed on his butt. He grabbed his left ankle in pain.

The Mexicans erupted into applause. "Bravo! Bravo!"

"Fuck you!" A companion, incensed at the humiliation, picked up the ball and kicked it. It sailed over the court and rolled between two old fence posts at the edge of the field.

Like a Univision crescendo, a roar of "Goooooooaaaalll!" filled the air. The two "good old boys" grasped their fallen comrade and carried him away with his arms draped over their shoulders. The Mexicans retrieved the ball and continued the game.

The same meanness ingrained in the trio in the park leaped across twenty years to reside in the hunters. Robert was unsure if verbal insults would escalate to physical abuse, but it was a distinct possibility. The rifles made him very uncomfortable.

The first hunter spoke again. "Know whut?"

"Whut?" The second hunter drew out the monosyllable for effect.

Stained-Glass Curtain

"These here ladies should perform for us."

"Lak put on a show?"

"Yup. Ah want to see how it's done. And Ah jest know they's willin' to oblige." He turned to Mother Superior and stroked the stock of his rifle. "Ain'tcha now?"

Instinct took over. Robert emerged from behind the oak and walked briskly down the path. He made a beeline for Mother Superior.

"Sweetie, am Ah glad to see you!" He kissed her vigorously on the mouth. She was too startled to resist. He pulled back with a broad smile. "Thought Ah'd never catch up to mah girls. Tetch of the runs a ways back." He turned to Czechmate and gave her a reassuring squeeze. "How you doin', Punkin?"

He held out his hand to the first hunter. "Hi, Ah'm Robert Martin. Nice to meet ya." The man waited several seconds before extending a tentative palm. Robert proffered his hand to the second hunter. "Hi." The hunter returned an unsubstantial shake. Like his friend, he did not speak.

Robert plunged on. "You huntin'?" It was a stupid question. The two rifles were in plain sight. Neither man answered. It was up to him to keep it going.

"That wuz dumb. It's obvious you're huntin'." His speech surprised him. His mother, offended by the dialect he acquired in grammar school, had painstakingly suppressed all traces of native patois in his speech. Now the tones and patterns of the rural South reemerged as protective coloration.

He searched for an area of commonality. "Whutcha huntin' fer?"

"Turkey."

Robert rushed to make the most of the first chink in the armor of reticence. "Okay! You're in luck. You know the gravel road just back yonder?" He pointed behind him.

The second hunter nodded slightly.

"'Bout three hundred yards beyond the church, up on the ridge to the right, ole Tom was a-gobblin'. Didn't know it at the time, but he was droppin' a hint fer me to pass on to you. That's not more'n fifteen minutes from here. If you hurry, Ah bet you can find him."

Robert's mouth froze in a friendly grin. He searched their faces. They seemed knocked off their perch by his whirlwind spiel. They stared back at him to verify his veracity. The first hunter cupped his hand over his chin. It was all Robert could do to maintain his façade.

"Y'say it's up there on Bartlett's Ridge?"

Robert smelled victory. "Yup, if that's whatcha call it. T'other side of the field from the barn, where the gate is. And he sounded good-sized."

He looked for affirmation in the guarded expressions. It was not yet forthcoming. It was time to close the deal. "Yeah, you better hurry after that turkey. He'll make a nice dinner." He shot Mother Superior a furtive glance. "And speaking of dinner, hon, we need to git to that shelter. Daddy is hu-un-gry! Let's go do our thang, and let these here men do theirs."

Mother Superior put her hand on Czechmate's pack and nudged her. Trancelike, she started up the trail. Mother Superior followed. Robert banked that he had enough credibility to turn his back on the hunters. He smiled once more. "Nice meetin' ya. And good luck with ole Tom!"

He followed the two women on the trail. From the outset of this affair, he had pegged the hunters' objective as humiliation, not homicide. His arrival had spoiled their fun. If he was wrong, he could get a bullet in the back. But like Lot fleeing Sodom, he wasn't about to turn around. He stared ahead at Mother Superior's pack and prayed the two nurses wouldn't turn around either.

They walked for several minutes, out of the swale and then down and out another. When they cleared the crest of the second ridge, Robert said quietly, "Let's stop."

Mother Superior breathed a long sigh of relief. "Thanks. That was an Oscar-winning performance. Your trail name should be Jed Clampett!"

They shed their packs. Czechmate rocked unsteadily, her arms wrapped tightly around her diaphragm. Her whole body shook with silent sobs. Mother Superior put both arms around her. "It's okay. We're all right now. It's okay."

Czechmate buried her face in Mother Superior's shoulder. Suddenly she lifted her head and staggered off, out of the way of her pack and poles. She began to vomit in recurrent heaves. Mother Superior rushed to her partner and steadied her until the contractions ended.

Robert felt warm and queasy. He had not allowed himself to relax with the hunters, appearing outwardly assured in spite of the tension gnawing at his insides. But now, out of harm's way, his pent-up anxiety overflowed. He sweated profusely. His heart raced, much like when he scaled Courthouse, Cheoah, and Roan.

The enormity sank in. He imagined what might have happened to Mother Superior and Czechmate if he had not come along, and to all three of them if his act had not played out. His stomach curdled in a way he had not felt since college, when he drank himself into oblivion at a fraternity keg party. The salty taste in his mouth telegraphed what was about to happen. He moved away from the packs and grabbed a small maple to steady himself. In one violent spasm, he vomited a stiff stream of orange into the doghobble beside the trail.

Robert continued to clutch the trunk for support. He spit to clear the lumpy residue from his mouth. Czechmate, still in the grip of Mother Superior, smiled at him weakly.

"Copycat."

Robert feigned disappointment. "What a waste of a carrot cake bar."

Mother Superior laughed. Her loud, long, guffaw dragged the other two into its infectious eddy. The two women, arm in arm, came to Robert and enveloped him. Inside the circle of release, they expelled their tensions with contractions of laughter.

When the purge was complete, Mother Superior spoke. "Let's get to camp. After all, Daddy, if you were hungry before, you're starving now."

"I'm having turkey and rice tonight. Tom turkey."

They stepped off again. For the first time Mother Superior led, followed by Czechmate. Robert brought up the rear. After a few minutes, Mother Superior turned to face Robert. "I forgot to say thank you."

"No, you did. Back there when we stopped."

"No, not that. Thanks for not throwing up until after you kissed me."

"If you want, I'll kiss you again."

"Not necessary. And wipe your chin."

They crested yet another ridge. There was a road below. A blue Ford Bronco was parked beside the trail. The front seat was occupied. Mother Superior stopped. Robert's stomach tightened. He searched for the composure that had served him with the hunters. "Odds are this is not a repeat. Walk on down like nothing's happened."

They proceeded to the road. The front door of the Bronco opened. A middle-aged man got out. He stepped to the rear and opened the tailgate. He retrieved a Styrofoam cooler and carried it around to the front of the truck. At the same time his lady, wearing a beatific smile, hopped out of the passenger seat and approached them. She carried a bulging paper sack.

"Hi there. Y'all like drinks and cookies?"

The three exhaled a collective sigh.

"Something wrong?"

"Oh, no!" Mother Superior exclaimed. "It's just that we weren't expecting trail magic. Thank you! We'd love some."

The woman pulled two cellophane packages out of the bag.

"Wow! Double Stuf Oreos!" Robert could hardly contain himself. "And Nutter Butters!"

The man opened the cooler. "Help yourself to Co-Cola and Sprite."

Robert looked at Mother Superior and Czechmate. "Did we just die and go to heaven?" He grabbed two Nutter Butters and chewed them quickly to overcome the sour taste in his mouth. He popped the top on a Coke and took several gulps. "Thank you," he said, first to the man and then to his wife.

Czechmate, clutching a handful of Oreos, walked over to him. She said nothing, but extended her free arm around his waist and gave him a tight squeeze. Reflexively, he encircled her waist and squeezed back. They stayed entwined, Czechmate eating Oreos, and Robert drinking his Coke.

Mother Superior couldn't resist. "The couple that hurls together curls together."

The lady produced a camera from the front seat of the truck. "Can we have a picture? For our club album."

It dawned on Robert they were volunteers. "Are you maintainers?"

"Right. I'm Imogene. He's Herbert."

Mother Superior chimed in. "You're our angels. We'd like pictures too. I'll get my camera from the pack."

"Thanks for the work," Robert added. "The trail's in great shape."

Imogene issued orders. "Herbert, you take pictures of me and them, with both cameras. Then I'll shoot."

When they finished, Robert offered a turn with the cameras. He took several pictures of the "angels" with his two friends. When he finished, he asked Herbert, "How far to the next shelter?"

"'Bout a mile. A little steep."

"Because of your kindness, it'll be the easiest mile we ever walk."

"*Ja*. Dank you for der drinks und cookies."

"Amen," chorused Mother Superior.

They shook hands. The three hikers headed for the shelter, and Imogene and Herbert returned to the Bronco.

Chapter 10

People are strange when you're a stranger,
Faces look ugly when you're alone.
The Doors

Two long poles, each adorned with the white blaze, buttressed a horizontal signboard above. Czechmate read its greeting. "'Appalachian Trail. Velcome to Damascus, Firginia.'"

"Ladies, we're making serious progress."

"Nurses rule!" Mother Superior walked under the sign. "And so do accountants. Let's find The Place. I want my shower."

They crossed the bridge over Whitetop Laurel Creek on to the main street of the renowned Virginia town. Several storefronts and eateries lined Laurel Avenue. They noted the location of the post office, laundry, outfitter, and pizzeria. After two blocks they spied the Methodist church. Behind it was their destination.

The Place was a rambling two-story house, surrounded by a large yard. The congregation had converted it into a hostel for AT hikers and for cyclists who biked on the Virginia Creeper Trail. It contained several bedrooms, upstairs and down, which were sparsely equipped with stacked bunks and foam mattresses. The luxuries included two bathrooms with showers, one on each floor, and a kitchen with a sink, table, stove, and refrigerator. A small study on the ground floor contained an eclectic library. The wraparound porch, with a swing and a clutch of rockers, invited guests to congregate and converse. The yard offered picnic tables and ample space for tenting. The church did not charge a fee but asked for donations. Most hikers gladly contributed something. The Place was perfectly adapted to their basic needs.

The three went inside and signed the register. Each dropped ten dollars in the contribution box on the desk. Czechmate found an empty bedroom that accommodated five. They dumped packs on the beds to claim the space and queued up for a long-awaited shower. After scrubbing and shampooing, they hung damp rain flies on the outside clothesline to dry. Socrates and Southern Bell soon arrived and wasted no time finding the shower.

Clean and refreshed, the quintet and dog made the pilgrimage to the laundromat. The next stop was the outfitter. They purchased some small items, including stove fuel, bootlaces, and insect repellent. In addition, Socrates and Southern Bell bought a two-person tent.

"Does this mean you're going steady?" Robert probed, with raised eyebrows.

"It means one tent is two pounds lighter than the two it replaces," Socrates replied. "Beyond that, it's none of your damn business."

The final destination was the post office. They picked up mail drops, and Socrates and Southern Bell sent their old tents home.

Errands complete, the five assembled on the porch. A party atmosphere broke out. Southern Bell hailed the passage of another state, Tennessee, four miles back. "Three down, elevun ta go!" They exchanged the mandatory high fives.

Socrates demanded, "How many miles, Mr. Accountant?"

"Four hundred fifty-five." Another round of high fives ensued.

What they celebrated most was their new status. Damascus was more than just another trail town. The attrition rate for hikers was the highest along the southern end of the trail. The Virginia town was a mythically significant waypoint. Those who reached it separated themselves from the pretenders who had fallen by the wayside.

Southern Bell put their feat in perspective. "They say only one outta three who start in Jawjah make it this far."

"We're survivors," Mother Superior boasted.

"We suhvived for the next test."

"What's that?"

"Endless Virginyah."

"Snaky," Socrates cut in. "How far is endless?"

"Five hundred fifty miles."

"Well, hell. If we're gonna take that on, we need pizza and beer."

Southern Bell fed, watered, and tethered War Eagle in the yard. The quintet hustled down Laurel Avenue for the classic trail town feast. The bouquet of cheese and pepperoni wafted up the street to meet them. Robert's stomach let out an audible rumble.

Socrates jumped at him. "What did you say, Snaky?"

"I say we split four large pizzas. Two for me. Two for everybody else."

"You'll eat like a pig and gross out the ladies."

"I've already barfed in front of two of them. I don't see how bolting pizza could be worse."

"Whatever. But your allocation sucks. I need at least two. I'm the growing boy."

Mother Superior interjected, "All I can say is you boys better not blink when the food comes."

They ordered a sausage and mushroom, a pepperoni with extra cheese, a vegetable medley, and two pitchers of beer. The bravado ended when the pizzas arrived. The succulent triangles vanished rapidly. As Mother Superior forewarned, the ladies took no prisoners in their determination to sate big appetites.

Robert reached for the last slice of sausage and mushroom. Southern Bell beat him to the prize. He pulled his hand back in mock pain, as if she had speared it with her fork. He shifted his claim to a wedge of pepperoni. "You're supposed to eat like a bird."

Southern Bell paused between sticky bites. "That suthern fiction has gone with the weeyund."

"Keep your Scarlett, Snakes," Mother Superior added. "But pass me the pepperoni."

"It's time to order another," Socrates declared. "What about ham, green peppers, and black olives? And another pitcher?"

"Go for it!"

When it was over, only a few remnants were scattered across the checkerboard tablecloth. The four aluminum platters were clean, save for an isolated sliver of olive or mushroom glued to the dish by a wad of mozzarella. Streaks of tomato sauce and strings of cheese were all that stuck to their plates. The pitchers were empty.

Socrates called Czechmate to account. "Matey, there's an inch of beer in your glass. Didn't your Mother teach you not to waste food?"

She pouted. "*Ja*! Und I don't need der Grik to remind me." She reached for her glass and guzzled the remains. She clanged the empty glass on the table triumphantly and let out a long belch. The other four applauded. She giggled. "Dat is my, how you say, post mortem on a delicious meal."

Southern Bell responded to Czechmate with a shot from the diaphragm. "As we say down in Alabamah, let's brang it up again and vote on it."

Socrates burped loudly. "As we say at Duke, it's better to belch and bear the shame than squelch the belch and bear the pain."

Mother Superior followed with a roof rattler. Czechmate ducked. "Just noise, dear. No flying projectiles."

Socrates challenged Robert. "What's the matter, Snaky? Are we too crude for you?"

Not to be outdone, he ended the refrain with a substantial belch and a final platitude. "Not bad manners, just good beer."

Socrates spoke again. "It's time for a round of farts."

Everyone groaned. Southern Bell pummeled him with both fists. "Let's leave. Before he starts."

Robert offered a suggestion. "On the way back, why don't I pick up ice cream? We can eat it on the porch."

"I scream, you scream, we all scream for chocolate!" Socrates shouted.

"What about chocolate chip?" Mother Superior proposed. "More than one flavor."

"*Ja*. Goot. I am still hungry."

"I can do chip," Socrates responded.

Southern Bell licked her lips.

"I'll take that as a yes." Robert reached into his wallet and dropped a ten and several ones on the table for his share of the feast. "Chocolate chip it is. Seeya on the porch."

Southern Bell licked her lips again. "Don't waste any tahme talkin' to the checkout girl."

—⁂—

Robert trotted up the steps to the porch, clutching a bag containing ice cream, plastic bowls, and spoons. He stopped suddenly on the top tread. Preacher knelt on the floor, stroking War Eagle.

"How old is he?" Preacher asked Southern Bell.

"Heyull be three in June."

"My golden retriever's four."

"Whut's his name?"

"Buff. Started to bring him on the AT. But with all my side trips, I decided not to. Now I wish I had."

"Ice cream!" Socrates shouted.

"Iss about time you got heer." Czechmate scurried toward Robert.

Preacher stood up. He wiped his hands on his shorts to remove War Eagle's saliva. "Hello, Dancing Snakes. Good to see you again." He approached, hand outstretched.

Robert passed the ice cream to Czechmate. "Matey, would you do the honors?" She grabbed the bag. Robert managed a smile and extended his hand for another bruising clutch. "Long time no see, Preacher. Where you been?"

"The question is where have you been? Always a step ahead, I guess. I thought I'd catch up in Hot Springs, but you guys didn't stay. I got to Erwin right after you pulled out. I left the trail there for a meeting at East Tennessee State. Been doing twenties since, trying to catch you." He looked at his watch. "Got to Damascus ten minutes ago."

Robert thought of Socrates Hare and Snaky Tortoise. It was hard to run off and leave somebody on the AT. "The weather improved. We did big miles to take advantage. So here we are. Obviously you met War Eagle and Southern Bell. What about these good folks? You remember Socrates?"

Preacher nodded in his direction. "Hi. I should apologize for the little spat at Mountain Mama's. WWJD? It's not good to carry a grudge."

Socrates flashed a quizzical expression. "WWJD?"

"What would Jesus do?" Preacher answered. "I have a quick temper. Asking that question helps to keep me from flying off the handle."

"Yeah, I guess," Socrates muttered.

Robert continued. "Over there in the swing is Mother Superior. Czechmate is serving the ice cream. Got it?"

"I'm bad with names, but I think so."

The group crowded around Czechmate. Robert continued to converse with Preacher.

"So how was your meeting at East Tennessee State?"

"Great! They called the other day. Saved five souls at their first retreat. Two guys and three coeds."

Robert steered the conversation away from soul saving. "Called? How'd they know where you were?"

"Cell phone. You don't carry one?"

"Too much weight." Czechmate passed him a big dish of ice cream, which he handed to Preacher.

"Thanks. I stay in touch with a lot of people. A cell's the best way. Mmm, I love chocolate chip."

"How many colleges are you working with?"

"Ten or so. I also talk with CBA."

"CBA? Doesn't ring a bell." Robert took the second dish from Czechmate and welcomed a cold, sweet spoonful on his tongue. He moved it to a spot on his palate that had been burned by a wad of hot mozzarella.

"Christians for a Better America. It's a political organization. We support candidates nationwide who sponsor our legislative agenda."

"Which is?"

"To enhance Christian and family values."

Robert again felt uncomfortable. Part of the allure of the AT was escaping provocations of modern life, like politics and religion. He did not want Socrates and Mother Superior to get started with Preacher. He sought safety again in the phone.

"What kind of coverage you get out here?"

"The phone? It's okay on the ridges. I hit dead spots in the hollows. If I keep walking I usually reestablish contact. You should carry one. It doesn't weigh that much."

"I don't call anyone but my kids, once a week. I just don't need it."

Socrates sidled up, holding a dish with gigantic scoops. He exhibited no residual hostility from their confrontation at Mountain Mama's. "You been doing twenties since Erwin?"

"Right. I have to finish in August. And I'll have more zeroes, when I go to meetings. I really need to cover ground."

Regardless of his opinion of Preacher, Socrates respected anyone who piled up miles over challenging terrain. "You did twenties over Roan?"

Preacher relished his envy. "I went from Erwin to Clyde Smith the first day. Then to Apple House the second."

"Snaky, how far?"

Before Robert could reply, Preacher answered. "Twenty-five and twenty. And the twenty includes that climb up Roan."

"Damn, I got to hand it to you. Those are serious miles. I can see it on mellow trail, like from Wautauga Lake to here. But over Roan?"

"I did twenties through Wautauga, too. To get back on schedule."

"What about the three hiking with you back in the Smokies? The Raggedies and that other guy?"

"The Boston Wrangler ran out of money. Left the trail at Hot Springs to go back to work. The other two, Anton and Andy, didn't want to do long days." He inhaled another spoon of ice cream. "Besides, I couldn't stay with them."

"Why?"

"They're fags."

"What?" Socrates demanded.

"You know, homosexuals."

"So?"

"I can't associate with them. The church is totally opposed to what they do."

Socrates changed from grudging admirer to devil's advocate. "Why? Did either one come on to you?"

"No. It's a good thing. I'd have punched him out."

"They left you alone. So what's the problem?" The volume of their dialogue had increased to the point where the women stopped talking to listen in.

Preacher seemed annoyed. "I don't approve of the lifestyle they've chosen."

"Chosen? You think they choose to be gay? Choose to get bashed? C'mon. Medical and psychological research indicates homosexuality is not a choice. It's an orientation, like being left-handed."

"That's your opinion. As for me, I don't fraternize with sinners."

"They're just being themselves. What's wrong with that?"

"Haven't you read the Bible?"

"Can't say I have, Preacher."

"Well, if you read it, you'll know that relations between members of the same sex is an abomination. When the people of Sodom engaged in homosexuality, God sent angels to destroy them."

"Snaky's my authority on the Bible. Tell me, man, is that what it says?"

Robert scraped the last bit of ice cream into his spoon, and licked it deliberately. "In Leviticus, a man having sex with another man is called an abomination. But the violation of many rules unique to ancient Hebrew culture, like dietary laws, was also called an abomination. In that context, abomination refers more to something dirty or unsanitary than to something inherently sinful." He motioned to Czechmate to ladle him some more ice cream. "Preacher, what kind of socks are you wearing?"

The question puzzled him. "Thorlos. But I don't—"

"No, not the brand name. What material?"

"Uh, they're a blend. Polyester, wool, and nylon. Why do you ask?"

"There's a similar prohibition in the Old Testament against wearing a garment made from two different kinds of cloth. By those standards, your socks are abominable. Even if you've just washed them."

Socrates and Mother Superior cackled. Preacher frowned. Robert continued. "Not picking on you. My socks are blended also. My point is you have to be careful about words from another culture and another time. Those words can have a totally different meaning and usage today. And Preacher, it's been a while since I read Genesis, but I don't remember Sodom quite the way you tell it."

"You can play word games, but the message is clear. God destroyed them because of their vile lust. This is where we get the term sodomite."

Robert had an intuition. "Preacher, you ever read the Sodom story?"

He waited a second too long to answer. "I've had sermons preached to me about it."

Robert continued. "You and I have a difference of opinion. Instead of what we've heard in the past, why don't we rely on the scripture?"

"You mean read the Bible? Here?"

"I'm sure there's one in the library. After all, this is a church building."

"No need," Preacher replied. "I have one in my pack."

Reluctant in the past to hear Biblical passages, Socrates was eager for it now. "Bell, Snaky's good at reading the Bible."

"Whattaya think?" Robert asked, looking at the nurses.

Mother Superior was indifferent. "What else is there to do?"

Czechmate glanced at him and said nothing.

"Ah can tell Momma Ah hayad Bible study on the AT," Southern Bell said. "She'd lak thayut."

"Get your Bible," Socrates urged.

Preacher extracted the Bible from his pack. He sat down in one of the rockers. "It's somewhere in Genesis." He flipped through several pages. "Here we go. Chapter nineteen."

"Read to us." Socrates posed as a child waiting for a bedtime story. His calculated eagerness vexed Preacher, who expected more reverence.

Preacher began. "The two angels came to Sodom in the evening, and Lot was sitting in the gate of Sodom. When Lot saw them, he rose to meet them, and bowed down with his face to the ground. He said, 'Please, my lords, turn aside to your servant's house and spend the night, and wash your feet; then you can rise early and go on your way.' They said, 'No; we will spend the night in the square.' But he urged them strongly; so they turned aside to him and entered his house; and he made them a feast, and baked unleavened bread, and they ate."

"Ah didn't know thayut," Southern Bell interjected.

"Know what?" Socrates inquired.

"Lot wuz the first trail angel."

Socrates and Mother Superior snickered. "Well, he wuz!"

"Hush, dear," Socrates admonished.

Preacher continued. "But before they lay down, the men of the city, the men of Sodom, both young and old, all the people to the last man, surrounded the house; and they called to Lot, 'Where are the men who came to you tonight? Bring them out to us, so that we may know them.'"

Preacher interposed, " 'Know' is the Old Testament way of saying they wanted sex."

Socrates slapped his forehead. "That's why I always want to be in the know!"

Southern Bell swatted him on the forearm. "Now, you hush!"

Robert looked at both sternly. "Can we hold comments until he finishes?"

Preacher began again. "Lot went out the door to the men, shut the door after him, and said, 'I beg you my brothers, do not act so wickedly. Look, I have two daughters who have not known a man; let me bring them out to you, and do to them as you please; only do nothing to these men, for they have come under the shelter of my roof.'"

This time, Mother Superior interrupted. "Save the men. The hell with the women. They're always expendable."

Czechmate was silent, but her expression was troubled.

"Chicks up front," Southern Bell drawled sarcastically.

"Please," Robert begged. "Let him finish." Mother Superior stuck out her tongue and bit down on the tip to indicate that she would stay silent. Southern Bell shrunk into a ball of affected contrition.

Preacher continued to read. "But they replied, 'Stand back!' And they said, 'This fellow came here as an alien, and he would play the judge! Now we will deal worse with you than with them.' Then they pressed hard against the man Lot, and came near the door to break it down. But the men inside reached out their hands and brought Lot into the house to them, and shut the door. And they struck with blindness the men who were at the door of the house, both small and great, so that they were unable to find the door. Then the men said to Lot, 'Have you any one else here? Sons-in-law, sons, daughters, or any one you have in the city—bring them out of the place. For we are about to destroy this place, because the outcry against its people has become great before the Lord, and the Lord has sent us to destroy it.'"

Preacher looked up from the Bible. "That's the gist of the story. The angels sent Lot and his family away from the city and warned them not to look back. God rained fire and brimstone on Sodom and Gomorrah. Lot's wife disobeyed. She looked back and became a lump of salt."

"Taking it out on the female again," Mother Superior pointed out.

Robert ignored her protest. "Okay. That's the scripture. Comments?"

Preacher spoke first. "It's clear as a bell. The men of Sodom wanted sex. Homosexual sex. But the angels turned them away, and God destroyed them for it."

Socrates responded, "Preach, this sex they wanted. Was it consensual?"

"What does that have to do with it?"

"Every man and boy in the city shows up at the door, demanding sex. Is that consensual? Is that one-on-one partner sex?"

"No, I guess not."

"What would you call it then?"

"They were going to force themselves on the two angels."

"It's called rape. In this case, gang rape. Mob violence. Like an old-fashioned lynching party, but with a twist."

Robert spoke up. "There are several translations of this passage. The King James and the Revised Standard use the archaic circumlocution 'know.' Other translations say 'to know carnally,' 'to have sex with,' or 'to rape.'"

"How do you know all this?" Preacher demanded.

"I teach a Sunday school class for high school kids. We studied this a few years ago. They asked a lot of questions. I read up on it to understand the context in which the word is used. I agree with Soc. The men of Sodom weren't thinking about sexual gratification. Lot and the two angels were strangers in their neighborhood. The mob wanted to humiliate them. To send a message. 'Git your foreign ass out of town and don't come back!'"

Preacher retorted, "You guys are trying to read their minds. The scripture doesn't tell us what they were thinking. It tells us what they wanted to do."

"The sin is rape, not homosexuality," Socrates reiterated. "Psychologists and psychoanalysts have concluded from case studies that rape is not a sexual act. It's a manifestation of hatred or the need to dominate."

"They weren't motivated by hatred. It was uncontrollable lust. I have a big problem with all your complicated interpretations. First A equals B, and B equals C, and C equals D. In the end you tell me A must equal D. It's a house of cards. It makes more sense to have a straightforward standard."

Mother Superior challenged him. "What's your straightforward standard?"

"The Bible says so."

"The Bible says so?" Mother Superior was skeptical. "I know a lot about standards, Preacher. From the army and from medicine. A good one always passes the test. Let's try yours out."

"Fire away."

"Say it's twenty years from now. You're married with two teenage daughters. God comes to you like He did to Abraham and tells you to sacrifice your oldest daughter. Would you do it, the way Abraham was willing to do with Isaac?"

Preacher thought for a moment, and responded calmly, "God has a purpose for me and my family. I wouldn't question that purpose."

"Okay. Different situation. You have out-of-town male guests. You're talking with them on your front porch. A biker gang rides up and demands sex with them. You say 'No, but you can have your way with my sixteen- and fourteen-year-old daughters.' Since Lot said essentially that in the Bible, you wouldn't give it a second thought, right?"

"That's absurd. The two examples are like apples and oranges. One is a command from God. The other is a wish from a depraved mob."

"I agree with you, Preacher. The context is totally different," Robert said. "But they are alike in that the Bible said it. That meets your criteria."

Preacher reiterated, "God does not mean for me to give my daughters up for rape."

"Then we have a new criteria," Mother Superior concluded. "A common-sense test. What Lot was willing to do with his daughters doesn't make sense to you. Intuitively, it does not appear to be in accordance with God's plan. So you use judgment to understand and apply the scripture."

Robert added, "There's a big difference in the way women are viewed today, from Biblical times. Back then they were property, under total control of the patriarch of the family."

"Some might say that attitude still prevails today," Mother Superior interposed.

Robert made a thumbs-down gesture to her. "Thanks for trying to negate my argument. And also your own. But you or anyone else wouldn't deny that women have a much higher standing in Western society today. We value them as individuals, with lives and souls just like men." Robert turned to Preacher. "Right?"

"I guess so," he answered unenthusiastically.

"You told me at East Tennessee State, they saved five souls," Robert countered. "Two males and three females. Did the males count for more than the females?"

"No, of course not."

"Then there's no guessing involved. In God's eyes women are just as important as men."

"Okay, okay."

The group was silent for several seconds. Robert continued. "What about the point Southern Bell made?"

Puzzled, she spoke up, "Whut was thayat?"

Robert shouted over the laughter. "Trail angel! I'm serious. Lot offers to feed the angels and put them up for the night. Otherwise they spend it in the street."

"There weren't any Holiday Inns in Sodom," Socrates offered.

"Exactly. No public accommodations. And strangers were regarded with the highest suspicion. The Bible charged the Israelites to offer hospitality to strangers, because they'd been strangers themselves in Egypt."

"Lot sure takes it to the extreme," Socrates interjected. "Offers up his own daughters to protect strangers."

"This is pretty weird to us. We go months or years without speaking to our next-door neighbor. We certainly won't sacrifice our children for someone we don't know. But it was consistent with the rules of hospitality in Israelite culture. Contrast Lot with the men of Sodom, who would brutalize defenseless travelers. That was another tradition on how to treat strangers. Physical humiliation. Injury, even murder. Unfortunately, it was rather common."

"Where'd you get all this stuff?" Preacher asked.

"I read a lot of books for that Sunday school class."

"What's the point of it?" Preacher was growing impatient.

"My point is this. You can't read the Bible and accept the surface meaning of each word or phrase. You have to exercise judgment, like Mother said."

"I will agree there are times you can clarify the Word through study and prayer. But the Bible is what it says."

"Lemme ask you something. At the start of this discussion, you equated the behavior of the men of Sodom to what Raggedy Anton and Andy, or other homosexual couples, do in a loving relationship. How do you make a connection between rape and love?"

"You aren't going to quit, are you? The act, whether motivated out of violence or out of love, is still sinful. God calls it an abomination."

"You believe God destroyed Sodom because the men were homosexuals?"

"I do."

"The Bible doesn't say that. God tells Abraham in chapter 18 that he is sending the angels to destroy Sodom. Before the incident in chapter 19 ever happens. The attempted rape is just the last straw."

"You keep substituting attempted rape for homosexual lust."

Robert paused. "If the Sodom story is a rebuke of homosexuality, don't you think that concept would be reinforced elsewhere in the Bible?"

"It is."

"Not so. Granted, there are several references to Sodom in the Old Testament. The prophets, like Ezekiel, Isaiah, and Jeremiah use Sodom as a whipping boy, anytime they want to make a point about unrighteousness. They condemn Sodom for a bunch of sins: wickedness, injustice, adultery, pride, inhospitality ... there you go, Bell ... even insensitivity to the poor. But never homosexuality."

"What about the New Testament?"

"A passage in Jude castigates Sodom and Gomorrah for sexual immorality and perversion."

"There you go. Homosexuality is a sexual perversion."

"But it doesn't specifically say homosexuality. If you infer homosexuality from perversion, you are making an A equals D argument."

Preacher rose from the rocker. "This discussion isn't going anywhere. Thanks for the ice cream. It was good, but it won't hold me any longer. I need a shower and something to eat. See you guys later." Preacher bent over and stroked War Eagle once more. He hoisted his pack, left the porch, and went inside.

Mother Superior broke the silence. "Snakes, I'm impressed. Where did you learn all that?"

"I know," Socrates echoed. "When it comes to the Bible, you're a damn search engine."

Robert laughed. "I wasn't kidding about Sunday school. The kids and I spent several weeks on that chapter. If he'd brought up some other passage, I wouldn't have known squat."

Czechmate sat huddled in a rocker off to the side. Robert walked over and kneeled by her chair.

"You all right?"

She frowned. "Vat he read upset me. How could a father treat his daughters like dat?"

"It was another time and culture," Robert consoled. "I'd like to think we're beyond that today."

She shuddered. "I'd like to dink dat, too. But I don't."

Her pose reminded him of her spell in Tennessee, after the encounter with the hunters. He reached up and took both of her hands. "You know that I, that all of us, will look out for you."

She squeezed his hands tightly. "*Ja*, I know."

Her attempt at conviction did not mask her inner disquiet. Robert concluded she needed more time to get over her recent trauma. He smiled at her. "What say we finish off the ice cream?"

Chapter 11

I don't care what they may say, I don't care what they may do, I don't care what they may say, Jesus is just all right, oh yeah.
The Doobie Brothers

The panorama from Chestnut Ridge was an unanticipated pleasure, like finding a coveted volume in a used bookstore. Ridges and valleys stretched southwest for miles and miles, to Mount Rogers and Whitetop in the distance. Had there been a nearby tree to climb, Robert might have seen all the way back to Damascus.

Mount Rogers and the surrounding Grayson Highlands were open high country, described as "Montana in Virginia." The rocky, grassy ridges were straight out of western cinema. Wild ponies roamed the highlands. Two had approached him near Rhododendron Gap, to yogi for food. Only chest high, they reminded him of the Shetlands at children's petting zoos.

The unique terrain and wildlife of the Highlands had lived up to its advance billing. Conversely, Chestnut Ridge had no prior advertisement. It was Virginia's best-kept secret, revealed without fanfare. He had burst from the confining forest into a grassy meadow. To the right were the rows of flattop ridges, paralleling the trail as far as he could see. He felt like a novice to whom the innermost secrets of the order had been divulged for the first time. Virginia had acknowledged his miles of probationary labor, and initiated him into its private chamber of beauty.

Robert liked hiking in the Old Dominion. Georgia, North Carolina, and Tennessee were a sequence of roller coasters. The ridges rose to high peaks and plunged into deep gaps, only to climb again to the next peak. The profile for the three states resembled the EKG of an irregular heartbeat, whose arrythmia was easily discernable.

By comparison, Virginia's heart beat slowly, in regular blips that only occasionally altered the "flatline." Its ridges were rounded and softened by millions of years of wind and water. Periodically the trail descended from one ridge, crossed a valley through a farmer's field, and then climbed to the next elongated crest. The less frequent ups and downs were interspersed with long sections of easy walking.

Why was Virginia different? Retreating glaciers? Tectonic plates? Whatever the geological reasons, he was not complaining. Virginia was mellow. He traversed more miles each day in the same amount of time, while expending less energy. Contrary to trail lore, Virginia gave him no reasons to feel "blue."

A mile short of the shelter, he stopped at a pipe spring beside a small pond and filled his Nalgenes and camp bladder. Water on top of the ridge was another welcome surprise. He didn't have to plunge hundreds of yards down the mountain to top off.

He walked toward the shelter on the knob. Caught up in Chestnut magic, he didn't notice the weight of his pack or the extra five pounds of water in the bladder. The field was alive with butterflies. Near Mount Rogers, War Eagle had chased them across the high pasture. Robert cavorted in the same manner. After a full day's hiking, he had enough residual energy to dance.

His mind ran free. A figure ran toward him in the afternoon sun. Hans the goatherd, ready to throat his yodel? No. The apparition wore a long skirt with petticoats. Hans's sister Heidi, coming to serenade him with an alpine rondelet? She launched into a pirouette with arms outstretched, and exploded his senses with a stereophonic soprano. "The hills are alive ..."

The stone shelter loomed and ended the Maria interlude. The building was a converted fire warden's cabin. The front wall featured a door and windows that opened and closed. It was a step up from the typical three-sided lean-to, but well short of a motel. He placed his pack and bladder by the door and leaned Old Hickory against the external wall.

Beyond the shelter, on the north end of the knob, the trail descended back into the ubiquitous Appalachian grove. On tomorrow's hike, the captivating pasture would revert to common forest.

The familiar Eureka nestled under the branches of the first line of trees. As was their custom, Mother Superior and Czechmate had selected a site on the circumference of an imaginary circle around the shelter. In the last week the radius of that circle had grown longer. Preacher was hiking with the fivesome, not by invitation but by default. In the egalitarian society of the trail, no one presumed to say what another could or could not do. His mileage approximated theirs, and he camped nearby at the end of the day.

Preacher was partial to shelters. The two couples, inveterate tenters, ceded the area to him and pitched a tolerable distance away. Robert faced a dilemma. He refrained from camping near either duo, not wanting to impinge on their privacy. As a result, he was consigned to stay in the shelter with Preacher, or pitch his tent an awkward distance away. He felt incapable of such a snub. He resigned himself to being one part of "the odd couple."

In the eyes of the others, Robert's prior history with Preacher dictated that he take responsibility for the current situation. He would be the buffer. He had held his own in the Damascus forum and seemed immune to Preacher's sermonizing. His duty was to guard the drawbridge and quarantine Preacher inside the moat.

Robert wondered why Socrates and Southern Bell had not caught up. Perhaps they stopped at the spring to camp under the stars. And Preacher, the cause of all this maneuvering, was also a no-show. He had stopped to talk to a group of southbound teenagers. Their meeting had apparently become a trailside revival.

Preacher was unlike most thru-hikers. He never expressed any feeling about the natural beauty along the trail. Animal sightings usually elicited spirited recounts from Robert's companions. Preacher never volunteered that he had seen a deer, a groundhog, a cardinal, or a black snake. When Robert mentioned his tête-a-tête with the ponies, Preacher showed no interest. His indifference was not limited to animals. He never waxed about a sunset, a native azalea, a trillium, or a waterfall. What he talked about was what he did away from the trail at his last stop, or what he planned to do on his next. Occasionally, he spoke about football, particularly his younger brother, Luke, an all-district running back at a Colorado high school. He also pined for "Buff." Their remaining discourse was limited to recollections of the Konnarock crew or to daily concerns like food, water, and weather.

To Robert's relief, Preacher was considerate about their Hobson's pairing. He had refrained from more proselytizing and the "Damascus debate." Robert hoped the evangelical hiatus would continue, but he doubted it. Preacher would report on his efforts with the teenagers and then start in on him.

Robert looked again at the tent below. The nurses must be resting inside. He sorely missed the companionship of the others, on the trail and around the camp stoves. From Hiawassee to Damascus, he had shared evenings with a person of his choosing, but no longer.

To the left of their tent, he spied a vista. In no hurry to unpack for the night, he walked to the promontory and peered into the valley below. The emerald dale stretched for miles, ringed on all sides by high ridges rushing to don a spring mantle. The valley was dotted with farmhouses and barns. The meadows were unplowed. He guessed the inhabitants were dairy farmers. What made the scene even more pleasant was what he did not see. There were no strip malls or parking lots, and no high voltage lines or wide highways. He could have passed this way a century ago and discovered essentially the same setting.

"What are you looking at?" Preacher peered over Robert's shoulder.

"Sit down. Take a load off." Robert waved at the panorama. "This is Burke's Garden."

"Looks like a valley full of farms. Why do they call it a garden?"

Preacher's denigrating tone irked Robert. A person hiking two thousand miles through the mountains should respond to the surrounding beauty. Perhaps he had a latent interest in history.

"Here's the story, Preach. A hunter named James Burke came to this valley in the 1740s. One night he fixed potatoes for dinner. He buried the peelings."

"Leave no trace, huh?"

"Sorta. He and his friends returned the next year. The peelings had sprouted into a potato patch. As a joke, the others called the place Burke's Garden. Just like that, he was immortalized. They eventually ran off the Indians and settled the valley. Been there ever since. You could go down there today and probably find James Burke the umpteenth tending his cows."

"Like I said—a valley full of farms."

"Preacher, that's the point. It's a beautiful, undisturbed farming community. Neon-free. Not a McDonald's in sight. It's looked the same for two hundred years."

"I grew up in a place like this. It's not like it's something new. I'm not impressed."

"Well, others have been. You've heard of Biltmore Estate?"

"That palace in Asheville? Yeah, some spread. I took one of my groups there last year."

"George Vanderbilt, the tycoon, wanted it here. Burke's Garden was his first choice. But these farmers refused to sell out, so he built the estate in Asheville instead. Proves every man doesn't necessarily have a price."

"Or that Vanderbilt didn't offer enough money."

Robert's frustrations rose. Preacher had not responded to the intrinsic beauty of the valley, or to the historic testimony of a community fighting to remain intact. He tried again. "This place has a nickname."

"Really?" Preacher replied perfunctorily. "What?"

"God's Thumbprint."

He perked up marginally. "Why do they call it that?"

"Take a look. The valley's a circular depression, surrounded on all sides by mountains. Like God pressed His thumb into the earth. It's a unique place with its own creation story."

"Dancing Snakes, where do you find all this stuff?" His question revealed annoyance more than curiosity.

"In the AT guidebook for southwest Virginia."

"Nice to have information. But it won't get me to Maine."

Robert gave up. "What say we eat?"

They cooked in lingering sunlight. Preacher ate his staple meal, a pot of ramen noodles mingled with a pasty instant soup. He chased it with two Reese's cups and a giant Snickers.

"How can you survive on that junk? If I ate that crap, I'd be seriously malnourished. And seriously depressed."

Preacher laughed at Robert's exasperation. "I travel light to pile up the miles. I eat only enough to get to the next town. Then I pig out on real food. Tomorrow, I'm going all the way to Bland. Some friends'll meet me and we'll go to a college in Bluefield. I'll eat like a king for two days."

"I hope so. Eat like this and you won't do tens, much less twenties."

Preacher's cell phone rang. The ring tone was a chime, not a buzz. Nonetheless, Robert found it grating. In his Chestnut paradise, any interruption was discordant babel. Preacher talked for several minutes. Robert gleaned that the other party would meet him tomorrow evening at Route 21 near Bland. Preacher ended the call and pocketed the cell.

The telephone ate at Robert. "Mind if I ask a question?"

"Not at all." Preacher chewed the last of the nougat.

"Why are you out here?"

"Whattaya mean?"

"Why are you thru-hiking?"

Preacher took his time to reply. "So I can say 'I did it.'"

"But you're not enjoying it."

"Why do you say that?"

"You don't talk about the flowers. Or birds or animals. To you the views are 'just another farm,' or 'just another mountain.' You never become a part of God's beautiful creation. Instead, you're on that damn phone every day, connected to the world the rest of us came out here to get away from."

"I need to keep in touch with my college contacts."

"You live for the next road crossing, to go into town and get away from the trail. Why don't you just drive from one college to the next? That would be more efficient. And more enjoyable. I'm back to my original question. Why are you here?"

Preacher chortled. "It started on a bet with my two buddies in Colorado. They didn't think I could do this. Well, nobody should say 'you can't' to me. It just makes me more determined. At first I wanted to do the Continental Divide Trail, but I couldn't juggle it with work. The AT fits. I can combine this hike with mission trips. My boss loves the idea. It creates interest among the students. It's already resulted in several professions of faith. I've been able to stay on schedule without any problems. Now my buddies are worried I'll go all the way."

Robert could not resist the Faustian comparison. "Did they bet their souls?"

"They're Christians. They wouldn't do that. I said bet, but it was more like a dare. No money involved. But they'll be sorry."

"You answered my question. You're not out here because you love the trail."

"I'm winning the bet and doing my job. And staying in shape."

"Then why Konnarock? Most volunteers have some attachment to the AT that lures them out."

"I read about it at school. I thought most of the crew would be college kids, like me. I'd be able to win some converts. Turned out it was mostly old—uh older—people like you. And you weren't receptive to my message."

"I'm receptive to God's message."

Preacher's face turned a dark shade of crimson. "My message comes straight from the Bible, the inerrant record of God! How can you not be receptive to that?"

Robert had pushed a button. "Preach, I have trouble with that word 'inerrant.'"

"Then what kind of God do you believe in?"

"God's not the problem. God is inerrant. I mean, He's God. He can't be wrong. And the message He delivers is inerrant. It's His message. But I ask you: does He deliver it to you personally?"

"He answers my prayers."

"Not what I mean. Did He deliver the Bible to you personally?"

"No. He sent the Word through the prophets. Disciples, apostles."

"Did He recite It to them in English?"

"They spoke Aramaic." He added, "Where are you going with this?"

"The Bible starts with stories, passed down orally. Then they are transcribed. Then translated into different languages. Like sequential electronic copies, they get blurred and grainy. Hard to make out."

"You're denying these people were instruments of God?"

"No. They were inspired by God. Acted in His name. However, they were human beings. Errant by definition. They made mistakes. Just like we do."

"You don't believe God overcame their shortcomings?"

"Look at it this way. A first-century Greek is transcribing an Aramaic parchment. He has a fight with his wife. Then his teenage son totals his new chariot. He doesn't have his mind totally on the task at hand."

"You've created a hypothetical situation to justify your argument."

"There's always the possibility of distraction. And other outcomes."

"Like what?"

"The scribes who passed the Word on to us also passed on their own ideas and opinions."

"The Biblical writers weren't free agents! God guided them."

"Say for a moment I agree. I don't, but just say I do. The narrators, the scribes, and the translators were guided by the Holy Spirit. They faithfully and accurately passed on the Word of God. And only the Word of God. Exactly the way He wanted it. We still have a big problem."

"What is it now?"

"The hearers and readers of the Word. Several billion of us, over two thousand years, trying to understand that message. There's room for huge disagreement."

"I don't have a problem understanding the Bible. It says what it says. I take it at face value. For some reason you can't. In Damascus you nitpicked every verse of scripture. Why do you have to analyze the Bible so much? Why can't you accept it?"

"Preach, I have a daughter. I can't accept that God wants me to turn her over to a raping mob. And you said you couldn't either."

"We've been through that. There are some passages where you use common sense."

"Then some words are more inerrant than others."

"I didn't say that."

"But that's the only logical conclusion. Lemme illustrate. When you were preparing to hike the AT, did you read any 'how-to' books?"

"I read up on equipment. Packs, tents, boots."

"Did you read about George Mallory?"

"Who?"

"The English explorer. He died trying to climb Mount Everest."

"Wait. I did see a PBS program about him a few years ago. But what's climbing Everest got to do with the AT? I mean, it's night and day. I don't see you or anybody else out here carrying ice axes or oxygen bottles. And he lived a long time ago."

"I think he died in 1924."

"Why would I be interested in his stuff? The improvements in equipment since then are incredible. I mean, when I bought my pickup, I didn't get an eight-track. I got a CD player."

"I agree. Everest and the AT are apples and oranges. Or as you say, night and day. Studying Mallory's gear list is a waste of time."

Preacher was impatient. "How do we get from reading the Bible to Mallory?"

"Use the same logic you applied for Mallory. Or as you say, use common sense."

Preacher looked at Robert warily. "What are you getting at?"

"High altitude equipment is out of context on the AT. Agree?"

"Yes."

"And hiking gear has advanced from eighty years ago."

"Okay."

"Sacrificing daughters is incompatible with modern morality and practice."

"Are you looping back to the homosexuals?"

"There's no ethical correlation between that mob of rapists in Sodom and a modern-day, same-sex couple in a loving relationship. In your words, they are night and day."

"You're twisting my words! And worse, twisting the Word of God."

"No. The Word of God is the Word of God. It's untwistable. What twists is how you, or I, or anybody else understands it. To say Biblical interpretation can't change over time is like saying we have to wear Mallory's heavy woolens instead of Polartec and Gore-Tex. We draw conclusions based on the body of knowledge available. Soc made a good point in Damascus. Scientific and medical knowledge about homosexuality is much advanced from a century ago, and light-years ahead of four thousand years ago, or whenever Sodom was."

"You place more stock in scientific theory than in what the Bible says."

"I'm saying my understanding is errant. There's a huge gap between inerrant God and errant me."

"That's what Christ is for, to bridge that gap."

"I know my shortcomings. I know I need help. But I'll try like hell to understand before I take that leap of faith. I'll study the Bible, but I'll also study science, history, art, and literature. The more I know, the better I'll understand the Bible."

"I don't see how this other stuff is helpful."

"Think about it. In the past, the Bible was used to justify slavery and segregation in America. Some people may still believe that, but they are on the fringe."

"I certainly agree it was wrong."

"I'm not asking if you agree with the concept. Do you agree that slavery and segregation are no longer the prevailing opinion?"

"I agree."

"Okay. What changed? Did God change?"

"No."

"Did the Bible change?"

"No."

"Then what changed is how American Christians understand Biblical teaching. Agree?"

"Yes." Preacher grimaced.

"The old ways of thinking are eight-track. The new ways are CDs and DVDs. Like technology, our understanding has improved."

"How can you build a revisionist case for Sodom? God destroyed them."

"There is a parallel. We don't celebrate Mallory for what he wore or slept in or cooked with. We celebrate his indomitable spirit. And God did not condemn Sodom for any particular sin, but for their deliberate turning away. Hardheaded unrighteousness is what got them destroyed. Not same-sex rape. Remember, God would have spared the city if it had just ten righteous men."

Preacher paused for several seconds. "Okay, let's say I agree with you about Sodom. I don't, but like you said, let's do a what-if. Sodom is Old Testament. You've still got the New Testament. The teachings of Christ say homosexuality is wrong."

"The references to homosexuality in the New Testament are all in Paul's letters."

"You don't disagree."

"You said teachings of Christ. The life of Christ is in the four Gospels. Matthew, Mark, Luke, and John. There's not a single word, pro or con, in the Gospels about homosexuality. Christ never spoke about it."

"You sure about that?"

"The only place you'll find anything is in Romans, Corinthians, and Timothy."

"Okay, it's not in the Gospels. But there are statements condemning homosexuality in the New Testament."

"Not exactly what I said. Lemme ask you another question. Is every word in the Bible as important as every other word?"

"Well, since it's all inerrant, yes. And since it all came from God."

"There are no good parts that people read more than others?"

Preacher smiled. "Like John 3:16?"

"Yeah, or Psalm 23."

"I see where you are going. Obviously we have favorite passages, but that doesn't mean the others aren't important. Or less important."

"You ever been in the armed forces?"

"No. Why do you ask?"

"The army has a method for teaching recruits. Every lesson has three parts. In part one you tell them what you're going to say, in part two you say it, and in part three you tell them what you said."

"So?"

"The Bible's like that. In the Old Testament God reveals what He's going to do, in the Gospels He does it, and in the rest of the New Testament He tells everybody what He did."

"I agree with that."

"And you agree the Bible is Christ-centered? After all, part two is all about Him. And we call ourselves Christians."

"You trying to set me up?" Preacher flashed a grin.

"Not at all." Robert smiled back. "I'm telling you what I believe."

"That's a switch. I didn't think you believed. I thought you just analyzed."

"I believe when we read the Bible, we ought to pay particular attention to the Gospels. That's where it's at. Or more accurately, where He's at."

"You don't read the rest?"

"Yes, I read the rest. But I emphasize the Gospels. Because if I find a conflict between passages in the Bible, I use the testimony of the Gospels to resolve it. I'm not much for your brand of religion, but one thing you say is dead-on."

"Really? What's that?"

"WWJD. What would Jesus do?"

"So you like that, huh?"

"You ever see a bumper sticker that says 'What Would Lot Do?' Or 'What Would the Levites Do?' Or even 'What Would Paul Do?' Jesus is the moral standard we live by."

"Amen."

"It's easy to accept that conclusion. But from then on it's hard."

"What do you mean?"

"Some tough standard. Living up to Jesus is impossible."

"That's why we pray for forgiveness."

"WWJD. I tell you what He does. He makes me uncomfortable."

"He makes me very comfortable. He's my savior."

"What I mean is, just when I think I may be a reasonably good person, I read that He comforts a prostitute, or eats lunch with a tax collector, or entertains the lepers and other so-called scum of the earth. He's sending me a message. It's not okay to sit on my butt and be happy with myself."

"I hear God's message and rejoice. You hear it and get miserable."

"Remember something that Jimmy Carter said. He once liked to think God must love his daughter Amy more than He did the starving children in Africa. The ones with the swollen bellies you see on TV. A natural reaction for a father, I guess. But Jimmy knew, deep down, that God loves all of humanity equally. He demands, and Christ demands, that we do, too. I think that's why Jimmy's made the effort to help the downtrodden people in the world. Sometimes I think I'm better and my family is better. Quite often in fact. Then I catch myself. The self-centeredness is what makes me uncomfortable."

"Are you uncomfortable now?"

"Have you heard the phrase 'tyranny of the majority'?"

"Yeah, somewhere in high school or college."

"De Toqueville. *Democracy in America.* I think his phrase applies to how straights feel about gays."

"Why do you keep coming back to that? Straights feel that way because it's the right way to feel."

"No, think about it. Straights are an overwhelming majority. Anywhere from ninety to ninety-five percent of the population, depending on whose estimate you believe. And we Christian straights are saved, even though we are totally unworthy. Then we face the impossible standard of WWJD. We can never live up to it. We drive to McDonald's and fill up our stomachs and feel guilty when we see those swollen bellies on TV. We enjoy our new houses until we meet a homeless person on the street. To compensate, we seek comfort in the fact that maybe there are some who are more totally unworthy, as illogical as that is. We're bad, but thank heavens, others are worse. Like with slavery and segregation, we look to the Bible for justification. And we find that we can single out this group, this five to ten percent of the population. It makes us feel better. We're no longer quite as intimidated by WWJD."

"The Bible singles them out. Homosexuality is an abomination."

"It doesn't really do that. They're mentioned only five or six times. Mostly obscure references, in the Old Testament and in Paul's letters. They all tie into the Torah, the ancient Jewish law. And the New Testament tells us the Torah is transformed by the coming of Christ. But we in the majority cling to the idea that homosexuality is worse than any other sin."

"Worse than what?" Preacher challenged.

Robert thought for a few moments. "Christ does talk about marriage and divorce. Man and woman become one flesh. What God joins together, let no man put asunder. What would Jesus do? Pardon me, but it's damn clear. But we in the ninety percent can't handle it. We cut ourselves some slack. Divorce has become acceptable. And not just in Hollywood. I mean, how many famous preachers are divorced? But do we cut any slack for same-sexers? No, even though Christ never condemned them. I don't think it's because of Biblical teaching. I think it's because of the tyranny of the majority."

"And I think you're caught up in another scenario. Pure rationalization."

"Preach, do you believe God created heaven and earth?"

"Yes. Says so in the Bible."

"Then he created homosexuals. Like every other living thing."

"You're crazy. He created them whole and they brought their sin on themselves."

"I don't think so. God's done some radical things. Like impregnating an unmarried teenager. You believe in the Virgin Birth?"

"Yes. Of course."

"Well, if God could do that, why couldn't He create homosexuals? God can do anything."

"Just because He can doesn't mean He has."

"Maybe he has, Preach. And we just haven't been able to fathom it. Paul says there's neither Jew nor Greek, slave nor free, male nor female. Maybe he means there's neither gay nor straight also."

The muted chime of Preacher's phone rang out again. This time the cell violated not only natural tranquility, but also the crux of Robert's argument. Preacher talked briefly to another colleague. He hung up and yawned. He stared at the diffuse glow penetrating the rainfly of the tent below. "Tell me something. Are Czechmate and Mother Superior lesbians?"

"I haven't asked. They haven't told. If it's important to you, why don't you ask them?"

"Maybe I will."

"Be prepared for Mother Superior's answer."

Preacher chuckled. "I know how to duck." He gathered his stove and cookware. "I need to start early tomorrow to meet my ride."

"Don't forget your ice axe and oxygen bottle."

Preacher smiled. "See ya up the trail." He walked inside the shelter.

The day was incomplete. Robert needed resolution. The stars above articulated themselves in the darkness. He gazed across the constellations to find a cluster that reminded him of Angie. He probed the heavens, searching for her familiar face. His imagination did not fail him as it had with Grandfather Mountain. He fixed on a likeness directly overhead.

Hello, Starshine.

The game was fun. For the next round he tried to imagine what his grandchild would look like. He combed the skies from horizon to horizon. He tried several combinations until he settled on one that pleased him. Only then did he realize that the star grouping was the same he had selected as Angie's best likeness. It was the perfect way to end the day.

Chapter 12

Hummingbird, don't fly away, fly away ... don't fly away.
Seals and Crofts

Robert entered the clearing in front of the shelter. Before he could remove his pack, Czechmate confronted him.

"Snecks, did you see der goats?"

"Actually, they saw me. Then they had their way with me. What about you, Mother?"

"They licked every drop of sweat off my legs. They must really be starved for salt."

"Dey come right up und lick my knees! It vas creepy! The big one tried to eat my shorts!"

Robert dropped his pack on the platform. "Did that turn you on?"

"Ugh. Iss that all you men think about?"

"Well, did it?"

"*Scheisskopf!*" Czechmate scooped up a handful of pebbles and hurled them at him in rapid succession. Retreating, Robert threw up his hands in mock horror. "When you start with German, I'm in big trouble."

Czechmate relaxed. He edged back warily to get a drink from a Nalgene. "That's just their way of being friendly. Or maybe they're horny as all get out. After all, we're talking about goats here."

She pouted. "It iss all you think about."

The experience had been surreal. The trail rambled over another Virginia ridgeline, Sinking Creek Mountain. Along the crest, veins of jagged rock erupted between the scrubs and small trees. The elevation on the ridge rarely changed, but the uneven footing demanded constant attention. Robert had stopped for a moment's relief from the continuous scrambling. From the high point he traced the meandering path of Sinking Creek, which snaked through the valley below. He heard a scuffle behind him. It was too early in the day for Socrates, Southern Bell, and War Eagle to overtake him. He turned to investigate.

A trio of goats hopped toward him over the rocks. The largest stood waist-high on Robert's six-foot frame. It sported an impressive charcoal coat and tufted goatee. The other two were shorter and wore less-distinguished sallow jackets. The goats were emboldened by the naked skin between the hem of his shorts and the tops of his gaiters, and they made a beeline for his exposed kneecaps. He was perspiring freely in the warm May sun, and the opportunistic threesome took advantage of his salty flow. Their brazen lapping initially stunned him. Then the tongues flicking on his skin excited him, particularly when they tickled the creases below his hamstrings.

A few seconds of passive bestiality was enough. He stepped away to end the intimacy. To discourage his suitors, he swung Old Hickory gently in a wide arc. "Don't worry, billies. The next salt lick will be along soon."

"Sooo creepy." Czechmate was still animated. Robert sat down between her and his pack and dug into the top pocket for gorp.

"I vonder vat they did to Bell. She hass such long legs."

"War Eagle probably scared them away. But I tell you something. If they made a play for Soc, they are sick, sick, *sick*."

"Did I hear my name? Spoken in vain?" Socrates walked in from the trail, closely followed by War Eagle and Southern Bell.

"Just talking about the goats. Since you sweat olive oil instead of salt water, we figure they left you alone."

"Wrong, Snaky. I'm a Capricorn. They sensed the kinship. Just ask Bell. It was spellbinding to see us exchange bodily fluids."

"Yeayah, right. They licked you once or twice and gagged. That stiff black hair on your laigs turned them off. They thought you wuz a pork-u-pahn."

"You're jealous. You didn't get a tongue massage."

Southern Bell sat on the edge of the platform and called for War Eagle. Panting, he rushed to her and licked her knees. She scratched behind his ears. "Those ole goats knew who these knees belonged to, didn't they? Nobody but mah baby gets to lick these laigs!" She looked at Socrates with a coquettish grin. "And who's jealuss now?"

War Eagle rubbed his snout against the inside of her long, shapely thighs. Socrates winced. "Trumped. By the favorite feminine card." He turned to Robert. "So, Snaky? Did they come on to you?"

"Passionately. Closest thing I've had to sex in over a year."

"I'll rephrase the question. Did you come on to the goats?"

"The thought entered my mind."

"Snaky, you poor thang." Southern Bell consoled. "You need a female companyun."

"Tell me about it."

She sensed a matchmaking opportunity. "When we git to the Shenandoah, Ah'll ask Bessie to come over from Staunton. You'll lak her."

"Since you're a vet, Bell, please elaborate. Is Bessie a cow?"

"You are bayud! She's hyooman. More than Ah can say fer you. Bessie's mah real purty roommate at Auburn." She stopped for emphasis. "Besides, she's got this thang for older men."

"He definitely qualifies," Socrates responded. "Snaky, just flash your AARP card, and you're in."

Robert ignored his remark. "Bessie sounds wonderful, Bell. Just give me two days' notice. I'll need that long to clean up."

Mother Superior took issue. "I don't know, Snakes. You had a tongue bath today. You can go three more days before you'll need a shower."

―∞―

The quarantine was over. With his pals again, Robert could rejoice and be glad. In its infinite wisdom, the AT made things right. His pack felt several pounds lighter.

He had tried to befriend Preacher, but they had little in common on which to build a lasting relationship. If, according to conventional wisdom, men were from Mars and women from Venus, then he and Preacher were from different galaxies. Their simplest conversations were destined to end in argument. Preacher's mind was made up at the outset. He was never receptive to Robert's reasoned positions. Conversely, Robert was sure Preacher saw him in the same light, an unyielding, unresponsive foe. Preacher must have been a point guard also, because they engaged in an unending game of one-on-one.

Weary from their differences of opinion, Robert nevertheless found a silver lining. The week from Damascus to Chestnut Knob had engendered mutual respect, the grudging acknowledgment of well-armed adversaries. They did not break through to friendship, but they did attain professional accommodation.

Their discourse had tapped into a long-dormant zeal. Robert could still get worked up about what he believed in. To back up his convictions, he had summoned forth all the knowledge from his years of study. The reemergence of this intellectual passion excited him, as had his physical prowess going up Cheoah. All his systems were in top form.

The days with Preacher underscored how much he had missed the easy camaraderie of the Fab Five. It was nice to banter freely with his buddies, knowing he wasn't about to set anyone off. Hiking was much easier in a relaxed atmosphere.

Preacher might catch up again, but only if he hiked diligently. The group had reeled off a twenty going over Sinking Creek and Brush Mountains. They paused on the first just long enough to take their "licks," and on the second to view the monument near the site where Audie Murphy, the war hero and actor, had died in a plane crash thirty years earlier. The next day they punched out eighteen challenging miles, beginning in the morning with Dragon's Tooth. The southern approach to the peak was rocky, but otherwise unremarkable. However, to the north the stone monolith fell off precipitously. The descent required all fours. The maintainers had anchored metal handholds and footholds in the cliff face to help hikers traverse the steep pitch without falling onto jagged boulders.

Mother Superior alerted them to what was to come. "If you think this is tough, wait till New Hampshire. The whole damn state's like this. And most of Maine."

"War Eagle, Ah need yowah four laigs to scampah over these rocks."

They reached MacAfee Knob. A massive, cantilevered rock jutted into the sky high above the Catawba Valley, seventeen hundred feet below. At first singly, and then in pairs, they walked onto the overhang for the requisite photographs. Socrates and Southern Bell ventured far out on the ledge, near the precipice. Robert proceeded cautiously, accommodating his fear of edges. Perched a conservative distance from the rim, he snapped several photos of the sprawling landscape. At first, the lush green valley reminded him of the pristine farms of Burke's Garden, but the roads, power lines, and buildings of Catawba, although dwarfed by the distance from the towering peak, were visible to the naked eye. Burke's Garden remained his favorite glen.

"Okay, guys, listen up!" Mother Superior summoned them to attention like a drill sergeant. "Today we celebrate a monumental event. Right here on top of the world. It's Czechmate's birthday."

Southern Bell exclaimed, "Lemme give you a big ole bear hug!"

When she loosened her embrace, Czechmate exhaled with exaggeration. "Today. May four. I am twenty-two."

"Like hell you are, Matey." Socrates chided her. "You're too pretty to lie about your age. C'mon, tell us the truth."

Czechmate adopted the pose of *The Thinker*. "Okay," she admitted. "I am twenty-four."

"Snaky, when it comes to telling their age, women have no conscience."

"No, they don't. And they bet we don't have the balls to call them on it."

Mother Superior took several pictures. Southern Bell led them in a "Happy Birthday" serenade. After the chorus, the group hiked another mile to a shelter and campsite.

Robert inventoried his food. There were two carrot cake bars left in his dwindling store. Resupply was the next day at Daleville. He had planned to eat one after supper and the other at lunch tomorrow. Now he had a better idea. He carefully pulled apart the foil wrapper from one of the bars and flattened it into a thin tray. He laid the bar in the center of the foil. He pressed the wooden end of a match through the crust of the Clif bar so that it stood erect. He carefully concealed the creation inside a stuff sack. Cradling his masterpiece, he made his way to the table where Czechmate and Mother Superior were preparing dinner. He announced loudly, "Okay, troops. Come here a minute!"

Socrates walked over, his arm draped around Southern Bell. "Whatcha got in the bag, Snaky?"

He pulled out the carrot cake. He lit the candle with another match and held up the sparkling confection for all to admire. "It's not a proper birthday without a cake."

Southern Bell burst out again in song. "Happy buthday to yew!" The others joined in robustly. The sopranos, the baritone, and Robert's monotone blended in the warm evening air. He presented the flambeau to Czechmate. She beamed at the attention. When the chorus ended, she acknowledged Robert's gift with a kiss on his cheek.

"Awwww!" Socrates mimicked the female gush of approbation.

"Awwww!" The others echoed.

"Speech! Speech!" Mother Superior commanded.

"Okay, okay, but it vill be short." Czechmate assumed a pose of profound seriousness. "I vas not telling the truth. Ven I said I vas twenty-four." She paused for effect. "I am tventy-six."

War Eagle had watched the entire ceremony in silent detachment. Suddenly he let out a rumbling bark. The group whooped at his impeccable timing. Blushing, Czechmate shouted above the din, "Okay, okay! Tventy-sefen!"

—⁂—

God, I'm a thru-hiker. Today I want to go from Campbell Shelter to Daleville. Give me wisdom, patience, and perseverance. And thank You for letting me walk in Your world. Please get me through this day.

Robert was the first on the trail. He had slept restlessly and rose before dawn. Mother Superior and Czechmate normally left before anyone else, but they were still folding their tent when he departed.

The heavy morning stillness along the spine of Tinker Mountain absorbed his footfalls. On occasion he could see through the trees to the Catawba Valley below. Its dark green carpet soaked up the early light like blotting paper.

The path cut through a dense garden of mayapple. Hundreds of stalks burst from the ground in springtime profusion. The twin green umbrellas thrust themselves up to meet him. One specimen leaned into the treadway, and he gingerly lifted one of its multilobed leaves. Underneath, where the two leaves forked, a small, white bloom with yellow anthers nodded from the stem. The intricate and delicate flower was no more than an inch across. He counted eight white overlapping petals, perfectly formed and undisturbed. The lobes of the large leaves, as designed by nature, protected the bloom from the sun, wind, and rain.

Robert resumed walking. Images of flowers from thirty-five years ago, Angie's flowers, burst into his thoughts.

"I want an outdoor wedding."

"Angie, be serious!" Her mother, Elizabeth, had groaned in disbelief. "In Texas? In May? Think of what can go wrong. Wind. Rain. Heat. Humidity."

"Don't forget the plague of locusts," Warren added with tongue firmly in cheek.

"Think of the flowers!" Elizabeth continued. "Think of your hair!" With one final tug on the cord of guilt, she exclaimed, "You're our only daughter. Our one chance at a wedding!"

Angie loved the brick courtyard at her Austin church. It was shaded by a massive live oak growing in the middle. Its branches stretched to the sanctuary on one side and to the Sunday school building on the other. He came from Fort Hood one evening to pick her up after choir practice. Under those branches, they declared their love for the first time.

Angie remained resolute. She would not be scared off by the vagaries of Texas weather or by Elizabeth's apprehensions. She told her mother that if the weather misbehaved, they would move the ceremony, along with whatever flowers they could grab, into the sanctuary. As a compromise, she agreed to a morning wedding, when the weather was less capricious, and to a reception in the air-conditioned fellowship hall.

May 5 dawned calm and cloudless. The wedding went off without a hitch in the crowded courtyard. The minister attributed the blue sky to divine intervention. Wearing a long white dress and holding a bouquet of yellow roses, Angie was as delicate as the mayapple, shielded from the elements by the leaves of her live oak umbrella. Its branches filtered the sunlight so that the few beams that penetrated the canopy spotlighted the radiant bride. Robert took her hand from Warren and whispered in her ear, "I'm the luckiest man alive."

The only negative was the morning coat. When she informed him that all the men in the wedding party would wear one, he objected. The only animal that should wear wool in Texas in May was the sheep itself. But like any other groom, he capitulated to superior forces. Warren also labored in the heavy nuptial garb. They commiserated later when safely ensconced in the air-conditioning. Enthralled by the ceremony, Elizabeth allowed that the wedding had suffered none of her imagined catastrophes. However, she reminded them frequently through subsequent years that Austin received a thunderstorm with two inches of rain on the following morning.

Robert pressed on up the path to Tinker Cliffs. At certain points, the trail skirted the rock ledge. He watched his footing carefully to avoid a misstep that might pitch him over the edge. When he could, he looked up to the sheer sides of the cliffs ahead at the high point of the ridge.

On their honeymoon in Acapulco, they had wandered out to some high cliffs to watch the local divers. Each launched himself in a textbook layout into the roiling ocean below. Angie and Robert held their breath until the diver surfaced near the rocks, and they marveled as he made the long climb back to the top for another plunge.

Later that evening, after many cervezas, Robert mounted the footboard of the bed in their hotel room and announced that he would dive into her arms. Like Lucy holding the football for Charlie Brown, she lay there until the last second, egging him on. Only when he was spread-eagled in midair did she roll away to safety on the floor. He belly-flopped on the mattress, cursing her duplicity. She drowned his complaints with peals of laughter.

He slid off the side of the bed to make love with her on the cool tile. "Let me get on top," she pleaded. "You won't love me if my butt has bruises." Humoring her aversion to the hard surface, he rolled over and pulled her onto him. He was so caught up in her he could have laid on a bed of hot coals.

He reached the high point of Tinker Cliffs. He paused to look into the Catawba Valley. The risen sun had burned away the morning shadows, and the daily haze was beginning to form. He tried to summon more memories, but his screen was fogged. For a frantic second he was terrified. He had forgotten what she looked like. Then her face materialized, close above as he lay on the Mexican travertine. She smiled with smug satisfaction. "Fortunately, Bobby, you're a much better lover than a diver."

Robert wiped away the tears in the corners of his eyes.

I miss you, babe. God, I miss you.

The trail descended in switchbacks from Tinker Cliffs to Scorched Earth Gap. The name intrigued him. Had there been a fire here, like the one south of the Beauty Spot? If so, it had happened long ago. Belying its name, the gap was lush with spring foliage. He followed the trail further down the ridge, beside a small creek. The forest, sparse and open along the cliffs, enveloped him here in deep shadow. He welcomed the veil of the overhead canopy. It would stifle more poignant reminders.

Suspended in the thoughtless rhythm of going forward, he walked several paces beyond the side trail leading to a shelter. He caught himself and backtracked quickly. He had already depleted one Nalgene in the warm and humid air, and he needed to refill at the nearby stream.

He found a spot where the water tumbled over a large rock. There was enough space below to insert his empty bottle. He squatted and filled the Nalgene quickly in the falling rivulet. After capping the bottle, he scooped two handfuls of the cool water and washed the sweat from his face and neck. Refreshed, he carried the water to the shelter and sat down on the edge of the platform. He retrieved the little brown vial and treated the water with two capfuls of iodine. He shook it vigorously to mix the contents and placed the Nalgene and vial back in the mesh pocket of the pack. He noted the time. In thirty minutes the water would be safe to drink.

All his friends used a filter. Southern Bell had asked how he abided the chemical taste of the iodine, day in and day out.

"It's a trade-off, Bell. My crystals weigh two ounces. Your filter weighs twelve. I endure the taste to save the weight. Besides, I mask it with powdered tea or lemonade."

He grabbed the other Nalgene and his bag of gorp and stretched out on the floor for a midmorning snack. In front of the lean-to, the ground was bare from the tread of bootsteps, but the forest floor to each side was plush with new spring green. At the edge of the small clearing, where the sun was strong, poison ivy burst forth, ready to torment any unwary hiker. Behind, in deeper shade, Virginia creeper launched its climbing tendrils. Ferns pushed tender fronds through the duff. Their uncurling shoots resembled retractable paper horns, like those his family had tooted at childhood birthday parties.

Overhead, in the branches of newly minted leaves, a songbird warbled a distinctive melody. Robert had heard its call several times over many days, but the shy creature had not made itself visible. He repeated the sequence to commit it to memory. He would ask Socrates to identify the bird.

His senses had dulled when he was away from the trail, but after two months in the woods, they were sharp again. He was really "seeing" and "hearing."

He saw the blur and heard the buzz simultaneously. From out of nowhere the hummingbird darted over his head and hovered in the air, beating its wings furiously to stabilize its tiny body. The deafening drone reminded Robert of the buzz from a low-flying military jet on a mountainside in Georgia. The sound penetrated his pores and vibrated down to his bones. In the split second the bird remained suspended before him, Robert made out the red blush on its throat, a stark contrast to its metallic green body and black, needlelike bill. Just as quickly as it arrived, the bird rushed away, doppler-like, into the dappled forest.

Their bedroom, once a place of warmth and love, was now home to agony and suffering. Robert was limited to waiting for the inevitable. No matter how much sunlight streamed through the window, the room seemed dark. The hospice nurse had told him "to do whatever makes her happy and comfortable." He searched for something to lift her spirits and make her forget, if only for a moment, the pain that racked her wasting body.

He thought about the hummingbirds. Angie had always been captivated by their perpetual motion, the beauty and majesty of their diminutive bodies as they flitted from tree to bush to flower. She put up three feeders on the back deck to attract them. When she returned from work at the florist shop, she would plop on the couch in front of the window, kick off her shoes, and watch them fight each other for a perch.

The thirsty birds lit near a portal below the glass globe and inhaled the liquid through their long, thin beaks. Angie counted the bubbles that rose through the sugar water in the reservoir. Fifteen bubbles was the record, an indicator of nutrients needed for perpetual squabbling. At one point she counted eight birds stacked in a holding pattern, impatiently waiting to land on any unoccupied perch.

One bird established his dominance at a feeder and parked himself close by to drive off any others who tried to light for a drink. He relented only for a female who Angie assumed was his mate. He was such a warrior she named him "Attila the Hum." She laughed at the energy he spent protecting his territory. Cooperation would have been much less exhausting.

Robert took down one of the feeders hanging from a post on the deck. Climbing up the extension ladder, he removed the screen from the bedroom window and suspended the feeder from a hook he mounted in the cedar siding above. It hung squarely in the middle of the pane, directly in Angie's line of sight. He freshened the sugar water daily to make the feeder as alluring as possible. He sat at her bedside and prompted her to look whenever a ruby throat arrived for feeding. She said nothing, but her eyes confirmed that she enjoyed the performance. It was her final pleasure.

Autumn, like death, approached. Robert prayed each night to postpone the cold snap that would send the birds winging southward. September turned into October. The Georgia summer lingered. They held hands and watched the hummingbirds dance.

The temperature, like her spirit, conceded to the march of time. The thermometer read in the low forties when she slipped into unconsciousness. He sat in the chair, staring at the vacant window. The hummingbirds had left. The next morning she left him also.

Robert stood up. He lifted the Nalgene to lubricate his scratchy throat. He filled his mouth, but could not swallow. Waves of grief smashed into him like the incoming tide. The mind games he had played to convince himself he was over the pain of her death were swept away like a flimsy beach house before the hurricane. He spit the water out on the ground and collapsed back onto the floor of the shelter.

The stark reality of her death registered with unparalled intensity. His previous grief seemed a calculated dishonesty, a feeling expressed to others because it was expected of him. Now he stood face-to-face with it, and it flattened him under its surge. He buried his face in his hands and struggled for breath.

He was unaware how long he cried. His consciousness of time and all sentient impressions were swept away by the tsunami. He was left with a numbing ache in his viscera. Drained of energy, he had only enough strength to breathe.

"Snakes, are you okay?"

The voice reverberated from the far end of a long tunnel. A hand rested lightly on his shoulder. He raised his head to see Mother Superior, her brow lined with concern.

Czechmate knelt by him on the other side. "Your face, it is red and puffy. Vat happened?"

"Honey, he's been crying. Snakes, can you get up?"

Robert grabbed her hand. He placed his other hand on Czechmate's shoulder and stood up slowly, on wobbly legs. After several deep breaths, he spoke in a low voice.

"Today's our anniversary. The first ..." he sniffed, "... the first since Angie died."

The salt stung his eyes, but he did not break down again. He felt better having said it, and much better because he was no longer alone. The waves relented.

Czechmate circled his waist with her arm, as she had done in Tennessee. She said nothing, choosing to transmit comfort by touch. Mother Superior let him stand with her until the crisis passed. After an appropriate interval, she moved into take-charge mode.

"Hanging around here won't do you any good. You need to move. Can you hike?"

Robert smiled weakly. "I'm a thru-hiker. It's what I do."

"It's ten miles to Daleville. You need to get to the motel. And take a nice, long shower." She continued to bolster him. "Then stuff yourself at a restaurant. Can you make it?"

"Yeah. I'll feel better once I'm hiking."

Czechmate grabbed his hands. "Snecks, you need carbs. I haf just the thing for you. Strawberry Pop-Tart." She turned so that Mother Superior could unzip the top pocket in her pack. "It's in dere," she indicated with a toss of her head.

He realized they still had their packs on. He was imposing on them. He let go of her hands. Mother Superior fished into the pack and handed him the Pop-Tart.

"Thanks."

The concentrated sweetness overcame the salinity of his tears. He ate a second bite and sat down on the edge of the shelter floor. Mother Superior was there also, writing in the register. Two months of habitual conditioning prompted him. "Let me have the book when you finish."

She retracted the point with a click and handed him the pen and the notebook. All she had written was the date and her name, proof for those who followed that she had been there.

He silently thanked her for not reporting what she had found at the shelter. He collected himself and wrote.

05/05/02. Give me a triple shot of perseverance today. Dances with Snakes.

He handed the book back to her. He ate the last of the Pop-Tart. Like a robot he found his pack. He policed up his water and gorp, placing them in their designated pockets. He hoisted the pack onto his back and checked the load levelers for proper adjustment. The routines of hiking comforted him.

"Ten miles?"

"About that," Mother Superior replied.

"I put one foot ahead of the other. Right?"

She smiled. "Right. Ten miles or two thousand. Doesn't matter. Every journey begins with a single step."

"Then let's go north."

Chapter 13

If you can't be with the one you love ...
Stephen Stills

"Snakes, you're slowing down."

"Sorry. I didn't notice." Like her voice, his was a distant echo.

"Just a few more miles. We're going to Daleville, not Katahdin."

He walked in a trance, oblivious to pace and the mechanics of hiking. Normally an eager observer, he did not notice the birds, animals, or flowers. He had chided Preacher for indifference to his surroundings. Today he was equally as guilty.

The trailing duo caught up shortly before Daleville. The cryptic entries in the register had alerted them that something was wrong. Czechmate, in *sotto voce*, apprised Socrates and Southern Bell.

They arrived at the motel. Mother Superior complimented Robert. "You made it. You persevered."

"If you say so."

"But it's good we didn't meet a rattlesnake. You're in such a fog you'd have stepped on him."

"Might have been good for me. I need a shock."

Czechmate offered comfort. "You'll be more like yourself ven you clean up. Und after you eat."

Socrates escorted his buddy to the motel room. "Can I do anything? What about laundry? They have machines here."

"Yeah, thanks. I don't have much stomach for it."

"That's okay. And gimme your fuel bottle. I'll fill it up."

Robert pulled dirty clothes from his pack and stripped off what he had on. After Socrates left, he showered and shaved. He lay on the bed, waiting for his clothes. Following his earlier emotional exposure, being naked seemed appropriate. He stared at reports on the news channel without watching or listening and dozed fitfully.

The rap at the door startled him. He jumped up and let in Socrates. He carried the clean laundry, replenished fuel bottle, and Robert's mail drop, which he had picked up from the motel desk clerk.

"Gee, what service. I should fall to pieces more often."

Socrates kept the conversation upbeat. "Dances with Godiva. You in training for 'Hike Naked on the AT Day'?"

Robert grabbed a pair of shorts and a tee from the pile of laundry. He held them to his nose and inhaled. "Nice and clean." Czechmate was right; the shower and the freshly washed clothes made him feel better. "By the way, smart ass, what did you wear while your clothes were in the wash?"

"My rainfly. The lady who walked in on me has a story to tell to her sewing circle. Her daughter came in later. Not bad looking. Had on short shorts."

"Did you remember to zip it up?"

"The tent pole didn't hang out, if that's what you mean."

"Did you keep it telescoped?"

"At least until the daughter bent over to get clothes out of the dryer. Then the sections started popping into place. You know how shock cording works."

"Remind me to tell this to Bell."

"Like hell you will. But speaking of her loveliness, she's checked out a restaurant down the road. Sounds promising. Wanna go to dinner?"

"Sure. Lemme get my sandals."

The five walked to the nearby restaurant. The hostess seated them at a large round table. While waiting for the food, the others shared the news they had heard on TV. Their chatter was reminiscent of water cooler conversation at the office on Monday morning. Robert said nothing, satisfied to be in the company of friends.

Dinner came. His appetite surprised him. Regardless of his mental and emotional state, his body demanded calories. He ate generous portions of roast beef, baked potato, salad, and cornbread, and topped off the meal with a large piece of coconut cream pie. The food was good, but lacked its usual gusto. He felt like the condemned man who ate a hearty meal.

They left the restaurant. Czechmate pointed to the market down the street. "Ve are going to the grocer. You vant to come?"

Southern Bell replied, "Yayah. We could use a few more thangs. What about yew, Snaky?"

"Stick a fork in me. I'm done. I'll be at the motel."

Southern Bell prompted him. "Remembah. We leave latah in the mawning. So we can go by the post office."

"Thanks for reminding me. I need to mail some maps back to Atlanta." The memory of a sweet moment dawned on him. "Czechmate?"

She pivoted to face him. "*Ja?*"

"Could you get me some Pop-Tarts?"

She grinned. "Strawberry?"

"You read my mind."

Back in the room, he realized he should have gone with them. He needed diversion. He busied himself with the odd jobs he had disdained that afternoon, starting with the mail drop. He put the new maps for central and northern Virginia into a Ziploc, which he then put in the top pocket of the pack. He stowed the two plastic pharmaceutical vials containing a month's supply of Lipitor and multivitamins inside the plastic bag with his toiletries. He separated four days of food into piles for breakfast, lunch, and dinner, and then he packed each pile into separate stuff sacks. There were five Clif bars left. He put two in the pocket with the maps and the other three in the lunch bag. He slid his clean clothes into large Ziplocs and compressed the bags to squeeze out the air.

To stay busy, he tended to equipment. He spread the sleeping bag over the back of a chair to fluff it up and air it out. He wet one of the motel washcloths and wiped down his Thermarest. He washed his cups, pot, spoon, and water bottles in the bathroom sink. Finally he rejuvenated his boots with a coat of Sno-Seal. Everything was ready for the next day's departure.

He turned on the Weather Channel and plopped on the bed to watch the local forecast. He waited for the national coverage and the commercials to play out. His mind wandered, and he began to replay the day's events. As much as he wanted to avoid it, he had to face what had happened.

I had a great anniversary, Angie. How about you?

Stained-Glass Curtain

The gut wrench at the shelter was over and also the emotional coma that followed. What remained was unrelenting loneliness. He tried to reprise memories of Angie, as he had done on Tinker Mountain. He summoned only fleeting images. The tears returned. He walked to the bathroom and blew his nose. Hoping for a pick-me-up, he doused his face with cold water.

The local forecast scrolled across the screen. Inattentive and preoccupied, he missed it. He had to endure another ten-minute cycle. He lay down on the bed, determined to concentrate on the TV. The voice droned about late spring snows in the Rockies. He forced himself to listen to the report of ten inches of snow at Loveland Pass.

He heard a quiet knock. He navigated through the strewn equipment and opened the door. The outer passageway was illuminated by a harsh artificial light, which made him blink. Czechmate stood in the glare.

"I haf your Pop-Tarts."

He stared without speaking. She wiggled the box from side to side to get his attention. "Oh, yeah. Excuse me. I forgot."

She stared at the telltale redness around his eyes. Embarrassed, he had to look away. He took the Pop-Tarts gently from her hand. "Thanks."

He looked at her again. Her eyes were riveted on his. Her small voice broke the gravid silence. "Robert, may I come in?"

He stepped back without thinking and held the door for her to pass. It clanged shut. The gear spread across the room caught his eye. "Let me clean this up."

He tossed the Pop-Tarts on the shelf above the clothes hangers in the entryway and rushed to clear a place for her. He picked up the mummy from the chair. On his way to turn off the TV, it hit him. Holding the bag in a jumbled wad, he faced her. "That's the first time you ever called me Robert."

She walked to him. She took the bag from his hands, tossing it gently onto the Thermarest. Her blue eyes leveled at him once again. "Dat's your name." She reached up with her right hand and gently stroked his cheek. "Now. Vat's mine?"

Her touch was warm. Absorbed in the sensation, he did not immediately answer.

"Vat's my name?"

"Czechmate."

She put her finger on his lips. "Na, na," she chided. "It is May five, Robert. Who am I?"

A wisp of blonde hair circled her right eye and lay on her cheekbone. Instinctively he reached to brush it away. He looked into the eyes that had been staring so hard at him, to find the answer to her question. They were no longer blue but hazel. The roving lock of hair had darkened to brown. He breathed in audibly. "Angie."

"*Ja.* Tonight."

Her revelation was unreal. The weather Muzak and the flickering images from the TV were unreal. Everything about this day had been unreal. But the touch of her hands on his skin, and the faint aroma of herbal shampoo in her hair compelled him to embrace unreality. He looked once more into her eyes. They demanded that he believe her.

"Angie."

He clutched her waist and pulled her to him. Her nipples pressed through the Coolmax into his chest. He kissed her, gently at first and then probingly. Her lips opened in a silken response. A wave of desire broke over him. He wrenched his glasses from his ears and tossed them into the pile of down. He cradled his hands under her hips and lifted her off the floor. Her legs circled him. With a soft moan he stepped backward and fell onto the bed.

—⚍—

The sun streamed in around the edges of the curtain and bounced off the scattered piles of gear. On the TV, a jet-stream pattern moved west to east across a map of the United States. Robert sat up in bed. He searched the room, from the outside door to the bathroom alcove. He was alone. He must have been dreaming.

He dropped facedown on the pillow and inhaled deeply. A bouquet of herbal shampoo filled his nostrils. He bolted upright. His shorts, turned inside out, hung precariously on the spread at the end of the bed.

Visions of Angie and Czechmate bombarded his consciousness. Each clamored for recognition. How was it that last night they blended together into a perfect confluence? Instinctively he felt the band on his ring finger. Angie appeared in the white gown with yellow roses.

I wasn't unfaithful. I was with you. I love you.

The image blurred. A blonde angel of mercy commandeered his thoughts. The angel segued to the mistress of passion. She undulated above him as he shuddered inside of her.

Angie reappeared.

Okay. It was her. Not you. On our anniversary. And I loved it. But I'm still in love with you.

Both were in bed with him. In the throes of orgasm with Czechmate, he held up the ring to Angie. Through his spasms of pleasure he shouted out its inscription: "Five—five—sixty-seven!"

He could barely hear her above his moans. "Hike for me. Hike for us."

There was a loud knock at the door. He welcomed the intrusion, which stopped the disturbing parade of images. He jumped out of bed and into his shorts. He retrieved his T-shirt on the floor on the other side of the bed. He turned off the TV and walked to the door.

The early morning sun blinded him. He stepped back to shield his eyes.

Mother Superior stood in the passageway. "Morning, Snakes. Did you sleep well?"

"Ah, yeah. Slept great. Guess I needed it."

"We need to talk."

"Sure. Come on in."

He motioned her to take the chair in the middle of the room. She cast a long look at the unkempt bed. He wondered if she could smell the shampoo on the pillowcase.

She bent over the sleeping bag on the floor and plucked his glasses from the pile. "Put these on. I want you to see clearly."

Everything in the room screamed what had happened the night before. He looked for a way to ease the tension. He pointed to the motel's coffeemaker. "Like some coffee?"

"No, thanks. Had some earlier." She motioned him to sit down on the bed. "Let's get to the point. Yesterday was a helluva day for you."

He laughed nervously. "In more ways than one."

"Well, as far as I'm concerned, what happened, happened. You were really low and needed a boost. I presume you got one."

"Two, actually."

"You asshole! How could you take advantage of her?"

He jumped up to confront her. "Just a damn minute! I don't know how much she told you. She asked to come in. She approached me.

It was her idea for me to think of her as Angie. Granted, I didn't do anything to stop it. But I'm no predator."

"She did all that?"

"Yes." He hesitated and added, "And with great passion."

"No. With great empathy. She has a genuine compassion for those who are suffering. That's why she's a good nurse." She pondered for several seconds. "You have no idea what it took for her to do that."

"Yeah. Red eyes. Runny nose. I wasn't exactly irresistible."

Mother Superior's eyes flashed. "Just like a man. So self-absorbed. I wasn't talking about you. I was talking about her."

"What do you mean?"

She paused. "This doesn't leave this room. And in particular, don't you ever tell her I told you."

Intrigued, he sat back down on the edge of the bed. "Agreed."

"I'm telling you this because, as we used to say in the military, 'you have a need to know.' Also, I don't want this hike to go south on us." She took a long breath. "Her name is Hana. She's the youngest of a large family in Czechoslovakia. Two older sisters and three older brothers. They all lived in a tiny apartment in Prague. Two bedrooms. The sisters were teenagers when she was born. They left home by the time she started school. One went to college and became a teacher. The other got married in her late teens. She wasn't close to either one. Her father was a supervisor in a garment factory and worked long hours. She never said as much, but I think he ran around. At any rate, he was never home. He left it to her mom to raise the kids. There wasn't much for a bored housewife to do in Communist Czechoslovakia. Particularly when she's strapped for money. Being a German, she must have felt even more isolated. Anyway, she hit the bottle. Hard. When the older girls left, the boys and Hana had to learn how to take care of themselves."

"Her mother didn't do anything?"

"They'd come home from school and find her sitting in front of the TV with a bottle in her hand. Or passed out. The kids became proficient in shopping and cooking. Otherwise they'd have starved."

"That's awful."

"Bad as that was, it wasn't the real problem. The oldest brother was. When he was fifteen, and she was nine, he started molesting her. When they got home from school, he sent the other two boys out to play. He checked to make sure Mom was zoned out, and then he cornered Hana in the other room. He started out fondling her. But he got bolder and meaner. He raped her. Sodomized her. Forced her to give him hand jobs. Blow jobs. Every stinking thing he could think of. Said he'd kill her if she ever talked."

A new image supplanted the cavalcade that had streaked through his mind just minutes before. A frightened little girl with a blonde ponytail cowered before an advancing monster. He felt the revulsion in the pit of his stomach. "Could she find any help?"

"One day her mother wasn't as drunk as usual. She caught him in the act and told the father. He beat his son up pretty good. Told him he'd carve him up if he ever did it again. It scared him for a while. But with Dad rarely there and Mom in a fog, he started up again."

"How long did this go on?"

"Two years. One day, she resisted. He lost his temper and beat her up. Bloodied her nose and cracked her cheekbone. Broke two ribs to boot. She said in retrospect it was worth it. He got scared and ran. She never saw him again. He was caught shortly afterward, stealing from a clothes store. They sent him to prison."

"Was she okay?"

"The doctors fixed her face and ribs. But what she really needed was tender love and care. She couldn't get it from her parents. Her other two brothers really looked up to the older brother. In their minds it was her fault he left. She had to deal with this all by herself. She lived in virtual isolation for three or four years. She went to school, came home, read books, went to bed. She didn't have any friends. I think she was afraid to commit to anybody. She totally withdrew into herself. Didn't do well in school. She fell behind and had to repeat some classes."

"She seems so well-adjusted now. Something must have happened to help her get over the trauma."

"Her mother died of cirrhosis when Hana was fifteen. Her aunt Greta in Munich volunteered to take her. She was a goodhearted Catholic widow. Gave Hana the first taste of love and security she ever had. She responded to her aunt's kindness and gradually came out of her shell. Greta sent her to a convent school. She thrived in that environment. She was twenty when she finally graduated from high school, or whatever they call it in Germany. She started work as a nurse's aid at a Munich hospital."

"After all that, she wanted to help others."

"Like I said, she has great empathy. She lost her childhood, Snakes. But once she got out of Prague and found a sheltering home, she became a caring, functioning adult. Three years ago her aunt died of cancer. Left her some money. She made a big decision. She applied for nursing school in the United States."

"What a story. Czechmate's a survivor. She willed herself to be somebody."

"Yeah, she's a top-notch student. Will be a top-notch nurse, too."

"I can see that. And I see why you think I have a need to know."

"You need to know so that you won't fuck things up."

Admonished, Robert sat up straight. "Okay. You have my attention."

"The first consideration is the hiking group. The Fab Five. When Czechmate and I started hiking, we figured we'd do it alone. We thought we'd never find anyone compatible. But we really enjoy you guys."

"The feeling's mutual."

"But groups are fragile. Witness the Preacher. When he was on the scene, we lost you for a week."

"Yeah. I really missed you guys."

"And we missed you, too. When a new element gets introduced it changes the chemistry."

"And the new element that worries you now?"

"Snakes, you're a man. By your own admission, you had a great lay last night. If you follow form, you won't make it to Katahdin without wanting more. If you chase her butt up the trail, there goes the chemistry."

Robert started to blurt out, but bit his tongue. Mother Superior gave him a chance to collect his thoughts. He spoke in measured words. "I won't deny it. I've been attracted to her since I first met you guys back at the Beauty Spot."

"I suspected as much. Thank you for being honest."

"Mother, you guys are partners. From everything I see, you love each other. Do you realize how lonely it is to crawl into a sleeping bag by yourself, night after night? Particularly when I had a partner I loved with all my heart? Last night was the first time I had sex with anyone but my wife in over thirty-five years. And in that drama Czechmate and I performed, I was still having sex with Angie. When I woke up this morning, I spoke her name first. Not Czechmate's."

"Can I trust you? Was last night a one-act play?"

"You don't need to dump any guilt on me. I'm doing that. I have a lotta things to work out. Sure, chasing Czechmate's butt up the trail is an attractive proposition. But after what you've just told me, I don't think I could come on to her. And she must be awfully skittish around men."

"This gets to my second consideration. Much more important than the first. It's Czechmate herself. I'm not positive, but I'm guessing, with the exception of her brother, you're the only man she's ever had sex with."

"Given her past, I don't understand how she did what she did last night."

"Nor do I." She paused before she continued. "My only clue is what she's said about you."

"What?"

"After you intervened with the hunters in Tennessee. And after you took on Preacher in Damascus. You are the only man she's ever known who stood up for her. She's seen so little kindness. She really responds to it."

"She certainly responded to me."

"And that's the whole point of this conversation. What she gave you last night is as pure a gift as you will ever receive. A present from her heart. If you treat it as anything else, you'll destroy the unique relationship you have with her, and you may destroy her too."

"Do you really think I'm that kind of person?"

"So far, no. Remember, I thought we'd never find someone compatible out here. That went double for single men. You are a surprise."

"I'm not really single. Not even last night."

"But you drank from her fountain. You may get thirsty again. Let's just say it's my job to protect her. I intend to do just that."

Robert stood up from the bed. "I've leveled with you. So I think I'm entitled to ask this question: Do you see us in competition?"

She shot him a look of disgust. "That too is just like a man. I thought we were concerned with her mental and emotional welfare. You want to turn this into some sort of sexual contest."

"Mother, I give you my word. I will never take advantage of her. That's my present from the heart, to Czechmate and to you. I love her and respect her too much to hurt her. What I meant was, I'm talking to the woman who'd be the first female Yankee catcher. The first Jorgina Posada. Competitiveness is not exclusively masculine. You certainly got your share. Level with me. Are your motives compromised by how you feel for her? I'm not saying that's wrong. I just want to know."

"I'd like to think I can love her and still do the right thing by her."

"I'd like to think that, too. And think the best about everybody. I want them to think the best about me, too."

Mother Superior stood up. "Okay. That's done. It's time for breakfast, and I need to get my stuff together for the post office. You coming?"

"Yeah, it won't take me long. I don't have much." He felt relieved, but he wasn't sure if she held any residual resentment. "Mother?"

"What?"

"Should I speak to her about this? To make sure we understand each other? I don't have a problem doing that, but I'm not sure it's appropriate. You can cheapen something by talking about it."

"I'll talk to her. I'll tell her you enjoyed the play. But there will be no curtain calls." She opened the door and stepped out. With her hand still on the knob she leaned back in. "One more thing." A smile flirted with the corners of her mouth.

"Yeah?"

"The mind that comes up with Jorgina Posada can't be all bad."

She closed the door.

Robert digested her disclosures. He recalled the experiences he had shared with Czechmate: her violent shaking after the confrontation with the hunters; her disquietude about Lot's daughters. The significance of her reactions crystallized. What had it been like as a child, living with constant fear, wondering why God let such things happen? After enduring that, what kind of resilience did it take to live a normal life?

His thoughts were interrupted by another knock. His door had become a turnstile at Grand Central Station. He opened it. Socrates burst in. "Okay, suppose you tell me what the hell is going on."

"What do you mean?"

"Don't be coy. That quality in snakes went out with the Garden of Eden."

"I was just talking to Mother about something."

"Well, why don't you talk to your buddy Socrates about something? Like last night, around midnight, when I took War Eagle out to pee. Czechmate comes out of your room, barefoot with shoes in hand, and walks back to hers. And then you and Mother talk in your room, bright and early this morning."

"We talked about the Braves and the Yankees. Smoltz versus Pettitte."

"Try again, Snaky."

"It's a long story."

"Gimme the short version. You get any last night?"

"A gentleman doesn't tell."

"You old cocksman! You got laid! Bell's said all along there was a spark between you two. She's got this sixth sense about animals in heat."

"Asshole. We're not talking about a barnyard coupling. It was an act of love and compassion."

"Highbrow sex is still sex. How was it? I bet she's hot."

"You're missing the point. Yesterday was not good for me. She found a sweet and tender way to help me."

"A mercy fuck."

Robert picked up the first thing he could find, one of his boots, and threw it at Socrates. He dodged the missile. "Whatever you call it, it didn't improve your aim. Lemme get you back on target. In five minutes you're going out that door. To face her. You figured out what you'll say?"

"I think so. Mother helped me."

"Mother? Helped you?" Socrates was incredulous. "I got to hand it to you, Snaky. You screw a beautiful woman and then get her partner to come down on your side. Maybe you should be secretary of state. Frankly, I thought she would castrate you."

"I told you, this is a long story. It has a superficial level and a profound level." For the first time, Robert smiled. "You're barely scratching the surface."

"You know damn good and well the surface is where all red-blooded American males operate. Look at you. You can talk about tenderness and compassion, but that shit-eating grin tells me you scored in a big way."

"There was a lot more to it than that."

"Okay, but when your head hits the pillow tonight, I bet you won't be thinking about that 'lot more' part."

"Actually I'll be thinking about herbal shampoo."

"She smelled good, huh?"

"A smorgasbord of sensations. All five senses got a workout."

"Sounds like you want more."

"You need to understand. This was a one-timer."

"Really? That's a bummer."

"I have issues to settle. Before I can have another relationship. I love Czechmate, but we won't make love again."

"That makes no sense. But most of what you say doesn't. Say, you get a haircut?"

"No. Why?"

"Your hair's lying down nice and flat. You finally got rid of those horns!"

Robert picked up his other boot and flung it at Socrates. It bounced off his shin. The blow did not stop him from laughing. He tossed both boots back in Robert's direction. "Get these on and let's go for breakfast."

They walked out the door into the courtyard. Czechmate, Mother Superior, Southern Bell, and War Eagle waited in the sunlight. Czechmate was blonde, slender, and beautiful. She also seemed tense. It was up to him to put her, and everyone else, at ease.

He approached Southern Bell and mustered a serious expression. "Bell, you're the only one here who hasn't seen my motel room. Would you and War Eagle like the tour?"

The others chuckled, nervously at first and then heartily. Through their laughter, Southern Bell shouted, "No, Snaky! May it forevah be a mystry!"

Robert approached Czechmate and grasped her hands tenderly. "Thank you, Angie."

Her apprehension evaporated into the morning air. "You're velcome, Robert."

He bent over and kissed her lightly on the cheek, savoring another breath of his favorite herbal scent. He faced the group. "Czechmate says she's starving, and so am I. Let's get breakfast. I'm thinking two eggs and eight pancakes."

Socrates asked innocently, "What did you two do to work up such an appetite?"

Southern Bell poked him in the stomach. "Can't yew keep yower mouth shut?" He doubled over, more in laughter than in pain.

"Iss okay, Bell. Ve played charades. Snecks is goot at this game."

Robert walked with Czechmate to the restaurant. It was his turn to play the naif. "By the way, what's the weather like the next few days? I never got the forecast. Something distracted me."

She rattled his ribs with a sharp elbow. "Snecks, it vill be sunny for us. But for you it vill be donder und lightning!"

Chapter 14

God made the wild animals of the earth of every kind ... And God saw that it was good.
Genesis 1:25

Socrates swigged heartily from the long-neck. He rubbed his stomach with satisfaction. "They have good beer in Waynesboro." He underscored his endorsement with a loud belch. "And good pizza."

"They hayuv good showahs, too. Ah'm so happy yew found one."

"You weren't exactly Miss Cashmere Bouquet."

"We were in the woods forever," Mother Superior interjected. "We all stank."

"But not like mah Greek philosofah. He was pohsitively putrid. Remembah, Ah was sleepin' with him. Ah almost called Momma, to send me back mah little solo tent." She fingered the sleeve of Socrates's tee. "Ah can't believe this shirt came clean."

"You overestimate my body odor. And underestimate detergents."

"Sweetheart, Ah assure you Ah overestimated nothing. But maybe Ah did sell that Tide short. We Auburn people just natraly think anything called 'Tide' is no-count."

"Longest I've gone without a shower. Snaky, how many miles from Daleville?"

Robert answered through a mouthful of pizza. "Don't know offhand. But I got the data book here." He wiped his hands on a napkin and flipped through the pages in the trail outline.

Socrates feigned impatience. "You used to know this stuff right away."

"Don't get your shorts in a wad." He put the book down. "One hundred and thirty-two miles. Smelling you the last few days made it seem like two thousand."

"Boys, be nice. Ve are clean und fresh again. Vat's important, ve are makink really goot time." Czechmate put her hand on Mother Superior's arm. "Soon ve can fisit our friends in Baltimoor."

"Slow down, partner. Let's get through the Shenandoah first. If you guys have finished sparring, we need to buy groceries. Snakes, don't you have a mail drop here?"

"No. And with good reason. I'll let you in on a little secret."

Southern Bell perked up. "This sounds int'resting."

"Gather 'round, ladies. And college boy. The old fart will enlighten. You wanna slack pack?"

"Whut do yew think?"

"The Smokies was seventy miles long. The AT ran down the middle. The Shenandoah is a hundred. The Skyline Drive runs down the middle. It has the AT, too, but it caters to car campers."

"So what's your point?"

"There are four or five restaurants on the Skyline Drive. Each is close to where the trail crosses the road. Also several campgrounds with convenience stores. If we plan right, we can pack light all the way through the park to Front Royal. We stop at restaurants to pig out and at stores to resupply. Slack packs and town food!"

"Snakes, you're cooking! And I'll go you one better. How far from Front Royal to Harpers Ferry?"

Robert perused the data book again. "Fifty-four miles, Mother."

"One of my nurses can drive over from Baltimore and meet us where the AT crosses the interstate. I'll ask her to bring two days' worth of food, and that should get us to Harpers. That's one hundred fifty miles of slacking."

"Dat's great! Ve haf vorked hard. Ve deserf to go light."

"There's mellow trail in the park, too," Mother Superior said. "No Roan Mountains. We should make serious time."

"You know vat I really vant? A bear! Tell me I vill see a bear!"

"We're overdue. I thought we'd see 'em in the Smokies, but they didn't come out in the rain. They're smarter than thru-hikers. Our chances should be better in the Shenandoah."

Socrates growled menacingly. *"Czarny niedwiedz."*
Southern Bell poked him. "Whut's thayat?"
"Black bear. In Polish."
"How'd yew know thayat?"
"I have a link with the noble beast. I know it in many languages. *L'ours noir. Oso negro.*"
"Well, Ah don't want any links with bayahs. Speakin' of which, yew look lak one. If yew want to keep tenting with me, yew bettah git a haircut. And trim yower mustache."

—⚇—

"Look up there!"
A scarlet tanager perched high above them on the limb of a dying oak. Its fiery plumage shone like a beacon through the sparse foliage. After a few seconds the bird took flight. The deep blue sky magnified its brilliance, until it disappeared into the vastness.
"That boy was so bright red he actually hurt my eyes," Mother Superior exclaimed. "It's a shame he didn't hang around longer."
Later that day they surprised an indigo bunting. It hopped in and out of the fractured light in the laurel bushes beside the trail. In the waning sun and lengthening shadow, the elusive bunting was an iridescent chameleon—one moment azure, then sapphire, and then ink. Southern Bell was enthralled. "Blue boy, stay in the sunlight! Yew'll put the sky to shame."
That night, Robert lay on the Thermarest, resting his neck on his unrolled sleeping bag. He thought about Angie and Czechmate, as he had every day since Daleville. His emotions ran the gamut from desire to sadness to regret.
He longed for his ordered, idyllic life with Angie. She had been his magnetic north, a thirty-five-year locus of love and companionship. He had steered his course from that waypoint. But she had left him. Bereft of her collimation, his bearings were now calculated by dead reckoning.
In contrast, Czechmate was a palpable presence. Every sight of her triggered the phosphoric moment in the motel room. But she couldn't be his new navigator. Their night together, and the subsequent revelations, had transformed her. Her past stood between them, as did

the promises he made to himself and to Mother Superior. Formerly the catalyst for his reemerging libido, she was now an untouchable.

Angie was the tanager. She perched high above, fierce and crimson. He could pinpoint her only for a few moments of rapt remembrance before she vanished indifferently into the blue sky. Earth bound, he could not fly away with her.

Czechmate was the bunting. She flitted along the trail, almost close enough to touch, but then she would skitter away into the protective undergrowth. He had to wait passively for her to hop into the light and expose her resplendent indigo.

On that one night of tenderness and fervor, the bunting had lighted on him, molted into the tanager, molted back, and hopped away. Blue to red. Back to blue. And gone.

Czechmate would never settle on him again. Such fortuitous magic happens once in a lifetime. In her tantalizing way she had become, like Angie, another memory. The two, so different in what they meant to him, were painfully alike. He couldn't have either one.

The new day that the Lord had made was a chamber of loneliness. How to rejoice and be glad about that? Harsh reality threatened to convert the Bible verse from a statement of faith to an irrelevant platitude. It was up to him to take charge of this reality. But how? How would he steer through the desolation? He was certain it would not be a short cruise, but a long voyage. He really would need wisdom, patience, and perseverance.

He slid into the mummy and closed his eyes. The fatigue from the day's exertion became his friend, and sleep became his sail.

―⁓―

The ensuing morning ushered in another avian performance. Czechmate, the lead hiker, flushed out a ruffled grouse and her large brood. The shadows made an exact accounting difficult, but at least eight chicks scurried for cover, to the delight of Czechmate. "The biddies are eferywhere!"

The hen commenced her routine by drawing attention to herself and away from the chicks. She hopped in the middle of the trail and bent her right wing under her body in a painful contortion. She bleated mournful cries. Her ruse completely convinced them. Czechmate, the caregiver, inched toward her to help. Satisfied her little ones were hidden from the outsized intruders, the hen ended the stratagem and flew away from Czechmate's outstretched hand. Both wings fluttered perfectly.

The three were mesmerized by her turn at center stage. "Best performance by an actress," Mother Superior declared. "The Golden Grouse Award."

Later that day, they traversed an area where many white oaks had been killed by an infestation of gypsy moths. Sunlight had penetrated the thinned canopy and sparked a profusion of white blossoms on the mountain laurels lining the trail.

The laurel was Robert's favorite flower. He stopped to admire the clusters of intricate, bowl-shaped blooms. Each tiny saucer was splattered with pink where the stamen emerged, and also on the dimpled petals where the stamen reattached. The flower was a textbook case of fine engineering. Bees feasted on its sweet nectar and in the process broke the stamen. They moved on and transported pollen to the next bush.

This method of pollination was a huge success. *Kalmia latifolia* covered Virginia like weeds. Several days earlier, near The Priest, they had walked through hundreds of yards of laurel pressing into the pathway on both sides. Robert coined the term "laurel gauntlet," to describe the narrow passageway. From a distance, the thicket of blooms looked like snowfall.

A brief but heavy thunderstorm doused them. The sun returned and paired with the steaming humidity to drench them again. The trailside foliage, weighed down with drops of water, squatted menacingly in the right of way.

"Another gauntlet here," Robert spoke over his shoulder to Mother Superior. "Want to lead for a while?"

She surveyed the saturation that awaited the first to plow through the pendulous laurel. "That's okay. You're doing a great job on point."

He plunged into the bushes. He thrust Old Hickory forward to deflect the branches, but they patted him on all sides, depositing cool drops of water on his head and arms. Like a dirty auto inside a car wash, he was slapped by a myriad of bristles. He walked fifty yards through the soaking laurel before the bushes finally receded. He took advantage of the opening to brush the water off his body and to dislodge the beads on his pack cover.

Preoccupied with drying off, Robert neglected to watch the trail with his usual attentiveness. He was jolted by a singular alarm, a chilling combination of a hiss and the click-click of castanets.

Robert shivered and stumbled backward into Mother Superior. "What's the matter?"

"Rattler."

The snake was perfectly camouflaged in the mottled light on the forest floor. It lay directly in the trail, less than six feet in front of him.

"Where?"

"There." Robert pointed charily at the snake with Old Hickory. The motion of the stick caused the rattle to intensify. "Wow! Look at that tail! Must be eight to ten buttons."

"That is one beautiful animal. He's what, about four feet long?" Mother Superior examined the wary viper. "Tan and brown. All black at the tail. Blends in perfectly with the leaves."

"I never saw him. If he hadn't rattled, I would've stepped on him. He hasn't coiled, so he's not really that agitated. He's saying 'I'll keep cool if you do.'"

Czechmate peered cautiously around Mother Superior. "The body. Iss huge!"

"Characteristic of pit vipers. Thick body, compared to a black snake or a garter snake." Robert pointed again with his stick. "Another tip-off is the triangular head."

The head was fixed on them. The only movement was the occasional flicking of its black forked tongue.

"Vat ve do?"

"Nothing. He's in charge. He's not riled enough to strike. Let's hope he just slithers away. Like Mother said, he's a beautiful specimen. Get some pictures for your friends in Baltimore." Robert stepped back a few more paces and took off his pack. He retrieved his camera. The others followed suit. For several minutes they photographed their subject. Finally, the rattlesnake, bored with the shutterbugs, slid off into the ferns and deadfall.

Robert exhaled with exaggeration. "Best way to meet a rattler. You see it or hear it before you get too close."

"I'm disappointed in you," Mother Superior said sternly.

"*Ja*, me too," Czechmate chorused.

"Why?"

"You didn't dance with it."

Robert laughed. "I only do that with copperheads."

—⚎—

The quintet stopped for the night at Rock Spring hut. Robert's first priority was to dry his clothes. He strung a nylon cord tautly between two trees beside the shelter, and invited the others to hang their wet things. The line soon sagged under the weight of damp shirts, shorts, socks, and underwear.

Robert admired his creation. "Ma, Pa, and the younguns hang their duds out to dry. Gives the place a homey touch."

The conversation turned to food. The plan to take advantage of restaurants and stores in the Shenandoah was on schedule. They faced a short stroll of four miles in the morning to Skyland. Robert salivated in anticipation. "I'm ordering the biggest breakfast on the menu."

"Maybe a Denver omelet. Or *huevos rancheros*. You think they have something that exotic?" Socrates asked.

"Dunno, but yew can probly count on grits and country ham. How 'bout mac and cheese tonight, to git ready for it?"

They busied themselves with dinner. In short order, three camp stoves hummed in polyphonic rhythm. Southern Bell pointed to the grass across the clearing. "Look ovah theyah. A doe and a fawn. This place is crawlin' with deer. They aren't even spooked by War Eagle." She petted the lab, who chewed his dinner contentedly.

"How many since ve entered the park?" Czechmate asked.

"Girl, I stopped counting at twenty," Mother Superior said.

Socrates added, "The habitat's perfect for them. Lots of grass and acorns. And it's a sanctuary. Nobody's shooting at Bambi."

"I can't beliefe anyone vould vant to shoot a deer. Dey are so graceful."

Southern Bell looked up from cooking. "Shiyut! The damn thing's eating mah panties!"

No more than twenty feet away, a fearless doe had approached the clothesline, and selected Southern Bell's underpants from the *a la carte* menu. Just a few feet down the cord, a second feasted on Czechmate's briefs.

"Domm you!" Czechmate shrieked. "Get avay!"

Southern Bell charged the deer. "Shoo! Shoo!"

The animals dropped their entrees on the ground and bolted into the forest. Southern Bell and Czechmate returned to the shelter with remnants of panties in hand.

Southern Bell held hers up with disgust. "There's a big ole hole right in the crotch."

Socrates and Robert exploded. Mother Superior joined them. The trio rolled uncontrollably on the floor of the shelter. Southern Bell and Czechmate stewed in rising indignation. Socrates stopped laughing, only to add insult to injury. "Ventilated. The new style." There were more shrieks.

Robert teased. "A fly. Now the girls can pee like the boys."

"Shut chor mouth. I thought yew wuz a gentleman, but yew're as bayad as he is."

Fuming, Czechmate inspected what was left of her underwear. "Iss not funny. If I catch that deer, I kill it."

Mother Superior did a perfect imitation. "I can't beliefe anyone vould vant to kill a deer. Dey are so graceful."

When the laughter subsided, Czechmate asked a question, to nobody in particular. "Vy dey vant to eat my dirty undies?"

The zoologist answered. "Matey, don't think like a human. Think like a deer. They have a continuous craving for salt. Remember the goats, back there south of Roanoke? Deer need salt even more. And a prime location for collected salt is the crotch of a woman's panties. Plenty of perspiration and urine residue. I suspect they sniffed everything on the line and went straight for the good stuff. Given time, they would have moved on to our shorts and then to all the T-shirts. By eating yours first, they paid you the supreme compliment."

Robert chimed in, "Life is short—eat dessert first."

Czechmate was glum. "I only haf one pair now."

"You can hike without them," Socrates offered. "It'll be cooler. And it would make Snaky's day."

Mother Superior intervened. "Nancy can bring you another pair when she comes from Baltimore with the food."

Robert could not contain his amusement. "Wait a minute. You mean there really is a nurse Nancy?"

"Yes, and if you say that to her, she'll bust your chops."

Socrates finally showed concern for Southern Bell. "What about you? How you fixed for unmentionables?"

"Ah only have one pair too."

"Saw a fig tree back a ways. If you like, I could twine some leaves together. We could call you Eve."

"And we could call yew Leave, as in 'leave me be.' Mother, could yower freeyund bring me a pair too? Polyestah. Size five."

The quintet left Skyland, sated by generous helpings of omelets and pancakes. They took a short detour to the top of Stony Man Mountain, to ooh and aah at the Shenandoah Valley and the town of Luray, far below. Then it was back to heading north on the AT.

Robert noted that it was unusual to be hiking early in the day with Socrates and Southern Bell. "It's a pleasure to have you two in our morning company."

"Yes, she's a real dear, isn't she?" Socrates needled.

"Yew are smellin' a whole lot worse now than yew evah did befowah."

"I'll tell you something, Bell," Robert said. "Might make you feel better. I had to get up in the night to pee—"

"Imagine that," Mother Superior interjected.

"—and I went in the grass a few feet off the trail. When we left this morning, I noticed that spot had been browsed heavily, more so than grass around it. Soc's right about this salt thing. Bambi craves it."

"Well Ah don't mind if they feast on yower pee, so long as they leave mah bloomahs alone."

"Shhh!" Mother Superior pointed into the dense greenery. Robert scanned the thicket for signs of movement. A black mass heaved at the base of a large white oak, twenty-five yards away.

"Bear," he whispered.

The beast grunted loudly. A dozen eyes riveted on the large head, tossing from side to side. Southern Bell drew in the leash on War Eagle. "Easy, boy." He growled, but did not bark.

"Look!" Czechmate exclaimed. "Two cubbies!"

The jittery cubs sought the refuge of their mother's body. Eyeing the strangers warily, the sow marshaled her offspring. Concerned at the number and the proximity of the intruders, she gave them a signal. The cubs shinnied up the trunk to a limb some thirty feet off the ground. From the newfound sanctuary, they looked down with curiosity at their spellbound audience.

Robert was agape. The cubs needed only a few seconds to scurry up the tree. He thought of the young swain, testing his strength on the carnival midway to win a prize for his girl. He swings the hammer and propels the clapper up the pole to ring the bell. The bears had ascended as if rocketed by a similar force. Their strength, speed, and agility were sobering.

"Remember the guy who said if you were ever chased by a bear you should climb a tree?" Robert asked.

"He was full of it," Mother Superior responded.

"I vant a picture." Czechmate retrieved her camera. She tried for a clear shot of the cubs through the intervening foliage. Spying a possible opening, she took several steps into the woods for a more unobstructed view. She held the camera up to frame the shot. The sow raised her head and growled.

"Matey, get back here! You're pissing her off."

Czechmate retreated to the trail. The growling subsided.

"Sweetheart," Mother Superior scolded, "the one thing you must not do is make the mother think you'll harm her cubs. Admire them from a safe distance."

Chastened, Czechmate replied, "I joost vanted some pictures."

"This is one of those times you let your eye be the camera and your memory be the photograph," Robert explained. "You wanted to see a bear. Now you have. Plus two of the cutest cubs in the forest. Enjoy them. There'll be other chances for pictures."

She sighed. "Are you sure? I vant photos of cubbies for my friends in München."

"Let's hope so," Mother Superior said. "But you have to be satisfied with what nature gives you."

"Mandy!"

"Hi, Dad! It's been a while. I was getting worried. Are you okay?"

"I'm fine. Hiking gets better the longer I go. I'm almost through the Shenandoah. But what about you?"

"The doctor says I'm fine. And the baby, too. My weight's okay, though I'm really beginning to show."

"Good. It sounded like something was wrong."

"Something is, Dad. Cissus died two days ago."

Robert felt pangs of sadness, tempered with resignation. Narcissus had been Angie's cat for fifteen years. He had never been the same since she died. Somehow his death seemed foreordained.

"Do you know what from?"

"Just old age, I think. He hadn't been very frisky. Just laid around in the sunlight coming through the window. Wherever it was warm."

"Did you have to take him to the vet?"

"No, thank God. We talked about it, but he didn't seem to be in pain, so we held off. Then Sunday morning Steven found him in the kitchen, curled up on that little rug under the breakfast table."

Before the hike, Robert agonized over what to do with Cissus. Mandy offered to take him, solving the dilemma. The cat, a small black Persian, had never been out of their Atlanta home. Angie had adopted him, the runt of a litter of five. The mother belonged to one of her clients. She and the kids debated for days over what to name the kitten. Angie had a full-length mirror on the inside of her closet door. Whenever it was open, the kitty rushed to it and jumped up on its hind legs in front of the mirror. A student of mythology, Mandy came up with "Narcissus," a name instantly adopted. As he aged, Cissus would no longer paw the glass with youthful enthusiasm but spent extended periods admiring his long, lustrous coat in the reflection. Angie remarked that if the cat were Will Rogers, he would have said, "I never met a mirror I didn't like."

When Robert drove him to Mandy's house in Jacksonville, Cissus went to every car window to check himself out. Dissatisfied that his image was reflected so poorly in the window glass, he lay down on the back seat and slept for the rest of the trip.

Dwelling on memories, Robert failed to hold up his side of the conversation. "Dad? You okay?"

"Yeah. Just thinking about the mirror on the closet door. Hey, I'm sorry I put you through this. I was worried this might happen. I just didn't know where else to leave him."

"Don't worry. We enjoyed having him, although he seemed out of his element down here."

"It wasn't where he was, hon. He missed your mom."

In her last months, Angie had sat in her favorite chair in the den, and Cissus would bound into her lap, seeking her warmth. She had a way of scratching him under his chin that left him mesmerized. Like any cat, he assumed his presence alone was sufficient recompense for her hours of unbroken attention. Later, when she was confined to the bed, he moved with her, curling up on the down comforter in the precise spot where she could reach his chin without straining. And at the end, when she could no longer lift her hand to pet him, he moved to her side, to feel her ebbing warmth through the comforter.

"Maybe he died of a broken heart."

"He was by himself a lot here, you know, with us working. I tried to scratch him and all. I guess I was a poor substitute."

"What did you do? Have him cremated?"

"No, we buried him. Steven dug a hole in our backyard. I found a shoe box he fit into. I put two things in the box with him." There was a catch in her throat. "One was a small makeup mirror I carried in my purse. The other was a picture of Mom."

Robert wiped tears out of his eyes. "Beautiful. You did exactly the right thing. She's smiling on you."

He pictured his young son on the stairway landing with his fishing rod. He had cast a line to which he had tethered a crumpled ball of aluminum foil. He bobbed it in spurts and starts, just beyond the extended paws of the leaping Narcissus. "Have you told Rob?"

"I tried to call him. No answer. I think he's out on maneuvers again. I sent him an e-mail."

"I couldn't raise him the last two times I called either. Say, could you do me a favor?"

"Sure."

"Send him an e-mail for me. Tell him I'm doing all right and hope he is too. And ask about Jennifer. He never volunteers any information."

"I know. He's so secretive about her."

"Oh, and tell him I love him."

"Got it."

The others were queued by the phone. "I need to be going. My friends are waiting to make calls. Give my love to Steven. Tell him my teeth are thriving on raisins, M&M's, and candy bars."

"He's penciled you in for a September appointment."

"Take care of yourself. And the baby. I love you."

"Love you, too. Bye."

—m—

Robert pondered why grief was so unpredictable. The casual sight of a hummingbird in the forest had triggered the most painful moment of his entire life. Yet the death of the family cat, for fifteen years a source of joy and companionship, had induced only a few tears. Cissus had been *her* cat; his passing severed another living link to Angie. It seemed he should be taking this loss harder.

Perhaps he didn't want to take on any more sorrow. He had turned off the spigot because the glass was full. Or perhaps he was getting used to the idea of no more Angie, used to the tanager on the high branch. The death of Narcissus was nothing more than another bridge burned behind him. He was happy for the cat. He had lived a long and comfortable life, basking in the warmth and love that all of them, but particularly Angie, had shown. Cissus had missed her. Now he would miss her no more.

I still miss you, babe.

He thought again about the "Czechmate anniversary." It was not the way to honor their thirty-five years. Yet he had to accept the reality. Angie was gone and never coming back. He was still here.

He didn't like that finality. Their life together wasn't over. It was only suspended. Someday it would resume. It was up to him to preserve that eventuality.

His new life had a different set of possibilities. Like the old, it was also legitimate. Each life could exist without negating the other.

For everything there is a season, a time to seek and a time to lose, a time to keep and a time to throw away.

He remembered the pep talk from Socrates in Gatlinburg. His mind kept muddling up the clarity. He needed to live in the past and live in the present also. The trick was how to get it right, how to keep it in balance. He had three more months and twelve hundred miles to perfect the mix.

"Snaky, what gives? You haven't said anything for miles."

"Mandy told me our cat died last week."

"That's too bad. How old was it?"

"Fifteen. He had a full life. He had his time."

"Will you get another when you finish the hike?"

"I don't know. I need to do other things first."

"Like what?"

"Like see my kids. Have Christmas with my grandchild. Watch Tech beat Duke for the ACC championship."

"Never happen."

"Will too. A wise sage once said 'man cannot live without hope.'"

"Snaky, don't confuse hope with delusion."

Chapter 15

Your lips move, but I can't hear what you're saying.
Pink Floyd

"Listen up! We meet Nancy tomorrow at nine, where the trail goes under the interstate." Mother Superior tugged at the bill of her Yankee cap, riding low on her wet hair. "Three miles from here. Soc, we need to leave by 7:45."

Writing in the register, Socrates ignored her exhortation.

"Don't yew worry, Mother. Ah'll get him up. Ah want mah new panties."

The group sprawled on benches in front of the Denton shelter. Robert, Mother Superior, and Czechmate lounged in the late afternoon sun. Across the wooden deck, Socrates and Southern Bell curled under the advancing shade. War Eagle, fresh from swimming in the nearby creek, lay damp and content at their feet.

The shelter featured a primitive, gravity-fed shower, piped from the creek. Like War Eagle, the five had washed away several days of dirt and sweat. Clean and refreshed, they celebrated.

"The Shenandoah is behind us, and endless Virginia is about to end," Mother Superior declared. "Hard to believe, but one-fourth of the AT has been in this damn commonwealth."

"But it was too pretty to get the blues," Robert added. "How could anybody be depressed with all that mountain laurel?"

"Und der bearss. I saw my bearss."

"Ah tell yew whut lights me up. When we get to Harpahs, we've hiked a thousand miles! Ah'm gonna celebrate with a big ole strawberry shake at the Dairy Queen."

Socrates put down the pen and the register. "Snaky, we do four states in less than a week, right? Out of Virginia. Through West Virginia and Maryland. Then into Pennsylvania."

"Bang, bang, bang, bang."

"We're hauling ass. Where's that halfway point again?"

"Pine Grove Furnace State Park. In Pennsylvania."

"Once we get there we're over the hump. All downhill from then on."

Mother Superior took issue. "Don't get overconfident."

"Look, ninety-nine percent of hiking is attitude. With the right frame of mind, you're over a mountain before you know it. And if you're with friends, you can bag several mountains every day."

"Speaking of friends, are you guys okay with a day off in Harpers? While Czechmate and I go to Baltimore?"

"No problem, Mother. Enjoy your girls' night out. We haven't had a zero in ages. Besides, Bell's a great tourist." Socrates spun the dampened end of one of her pigtails between his fingers. "Wanna go sightseeing?"

She stroked his chin whiskers. "Can we see John Brown's body?"

"Don't know, dear. My guidebook doesn't cover morbid attractions. Snaky, what about it?"

"Don't think he's buried there. But instead of cruising the cemetery, let's go by ATC Headquarters. Get our picture taken for the official rogues' gallery of thru-hikers."

"Good idea. We five should be photographed together."

"You mean six, don'tcha?" Southern Bell patted the chocolate coat of the Lab, which glistened from the recent swim.

"Of course. Didn't mean to slight you, War Eagle." He acknowledged Mother Superior's solicitousness with a large brown-eyed stare.

"We aren't the Fab Five," Socrates asserted. "We're the Six Pack. It'll be a helluva picture."

"Do they hayav movies in Harpahs?"

"Don't know, Bell, but we'll soon find out."

"It's been so long. Ah can't remembah the last movie Ah saw."

"*Gone with the Wind*?"

"Shush!" Southern Bell poked Socrates in the ribs.

"*Spiderman*?"

"Nooo." She hit him again. "I don't lak dumb action movies. Ah lak love stories."

"*Silence of the Lambs?*"

Southern Bell pummelled him with both fists. "Yew are sooo bayad!"

War Eagle cocked his ears. There were footfalls on the trail from the south. A figure moved through the trees toward them. Mother Superior recognized the approaching hiker and mumbled under her breath.

"Oh, shit."

"Hi, guys."

Robert hid his chagrin. "Hello, Preacher. Been a while."

"Several weeks. Got to hand it to you. You been tearing up this trail. Whenever I thought I'd catch up, the register would say you were still a day ahead." He took off his pack and flopped near War Eagle. "Hiya, pup." He opened the lid and drained the water in his liter bottle. "You like swimming, huh?"

War Eagle thumped his tail twice on the wooden deck.

"Thayat's a yes."

Robert replied, "Yeah, we've been moving out. Virginia's been nice, but it's time to hike somewhere else. Maryland. Pennsylvania. Some of us need to finish in August, like you."

"Actually, I have more time. My plans changed."

"How so?"

"Where was it we talked last?"

"Right before Bland. You were going to a college in West Virginia."

"Yeah, Bluefield. Good meeting. Fifteen professions of faith. But that's not what changed things. When I got to Roanoke, I went to the CBA national symposium."

"You a basketball player?" Socrates asked.

"Nice try," Preacher replied. "CBA stands for Christians for a Better America."

"What's that?"

"I thought I told you."

"You told me," Robert interjected. "I didn't mention it to anyone else."

"It's a political organization. We support candidates and legislation that promote the preservation of family values."

"What's a family value?" Socrates asked.

"Whaddaya mean?"

"Give us an example."

"Okay. The right to life for an unborn child."

Mother Superior spoke with authority. "You are certainly entitled to your opinion, Preacher. But I want a nice quiet evening where we all rest up from a hard day. So let's not get into that subject."

"Okay." Socrates intentionally stretched out the two syllables. "Preach, pick a different family value."

"The right of every child to pray at school."

Socrates replied, "No problem. Assuming the school doesn't sponsor the prayers. And the child prays voluntarily, without coercion. And whenever and wherever he chooses."

"And to Whomever she wants. God, Jehovah, Allah, the Virgin Mary, the Wiccan Goddess. Whomever." Mother Superior added, "This is America. There have to be multiple choices. If that's what you're selling, then I'll buy."

"Actually I was thinking about praying to Jesus."

"That's understandable, Preacher. No one here doubts you're a committed Christian." Robert added, "But tell me, is religious tolerance a family value?"

"I believe the only true message is the gospel of Christ. I do my best to make sure everyone hears it."

"You didn't answer my question. Or maybe you did. But enough about family values. What happened in Roanoke?"

"We talked about the elections this fall. The big issue was where to concentrate our resources. You know, the biggest bang for the buck. Our keynote speaker pointed us in the right direction."

"Who was that?" Mother Superior asked.

"Senator Fairchild."

She raised her eyebrows. "Senator Rosemary Fairchild? From Oklahoma?"

"She's our honorary president. She's quite a motivator."

"Yeah, I guess. If you're a shock troop for Genghis Khan."

Preacher parroted her earlier remark. "You are also entitled to your opinion. But if you want that pleasant evening, then don't make disparaging comments about the senator."

"Her positions are diametrically opposed to everything I believe."

"Personally, I think she's the moral compass of America. She's also vice presidential timber, perhaps for 2004."

"I'm not surprised you feel that way. What did she say at this meeting?"

"She helped us select the top congressional races. Where we can pick up seats for candidates who support our platform. One's in Colorado. I was all set to go back home and work there. Then she told us about an election in Vermont. It's just as important as the federal races. Maybe more so."

"Why Vermont?" Socrates asked.

"A court case in the late nineties. Two lesbians wanted to get married. Vermont wouldn't issue them a license, so the women went to court. The state Supreme Court ruled Vermont had discriminated. Directed the legislature to provide for same-sex marriage, or some equivalent. Under the gun, the legislature passed a civil union law. Made a travesty of the institution of marriage. Since then, three thousand gay and lesbian couples have applied for licenses and gone through with these ceremonies. Most don't even live in Vermont."

Socrates interrupted. "So? I don't see how this law hurts you or anybody else. To the contrary. Religious conservatives always complain that homosexuals lead a promiscuous lifestyle. Now two people enter into a lifetime monogamous commitment, and you bitch about that also."

"The Bible holds that marriage is a holy union between a man and a woman. It does not sanctify a union between a man and a man or a woman and a woman. What Vermont has done defies these teachings."

Mother Superior sighed. "There goes our pleasant little evening. Preacher, you seem to have a problem with the separation of church and state. What Vermont has done is to create a civil ceremony. No involvement by any church. Right?"

"Thank Him for that."

"Other states don't have to recognize these unions."

"As I understand it, yes."

"And the Vermont decision doesn't extend to rights guaranteed to married couples under federal law."

"Yes, because Congress passed the Defense of Marriage Act."

"Let's say a couple from Ohio goes to Vermont for a week, gets a license from a town clerk, and has a justice of the peace perform a ceremony. Then they go home. From a legal standpoint, nothing's changed. That is, unless Ohio recognizes the Vermont union."

"I guess so."

"But to that couple everything has changed. Their relationship now bears a stamp of legitimacy that to this point has been denied them. They have responsibilities and obligations to each other, just like other couples. What's so wrong with that? The state performed a function, and did not involve your church and its rules. It's typical First Amendment."

"My church and its rules are what's stopping this cancer from spreading across America."

"A cancer it once condoned. Did you know that in the Middle Ages, there was a formal ceremony for same-sex unions, as a part of the liturgy of the church?"

"No way."

"It's true. In both the Catholic and Greek Orthodox traditions."

"Well, we don't have that now. Not in my church. Or most any church in the United States. The American family, husband, wife, and their children, that's the cornerstone of our society. Kids with both a father and a mother do better in life. When gays and lesbians adopt or have children, these kids are put at risk."

"Preacher, that's bullshit. I bet I see more families in my line of work than you do. Heterosexual couples, same-sex couples, single mothers, and single fathers. You know what makes a family work?"

"A lot of things. Love, faith, respect. Fear of God."

"The parents, regardless of sex, regardless of number, or regardless of orientation or religion, take the job seriously. That's what. And they show love and affection for the child. I've seen lousy parents who happen to be a traditionally married couple. I've seen great parents who happen to be same sex. And vice versa. It's the same with single parents. One person who takes responsibility is far better than two who don't. You cannot say a child's at risk simply by the type of family it belongs to."

"The way to bring up a child is in a family with a father and a mother. I realize it doesn't work out that way all the time. People die. People get divorced. Although a lot of them take the easy way out, rather than trying to make their marriage work. But it's anathema to see laws put on the books encouraging people to experiment with sinful liaisons, and forcing this lifestyle on innocent children."

"Experiment? Force? You still don't get it. Sexual orientation is not a choice. Same-sex orientation occurs in about 5 percent of the population. People do not choose to be in this minority. No one who sees firsthand how the other 95 percent act toward gays and lesbians would willingly opt for this. And even if they wanted to, they couldn't force anyone, including a child, to change his or her orientation. What they can do is choose to accept who they are. The Creator endowed them with homosexuality. They go ahead and live out the gift He gave them. Just like the 95 percent who live as straights."

"You're the one who doesn't get it. To say homosexuality is a gift of God is blasphemy."

The deck was silent for several seconds. Mother Superior sighed again. "I have as much chance of changing your mind as you do mine. Let's talk about something else. What's the objective for this Vermont campaign?"

"After the 2000 election, there were enough votes to repeal the legislation in the Vermont House, but not in the Senate. Our goal is to hold our own or increase the margin in the House, and get the necessary turnover in the Senate."

"How many votes do you need?"

"About five."

"What about the governor? He signed the first bill. Won't he veto an attempt to repeal?"

"Governor Dean's not seeking reelection. He's running for president. We hope to elect a friendlier candidate."

"Another thing I don't understand. The Supreme Court in Vermont mandated this law. How can the legislature repeal it?"

"That's not the plan. With majorities in both houses, and a consenting governor, we can pass a constitutional amendment that explicitly defines marriage as a union between a man and a woman. That amendment would take precedence over the court decision. That happened in Hawaii and Alaska a few years ago. Overturned some bad rulings from activist judges."

"What are your chances? Realistically?"

"Slim. But as you New Yorkers say, 'You gotta believe.'"

"That's the other New York team, Preacher. Yankee fans don't have to believe. They already know. So when are you going to Vermont?"

"They want us around Labor Day. It's a small state. We should be able to canvass the towns and cities, and get our message into all the media outlets in two months. I'll have time between finishing the trail and starting the campaign. I'm going home." He smiled at Robert. "And collect on my bet."

"You said there was no money involved."

"There isn't. But I do want to extract my pound of flesh."

"Preach, we don't get to the halfway point for another week, and you're already crowing about finishing. You never know. You can fall and crack your head tomorrow. It's all right to make plans, but don't talk like it's a done deal."

"Cautious. Always cautious. Can't you accept something straight up, without caveats and conditions?"

"Prudence is a good thing. It helps you see angles you might otherwise overlook. We had this discussion on Chestnut Knob, remember? About the Bible."

"Yeah. You weren't totally honest with me."

Robert was taken aback. "How so?"

"You conveniently overlooked the first chapter of Romans."

"I don't follow you."

"You went on about how there's nothing in the Bible that condemns homosexuality. Except for outdated references to peculiar Jewish laws. You seemed to have ignored the apostle Paul."

"I wasn't sweeping him under the rug."

"Really? I'll get my Bible. I want to read it to you."

"You mean Ah'm gonna git more Bible school?"

Socrates muttered, "'Fraid so."

Preacher retrieved the Bible from his pack and searched for the passage. "Here. First chapter of Romans, verses twenty-six and twenty-seven." He emphasized several words as he read. "For this reason God gave them up to *degrading* passions. Their women exchanged natural intercourse for *unnatural,* and in the same way also the men, giving up natural intercourse with women, were consumed with passion for one another. Men committed *shameless* acts with men and received in their own persons the due penalty for their error."

He put the Bible down. "Degradation. Shame. Both gays and lesbians, going against nature. And as a result, the retribution of the Lord. They got what was coming to them. It's very clear what Paul is saying."

"I agree, Preach. That's a clear statement. And a very strong one."

Preacher was skeptical. "If you really mean that, then it's a first."

"I mean it. Paul condemns those people."

"So you finally agree with me?"

"Just one thing. The cart's before the horse. Go back and reread the first words of verse twenty-six."

Preacher picked up the Bible and relocated the passage. "For this reason God gave them up ..."

"What reason? Aren't you the least bit curious why God would give them up? After all, He's supposed to be a loving God. Go back a few verses and read why."

Preacher studied the text. "Verse twenty-two: Claiming to be wise, they became fools; and they exchanged the glory of the immortal God for images resembling a mortal human being or birds or four-footed animals or reptiles. Therefore God gave them up in the lusts of their hearts to impurity, to the degrading of their bodies among themselves, because they exchanged the truth about God for a lie and worshiped and served the creature rather than the Creator, who is blessed forever! Amen."

"What's the verdict?" Robert asked. "Why did God give them up?"

"Sounds lak ahdolatry to me."

"I agree, Bell. What do you think, Preacher?"

"They turned away from God."

"And what is the first commandment?"

"Thou shall have no other Gods before me."

"And the second?"

"No graven images."

"They were guilty as hell on both counts. That's why he gave them up. They were hopelessly unrighteous. Any subsequent behavior is derived from this primary sin of turning away."

"But it's still sin."

"Paul condemns this behavior. But what specific behavior is he talking about?"

"C'mon, Snakes, he's talking about homosexuals. You can't see that?"

"Remember, he's writing two thousand years ago. There were some particularly disgusting religious practices of that time."

Socrates spoke up. "You mean the temple prostitutes?"

Southern Bell gasped. "Where did yew come up with thayat?"

"The learned Greek," Robert replied. "Talk to us."

"It was a common practice in Egypt, and later in Greece and Rome, to have same-sex prostitutes reside in the pagan temples. They threw orgies for the faithful. The revelry was tied to the worship of their deities. I saw this stuff in one of these made-for-TV movies, back in Waynesboro. A real heavy-breather."

"Yew said it was trash and Ah shouldn't waste mah time watchin' it." Southern Bell pouted.

"And I was right." He nodded toward Robert. "Who knew there'd be a tiny kernel of knowledge in all the sleaze?"

"If it's trash to you," Robert added, "think of how it seemed to Paul. He's a Christian and a Jew. No wonder he lambasted them for fornicating in the name of their God. A particularly reviling way of taking the name of the Lord in vain. How many commandments have they broken so far, Preacher?"

"Three."

"Carousing with prostitutes in the temple on the day of worship does not exactly remember the Sabbath and keep it holy."

"Okay, four."

"We could keep going, but it's safe to say Paul didn't think much of prostitution in the temples."

"But that's not the only type of homosexuality that occurred," Preacher countered. "You're being selective to prove your point."

"Maybe Soc can regale us with more of his knowledge. What else might Paul be talking about?"

"Nothing comes to mind."

"Think about your namesake."

"My great-great-great uncle Socrates?"

"Yeah. Socrates, the mentor."

"Oh, yeah. Pederasty."

"Pederasty? What's that?" Preacher demanded.

"The Greeks felt hanging out with other men was infinitely superior to the company of women. If a male youth listened to his educated elders and participated in their discourse, he would increase in wisdom and knowledge and be prepared to enter manhood." Socrates paused. "What usually happened was an older man took a youth under his wing to train him. In its pure form this was supposed to be a Platonic arrangement."

"Let me guess," Mother Superior retorted. "Something more than wisdom and knowledge got transferred."

"The relationship was not one of coequals. The opportunity for the teacher to take advantage of the pupil was a constant temptation."

"Like with priests and altar boys."

"Another gold star for you, Mother. When the older man got around to having sex with the boy, he did it in the classic way. Intercrural intercourse."

"Inter-what?" Preacher could not hide his repugnance.

"A lot of new words tonight." Socrates stood up and spread his legs slightly, and bent at the knees. He undulated for a few moments to illustrate. "Between the thighs."

"Ugh. Ah imagine thayut's messy."

"Yeah, and I don't think it's particularly satisfying either."

"Certainly not for the boy." Mother Superior shook her head in disgust. "He stands in this demeaning crouch and is rewarded with semen running down his legs."

"I doubt the older man enjoyed it either. Most relationships soon deviated from intercrural to anal sex."

Mother Superior retorted. "The young man's the vessel for the elder. The seeds of wisdom and knowledge are planted right up his ass."

"Do yew evah watch 'Sex and the City'?"

"Bell, what the hell does that have to do with what we're talking about?"

"Yew know Charlotte? The brunette. She's mah favorite. Anyway, one of her boyfriends wanted to have anal sex. She refused. She didn't want to be remembahed as the 'up-the-butt girl.'"

"You guys are hitting on all the objections to pederasty." Robert continued. "One-sided. Nonconsensual. An abuse of authority. The emotional damage to the youth exceeded any educational benefits that were supposed to accrue."

"Wait a minute!" Preacher was obviously irritated. "How can you say that Paul is condemning only this pederasty thing? Or that he writes just about temple prostitutes? You don't know that."

"There's a lot I don't know. And a lot you don't know either. Some scholars think Paul picked on the Greeks deliberately, to lull the Jews into a false sense of security. You know, 'We're better than those people.' Then he zaps the overconfident Jews for their own unrighteousness, in the next chapter of Romans."

"Do you have proof of that?"

"No. But one thing I'm certain of. Paul's primary concern is our broken relationship to God. We are unrighteous. And we are literally consumed by the passions that result. To Paul and his audience, the prostitutes and the pederasts were familiar examples of those who turned away from God. But just because some who turn against God practiced homosexual behavior, Paul does not mean that all homosexuals are unrighteous. If they are righteous, Paul's not writing about them here. God forgives those who fear him."

"That's a neat conclusion," Preacher responded. "But I don't buy your easy forgiveness."

"Remember the two criminals crucified with Jesus? One asked to be remembered, and Jesus told him that he would be with Him in paradise. Would Jesus accept a criminal but refuse a gay or lesbian?"

"Con ve talk about somethink else now?" Czechmate spoke wearily. "Efery time ve are together ve talk dis."

"I'm sorry," Preacher responded. "But I feel very strongly about this. And I can't believe the way he's splitting hairs."

Robert chastised himself for his insensitivity. "Czechmate, I'm sorry, too. But you make a very good point."

"Vat?"

"Paul talked about a lot of other sins."

"What other sins?" Preacher asked suspiciously.

"Hand me the book." Preacher passed the open Bible to Robert. "You stopped reading at twenty-seven. I'll read the next few verses."

"Why?" Mother Superior questioned. "I'm getting tired of this too."

"It won't take long. Verse twenty-eight: And since they did not see fit to acknowledge God, God gave them up to a debased mind and to things that should not be done. They were filled with every kind of wickedness, evil, covetousness, malice. Full of envy, murder, strife, deceit, malignity, they are gossips, slanderers, God-haters, insolent, haughty, boastful, inventors of evil, rebellious toward parents, foolish, faithless, heartless, ruthless. They know God's decree, that those who practice such things deserve to die—yet they not only do them but even applaud others who practice them."

"Snaky, that's Letterman's top ten ways to piss off God."

"No. That would be the Ten Commandments. This tally sheet is called a 'vice' list. But the point is, when Paul talked about what humans did after turning their backs on God, he listed a cornucopia of transgressions, not just homosexual conduct. As Czechmate says, let's pay them equal attention."

"Sin reminds me of infinity."

"How so, Soc?"

"It's a whole. You can't break it into pieces, or say that one piece is bigger than the others."

"Dat's nice to know, but not vat I meant about changing the subject," Czechmate said. "Iss time to cook dinner. I am hungry."

Socrates snatched the Bible from Robert. He picked up the shelter register and pen from the deck and tore out a blank page from the back of the spiral notebook. He began to scribble furiously.

Southern Bell stood up and stretched her long legs. "Lesson's ovah for me, too. C'mon, War Eagle. Let's git you some suppah." She made her way to her pack in the shelter.

"Very interesting," Mother Superior said. "The media Christians never mention that other stuff. But dinner's on my radar screen also." She rose to join the other two. The three women fired up their stoves and began to prepare dinner. Socrates remained on the bench, writing on the paper.

Robert reluctantly accepted that the others could not sustain a passion for theological discourse. He fished the stove from his pack and began to assemble it.

Preacher hovered nearby, waiting for an appropriate moment. While Robert primed the stove, he spoke up.

"Dancing Snakes?"

"Yeah?"

"Would it be okay if I hiked with you guys again?"

Robert struggled to understand Preacher's motivation. Why would he want to be in their company? They were opposed to his beliefs. They took issue with everything he said. Perhaps he was lonely. He had hiked by himself for a long time. They may not have befriended him, but at least they engaged him. Robert looked around. His friends were absorbed in busywork. It was up to him to answer.

"Preacher, everyone out here is free to do what he or she wants. You know, hike your own hike."

"Right. It's what I'm trying to do."

"The five of us want to hike our own hikes also. And what we want more than anything is to enjoy each and every day."

"So do I."

"This is what worries me. Every time we hook up with you we get into big arguments. They cut into the enjoyment."

"I'm not trying to start any fights."

"Not saying you are. But the reality is you're the match and we're the gasoline."

"What do you suggest?"

"Well, you and Mother Superior agreed to a truce. No talk about right to life or Senator Fairchild."

"You want to expand the truce?"

"Yeah. Nothing more about homosexuality. We've beat it to death. And in general, respect everybody's right to a hassle-free hike. Can you do that?"

"I can."

"Okay. Shake on it." He extended his hand for another firm clasp.

Socrates stood up from the bench, waving his paper. "Snaky, you're on my wave length. Okay. Listen up. I'm only going to read the rules once."

"What rules?"

"The rules of conversation. It's hard for all you opinionated bastards not to say what's on your mind. So I've drafted a code of conduct."

"Mistah numbah-one-opinionated bastard of all time, are yew including yourself in this code?"

"Yes, Bell. At the urging of Czechmate and Snaky, and with inspiration from Saint Paul, I've compiled the approved conversation guide for the rest of the AT. Pay attention. We've talked about homosexuality since we got to Virginia. We won't talk about it any more. For the rest of Virginia, we can talk about wickedness and evil. When we get to West Virginia, we can talk about covetousness. In Maryland, malice."

Southern Bell broke in, "Oh goody. One of mah favorite movies. Nicole Kidman and Alec Baldwin."

Socrates shook off her diversion. "For Pennsylvania, it's envy and murder, and for New Jersey, strife and deceit. In New York, we talk about malignity."

Mother Superior smiled broadly. "In New York, you have to let me talk about the Yankees."

"Special exemption. Mother gets fifteen minutes a day for the Bronx Bombers. Now where was I? Okay, in Connecticut, we'll speak only of gossips and slanderers, and in Massachusetts, haters of God. The Pilgrims will love it. We may even have another witch trial. In Vermont, we talk of the insolent and haughty, and nothing about constitutional amendments. In New Hampshire, we'll talk about the boastful. And being disobedient to parents."

Robert chided, "You'll need extra time on boastful, Soc."

"The final four are for Maine. Foolish, faithless, heartless, ruthless."

Mother Superior warmed to the challenge. "Katahdin is such a butt kicker. Why don't we save 'ruthless' for the final climb?"

"Done!" Socrates concluded, "Are there any questions?"

"Yes," Robert replied. "I'm surprised. You give Mother Superior a Yankee dispensation, but you don't work Duke in there anywhere."

"Wrong. I covet Duke. I gossip about Duke. I boast about Duke. I can be downright insolent and haughty about Duke. And ruthless. Oh baby, wait till we get to Maine!"

"Paul should have mentioned insufferable."

Socrates turned to Preacher. "Can you live with this?"

Preacher rose to the occasion. "In Virginia, I can talk about the wickedness and evil of Indiana, eliminating Duke in March Madness."

"You son of a bitch."

Robert laughed. "Soc, if you live by the sword …"

"This is the fust time since God knows when that Socks has held a Bible. Learn from this, Snaky. Don't yew evah give it to him again."

Chapter 16

For what you want, above all things, on a raft, is for everybody to be satisfied, and feel right and kind toward the others.
Huckleberry Finn

Preacher led them into the state park. He turned to face the line of hikers behind him. "Do we eat dinner first?"

"Ah don't know about yew all, but Ah don't want want mac and cheese in the way when Ah throw down ice cream."

Robert agreed. "Life is short. Eat dessert first."

The group congregated at a picnic table in front of the small store. They assembled wallets, spoons, and cameras, and then they placed their packs and poles out of harm's way.

Socrates drummed on the table impatiently. "What flavor?"

"Easy. Ah can eat strawberry ice cream till the cows come home."

"I thought you raised turkeys in Alabama."

"Just an expreshun. But yew know thayat, Smarty Pants." Southern Bell tethered War Eagle to one of the table legs. "Yew like strawberry too, don'tcha?" She caressed his snout. "Yew can lick the carton when Ah finish." She turned to Socrates. "So whut are yew havvin? Baklava ripple?"

"Don't make fun of my heritage, doll. As we Greeks always say, 'I can eat chocolate until the minotaur comes home.' And you, Snaky?"

"I love chocolate. But when I was a kid, I ate a wad of raisins and got real sick. Couldn't stand them for thirty years. If that happened with chocolate, I'd never forgive myself. So it's vanilla."

"What else from a risk-averse accountant? Grow a pair! Try the black cherry."

"I'd barf all over the place. We all know I'm good at that."

Socrates continued his interrogation. "Girls, you're quiet over there. Speak up. What's your choice?"

"Chocolate chip," Mother Superior replied. "One flavor by itself will be cloying. We might gag after the first quart."

"Whatever works. Preacher?"

"Butter pecan."

"That's not too rich?"

"No way. The only question is whether I go back for seconds."

"You're shitting me."

"A choice between ramen noodles and ice cream? It's a no-brainer."

The six filed into the store and surrounded the freezer chest. The proprietor, who wore a white apron with the name "Al" sewn over the small chest pocket, greeted them. "Welcome to Pine Grove, the halfway point on the AT. You guys want ice cream?"

"Al, how'd you guess?"

He laughed. "What'll it be?"

"Six half gallons. One vanilla, one chocolate, two chocolate chip, one strawberry, and one butter pecan." Socrates added, "Do you offer volume discounts?"

"Guys, I'd love to accommodate you, but I have to make a living. Besides, it's Hershey's. Premium stuff. Each carton is $4.99."

Socrates continued to bargain. "The legend says if you eat it all at one sitting, the ice cream's free."

"That was in the old days. Before so many of you crazies decided to thru-hike. I'm not running a government giveaway here. But we do have complimentary wooden spoons. They're inscribed. Here's one for each of you."

Socrates read the lettering on the small spoon. "Member of the half-gallon club. That's precious. Bell, you take it."

Al continued, "Got T-shirts for sale too, over on that rack. Only $13.95."

Preacher held up a shirt and read the inscription. "Official Member of Half-Gallon Ice Cream Club, Pine Grove Furnace State Park, Gardners, Pennsylvania." He flipped the shirt around. "What's this on the back?"

"That's a keystone. Pennsylvania's the Keystone State."

"Cool. I'll take this blue one. Extra large, I hope. Yeah." He looked at Robert. "My buddies'll die when they hear this story."

"What's the average time to eat a half gallon?" Socrates asked.

"It varies," Al responded. "Most take about forty-five minutes. Much longer and it melts. Would you like me to take pictures?"

"Yeah, man. That'd be great."

Outside, they sat on the benches around the table, and opened the cartons. Socrates read the label. "Calories per serving—160. Servings per container—sixteen. Do the math, Snaky."

"Okay, 1,600 plus 960. That's 2,560 calories. You don't want to know about the sat fat."

"I guess I won't need a candy bar after dinner," Socrates added.

"Ah hope this means yew'll be a little sweeter," Southern Bell replied.

"Sweets for the sweet." He looked at his watch. "Five o'clock. Dig in."

Al took two or three shots from each camera and returned to the store. Hot and hungry after eighteen miles of trail, Robert attacked the vanilla with gusto. He quickly polished off the first pint. The others also made what seemed to be effortless progress. Preacher had already consumed a quart. When his carton was half-empty, Robert checked his watch. "It's 5:20. This is a piece of cake."

Socrates shot back, "No, idiot. It's ice cream."

Preacher slammed his empty carton on the table. "One and done! Twenty-one minutes." He danced around the table, waving the container in the air. Mother Superior and Czechmate used the moment as an excuse to stop eating and take pictures. Preacher stopped dancing and disappeared inside the store.

The nurses set the cameras aside. "Give him credit. He didn't even flinch."

"Dat boy conn eat!"

The easy part was over. Robert wasn't stuffed, but the cloying sensation that Mother Superior anticipated had materialized. He had never imagined that the taste of ice cream could turn him off. He remembered drinking a gallon of citrate of magnesium two years ago, in preparation for a colonoscopy. The last four glasses made him gag. The ice cream was still palatable but wearing out its welcome. He regretted not selecting Neapolitan for a greater variety of flavor.

The others were laboring also. The rate of consumption had slowed dramatically. Czechmate had hit the wall. "I vill nefer eat ice cream again."

Robert encouraged her. "This time tomorrow you'll be screaming for more."

"I may scream, but not vor ice cream."

"I scream, you scream," Socrates rolled a large spoonful of chocolate on his tongue. "Yum!" He swallowed unconvincingly. "We all scream for ice cream."

Preacher returned from the store with another carton.

Socrates gaped incredulously. "Preach, what the hell you got there?"

"Moose Tracks," he replied, opening the lid. "I won a pie-eating contest at our county fair in Colorado. This is even more fun." He took a large bite of the dark brown delicacy.

Robert could not let his voracity pass. "Preacher, your gluttony can affect me in one of two ways. I can be intimidated and wimp out. Or I can be inspired and eat my way to fame." He dug into the remaining block and swallowed a large spoonful. "Watch me eat."

The ice cream had softened. The change in texture caused a slight variation in flavor. He welcomed the difference and took several more spoonfuls. He was spurred even more when a large swath with the spoon uncovered the bottom of the container. In a few minutes, he was done. He raised his arms over his head and wiggled the Lexan spoon victoriously in his right hand. "Forty-four minutes! Ahead of the curve!"

Preacher captured Robert's celebration on camera. The others concentrated on the task at hand. Socrates and Southern Bell were locked in a titanic struggle. At forty-eight minutes, with a pink stream oozing down her chin, she stood up and waved an empty carton. "Toldja! Toldja! Ah can eat strawberry forevah!" She tore open the container and handed it to War Eagle, who licked the syrup sticking to the sides.

Socrates stood up with his empty carton, flecks of chocolate clinging to his beard. "Forty-eight minutes, thirty seconds." He was delighted to have finished, but testy because Southern Bell had nosed him out. "Your momma would be ashamed of you. Eating like a pig in a sty."

"Tell her whutevah yew want. This wasn't exactly an ice cream soshal at the church. Ah finished first. It's not gonna hurt too bad to admit that, is it?"

He searched for a comeback. "What hurts is to see thousands of calories going straight to your slender hips."

"Guilt won't work, hon. And watch yower mouth, if yew want to sleep in mah tent tonight."

"Quit now, Soc," Robert advised. "You're just digging the hole deeper. How 'bout a picture of you together, holding each other and waving the spoons? Smile. Yeah, that's great."

Mother Superior, absorbed in chocolate chip, glanced at Preacher, who had made large inroads in the second half gallon. "I'm about to gag. But there's no way I'll let you lap me." She took another large spoonful and grimaced. "Three more bites."

"Close it out, Mariano," Robert exhorted. "Bottom of the ninth. Two outs. Three-two count. She winds. She pitches. Strike three! Ball game! Yankees win! Yankees win!"

She stood up, holding her stomach. "Fifty-three minutes. I don't feel like Mother Superior. I feel like Lake Superior."

Their attention focused on Preacher. After racing through almost a gallon of ice cream, he had hit the wall also. He rationed his intake with small, measured bites and increased the interval between spoonings. "C'mon, Preach," Socrates shouted. "You must be close to the Guinness record. Two in one hour is fabulous!"

"You can do this," Mother Superior urged.

Inspired, he found a cache in his distended stomach for the last of the Moose Tracks. He stood up and rested his hands on the picnic table for support. He did not dance as he had after the first carton.

"You're something else," Robert said, with admiration. "One gallon in fifty-six minutes, fifteen seconds. Al should give you the T-shirt for that."

Preacher sat back down on the bench with a thud. "I'm not moving. Ever."

"Look! Matey's almost finished!" Socrates hovered as Czechmate meted out another spoonful. The lark had turned into a formidable chore.

"This tradition of yourss, it does not sit vell mit my European sensibilities."

Mother Superior laughed. "What you mean is it doesn't sit well in your tiny little stomach."

Robert pictured her tantalizing concavity, now concealed under the untucked Coolmax. That waist had to survive this ordeal.

Czechmate circled her spoon around the bottom of the container and collected the last bit of chocolate syrup. Her eyes came alive. She licked both sides of the spoon with a fully extended tongue. "Ja! Ja! I did it! A haf gallon!" Mother Superior snapped away.

Socrates pointed to his watch. "Fifty-nine minutes and fifty seconds. All six in less than an hour. The few, the proud ..."

"The stuffed!" Southern Bell broke in.

Preacher groaned from the bench at the picnic table.

Robert shuffled slowly toward the store. "I'll ask Al to take a group shot. Halfway done. It's all downhill from here."

—m—

Rejoice.

Robert ascended the eastern face above Lehigh Gap. He pulled himself over the next outsized boulder and stopped on a flat, narrow ledge. For the first time in several minutes he stood with both feet side by side. He looked ahead to preview the coming attractions. The rocks seemed to have been dumped from a giant crane by a sadistic crazy who took fiendish pleasure in blocking his progress.

Be glad in it.

He laughed to himself. He was too deep into Pennsylvania to be surprised or outraged by what lay on its trail. Early on he had learned that the "Keystone challenge" was not high elevations, long climbs, or steep descents. It was rock: small rock, large rock, pointed rock, jagged rock, unforgiving rock. And when it rained, slippery, treacherous rock.

"Only thirty-five more miles in Rocksylvania!" Behind and below, Mother Superior struggled with the boulders. Her short, stocky legs propelled her body up the steep pitch in irregular spurts. Further back, Czechmate eased around a huge gray monolith that blocked the view of the trail further below. Socrates, Southern Bell, and the Lab, he presumed, were behind. Several hundred feet down, at the bottom of the gorge, the Lehigh meandered southward toward Allentown.

Across the river, the western incline rose less precipitously from the river to the blue sky. Grasses and scrubs grew up the slope from

Palmerton. The green blotches suggested that efforts to revegetate that part of the mountain were marginally successful.

Robert needed all fours for negotiation. Old Hickory was useless in this passage. He slid his stick over the next boulder and retrieved it after crawling over the obstacle. The morning sun was high enough to beat down mercilessly on the barren rocks. As a precaution he wore the cap and bandanna. He was also careful where he placed his hands and feet. Rocks in the sun were prime snake locations.

His great AT adventure had taken on a different character. At the outset in Georgia, the exhilaration of thru-hiking sustained him, even through his sorrows. A continuing sense of expectation enlivened him all the way through the Old Dominion. But now, plodding into the second thousand miles, his approach was businesslike. Of the three items he prayed for, perseverance rose to the fore. He blotted out any distractions that might arise and focused on the basics.

Eat, drink, sleep, and hike. Eat, drink, sleep, and hike. Moving up the trail became his regular job.

His partners made similar adjustments. June afternoons were warm. The prospects for July were even hotter. The coolest time of the day was early morning. To take advantage of lower temperatures, Socrates modified his routine. He and Southern Bell were now on the trail by seven thirty, sometimes even before seven.

Except for short bursts of climbing, like coming out of Lehigh Gap, they followed Pennsylvania's flat ridges and piled up big miles daily. Robert recalled the thrill at Mountain Mama's when they contemplated their first twenty-mile day. Now they chalked up twenties with regularity and nonchalance, often reaching camp before 4:00 p.m.

He cherished the free time in the late afternoon to rest his battered feet. Some hikers, like Mother Superior and Czechmate, quickly mastered the technique for navigating the rocks on Pennsylvania's Blue Mountain. They glided over the irregular stones and somehow avoided the protrusions that pounded, poked, and pinched the toes and heels of other hikers. Robert never figured out how they did it. He accused them of having trained for this torture by walking barefoot over a bed of nails.

The rocks angled in all directions and disrupted his rhythm. Often his boots caught between the stones, making him stop and restart. He longed for the fluidity of southern trails, hiking in dirt, with only an occasional concentration of rocks. In contrast, the rare strips of dirt in

Pennsylvania were cause for celebration. Stones were everywhere. He repeatedly congratulated himself for having bought a pair of gel insoles in Harpers Ferry. They were the last line of prevention for stone bruises. Even with them, his feet were screaming when he reached camp each evening.

He scrambled up to the top of the Blue Mountain ridge. Preacher sat on a large black rock, waiting for him and the others.

The relative tranquility of the past two weeks was amazing. When they left the Denton shelter, Robert worried how Socrates and Mother Superior would tolerate Preacher. No one shouted from rooftops that they loved having him, but neither did they grouse about it. And there were times, such as at Pine Grove, when they were open and friendly.

Preacher had no more conferences that would take him off the trail until Massachusetts. Apparently he wanted company on this stretch and was willing to squelch his outspokenness to keep it. Their steady progress across Pennsylvania fit into his plans. Like the others, he fell into the routine of making miles.

At camp each night all six joined for meals. Afterward, the couples withdrew to tents, leaving Robert and Preacher to fend for themselves at the shelter. The pairings were reminiscent of the week north of Damascus, except this time Robert was not so isolated.

After dinner, Robert and Preacher had time to talk. The "Socratic rules" placed the flash points off limits. The two usually chatted about sports, and particularly football, which was Preacher's favorite. While not a star like his brother Luke, he had played linebacker in high school and junior college in Colorado. He was a big fan of the Colorado Buffaloes and the Denver Broncos. Those teams were two time zones away, distant and infrequent rivals with Robert's favorites in the South. The possibilities for noncontroversial discussion were almost inexhaustible.

They both craved sleep, so they never talked late into the evening. Darkness arrived around nine, and they were often asleep by the last light of day.

"Preach, you shot up this hill like a deer. You must have calories left over from the Moose Tracks."

"No. It's the Ben and Jerry's I had last evening at the road crossing. How far back are the others?"

"A minute or so." Robert took off his pack and sat on the rock next to Preacher. He drank a big swig. "I should be nursing my water. It's fifteen miles to the next source."

"I know. I really tanked up this morning." Preacher rubbed his stomach to emphasize.

"You stretched that reservoir with all the ice cream."

"Like a camel." Preacher pointed north on the trail. "Looks like easy walking from now on."

"Yeah. And we'll stop some to take pictures of the moonscape."

Mother Superior and Czechmate cleared the crest and walked toward them. In a few moments, Socrates and Southern Bell followed. War Eagle bounded beside her, pleased with the flat surface under his paws. They congregated around the rock, devouring snacks and sucking on hydration tubes.

"Ready for the ecology lesson?" Socrates asked.

"Vat you mean?" Czechmate spoke between drafts of water.

"We're gonna walk through the EPA Superfund site."

"I read about this place," Mother Superior replied. "Pollution from a zinc smelter, wasn't it?"

"Yup. It operated for some eighty years. The prevailing winds blew the emissions this way. There's not much growing for the next three miles."

"Vy don't they shut it down?"

"They did, Matey. Twenty years ago. The pollutants were so concentrated the ground still won't support life."

Socrates led them across Blue Mountain. At first the degree of destruction was not readily apparent. The surface was covered with the same rocks and boulders they had seen on the side of the Lehigh gorge. But as they progressed into what once was a forested plateau, the landscape turned stark and brutal. There was no green. Limbs and trunks lay scattered at random on the ground, blanched by years of chemical exposure. The ground was a dull ocher, punctuated in spots with gray rocks. No birds flew about, and no mice, lizards, or insects scurried on the ground. Life had abandoned this corner of the world. The group marched across the desolation like astronauts strolling on the moon.

Socrates stopped at a bump on the ridge. He turned to Southern Bell. "Whaddaya think?"

"Ah thought Sherman marched through Jawja."

Robert piped up. "Speaking of Georgia, there's a place like this on the border with Tennessee, called Copper Hill. Piles of copper tailings. It's barren, but nowhere as stark as this." He nudged Socrates. "You still believe in the perfectibility of man?"

Socrates laughed. "Two steps forward, and in this case, a giant step back. I suppose you think this is proof why we need God."

Robert retorted, "It certainly gives one pause."

"If you believe in God, then why did He let this happen? He had one hell of a senior moment. Like for eighty years."

The barren scene disturbed Czechmate. "Iss like vat the Communists did in Eastern Europe."

"Matey, about all I can say is the country needed zinc, and folks around here needed jobs. That's all that mattered. Then people started raising hell about what was happening to the land. They eventually prevailed."

"But iss too late."

"For the last twenty years, they've tried different treatments to regenerate growth. Hopefully one day they'll hit on one that works. But for now it sure looks like hell."

"Soc, what are the sins we can talk about in Pennsylvania?"

"That would be envy and murder, Mother."

"This is environmental murder in the first degree. I'll talk about it in Pennsylvania and anywhere I damn well please. It's just stupid. We let this go on for generations, just so a few old men could make money."

For the first time since leaving Virginia, Preacher challenged her. "Mother, you can blame the owners for this, but blame all of us also. Zinc's one of the ingredients used to make the zippers on our packs. And hundreds of other products we use every day. They manufactured the stuff because we demanded it."

Socrates broke in. "Every American should be required to come here. To raise the national consciousness. And instead of arguing about why it happened, we should make sure it never happens again."

War Eagle sniffed a stagnant rain puddle near a stack of dead limbs that resembled a boneyard. The color of the water alarmed Robert. "Bell, watch out for War Eagle. He shouldn't drink anything up here."

"Come here, boy! Come to Momma." She twisted her hydration tube and squeezed a stream into his mouth and onto his long nose. He licked the cool drops gratefully. "Socks, can we leave? This place gives me the creeps."

"Good idea. We still have to go some to find good water."

"It should be okay at the next shelter."

"Right, Snaky. Let's get the hell out of ground zero."

Robert burst into the tent site, located under several tall pines near the shelter. "What's today?"

"Look at your watch, Snakes," Mother Superior chided. "It's the nineteenth."

"What day of the week?"

"Wednesday."

"The heavens are smiling on us!"

"You mind letting us in on your celestial vision?"

"You'll love this. We're twenty miles from Delaware Water Gap."

"Right. So?"

"Where the church is, with the hostel."

"The Church of the Mountain. Where've you been? We decided to shoot for it tomorrow. I can feel the shower already. And speaking of showers, get downwind. You stink."

"You're not telling me anything I don't know. But I can tell you something new. I just read it in the register."

"What?"

"Once a week the congregation hosts a family night dinner. And they invite all hikers who are there to join them."

Robert felt the heat of ten eyes. "Guess what day of the week the good people spread the food?"

Socrates sprang from his evening rock. "Tomorrow? Home cooking?"

"I ask again. Do you believe in a Supreme Being?"

"We get the good, Snaky, and sometimes the bad. Don't make this out to be anything more than it is."

"Ah just luv trail magic!"

"Ve get a shower und a free meal?"

"That's right, Matey. And maybe all the ice cream you can eat."

She screwed up her face and stuck out her tongue. "I vant some fegetables. Und some real potatoes."

Preacher licked his lips in anticipation. "This'll be the fastest twenty we ever do."

They reached the church by three the next afternoon. The hostel, located in the basement of the church, was full. Many hikers had arrived the night before and stayed over for the dinner. Rather than split up, the six chose to spend the night at the shelter, in the yard behind the church. They unpacked their Thermarests and sleeping bags to reserve their spots. Quickly they got their things together for a long-awaited shower. A step ahead, Preacher waited for the others on the edge of the shelter platform.

An elderly man, perhaps seventy, rounded the corner of the church, pushing a lawn mower and carrying a can of gasoline. The gentleman removed his baseball cap and wiped the sweat from his forehead with a wrinkled handkerchief. He replaced his cap and bent over to start the machine.

Preacher watched him fiddle with the mower in the afternoon sun. "Guys, we ought to help him out. That grass is really thick."

Robert concurred. "Why don't we ask what we can do?"

"Y'all are right. Ah can put off mah shower for another hour. Ah mean, after all, they're gonna feed us tonight."

They walked across the grass. The man stood up when he saw them coming. He was short, thin, and wiry, and he greeted them warmly. "Welcome to the Presbyterian Church of the Mountain. My name's George." He nodded toward the shelter. "Is everything okay over there?"

Preacher responded. "Hey, we're fine. Thanks for asking. Actually, we wondered if you needed help with the yard."

Mother Superior added, "George, we'd like to work for our dinner."

He hesitated for a moment, reluctant to impose on church guests. However, he was clearly desirous of help on a hot day. "There's an awful lot to do," he warned.

"There are six of us. With that many, it should go quickly."

"Okay, if that's what you want. Let me get the other tools."

In a few minutes, they were at work. Preacher manned the lawn mower, while Socrates trimmed the borders with an electric edger. Mother Superior and Czechmate pruned several pieces of shrubbery with manual hedge clippers. Robert and Southern Bell trailed the others with yard rakes and plastic bags, collecting the various clippings. Delighted to be a latter-day Tom Sawyer, George offered encouragement to his conscripts. Despite the afternoon heat, they finished the tasks and put the tools away by four thirty.

George thanked each of them, shaking their hands with vigor. Southern Bell planted a big kiss on his cheek, and he beamed from ear to ear. "Here's what I want you to do. Dinner's at six. I'll save a table for you in the fellowship hall, over by the window in the corner. Make sure you sit there. I'll tell the ladies to take real good care of you."

They showered and changed and made it to the serving line just in time for the pastor's blessing. The spread was impressive. The entrees were barbecued chicken and honey-baked ham, flanked by mashed potatoes and a sweet potato casserole. Czechmate went crazy for the assorted vegetables, which included beans, peas, yellow squash, tomatoes, green peppers, candied carrots, cole slaw, and a broccoli/cauliflower casserole dripping with melted cheese. Preacher and Socrates loaded up on homemade cornbread. George was true to his word. The ladies kept their glasses full of ice-cold lemonade and brought all the dishes around for seconds. Southern Bell placed her hand on the arm of one of the servers. "Thank yew. Yew've given us about anything a body could want."

Her hostess smiled. "Everything but pasta. We figure you're tired of macaroni and cheese. But save room for apple pie and watermelon."

George came around with the dessert. With great fanfare he scooped vanilla ice cream onto the plates of apple pie. Czechmate held her hand over the pie and shook her head. "None for me."

George would not take "no" for an answer. "How about a tiny scoop?"

Not wanting to offend someone so solicitous, she relented. "Okay. *Ja.* Joost a tiny one." She glared at Robert. "Don't you say a vord!"

Sated and content, Mother Superior offered her assessment. "This food would taste good under any scenario. But the hour in the yard seasoned it to perfection."

"Hear, hear," Socrates said, holding up his slice of watermelon.

"Preacher, this was your idea. We owe you our thanks." She tipped her glass of lemonade in his direction.

"Thanks, Mother. Thanks to everybody for working so hard."

"Do yew realize this is the end of anothah state? No more Rocksylvainyah! Gimme five!"

Chapter 17

Through the night with the light from above.
God Bless America

"One helluva thunderstorm last night."
"But it brought in dis crisp air! I can breeth again."
"I love Canadian highs. No heat. No humidity."
"Ja, dis is great ver hiking."

Mother Superior skipped up the trail, reclaiming the spring in her step that had vanished during the oppressive passage across New Jersey and New York. "Let's hope the wet bulb readings stay low."

"Roger that," Robert replied. "For the first time in a week, I don't stink to high heaven."

In the heat, he had perspired in cascades. His sweat permeated the shoulder straps, hip belt, and padding of his pack. The jungle environment spawned a putrid culture, reeking of ammonia. The stench in the saturated Newstar fouled his T-shirt, making him delightful company. He feared the nurses would invoke medical prerogatives and place him under quarantine.

One day, seeking drinks and snacks, they left the trail at a road crossing and walked to a nearby convenience store. A desperate Robert prevailed upon the store manager for a brush and a bucket of warm, soapy water. He scrubbed the pack to remove the imbedded salts. He dumped his shirt in the bucket and rubbed it vigorously. The scouring removed the bouquet, but only momentarily. The sultry weather continued, and so did his sweat. He had to wash his gear every night to check the noxious smell.

The excess perspiration created another problem. Back in Harpers Ferry, he had traded nylon shorts and briefs for a bathing suit with a thin mesh liner. Socrates held an impromptu ceremony to initiate him into the fraternity of male hikers who traveled "commando style." The streamlined outfit worked fine until the onset of heat and humidity. Sweat salts accumulated in the hem of his trunks. It chafed the inside of his thighs, and raised painful red welts. He spread Vaseline on his tender skin and walked bowlegged to minimize contact with the fabric.

Preacher mocked him. "Been in the saddle too long, cowboy?"

They had been overtaken in New Jersey by The Highlander, a fast-moving northbounder from Texas. He hiked in a kilt. A former victim of the same irritation, he had discovered the airy freedom of the tartan. He championed it as the perfect remedy for chafed thighs.

After he had gone by, Southern Bell lambasted the outfit. "Reyull men don't wear skirts. Particularly out heah."

"I think it's okay," Socrates replied. "As long as he gets a bikini wax."

Robert was not about to emulate The Highlander, but he was compelled to try something other than Vaseline. The jelly wore off too quickly. Mother Superior suggested Desitin ointment, the thick salve mothers spread on babies to treat rashes. He slathered it on his thighs in the morning, at lunch, and again at night. The oily emollient did the trick. The welts disappeared.

Socrates derided him. "I thought I made you a macho man when I got you to ditch the underwear. Now diaper rash! You're such a baby."

"I'm a comfortable baby. And that's what counts."

"You're a baby who smells like a dead fish."

Robert took additional precautions. When he stopped for breaks, he removed his T-shirt and wrung out as much of the accumulated sweat as possible. At one pause, he estimated he extracted a half-cup of perspiration. The frequent squeezing prolonged the time before the saturated shorts began to irritate him.

To avoid dehydration, he increased intake to six liters of water daily. On one beastly day he drank seven, and a twenty-ounce, ice-cold Coke proffered by an angel parked in her dusty SUV at a road crossing. The only plus to the voluminous sweat was curtailed urine. The frequent urges for which he was renowned abated to sporadic trailside sprinkles.

"We're so happy for you, Snakes," Mother Superior mocked. "You've finally graduated from toilet training."

"I don't know. With cooler weather, I'll be 'Old Faithful' again. Whiz every hour on the hour."

"Better you pee like a geyser than sweat like a pig. You smelled worse than Soc ever has."

"Und that is sayink a lot."

"Thanks. You ladies really know how to stroke a guy."

With the change in the weather, the polyester tee was no longer overwhelmed by torrents. It wicked away the sweat before the onset of discomfort, even on the steep approach to the summit of Bear Mountain.

"You guys are gonna love this place." Mother Superior spoke with excitement and pride. "I've been coming here since I was a kid."

"I knew the mountain was old, but I didn't think it was that old."

"You should talk. You probably were around before God made it."

"God did create Bear Mountain, but He left the Adirondacks for me."

"Vatch out, Snecks." Czechmate pointed toward the sky. "Dink of the innocent bystanders."

"If He wanted to zap me, he'd have done it last night, in the middle of that light show."

"Don't stand anywhere near him, honey. Or Soc either. They're lightning rods. Hey, look. The Perkins Tower. We're at the top."

They entered a clearing surrounding a gray stone tower. Preacher, who had sprinted on ahead, waited at its base. Several other hikers and tourists milled around the summit, soaking up the sunshine. Some had gone to the other side of the tower to the overlook.

Heretofore Mother Superior had bemoaned the thick haze that shrouded any views of New York City. Now she beamed. "We're in luck. We'll be able to see the skyline."

"Before ve sightsee, I vant a drink." Czechmate strolled over to Preacher and pulled off her pack. She plopped onto the ground and sucked several bites of water through her hydration tube.

Mother Superior betrayed her impatience. "Some tourist you turned out to be."

"Joost let me rest until the others cotch up."

Mother Superior scurried to and fro at the base of the tower. Socrates and Southern Bell arrived within five minutes, but it seemed like an hour to her. She became more agitated when they, like the others, wanted refreshment before taking in her view. War Eagle became an additional distraction, frolicking with two small boys who were visiting the mountain with their parents. Attracted to their spontaneity and artlessness, he raced three times around the base of the tower, egged on by their high-pitched laughter. Southern Bell stopped him before a fourth lap. "Dawg, Ah wish Ah had yower energy. But yew're scarin' all the toorists."

Mother Superior could wait no longer. "Off your ass, people. Time to see my city."

"You guys should take a look," Preacher interjected. "It's quite a sight."

Preacher's endorsement surprised Robert. "Hey, if Preacher raves about it, it must be good. Let's check it out."

The group walked around the tower to the overlook. Directly below, the broad blue river bisected the verdant Hudson valley, stretching southward for miles. The natural expanse triggered thoughts of Burke's Garden, and also of the picture postcard farms visible from the rocks on the Pinnacle, back in Pennsylvania. The sight of fields and forests gave way to an even greater attraction further south. The haze had been blown into the Atlantic by the passing storm, and the New York City skyline, in crystal relief, was silhouetted against the azure sky. The buildings, perhaps fifty miles away, seemed no more than fifty yards distant. Mother Superior's Chamber of Commerce spiel had not done justice to the breathtaking sight.

By fortuitous circumstance they had reached this spot on a cloudless and smogless day. Robert reached out, like Angie at Blood Mountain, thinking he could grasp the city. Had he a pair of binoculars, he could have peered through the shiny glass of the skyscrapers and read the expressions on the faces of those inside.

"Toldja! I've seen this a dozen times. Nothing else like it." Mother Superior relinquished her role as booster and became a tourist like the others. Standing between Socrates and Robert, she rattled off the names of the more prominent skyscrapers. "The big one is the Empire State Building," she pointed. "And over there is the UN."

"Way cool," Socrates replied.

Mother Superior fell silent. The robust color drained from her cheeks. Tears welled in her eyes.

Robert put his arm on her shoulder. "What's the matter?"

She wiped the corners of her eyes. "The towers." She pointed toward southern Manhattan. "They were over there."

Her sadness was contagious. They all looked at the hole in the cloudless sky, in vain hope the twin spires might somehow reappear in the void.

Robert sifted through the ashes of his memories to recount the horror of September 11. At first, it had been difficult for him to join in the national grief. Consumed with Angie's advancing illness, he blotted out the agony and suffering of others. He could not handle the collective sorrow of the country heaped on top of his own personal misery. But after her death, after the funeral, after family and friends had departed and he had time alone, he connected to those in New York, Pennsylvania, and Washington. The images of unfortunate people, facing death like Angie, haunted him.

What was it like, sitting in the cubicle in front of the computer, to look up and see a 767 come through the window? What raced through your mind? A split second to frame an image of those you loved? An unvoiced prayer? There was no time to ask why, no time to lament what might have been. It was terrible to be snuffed out like that. But was it worse than being in tension with death for months on end, watching it inevitably exert its power over you as it took away your beloved?

He thought about the people above the ninetieth floor. As the searing heat and suffocating smoke drew closer, their lives came down to a despondent choice of waiting to be incinerated or hurling themselves to death on the concrete far below. He was certain there was bravery and integrity in making this choice. Angie had been brave. Could he have been?

Could he have been as brave as the passengers on the plane over Pennsylvania? With irrepressible spirit they chose how they would die. He remembered his father, who never surrendered his dignity as he fought his terminal battle with stomach cancer. Robert had marveled at his disposition in his final weeks, a precise combination of stoicism and serenity. Certain he was going to die, he seemed just as certain he had lived life well. He had reached this conclusion over many years and months. The passengers on Flight 93 reached it in minutes and seconds.

He thought about the firemen and policemen, who rushed into the buildings to rescue others. With their lives on the line, they never questioned their duty. If the time ever came when he was called upon to make a similar sacrifice, would he have their courage?

"I first came here when I was ten years old. The towers were always here ... until now." Mother Superior lowered her head. Robert gave her another squeeze.

"We'll build them back," Preacher said. "America will come out of this with flying colors."

Mother Superior sighed. "You can build them back. But it won't ever be the same. You can't build back thousands of lives."

Czechmate walked over and embraced her. Robert released his grip on her shoulder and stepped aside. "You haf been strong for me. Now I vill be strong for you." With her hand, Czechmate lightly combed Mother Superior's bangs to keep them from matting against her forehead. She blotted the tears that rolled down her cheeks. "They joost thought they could hurt us. Und maybe they did for a time. But ve vill come back stronger than efer."

Normally the caregiver, Mother Superior accepted the role as patient. "Thanks. You get an A for bedside manner."

Czechmate let out a little squeal and hugged her. "Dat's the first A you efer give me!"

With a deep breath, Mother Superior withdrew from Czechmate. She closed her window of vulnerability and reverted to professorial form. "C'mon. Let's hike down to the river. We can go through the zoo near the bridge."

"Zoo?" Southern Bell was intrigued.

"That's right, honey. The AT crosses hundreds of mountains and goes over and under interstate highways. It also winds through one little zoo."

"Wheyah?"

"Right down the mountain. On the banks of the Hudson. Nice collection of native species."

Southern Bell squatted and petted War Eagle's snout. Happy for the attention, he licked her hand. "Hun, yew want to see another bayah?"

He barked in anticipation.

"Sorry. He'll have to look through the fence. They won't let dogs in."

They spent the night at Graymoor, a spiritual retreat of the Franciscans. As a part of their ministry, the friars allowed camping on their ball field, located a few hundred yards off the AT. Hikers were welcomed at dinner each evening, but the six dawdled at the zoo and arrived too late to eat with the monks.

The field was equipped with running water, a bathroom, and a picnic kiosk. The group pitched tents and made themselves at home. After eating and cleaning, they gravitated to the benches of the open-air pavilion to enjoy the cool evening breeze.

Preacher donned earphones and surfed for news on a small radio. After futile attempts to find a national report, he shifted to a public radio symphonic broadcast. He played it through the speaker, a tuneful backdrop for their camp talk.

The hole in the skyline continued to vex Mother Superior, who refrained from joining the conversation. Finally, after a lull in the chitchat, she spoke up. "What's been happening lately? Any progress with the terrorists?"

"Don't know," Socrates admitted. "With the hike and all, I've lost touch."

Preacher responded. "I listen to news off and on. Nothing's happened. But we're gonna get that son of a bitch."

"Bin Laden?"

"Damn straight. It's just a matter of time."

"How can you be so sure?" Socrates asked. "Our best chance was last fall, when he was on the run in Afghanistan. It'll be harder to find him now. He has a jillion places to hide."

"We'll get him," Preacher reiterated. "What he did wasn't just a crime against America. It was a sin against God. Even in the eyes of his own God, Allah."

"I wish I could be that certain. But the facts don't bear it out. We've been chasing Eric Rudolph in North Carolina for what, five years now? And we're no closer to catching him. It should be a lot easier to track down a guy in the Appalachians than Afghanistan. Or Pakistan. Or wherever the hell he is."

"You have to keep the faith. God wants us to capture those fanatics. And restore peace in the world."

"Ah just wish it would happen soon. Ev'ry time we trap him he seems to melt away. He and that one-eyed moolah. They're craftier than the fox in the hen house."

"Bell, you mean mullah. Mullah Omar. Look at it from the standpoint of history, Preacher. Hitler, Mussolini, Idi Amin, Pol Pot. It takes time to get rid of bad guys."

"It took forty yeers to get the Communists out of Czechoslovakia und East Germany."

"Right, Matey. Preach, I disagree with you that God intervenes in history. There was no divine retribution with the Soviets. They just played out their string. Ran out of gas. Folded their cards. Whatever. But that won't happen with Al-Qaeda. There's too much fervor, too much hatred in the Mideast for this to die off."

"Not if we keep the pressure on." Preacher replied. "We never tried to run down the Communists. We just contained them. This is different. Keep them running and they'll slip up. It will happen, and soon."

"I agree with Soc," said Mother Superior. "It's not as easy as you think. Look at Castro. And Saddam Hussein. They're still hanging around, in spite of all our pressure. It may take fifty years to get rid of those bastards."

Czechmate nodded. "Only the goot die young."

"Okay, maybe it won't happen that soon. But the point is, we're doing the right thing by trying to bring them to justice. And God always comes down on the side of right."

"I guess I'm not as optimistic. I don't believe in this divine intervention stuff either. There'll be more dark days ahead."

"Maybe so, Mother, but there's no doubt about the final outcome. God will bless America. He always does."

Robert, drinking tea from one of his Nalgenes, sputtered loudly.

"Choke on something?"

"The tea, Preach. But I wish you hadn't said that."

"Said what?"

"'God bless America.'" Robert cleared his throat. "It's not what you said. It's how you said it."

"What could possibly be wrong with 'God bless America'?"

"Nothing. Nothing at all. I hope He does. I often pray He will. But when you say 'He always does,' you're taking too much for granted. That's an unsupportable conclusion."

"Here we go again. You can't accept anything without dissecting it like a frog in biology lab. Don't you trust God?"

"Preacher, this has nothing to do with trust. It has everything to do with presumption. We just don't know. We don't know if we're right in His eyes. Nobody knows the mind of God. Not me, you, or the Pope, or Billy Graham or even Mother Teresa. When you say He will always bless America, you're presumptuous as hell."

"Okay, I don't know exactly what He's thinking. But I know He rewards those who are righteous and faithful."

"Preach, I'm not attacking faith. And don't think I don't want to see bin Laden and Al-Qaeda brought to justice. What bothers me is that there are lots of people in this country who confuse national interest with divine will. They assume that what we do as a nation is right. Because we think it's right, God must think so, too. Therefore, He will automatically bless it."

"That's what faith is. You pray about something. Your prayers are answered."

Socrates broke in. "Well, it's obvious from the news bin Laden prays a lot. He thinks he's right, and that Allah will reward him. Seventy-two virgins. What's the difference between his faith and yours?"

"If you don't know the difference, you're in big trouble. The United States has a track record of getting rid of dictators and oppressors. That's what we're doing here. I mean, how can you possibly defend the Taliban? And how could you think God would defend them?"

"That's not the point," Robert replied. "I'm not talking about them. I'm talking about us. We get arrogant. Dammit, we know what's right. We have read the mind of God, and guess what? He agrees with us. We have determined what is Right, with a capital R. The president. Congress. The American people. It's this hubris that gets us into trouble."

"How? Give me an example."

"The Cherokee removal. Breaking treaties with other Indian tribes. Incarcerating Japanese Americans in World War II. Proud moments in American history."

"Yeah," Socrates added. "Holding hundreds of people in jail without access to counsel. Even American citizens. What happened to the Bill of Rights?"

"Don't forget it took ninety years before we freed the slaves," Mother Superior said. "And 130 to give women the right to vote."

"Sure, we've made mistakes," Preacher countered. "But those are the exceptions. On the whole, because of our Christian values, we've done the right thing. That's what I mean about track record. The results prove it."

"But we're not right all the time. And we go about it ass-backward. I would rather see us pray first for guidance." Robert continued. "We don't ask Him to show us what's right. We just ask Him to rubber stamp what we think is right."

Socrates broke in. "And dammit, God, be quick about it. Hurry up and bless or I'll kick Your Holy Ass."

Preacher cringed. Czechmate turned to Mother Superior. "You vere right. Ve should stay far away from them. To dotch the lightning."

Robert chuckled. "That's a might extreme, Soc. But I do think we, as individuals and collectively as a nation, manipulate God. We're impatient."

"Impatient?" Preacher snorted. "What would you have us do? Deliberate over the right course of action, while they systematically blow New York and Washington to kingdom come?"

"No. We had to go right after them. But what I'm talking about is how we use God. I'll show my age, but have you guys ever watched *M*A*S*H*?"

"That's not ancient," Mother Superior answered. "That's classic. We watched *M*A*S*H* all the time in the desert. I even taped some episodes to use in teaching my classes."

"*Ja*, I remember. Der corporal, he vas so cute."

"Snaky, Ah used to watch the reruns after suppah, right before *The Dukes of Hazzard*."

"Remember how Radar O'Reilly slid those papers under Colonel Blake's nose and told him to sign?"

"Yayah. Lak a three-day pass for Trapper and Hawkeye."

"A lot of Americans think like Radar. God is Henry Blake. Sure, he's the authority figure, but if we're clever like Radar, we'll get what we want. And you know, we're not really being that bad because we always want to do the right thing. That choir boy from Iowa doesn't have a sneaky bone in his body, and by golly, neither do we."

Preacher shook his head. "Where are you going with all this?"

"When we say 'God bless America,' is it a request? A prayer? Or as Soc said, an order? Maybe even an ultimatum?"

"It's a prayer. A simple prayer."

"What kind? Are we on our knees in awe and humility? Or are we like a kid at Christmas, praying for a bike?"

"The people I know who pray are genuinely grateful for what they receive."

"I dunno, Preach. I think we look to God for wish fulfillment. We sit in front of the keyboard, search through all the toys and order up some goodie from God like He's Amazon.com. All we have to do is press the 'buy' key. We fully expect in three working days UPS will ship it to our front door. Prayer answered. Gee, thanks, God. Your will be done."

"Good point." Mother Superior sat up from a slouch. "God is just another convenience. Like cruise control. We decide how fast we want to go and turn it over to Him. Click the God button and don't think about it any more. He'll get us there. But suppose we set the speed on seventy when conditions allow for only sixty? We crash. Is God at fault for being a shitty navigator? Maybe we should have consulted Him before deciding how fast to drive."

Preacher was animated. "What's the matter with you guys? Do you think every Christian in America is that shallow? That all of us manipulate God? Rather than revere Him? Nobody with faith thinks he can do a number on God."

"I do at least one number every day," Robert said. "I bet you do too."

"I said people with faith."

"Preach, just because I have doubts does not mean I'm faithless. To be true to myself I have to challenge God. It's part of my imperfection."

"I agree none of us is perfect. But I think we're basically reverent."

Mother Superior spoke. "Back in Baltimore last month, I saw this bumper sticker. Red, white, and blue, stars and stripes, like all the others. Except it said 'America, bless God.' It really got me thinking about reverence. And humility. It redefined the relationship."

"That's all I've been trying to say." Robert continued. "First things first. Like the first commandment. No other Gods before me. Honor God and everything else falls into place."

"You guys aren't making sense. You think just because we ask God to bless America, we're trying to pull the wool over his eyes?"

"I hate to say it, but if the shoe fits ..."

"You have to understand, Preach. Snaky is a Calvinist. According to him we are totally depraved." Socrates underscored his point with a thumbs-down gesture.

"We're all self-centered. We want it our way. Sin gets in the way of faith. Constantly." Robert paused. "Preacher, do you say a blessing when you eat?"

"Usually. Or someone does, if I'm in a group."

"It's good to ask a blessing at each meal. But sometimes they come across as less than sincere. Wooden, or even singsong."

"I guess. Some blessings get short shrift."

"Good bread. Good meat. Good God, let's eat!"

"Thanks, Soc. You can always serve as the bad example. Preach, say your Uncle Ralph is really hungry and wants to get on with the meal. He'll rush through the words so he can chow down. Or maybe we're all watching a game on TV, and the blessing goes in one ear and out the other."

"I admit sometimes we go through the motions with the blessing. We don't give God His due."

"Preach, that's what I mean about asking God to bless America. We say it so many times it loses conviction. We're just touching all the bases. Paying the premiums."

"Snakes, I like you, but you're a real doubting Thomas. What's it going to take for you? To see and touch the nail marks? If you had even a small amount of faith, you'd understand there comes a point where you stop questioning everyone's motives and just believe. The United States has people all around the world trying to track down these terrorists, because if left alone they'll destroy the earth as we know it. We don't want that to happen. We go after them. It's perfectly reasonable to ask God to bless that endeavor. If you've got a problem with that, then maybe you're the problem."

Socrates spoke up. "Easy, Preach. Don't get personal."

"I'm not insulting him. It's just the way I feel." He reflected for a moment. "Back in Virginia, what was it you said we could talk about in New York?"

"The Yankees!" Mother Superior broke in.

"Yeah, yeah. But what from the verse in Romans?"

Socrates responded, "As I recall, it was malignity."

"Okay. These doubts about whether we're doing the right thing are a cancer on the nation. They eat away at our resolve."

Robert countered. "That's your take. I think overconfidence and a lack of humility are also cancers. They blind us to reality and cloud our judgment."

Preacher reached for his radio and turned it off. "Man, I feel sorry for you. On Bear Mountain today, looking at New York, I thought you understood. But I'm not sure now. You don't have anything to believe in." He stood up and turned in the direction of his tent. "You're missing out on all that joy."

"That's where you're wrong, Preach. For something to be worth believing, you have to fight with it until you really understand. Trust me. I've been my fifteen rounds with God."

"I suppose you think you won."

"In a way, yes. Like Jacob, I came out crippled. But I came out a believer."

Preacher shrugged. "I hope so. It's time to go to sleep."

Robert called after him. "God bless America, land that I love."

He turned around. "Finally. Good for you."

"We always say 'God bless America.' We've cornered the market."

"Whaddaya mean?"

"We ought to share the wealth with other countries."

"I guess we could do that sometime."

"No. I mean right now. Each of us asks God to bless a country, other than America. Why don't you start?"

Preacher debated buying into the proposition. Finally he muttered, "God bless Australia."

"Good start," Robert replied. "Czechmate?"

"Okay. Gott bless Bangladesh."

"Mother?"

"God bless the Cameroons."

"Bell?"

"God blayuss Denmark."

"Soc?"

"I'm a nonbeliever. If I do this, I'm taking your God's name in vain."

"Just this once. It won't hurt."

"Okay. God bless Greece."

"Very good. My turn. God bless Nicaragua."

Robert let the words sink in. "There. It's okay to be magnanimous. God doesn't have to wear red, white, and blue. And I don't think we slighted America in the least. Good night, Preacher."

"Good night, Dancing Snakes." He walked across the ball field and climbed inside his tent.

Socrates spoke. "You know, even when he's nice, and he was very nice tonight, he still rubs me the wrong way."

Robert grinned. "Want some Desitin for that?"

"You may get me to sound like a fish, but I'll be damned if I'm going to smell like one."

Chapter 18

Make straight paths for your feet.
Hebrews 12:13

"Shiyut!"

Mother Superior stopped on the trail. "That has to be Bell."

Robert chuckled. "You think?"

"Shiyut! Shiyut! Shiyut!"

"The lady has a real issue." Mother Superior resumed walking. "I wonder what Soc's done now."

"A female rush to judgment," Robert replied. "He might be totally blameless."

"Get real. This is Soc we're talking about."

Preacher pointed through the bushes. "There's the lean-to."

"Let's see vat's the fuss."

The four entered the clearing. Southern Bell sat cross-legged on the shelter platform. Socrates hovered behind. She hunched over, scrutinizing the inside of her left thigh. Her index fingers and thumbs formed a diamond-shaped fence on the skin, as if to confine something dangerous inside. War Eagle paced back and forth, whining in empathy with his mistress.

"We okay here?" Mother Superior inquired.

"We are most sertonly *not* okay."

"We need you, Mother," Socrates entreated. "Bell's got a tick."

"Ah hate 'em! Hate 'em! Creepy, filthy bloodsuckahs. At least it's not big, lak the ones in Alabamah."

Mother Superior parked her pack on the inside wall of the lean-to. "Not big? That's not good."

"Whaddaya mean, not good?"

Mother Superior motioned for Socrates to move and sat down next to Southern Bell. She studied the small black dot from several angles.

"It's a deer tick. We need to remove it. Now."

"Is it bayad?"

"You ever heard of Lyme disease?"

Southern Bell frowned. "Yayah, but we don't get it in Alabamah."

"It's more common in the northeast. Named for a town here in Connecticut. It's caused by bacteria, passed on by the tick bite. That is, if it's a carrier. Not all deer ticks are."

"I was afraid it might be that," Socrates said. "But I wanted your diagnosis."

Southern Bell glared at Socrates. "Sometimes yew treat me like a mushroom."

"What does that mean?"

"Yew feed me shiyut an' keep me in the dark." She turned to Mother Superior. "What's this disease gonna do to me?"

"Easy, Bell. The odds of your getting it are low. When did you first notice the tick?"

"Fifteen minutes ago. When we got heyah. Why?"

"Usually it has to embed for thirty-six hours before it transmits bacteria into the blood stream. Can you recall the last time you looked at your leg and didn't see it?"

"Oh yayah. Last night. Ah gave myself a sponge bath. Scrubbed both laigs pretty good. Ah would have seen it."

Socrates grinned sheepishly. "I saw them last night. Up close. Don't remember a tick."

Mother Superior stared at him stonily.

"Don't ask," Socrates warned.

She turned to Southern Bell. "The prognosis is good. You probably picked it up today while hiking."

Southern Bell poked Socrates. "Ah knew it was yower fault."

"How can you say that?"

"Yew made me lead when we walked through that tall grass. A true gentlemun would have gone first and knocked off the ticks."

"I'm not Sir Walter Raleigh, okay? Besides, you wanted to lead."

"I was jus' trying to humah yew. Yew like to stare at mah butt."

"I love your butt! You gonna blame me for that?"

Mother Superior broke in. "It's been chewing on you for ten hours or less. Probably not long enough to transmit bacteria. Once we get it off, you should be good as new. Czechmate, there's a pair of tweezers on your Swiss Army knife, right?"

"*Ja.*"

"Sterilize them in a flame for a few seconds. Then bring them here. And some polysporin."

Czechmate took off her pack and rummaged for the requested items. Socrates changed the subject. "How was Kent?"

"Fine. Everything went okay."

The four had detoured that morning to buy provisions at the small Connecticut town, located a mile off the trail. Socrates and Southern Bell, who were better supplied, slept in while the others went ahead. The first destination in Kent had been the outfitter. They bought fuel, boot laces, a Lexan spoon, and batteries. Robert also bought a replacement for his pinch light, whose halogen bulb was in its last throes. While the others headed for the supermarket, Preacher volunteered to do the group wash at the nearby Laundromat. He borrowed a pair of used shorts from the outfitter "hikers' box" to wear while his clothes were in the machine.

"Here's your clean stuff." Robert tossed a T-shirt and pair of socks to Socrates. "Say, didya know Preacher's a quick-change artist?"

"Another Laundromat adventure?"

"It was easy." Preacher's eyes twinkled. "There was only one woman, plus the hostess, in the place. The dryers were in this little alcove. I went around the corner and slipped into the shorts while they were yakking about their kids. Same thing when the clothes came out of the dryer. Back into my own."

"That's a shame. Those ladies could have used some Colorado beefcake. Did you do Chippendale?"

Preacher held up muscular arms in the classic bodybuilder's pose. "Sat there the whole time without a shirt on."

"At least he didn't moon ev'rybody, lak yew did back in Pennsylvainyah. Before yew wrapped yowerself in the rainfly."

Czechmate approached with the tweezers and antibacterial ointment. Southern Bell sat up straight.

"Okay. Let's persuade this little critter to let go." Mother Superior gently maneuvered the tweezers around the body of the tiny tick.

Southern Bell tensed with trepidation. "The ones you have in Alabama are wood ticks. They're bigger, but don't carry the Lyme bacteria. The disease is almost unheard-of in the South. I'm not surprised you don't know much about it. The symptoms can be nasty. Fever, fatigue, headaches, muscle aches, joint pain. If it's not treated you can develop serious cardiological and neurological problems." Czechmate and Socrates watched with curiosity as she manipulated the stubborn insect. She twisted steadily with the tweezers. "There." Mother Superior held up the tick in the pincer for all to see. "Got all of that son of a bitch."

Socrates was impressed. "Nice technique."

Southern Bell exhaled with relief. She examined the tiny inflammation on her thigh where the tick had been dislodged. "It doesn't look too bayad."

"Here." Mother Superior handed her the tube of polysporin. "Apply this frequently over the next few days to fight infection. You should be okay. But if in a week or ten days you develop a red bull's-eye rash with swelling, or you have any of those symptoms I mentioned, you hurry to a doctor."

"Thanks. Yew know, Momma's at ease with me hiking with two nurses. Ah'll call her about this when we get to Sawlsberry."

"Wanna use my cell?" Preacher offered. "I have extra minutes."

"No, thanks. Ah'll wait a day to see how it does before Ah call."

Socrates extended his hand and helped her up. "You okay now, baby?" He bent forward and gave her a peck on the lips.

Southern Bell beamed at his solicitousness. "Ah just love it when you decide to be nice."

"By the way, Soc, with a gaping wound like that, there's always a danger of infection." Mother Superior's tone reeked with sarcasm. "Keep your dirty body off that thigh for at least two weeks."

"Gimme a break, willya? I have feelings for this woman."

"Exactly what I'm afraid of. In the long and storied history of medicine, no curative benefit has ever been attributed to semen."

"You're heartless. I'm a sensitive guy. I have other than sexual feelings."

"We know. You get hungry at least three times a day."

The others hooted. Put down hard, Socrates elected to change the subject. "Speaking of food, is anyone ready for dinner?"

Robert chimed in. "Not just yet. We had a big lunch." He paused for effect. "Would you like to know what?"

Socrates glared. "Get it over with."

"They were huge. At least a half pound. Right, guys?"

The others nodded.

"Oozing with cheese. With a big plate of fries, swimming in catsup. Bigger even than the one at Mountain Mama's. Really felt bad you guys weren't there to enjoy it. But somehow, in our sorrow, we forced it down."

"Your sincerity touches me."

"Oh, I forgot one little detail." Robert waited for another glare. "We had dessert."

"Big deal."

"Yeah, I guess you're right. It wasn't much. Just a pint."

"You didn't?"

"Oh, but we did."

"You sons of bitches go into town without us, eat Ben and Jerry's, and come back and lord it over us."

"Oh, are we lording?" Robert turned to Mother Superior, Czechmate, and Preacher, who were grinning from ear to ear. "How could he get that idea?"

"Screw you."

"Don't you want to know what flavors?"

"Bell, until today we called these people our friends."

"Ah know. This cruelty is uncalled for. Pahticulahly when Ah'm at death's door."

"Let's see. Preach had a pint of Phish Food. I had Vanilla Heath Bar Crunch. Mother and Matey split a pint of Chocolate Chip Cookie Dough."

Socrates winced as Robert named each flavor. "And I'm having ramen noodles for dinner. Tonight, when you're asleep, I'll throw you into the Housatonic, one by one. With burgers and ice cream in your bellies, you'll sink like stones."

"Actually, we did bring you something." Robert reached into his open pack and pulled out a clean, rolled-up T-shirt. Inside, cushioned from the bumps of the trail, was a sealed plastic tray containing a pint of fresh strawberries. Robert handed them to Southern Bell.

"Oooh! Yew remembahed how much Ah like these!" She rushed forward and gave him a big hug. "Yew're not so bad aftah all."

Socrates erupted. "You really are a snake. You eat ice cream behind my back, and now you're copping sneaky feels from my girlfriend. You're the first in the river tonight."

Robert reached into the pack. He extracted a bottle sheathed in one of his hiking socks. "And this is for you, Soc." He pulled the bottle out of the sock slowly, exposing only the green glass of the tapered neck. Socrates studied it intently, with rising expectations. Robert slid it back down in the sock. "Since you're acting so violently, this might not be a good idea."

"Snaky, you don't know what violent is. But you'll find out if you keep playing these shitty games."

Robert jerked the sock down, revealing the Heineken label. "Put it in the creek for thirty minutes, and it'll be cool enough to drink."

Socrates grabbed the bottle and rolled the beer across his cheek to his lips. "You're still a bastard." He planted a kiss on the label. "But a passably acceptable one."

—☙—

After dinner they walked from the lean-to back to the AT, which coursed for several miles along the west bank of the Housatonic. They sat on large boulders at water's edge and enjoyed the sights and sounds of the encroaching evening. The breeze was scant. Throngs of mosquitoes, who thrived in the moist environs, attacked them. Czechmate passed around a bottle of repellent, and all dosed liberally.

Socrates, mellow after several sips of beer, inquired about their day. "See anything interesting coming over on the trail?"

"Ve saw a hawk, circling in der sky."

"Sharp-shinned," Robert added.

"I thought it might komm after my candy bar, so I held my Lekis up in der air to fight it off."

Socrates performed a crude impersonation of Czechmate, flailing sticks at a diving raptor. "Bet you scared it shitless. Where was this?"

"Joost before ve came down the steep part."

"The St. Johns Ledges." Robert clarified.

"It was kinda tricky through there. Bet it's even worse in the rain."

"And ice," Mother Superior added. "I've hiked here in the winter. You need crampons for spots like that. Sometimes it's dangerous."

"I was impressed by the rock steps, though. Somebody donated a lot of time and effort."

"Yeah. They were a real piece of work."

"Snaky, is that what you and Preach did when you worked on the AT?"

"That's right! You guys did trail work," Mother Superior spoke with admiration. "I'd almost forgotten."

"The Konnarock crew, in Tennessee. Four years ago. I did a week."

"Two for me." Preacher nodded toward Robert. "He wimped out."

"I went back to work. Didn't have time on my hands like you carefree college students."

"You've piqued my interest," Mother Superior said. "Tell me about this Konnarock group."

"You gonna volunteer?"

"Depends on what you tell me."

"Well, essentially you help the local volunteers build trail. It's not easy. You get tired, dirty, and sweaty. Rained on. But there's great personal satisfaction when you see the new trail you just carved out of the hillside."

"Tell me what's involved. I mean, what do you do exactly?"

"If you remember, a lot of trail in the south is sidehill. In dirt. Not like that rock ledge we came down today. We didn't build steps on that project. We dug sidehill."

"How do you know vere to dig?"

"The crew leader lays it out. He or she carries a bunch of those small plastic utility flags. The bright orange ones. They mark where the trail's supposed to go."

"She? I'm even more interested."

"It so happens our leader was male. The assistant was female. The crew split about half and half."

"As I recall," Preacher interjected, "we had ten people. From age eighteen all the way to seventy-something."

"Yeah, they were all good workers. Anyway, the leader sets the flags about ten feet apart, along the lower edge of the trail. Each volunteer takes a section between the flags and clears it out."

"How do you do that?"

Preacher spoke up. "With Pulaskis and fire rakes."

"What the hell is a Pulaski?" Mother Superior asked.

"Forest Service uses it to fight fires. Named for Edward Pulaski, a ranger in Idaho. He got tired of lugging both an axe and a shovel to fight fires. He took a double-bladed axe to his forge and formed one side into a mattock. That way, he could chop trees and grub in the dirt with one tool. It's good for fires and also for trailbuilding. Very versatile."

"Forge?"

"Yeah. He was a blacksmith. This was about a hundred years ago."

"Preach, I'm impressed," Robert said. "Where did you find this out?"

"If you'd stuck around longer at base camp, you'd have learned something."

"You mentioned another tool," Socrates inquired.

"Yeah, the fire rake. It's about twice as wide as a hoe, but instead of one blade it has broad triangular teeth."

"Right, four teeth," Robert concurred. "They're strong and sharp."

"It rakes up leaves and twigs, but you can also chop in the dirt with it."

Robert continued. "When you start to clear your ten-foot section, you rake the leaves out of the way, up above where the trail will go. When you're through digging, you spread those leaves over the completed trail, to protect it from erosion. But I'm getting ahead of myself. After you rake away the leaves, you start digging with the Pulaski. In the southern forest, the first stuff you run into is decomposed organic matter. It can be several inches thick."

Preacher countered. "It's called duff."

"I know about duff," Socrates replied. "Decayed leaves. And rotted wood."

"As a renowned botanist, I figured you would."

Socrates acknowledged the compliment with a tip of his beer bottle.

Robert continued. "Duff's great for plants to grow in, but awful for trails. It's unsubstantial. It will undermine the treadway because it won't pack down. The dirt'll wash away with the first good rain, and the trail slips down the mountain. So you gotta get rid of it."

Preacher jumped in. "They say the most important step in building a trail is digging out the duff and throwing it down the hill. Then the fun begins. You chop the roots and dig the rocks. Chop and dig until you clear them out. Everybody has a technique. I started at the flag line and worked my way up and into the hill. That way I carved out a flat surface to stand on while I worked. That little ledge gives you valuable purchase, particularly if the hill is steep. Otherwise, you need to be a mountain goat."

"Whut's purchase?"

"Leverage, sweetie."

Robert broke in again. "Footing's important. Once, I jerked on this big root, and it popped. I did a backward double somersault with a double twist. Wound up fifteen feet down the mountain."

"That's a 2.5 degree of difficulty," Socrates estimated.

"*Ja*, he vould have von. Except the German judge, she marked him down."

"Damn, Matey, I knew it was rigged. But at least I didn't land in poison ivy."

Preacher continued the tutorial. "When you finally clear out the duff and the roots and the rocks, you get to what's called mineral soil. Red or yellow clay."

"Red clay. Thass whut the South's famous for."

"And what you want for your treadway, Bell. It's solid. Unlike duff, it holds together. You dig in the soil until the trail is flat and as wide as the length of a Pulaski handle."

"Why that wide?"

"So two people can pass. The treadway should outslope slightly, away from the bank, for proper drainage. If you inslope it, the water stays on the trail, causing erosion. Before you know it, your trail's a ditch."

"But you can't outslope it too much," Robert cautioned, "or hikers'll pitch off the side when they walk on it. Three to five degrees max."

"What about the inside bank?"

"It should slope at forty-five degrees, Mother. To drain well."

"It sounds lak yew need to be an engineah to get it right."

"Not really. With a little practice, you can eyeball the angles."

"And when you complete your ten-foot section, you have to tie it in to what the folks on your left and right have built."

"Ah can see why it should be level."

"Yeah, Bell. As smooth as you can." Robert continued. "The crew leaders emphasize quality over quantity. They don't rush you. They want the trail built right. The standard for the average volunteer is thirty feet a day."

"So the whole crew shoots for three hundred?"

"There's really no quota. If the bank's not steep, or if the duff and roots are thin, you can do more. But the key isn't *X* number of feet. It's compacting and sloping the mineral soil so it drains well."

Preacher followed. "Then you've got your obstacles. Stream crossings, boulder fields."

"Yeah. On a steep bank, you might have to build a rock or log crib to support the edge of the trail. These are all harder and take longer."

Socrates interjected. "You said boulders. How big?"

"Several hundred pounds."

"Jeez, Preach, howya move those?"

"You use rock bars to pry them loose. After they're free, several guys can move them out of the way. Or you can pry up the front end with a pick and leverage it from the back with the bar. You can only push it inches at a time, but eventually you'll get it out of the treadway."

"Sounds too much like work."

"Remember the steps on St. Johns? To move those rocks, they had to bring in more equipment. Grip hoists, wire ropes, and snatch blocks."

"Pulleys?"

"Yeah. To move that weight you need the mechanical advantage. The week after Dancing Snakes left we built a four-foot rock crib. We set up a line and moved several big rocks about a hundred feet to use as the base for the crib wall. Some of those suckers were three feet long and a foot thick."

"I didn't realize it was that involved," Mother Superior said. "How do you get the equipment on site?"

"Carry it. They try to park the truck as close as possible, but you always wind up humping tools to the site. Usually a mile or so."

"How much those rock bars weigh?"

"Twenty, twenty-five pounds."

"I carried the Pulaskis and the fire rakes," Robert confessed. "I let the horses like Preach tote the bars and the grip hoists."

"Would you do it again?"

"I don't know, Mother. With my schedule I haven't found the time. And this year, I wanted to hike."

"What about you, Snakes?"

"In a heartbeat. It's a way to give back to the AT for all the fun I've had hiking. I'll sign up for two weeks next year."

"I may join you."

"That'd be great, Mother! One thing Preach didn't mention. They really feed you. Hearty and healthy. And the locals usually put out a spread at the end of the week. The Tennessee club gave us a pizza party."

"Leave it to you to bring food into the discussion."

"Guilty. And so are you. You didn't think twice today about that giant cheeseburger."

She cackled. "The famous New England calorie rush. By the time we get to the Whites we'll be throwing down five thousand a day."

"Six, if you're a growing boy. Like Soc or Preacher."

"I don't mind. Particularly if I can get calories from ice cream."

"Hey, did I tell you what I found in the outfitter's hiker box?"

"No, Preach. What?"

"An unopened jar of extra-crunchy peanut butter."

"You've been holding out on us!"

"It's in my pack at the lean-to. Anybody interested in a bedtime snack?"

Southern Bell chimed in. "Ah've got saltines."

Preacher added, "I also have a package of marshmallows."

Socrates jumped up. "Too much! I have some M&M's left over from my last batch of gorp. We can make saltine s'mores!"

Robert joined the enthusiasm. "Fire up the stove! Toast the marshmallows! Melt the chocolate! Somebody record this in the register. We'll be famous up and down the trail."

"Saltine s'mores! Ah can see it now. The new flavah from Ben and Jerry's."

—⁓—

"Mandy?"

"Dad! Where are you?"

"Salisbury, Connecticut. I get to Massachusetts tomorrow."

"Gosh, you're really moving."

"The states are flying by. I'm having fun, so I guess that's to be expected. How're you doing?"

"Oh, I'm okay. But there is one thing."

"The baby?"

"No, no! We're both great. I'm rounder by the day. And it's starting to kick. Have you called Rob?"

"I never can catch him. I leave messages but obviously don't get any feedback. Why?"

"Well, he's done it now. Blew out his knee a week ago. Playing volleyball in the base tournament."

"How bad?"

"Torn ACL. They scoped him the next day. He was on bed rest, except for therapy. Now they have him on light duty. He may have gone into work when you called."

"But I thought you said—"

"Relax. The only thing he can do is sit in front of the computer with his leg propped up. He won't be in the field for a while. Or skiing. When they told him that, he almost cried."

"That means he'll get serious about rehab. What's the long-term prognosis?"

"He should make a full recovery. The doc didn't see any loss of range of motion. Oh, and Jennifer's taking extra special care of him."

"Really? I bet he milks that for all it's worth."

"I'd love to hear her side of the story."

"I'll keep calling until I reach him. I can give him pointers on how to cope with a bad knee. Apparently he's coping fine with the relationship."

"Is your knee okay?"

"I never felt better in my life. I can do twenty miles any day I want to. I get aches and pains, but I just swallow some naproxen, and they go away. Like the pounds. I'm down to one-sixty."

"That's awful! If this baby gets hungrier, I could catch up with you. Are you sure you're getting enough to eat?"

"Mandy, I'm on the perfect diet. I only eat everything I want, supersized. Been doing that since Virginia. Soc and I will eat a pint of every Ben and Jerry's flavor before we finish."

"I hate you. I'm already sick of nonfat sherbet. But how is Socrates? He still getting along with that other guy?"

"Preacher? They've been in a truce for what seems like forever. We still have spirited discussions. But they aren't personal like they used to be. At least nobody takes them personally. When we get to Dalton, Massachusetts, Preacher'll take a few days off to go to one of his meetings."

"Hiking makes for strange bedfellows. What about the nurses?"

"They're fine. Mother Superior just performed a tickectomy."

"Ugh. On you?"

"No, on Bell. She's okay. We all learned about Lyme disease. I inspect my body every night to make sure I have no unwelcome guests. So far, so good. How's Steven?"

"Great. He interviews tomorrow with a dentist here in Jax. I told you he aced his exams. The word's getting around."

"I'm already calling him Dr. Worth. It would be good if you guys didn't have to pick up and move, particularly since you're great with child."

"Yeah. I like where I am and what I'm doing. I don't want to go job or house hunting. With a baby, it would be hard to uproot."

"That reminds me. I don't want to impose, but may I come for a short visit after the hike? Say early or mid-September? I'll earn my keep. Cut the grass. Fix dinner."

"We'd love to have you. But you cook? I don't think so."

"Mandy, I boil water with the best of them. I never fail to get succulent bubbles rising in the pot."

"Tell you what. You can take us out. I'll be so big I won't be able to stand close to the stove."

"Deal. You know something, I don't think I've ever been away from my family this long."

"You really miss her, don't you?"

"Every day, hon. I still catch myself saying, 'I need to ask Angie about this,' or 'I bet she'd like that.'"

"I know. Sometimes I have to stop myself from trying to call Mom."

"We were in this small town, Kent, a couple of days ago. I passed a florist's shop. Right in the window was an arrangement that was the twin to the one your mom did for your wedding. You know, the one on the table by the reception desk. Same white roses, same greenery."

"What did you do?"

"Well, I thought about going in and telling the owner off. I was pissed, because that was a unique creation. By my unique wife for a unique event in my unique daughter's life."

"I get the picture."

"But the flowers were seated in a really tacky bowl. Looked plastic. Maybe acrylic. Some dirt on the surface. Immediately it lost its allure. Angie put your arrangement in a tasteful cut-glass vase, remember?

Really set it off. So I still had all my uniques. The unkempt zealot didn't have to go in and freak the florist."

"When it came to flowers she had the touch. She asked me what I wanted for the reception. Like I was going to think of something better than what she had in mind. I pulled out my checkbook and tore out a blank one and gave it to her. She laughed. After the disagreements we had about other facets of the wedding, she really appreciated the symbolism."

"I'm glad to see you're hitting on them too."

"Hitting on what?"

"The memories. When I started the hike, it seemed like all I could bring back were things that made me sad. I had to force myself to remember the good times. Did I tell you about my alter egos?"

"No. Were you hearing voices?"

"Sort of. I had Grief on one shoulder and Memories on the other. They took turns talking. At first I tuned in to Grief all the time. But the longer I walked the more I listened to Memories. All the good things about her. About all four of us. Now when I think of her, it's almost always a warm feeling."

"You're right. I don't let those last months blot out the Mom I knew for the rest of my life."

"You think we're healing, Mandy?"

"Yeah, I guess so."

"So hearts are like knees. We tear them up, but they mend."

"But not without scars. And a memory, even a good one, is a poor substitute for the real thing."

"Amen to that. There's only one advantage to living with the memory."

"What's that?"

"The memory doesn't complain when I've been three or four days without a shower."

"It's good you can find consolation in the little things." She paused for emphasis. "The really, really small things."

"What I take comfort in is you. And Steven. And Rob. And in your baby. I feel better every time I talk to you. But I gotta go. I'll call you again in a few days. Do me a favor."

"What?"

"No volleyball, okay?"

"Absolutely no worry there. I love you, Dad."

"Love you, too. Bye."

Chapter 19

This is no social crisis, just another tricky day for you.
The Who

"That's one bad dude."
"Und dat shameless hussy! In der skimpy pants!"
"Hide the women and children!"
The two interlopers stopped in front of the rambling two-story house and stared at the quartet on the wrap-around porch. "These ain't friendly townfolk, Maybelle."
"More lak desert rats, Black Bart."
"Check the roof for snipers."
She glanced at the gables. "Nobody up theyah."
"Listen close. I'll cover the two varmints on the left. You watch them tarts on the right." He grasped his Lekis, with the tips pointing downward, and assumed the gunfighter pose.
The big man on the porch stood up and advanced toward the strangers. Bowlegged, he gripped his hiking poles and mirrored his adversary. "Black Bart? I've heard about you. They say you're fast." He sneered. "They say that about me, too."
Black Bart eyed him skeptically. "What's your name, boy?"
"They call me the Colorado Kid."
"The Colorado Kid. I've heered talk about you too." He flicked his mustache. "And that's all there is. Just talk."
The Kid smirked. "Exactly whut them six other smartasses said, before they was carted off to Boot Hill."

"Well, Kid, seven's not gonna be your lucky number." Bart tweaked his mustache again, and glowered. "Draw, you yellow-bellied coward!"

They faced each other across a few eternal seconds. With a flick of his wrists, the Kid jerked his poles parallel to the ground, squeezed the grips and shouted, "Bang! Bang!" Simultaneously Bart raised his Lekis and spit out a retort. The two stared impassively at each other.

Mother Superior glanced at Czechmate and Robert. They nodded with gravity. She pronounced sentence. "He beat you to the draw, Black Bart."

"No way!" Bart sputtered in disbelief. "I've been robbed!" He reached over to Maybelle and ripped away the red bandanna covering her braided bun. He wadded the hanky and threw it at Mother Superior. "Black Bart challenges the ruling on the field that he was outdrawn."

Mother Superior picked up the bandanna. She walked to her pack, delved into the top pocket, and pulled out her black pack cover. With a grandiose gesture, she stepped away from the other two "officials" and draped the cover over her head. In the semidarkness, she manipulated a phantom panel of knobs and switches. Mimicking the obligatory crowd reaction, Robert chanted a chorus of boos. Finally she emerged and walked purposefully to the center of the porch. She reached to her waist and turned on her audio.

"After further review, the ruling on the field stands. The Colorado Kid outdrew Black Bart. The latter has no time-outs remaining."

Bart's disbelief slowly morphed to racking pain. Staring at his belly button, he dropped his Lekis and clutched the imaginary hole where the bullet tore into his stomach. He fell to his knees by the curb. Emitting a hideous death rattle, he toppled face forward into the grass between the street and the sidewalk.

With a shriek, Maybelle rushed to his side. "Bart! Don't leave me, Bart!" When she could not revive him, she turned in anguish to the Colorado Kid. "Why? Why? Why did it have to end lak this?" She buried her forehead in Bart's back and wept.

The victor was unmoved. "Another notch for the Colorado Kid."

"Gripping. Truly gripping." A voice sounded behind the screen door. "But don't anybody quit your day job." The door opened and a diminutive lady backed out. In her late fifties, she carried a large tray laden with six metal goblets. Each contained a heaping chocolate sundae, replete with syrup, nuts, and a cherry crown. The four on the porch gasped. Southern Bell immediately terminated the role of the grieving Maybelle. "Ooh! Ice creayum. Chocklat with a cherry on top!" She left the mortal pile beneath her and ran to the porch. The sundae buzz miraculously revived the prostrate Socrates. He scrambled to join the others.

Robert shouted, "It's a miracle! Like Lazarus, Black Bart is raised from the dead!"

"These must be the two you told me about." The lady put the tray down on a white rattan end table. She stepped back as Czechmate and Preacher lunged for a goblet and spoon. "Welcome to Dalton."

Robert remembered his manners. "Paula. This is Southern Bell and Socrates. Guys, this is Paula, our hostess for the evening. She's graciously allowed us to camp in her backyard or sleep here on the porch. And use the outside faucet for water."

"We pitched our tent out back," Mother Superior said. "Why don't you guys join us?"

"Ice cream first." Socrates grabbed Paula's hand. "Thank you, ma'am. You're a lady and a scholar."

Southern Bell also shook her hand. "No, silly. She's an angel, plain and simple. She brought us this chocklat deelight. Paula, thank yew."

They plopped on the chairs and the swing. Some sat cross-legged on the planked floor. They quietly devoured the sundaes, and Paula retreated into her home. Socrates plucked the cherry out of his goblet. Holding the stem between his fingers, he wantonly licked away the chocolate syrup and bits of pecan clinging to its skin. "This has been a great two days. Starting at Upper Goose Pond."

Robert concurred. "That was a neat place."

"Thank the glacier that carved out that little piece of heaven."

Czechmate raised a loaded spoon. "To der glacier." They all toasted with a spoonful and ceremoniously swallowed the chocolate.

Socrates continued. "Upper Goose Pond. A cool swim after a hot day. Followed by a moonlight ride in a canoe with my sweetie." He reached over and wiped a fleck of chocolate from Southern Bell's cheek. He sucked it off his finger.

Southern Bell took a swat at him. "Yew greedy thief! Whut's on mah face is mine, not yowers!"

"Would you like to lick the syrup in my beard?"

She did not look up from her dish. "Yew slob. Clean yower own chin."

Robert resurrected the conversation. "And what about that caretaker at the pond?"

"That's the best three dollars I ever spent." Mother Superior licked the spoon twice, so as not to miss her final morsel of chocolate. "The pond and the cabin alone were worth the money. But I couldn't believe it when he pulled out the watermelon last night."

"Und der pancakes this morning. He vas a good cook. I vas so full of energy I could have hiked a tirty today."

"Yeah," Socrates reiterated. "Great breakfast. And then twenty miles of mellow trail to Dalton. Took us what, eight hours? We weren't even trying hard."

"Don't forgit mah friend. The 'Cookie Lady!'"

"Another cherub in the host of angels."

About lunchtime, Preacher, Robert, and the nurses had reached a highway. Off the road to the right they spotted a farmhouse. The guidebook indicated the owners let hikers get water from a spigot on the side of the house. They trooped in to fill up their bottles and bladders. As they splashed the sweat from their faces, the mistress of the house appeared at the door with a plate of freshly baked chocolate chip cookies. The aroma was mesmerizing. Soon after, Socrates and Southern Bell charged in with noses high, like bears hot on the scent. After making short work of the cookies, they loitered in the shade of the house, ate lunch, and watched the butterflies frolic in the "Cookie Lady's" flower garden. Fed and rested, they resumed their easy walk into Dalton.

Socrates continued. "And just when I think we've had all the magic there is, here we sit on Paula's porch eating chocolate sundaes. So much for the journey of privation through the great north woods. Hell, I'll get gunned down in cold blood every day if it ends up like this."

Robert chimed in. "Nothing for us but kindness and hospitality. These Massachusetts folk took out all their hostility on the British, at Lexington and Concord."

"They really have spoiled us." Southern Bell countered. "I'm downright pampahed."

"I'd like to pamper myself with a bath and clean clothes. Didya hear what Paula said about the Dalton laundry?"

"Where is it, Preach?"

"Down Depot Street and to the right. A half mile or so. The neat thing is the lady at the laundry'll give us a clean towel. While we wait for our stuff to get done, we can wash up at the lavatory in the rest rooms."

"Soap, hot water, towel. Almost as good as a shower."

"Let's get it done," Robert added. He bent toward his armpit and made a loud sniffing noise. "Surprise, surprise. I'm gamy."

"*Ja*, so am I. I really vant to vash my hair." She touched her fingers to her scalp. "Iss matted like a dog."

Preacher rubbed the top of his scalp. "Paula says there's a barbershop on the way. Don't know about you guys, but I want to cut most of this off. Anything to keep cool."

Robert grasped the hair below his temple and pulled it down between his fingers. The ends hung well over his ear. "I'll join you. But I won't get skinned the way you do."

Southern Bell reached for Socrates's mane. "Hon, could Ah persuade yew to trim some of this bramble bush?"

"Will you make it worth my while?"

"Yew just might git lucky, boy!"

"All right!" Socrates turned to Robert. "Delilah just made Samson an offer he can't refuse."

"Let me change thayat. Ah should have said with a haircut *and* a showah."

"Maybe we all get lucky," Robert added. "On the way back from the laundry somebody might invite us in off the street for a home-cooked dinner."

"Thass probly too much magic to expect. Y'all pass me the spoons and the goblets. Ah'll take the tray in to Paula. Heaven knows that angel shouldn't hafta clean up aftah us."

―⁂―

The long July day receded into twilight. A faint breeze fought vainly to dissipate the sapping humidity. Robert and Preacher, each clutching a bundle of laundry, ambled back to Paula's through deepening shadows. Robert held a freshly washed Coolmax up to his nostrils. Despite the soaking in detergent, the polyester, impregnated with months of perspiration, emitted a stale odor. The fragrant suds were no match for its redolence. He yearned for the day when he could wear a cotton shirt that would not give off the telltale "poly-pew" bouquet.

He ran his fingers through his scrubbed, shorn hair. "Preach, we smell about as good as we're going to. Pity it will last for just one day."

"Yeah, clean is good. But not as good as the ham and potatoes." Preacher dwelled fondly on their dinner in a Dalton restaurant. "And the apple pie."

"A la mode at that. Hey, I almost forgot. You'll be eating well the next few days, won't you? No more ramen. Where is it you're going?"

"Brattleboro. I meet the coordinator tomorrow afternoon. The icebreaker and initial orientation are tomorrow evening with Senator Fairchild. Then two days of training."

"Three days off the trail? I bet you gain at least five pounds."

Preacher patted his stomach. "If I don't, it won't be for not trying."

The two walked over a bridge, alongside a spillway by an old mill. They paused in silence to watch the Housatonic churn downstream. Robert noted another milestone. Tomorrow the Fab Five would leave the river, an on-again, off-again companion throughout Connecticut and Massachusetts. They would hike away from Preacher also.

When Preacher asked to join them in Virginia, Robert had acquiesced with considerable reluctance. Realistically Preacher could not hike in harmony with the five. But he had reined in his compulsion to blurt out what was on his mind. Socrates and Mother Superior had also chosen not to ignite the fires of debate. They walked on eggshells at the beginning, but over the span of five hundred miles, a grudging respect arose among them. A lasting friendship was out of the question, but each learned to honor the other's quest to be a thru-hiker. That was the sacred common denominator, not subject to question or challenge, which kept them together. This circumscribed camaraderie, tempered by more than a month of sweat and strain toward a shared goal, had carried them to this point.

They turned onto Depot Street and walked to Paula's house. Leaving Preacher stuck in Robert's mind. It would not be easy to overcome a three-day head start, particularly in the rugged landscapes of Vermont, New Hampshire, and Maine. Unless there was an unforeseen injury or equipment problem to slow them down, Preacher would never overtake them. Robert searched for the right way to frame a goodbye. Nothing seemed appropriate, except that he should not make it a big deal. It was better to exchange the formulaic "seeya up the trail" in the morning and leave it at that.

They stepped onto the porch in silence. Robert tossed his laundry onto the Thermarest and sank into one of the rattan chairs. Preacher parked on the swing. He pressed his feet into the floor to preempt its reciprocating motion and to silence the squeak in the links of the chain. The evening gloom descended with a heavy stillness, broken only by the chirping of crickets and the occasional sound and light of a vehicle on Depot Street. Not wishing to talk, Robert leaned back in the chair and closed his eyes, rubbing them gently with the tips of his index fingers. Lost in thoughtlessness, he was aware of nothing but the harmonious cricket chorale.

Another noise penetrated his consciousness. Faint and intermittent, it had a pleasant modulation, like the cooing of a dove. It was strange to hear a bird call this late in the evening. By this time they had usually vacated the stage and left performing to the insects. The sound repeated, with more intensity. It wasn't a dove or any birdcall. The swell brought forth an epiphanous recognition. He opened his eyes to confirm he wasn't dreaming. The music was "Angie's serenade," the rising, rhythmic, pleasurable moan of a woman nearing orgasm.

He glanced at Preacher. His expression revealed nothing. Perhaps he did not hear the sound. That was unlikely, given its repetition and the stillness of the evening. Perhaps he didn't recognize it. Preacher never talked about girlfriends or boasted about conquests. Robert surmised he could have led a sheltered youth, what with his early commitment and calling. But he could just as easily be a ladies' man. He was nice looking, enough to be called a "hunk." With frequent contacts with friends and students, and the daily onslaught of mass media, he *had* to know what was happening in the backyard.

Robert recalled the scene between Socrates and Southern Bell at the barbershop. Socrates jumped on the idea of "getting lucky." He was first in the barber chair and asked for both a haircut and a trimmed beard. Afterward, Southern Bell checked him out. Both Robert and Preacher had witnessed her enthusiastic approval of the tonsorial outcome. She stroked his cheek and chin and planted a big kiss on Socrates's lips, an inviting target no longer hidden beneath the drooping tendrils of an untrimmed mustache. As they walked away, she kissed him again and caressed the nape of his neck, visible for the first time in weeks. It was a prologue to the main event now taking place inside the tent in the backyard.

Robert felt uncomfortable. They had passively invaded Socrates and Southern Bell's privacy. He had never been a voyeur, and he didn't want to be an eavesdropper either. He debated saying anything to Preacher, whose face betrayed neither condemnation nor approval of "the sound."

The moan occurred again, slightly muffled. Was she trying to suppress her pleasure? It was impossible to sit there any longer and pretend nothing was happening. And Preacher was staring at him.

Robert spoke in a hushed tone. "Sounds like Soc's getting lucky."

There was no reply.

"Correction. Bell's getting lucky."

"Yeah." Preacher's response was a whisper. Robert could not tell if he was upset, envious, or simply indifferent.

"It's kinda weird, sitting here. Think we should leave?"

"Good idea."

Before they could move, another series of muffled moans ascended. The pitch was higher, the chorus more rapid. Wistfully recalling "the serenade," Robert recognized the final throes. The peals of pleasure exploded in a climactic crescendo, with an unmistakably European flourish. *"Ja! Ja! Ja! Ja! Ja!"*

Robert endured several moments of conflict before breaking the bonds of his erroneous assumptions. He forced himself to accept the identity of the lovers in the backyard. He had seen them enter their tent many times, but when they closed the rainfly, they were zipped out of his senses. Before tonight, no explicit indicators had emanated from the nylon citadel.

Sometimes he had imagined what might be taking place inside, but it was a half-baked fantasy. Now reality had been piped to his unsuspecting ears, and it totally invalidated his inadequate imagination. The new serenade was graphically and sensuously real, real as any song Angie had ever sung, and more real than his night with Czechmate in Virginia.

A car drove by on the street, illuminating Preacher on the swing. His face was flushed and agitated. He stood up, and the links in the chain squeaked loudly.

"You guys are shit! I should have known better than to do this!"

"Preach, we should have left when we first heard them. They have a right to privacy."

"They have rights? What about me? Don't I have rights?"

"Preacher—"

"I have the right not to listen to that."

"It's unfortunate this happened. No one meant for—"

"I'm not so sure. You knew this was my last day. This is your idea of a sendoff?"

"Preach, get real. This wasn't a setup. Six people in close proximity, for weeks on end. Sooner or later something happens. It should have been private, but it wasn't. Leave it at that."

"I don't intend to leave it. That's why I'm going to Vermont. To make sure God-fearing people won't have to put up with this. I'm supposed to share an experience with them that explains why I'm there. Now I have something for show and tell."

"Are you serious?"

"You expect me not to talk about this? You flaunted it right in front of me! I guarantee those volunteers will be motivated. We'll spread the message across the whole state of Vermont. We'll get that constitutional amendment!"

Another car passed. Preacher's face was beet red. Robert hoped his anger was subsiding, but Preacher's tortured expression indicated the heat was still rising.

A rumpled Mother Superior appeared in the deep shadow at the corner of the porch. "Can you guys keep the noise down? Paula went to sleep early. She gets up early to go to work."

"You're asking *us* to keep the noise down?"

Her radar acquired his disapprobation. "What are you getting at, Preacher?"

"You know damn good and well what I mean!"

A car drove by slowly. The glow from the headlights illuminated their faces. Preacher's eyes had narrowed to slits, like the edges of a dagger.

"What? What?"

Robert ended the standoff. "We got back from dinner a few minutes ago. We were sitting on the porch while you ... well, let's just say we heard you and Czechmate."

She flashed a Medusan scowl. "You nosy little bastards!"

"Mother, I'm sorry. You're entitled to your privacy. When we realized what was going on, we started to leave. But it was too late."

"How convenient. You hung around and satisfied the ultimate male fantasy. Listened to two lesbians get it on."

"Gimme a break, will ya? It wasn't like that at all. I thought it was Soc and Bell. Until I recognized Czechmate's cry, uh, at the end."

"Was it good for you, Snakes? As good as Virginia?"

"That's not fair. This whole thing was an unfortunate coincidence. Don't try to read intent into what happened. We were just at the wrong place at the wrong time."

"You insufferable bitch!" The magma rising from Preacher's molten core spewed out in a pyroclastic shower. "You think I enjoyed hearing you? Your perversion makes me sick!"

Mother Superior shot back. "You're saying if it was Soc and Bell, everything would have been okay? It wasn't the sex that's wrong, but who was having it? I didn't see a sign in the back yard saying 'Sex is okay, as long as you're straight.'"

"You're disgusting! Sex is a union between a man and a woman, undertaken in marriage, ordained by God, with the ultimate goal of procreating the species. You and Czechmate do none of that. What you do is unnatural. It debases marriage. No way does it lead to procreation. And I resent having to listen to it!"

"Go ahead, Preacher. Put marriage on a pedestal. Where all you heteros can bow down and worship it. There's just one little catch. Jesus said, 'What God has joined together, let no one separate.' The real perversion is that half your sacred marriages end in divorce. That one statistic smashes your pedestal into a million pieces."

He tried to reply, but she continued. "And by the way, you're right. You won't see me and Czechmate procreating. You won't see us bringing kids into the world and then splitting up. You won't see us shunting those kids back and forth from one house to another, subjecting them to stress, doubt, isolation, and abuse. I'll tell you what's sick, Preacher. Your goddamn hypocrisy and your goddamn double standard!"

She was no more than three feet from Preacher's face. His muscles twitched, as if ready to spring. Alarmed at their intensity, Robert stepped between them. He pushed Mother Superior back a step. Her resistance let him know that she could take care of herself in a fight. He turned and confronted Preacher's muscular body. He put a hand on each of the powerful shoulders and gave him a gentle nudge. Preacher refused to budge.

"Ease off, Preach. We don't need a fight."

A few seconds of agonizing tension passed. Preacher relaxed and stepped back. He wiped the beads of perspiration from his forehead. He spoke, almost in his normal voice. "Soc said we could talk about 'haters of God' in Massachusetts. I want to thank him for that."

"Preach, we all hate God," Robert interjected. "It's the human condition. We don't like that He's in charge."

"We all sin, yes. But some willfully reject the natural order He established at the beginning of creation. They reject the two who become one flesh. Those are the real 'haters of God.' That's you, Mother. I mean, just look at your trail name. Mother. You're mocking Him. You know damn good and well you'll never be a mother. You and Czechmate are haters of God."

Mother Superior steeled herself with years of military discipline. "Preacher, you have so much hate inside that you can't see the real God, the One you say I hate so much. Because you don't understand. You don't understand He has so much love He can overcome my hate, and even yours, if we let Him."

A car drove by on the street. She waited for it to pass. "I don't want to talk to you anymore. It's time for you to go. This experiment didn't work. Go to Vermont. Go to your conference. Do whatever the hell you want. But leave me and my friends alone."

"What makes you think I'd want to stay?" He moved to his gear on the floor of the porch. He opened the valve of his Thermarest and deflated it. He stuffed it and his sleeping bag into his pack. Randomly he tossed his clothes and the rest of his gear into the maw. He snapped the pack shut and lifted it onto his back. Without glancing over his shoulder, he walked silently off the porch, across the yard, and down the street.

He vanished into the darkness. Another car passed. Its headlights revealed an empty sidewalk. Mother Superior delivered her epilogue. "Good riddance."

Robert tried to gauge her emotions. "Mother, are we all right here?"

"Yeah, now that he's gone."

"No, I mean you and me. I wasn't trying to spy on you. Not playing out any fantasy …"

"You didn't deserve that. I said some things in the heat of the moment. You had a right to be on the porch. We must have been louder than usual."

"You weren't that loud. At least not at first. But at the end ... Like I tried to explain to Preacher, shit happens."

She chuckled. "It sure hit the fan tonight, didn't it?"

With relief, Robert joined her in laughter. "Look, if you guys want to be alone, give me a sign or something. I'll pitch my tent over the next ridge. This damn trail's over two thousand miles long. We ought to be able to find enough space."

"Tell you what, Snakes. If I want you to make yourself scarce, I'll give you a military salute. You salute back, so I know you understand."

"Got it." The talk of future arrangements put Robert at ease. "And would you wait at least ten minutes after I leave before you get it on? I'm a horny old man. Out here all alone. Don't know if I could handle that sweet melody again."

Mother Superior jabbed him affectionately. "The nightingale really warbled tonight."

"My favorite tune."

She prodded his ribs again with a soft fist. "Snakes, you're a nice guy. More than I expected from any straight man. Angie was lucky to have you."

"Thanks. You've paid me the ultimate compliment." He put his arm on her shoulder and gave her a long squeeze. "But it really was the other way 'round."

They stood on the porch for a while. Mother Superior broke the silence. "Where the hell are Bell and Soc?"

"It's unlike them to be out this late. They must have found a party."

"We'll have to let them in on what happened."

"It can wait until morning."

"What if they come back and see Preacher's gone?"

"I bet they come back and walk right by the porch to their tent. Without noticing a damn thing. When I saw them last, the vibes were strong. They'll have one thing on their minds. Another nightingale will sing in the backyard tonight."

"For your sake, I hope the Alabama sonata is not as loud."

"You never can tell what a few beers might do. But if they notice, I'll just tell 'em he left early for his training. Tomorrow we'll fill them in on the details."

"Sounds like a plan. I'm turning in. Good night." She patted him on the shoulder and flopped across the porch to the corner of the house.

"Mother." He stopped her before she disappeared into the backyard. "I didn't see a salute. So it's okay for me to sleep here tonight?"

"Snakes, since you asked for it, I'll give you the universal salute." She held up her right fist with the middle finger fully extended.

He returned the gesture. "Good night, Mother. And love to you, too."

Chapter 20

*It's kind of a special feeling, when you're out on the sea alone,
Staring at the full moon, like a lover.*
Little River Band

They reached the hut at Lonesome Lake in midafternoon. One of several rustic inns in the White Mountains, it offered dinner and breakfast and dormitory-style sleeping on bunks with mattresses. Its guests hiked in on rugged trails like the AT to enjoy these comforts, set in the midst of the starkly beautiful New Hampshire landscape.

The hosts placed leftover pastries on a table in the dining room and made them available to all comers for a nominal fee. Thru-hikers made a point to graze for these delicacies. The five were rewarded with a sheet of tasty apple strudel, only slightly stale from hours in the mountain air. They devoured the pastry and washed it down with lemonade.

Socrates struck up a "Who do you know?" with Heather, a member of "The Croo," the students who staffed the hut during the summer. She had a cousin at Duke with whom he had shared a biology class. Their dialogue moved to the merits of eastern colleges and then to New England trees and wildflowers. The other four found the strudel more interesting, and the entire sheet soon disappeared.

Robert spoke half-heartedly. "I guess we should continue up the trail and find a campsite."

Heather spoke up. "Do you guys know about 'work for stay'?"

"Whut's thayat?"

"We let two hikers have free room and board. In exchange, they help clean up after dinner and breakfast."

"Ooh, thayat sounds reayull inviting."

"Sugar, I could go for that."

Robert took the hint. "Ladies, you wouldn't have to twist my arm to get me to stay here."

"*Ja*. I like der view. Und a soft bed."

"After scrambling over Moosilauke and the Kinsmans, I could be pampered for one night. Let's splurge!" Mother Superior looked at Heather. "Do you have three vacancies?"

"I think so."

"You take plastic?"

"All kinds. Mastercard, Visa, Amex, Discover."

"We three will register, and those two can do 'work for stay.'"

Socrates hugged Mother Superior. "Thank you."

"Thayat's the nicest thang you've evah done fer me. Except pullin' that tick off my laig."

After a delicious, hearty dinner, Robert and the nurses ambled to the lake and waited for Socrates and Southern Bell to finish their chores.

The moon dominated the charcoal sky, relegating the overmatched stars to distant insignificance. Its only competition was its own image, reflected in the placid pool of Lonesome Lake. Impaled by the twin shafts of light, Robert and the nurses sat motionless on large, flat boulders at the water's edge. Around the lake, the warm glow bathed the silhouettes of the northern forest and cast conical shadows onto the unrippled pond. On the horizon a stark massif rose into the heavens, a blackened wainscot framed against the umbral wall of sky.

"Vat iss dat big mountain?"

"Franconia Ridge, sweetie. We climb it tomorrow."

"Ooh." Czechmate pondered the daunting implications. "I should sleep vell tonight, *ja*?"

"You bet. It's a bear."

"This moon is something else." Robert marveled at the imposing globe, illuminating every cranny of the forest. "I've never seen it so bright."

"What a purty sight!" Behind them, Southern Bell unleashed War Eagle, who made a beeline to the intriguing aromas of the lake bank. Socrates kneeled and picked up a smooth pebble. He threw it underhanded over the still water. It skipped twice before sinking.

"You guys finish?"

"The dishes are clean. The tables are wiped," Socrates said. "This was a sweet deal. So much food, so little work."

"The perfect job for you."

"Ackchooly, we finished twenty minutes ago. Socks stayed to eat fower mowah desserts."

"Chance calories." Socrates rubbed his stomach. "Best kind of magic."

"I'm envious," Robert replied. "I'll have to try work-for-stay on up the trail. Maybe at Lakes of the Clouds. Y'all come sit on this rock."

Socrates measured Franconia Ridge, looming in the moonlight. "Look at that damn thing!" He skipped another pebble across the water. "Has to be tougher than South Kinsman."

"The Whites jus' keep gettin' bettah and bettah."

"It will kick our sweet arses. But if the weather holds, the view will be worth it." He sat down between Southern Bell and Mother Superior.

"Think about it," Mother Superior mused. "When we started in Georgia four months ago, didja seriously believe that one day we'd be standing here in the Whites? The biggest, baddest mountains on the whole AT?"

"Never a doubt, Mother. We just had to do it. And we have."

"Are you the Nike spokesman?"

"Just do it, baby! When we get through the Whites, there's only one more state. Maine."

"You sound like Preacher," Robert cautioned.

"I resent that! Whaddaya mean?"

"Taking the AT for granted, like he did. 'When we get through the Whites.' Man, they're the hardest part of the whole damn trail. You should assume nothing."

"After four months of hiking, I'm reasonably confident of my abilities."

"Take it one day at a time. I made a vow in Georgia never to say the K word until I was far into Maine."

"Vat you mean, der K vord?"

"Mount Katahdin. Right, Snakes?"

"Right, Mother. Look at that humongous ridge. We're gonna pay big-time getting up Franconia. No sense thinking any further ahead than you can see. My goal is Mount Lafayette. The high point. Right up there."

"One day at a time, huh? You have no sense of expectation."

"Hell, how can you bring up Maine with that thing over there staring us in the face? When we get to Lafayette, then I'll think about what's next. Mount Garfield. South Twin. And something called Mount Washington. Maine? I don't think so."

Socrates humored him. "Okay, okay. I get it. Caution is good."

"I prefer to call it respect. I don't want these mountains thinking I'm dissing 'em because my mind's on some summit up in Maine."

"Like these rock piles know what you're thinking."

"They're alive. And you know it."

"They're mountains, Snaky. Not humans."

"If all they are to you are rock piles, then why take six months out of your life to hike over them?"

"Hey, I don't get personal with each mountain, like you. But that doesn't mean I don't appreciate them. I'm just more scientific about it."

"Remembah whut Julia Roberts said in *Pretty Woman*?"

"Bell, we're holding our breath until you tell us."

"When Richard Gere furst picked her up, before they fell in love, she wouldn't kiss him on the lips. She said for a hookah that wuz too personal."

"Dammit! I don't like where this is going."

"Whattcha mean, sugah?"

"Pardon the expression, but this prostitute standard really sucks. According to Julia, and to you, when Snaky climbs a mountain, he can give it a kiss. It's personal. What about me?"

"Well, yew're obviously not in a serious relashunship."

"You're insinuating that I give it a blow job!"

Mother Superior hooted. "The perfect mountaintop experience!"

"Yew always twist mah words around. But since yew're such a little shiyut, I'll leave them just the way yew twisted them."

"Forget the whole damn thing. I didn't like the movie anyway."

"Why not?"

"Because in the real world, CEOs don't fall in love with whores."

"Whatevah happened to romance?"

"It's overrated."

"I think yew killed it."

"Snakes, back to the K word. I know you don't tempt fate by talking about Katahdin, but you have to give some thought to the end game. I mean, we're not the lost tribes of Israel, wandering for forty years. Six months, max. We're down to the last weeks. You have to think about what happens after K."

"Oh, I do, Mother. All the time. I have plans."

"What are they?"

"The first three months off the trail I'm booked. For a birth and a wedding."

"Hold on!" Mother Superior demanded. "We know about the grandchild. What's this wedding stuff?"

"Rob and Jennifer are engaged."

"Dat's goot! You vill haf a nurse in your family."

"Yes, great news," Mother Superior continued. "When did you find out?"

"A few days ago. Phone call back in Glencliff."

"What took you so long to share the news with your good friends?"

"No reason." Robert felt sheepish. "Just waiting for the right time. And the right place." He pointed skyward for justification. "Nothing like a full moon as a stage for a momentous pronouncement."

"When's the wedding?"

"Late December. They want to give Mandy some time to recover. It'll be an extended trip for her and the baby. At least that's the rationale for public consumption."

"What's that supposed to mean?"

"I think Rob has ulterior motives. He's waiting for his knee to heal. And for good snowpack in Canada. The honeymoon's at Whistler."

"A schemer. Just like his Dad. Where's the wedding?"

"Jennifer's from Seattle. It's in her parents' church."

"Are we invited?"

"Mother, I'm sure Jennifer would love to meet all the nurses from Rob's side of the family."

"Whut about me?"

"And also the veterinarians."

"Aren't you leaving someone out?"

"Sorry, Soc. They specifically said 'no Dookies.'"

"This marriage is doomed."

Mother Superior again steered the conversation. "The birth and the wedding are milestones. But near-term. What I meant to ask was what will you do in the long run?"

"You mean with the rest of my life?"

"At your age that's not a long time," Socrates added. "You need a plan."

"Socks, yew're just awful!"

"It's okay, Bell. I'm immune to insults." Robert eyed Socrates. "Since your life is so boring, you can live vicariously through mine. For starters, I've decided to sell my house."

"You're full of it tonight. That is, the momentous pronouncement."

"It's too big for me. Angie and I had even talked about downsizing before she died. The lasting impression from this hike is that I ought to simplify. If I can live for six months with what I carry on my back, I don't need to surround myself with things. The kids can choose what furniture and stuff they want. After they pick it over, I'll sell the rest. The mother of all garage sales. I'll keep a few items that give me the best memories of Angie, but the rest goes."

"Where'll you live?"

"There are lots of trails out here. I may keep on hiking."

"Get serious, Snakes. You can't be homeless. You have to have a base." Mother Superior continued. "Put it this way. The keepsakes that remind you of Angie. Where will they be?"

"I'm thinking a small place near Asheville. It's close to the AT and other places where I like to hike."

"Snaky, with your checkered background, we may not let you into North Carolina."

"Hey, I would immediately improve the Tarheel gene pool."

"Shit, the Teletubbies and the psychopaths could do that. Don't damn yourself with faint praise."

"Dukehole, I was talking about the state, not the university."

"To live in North Carolina, you have to be approved. By a graduate from a fine Durham institution."

"You forget. I'm a graduate of a fine Carolina institution."

"For that reason we'll probably let you in. On a provisional basis."

"What?"

"You become a Cameron crazy."

"No way. I'll live in Tennessee first. Or maybe Virginia."

"We'd be delighted to have yew in Alabamah."

"Thanks, Bell, but there aren't enough mountains down there."

"We hayuv a lot of friendly people. Plenty of the female perswayshun."

"You still trying to fix me up?"

"Wayull, we vets get calls all the time to mate bulls and cows. Stalyuns and mares. Sometimes Ah forget and practice on people, too."

"Watch out, Snaky. Before you know it she'll have you come in a cup."

"I don't inseminate on demand."

"But yew're such a nice catch. Smart. Handsome. Fit. Ah wonder, will yew evah get married again?"

"Thanks for the compliment. But no. I've had my marriage. It can't be duplicated. There won't be another."

"Whut about girlfreeyunds?"

"I said no more marriages. I didn't say I was going into the priesthood. I like women too much to swear off your company."

"Horny to the end."

"What can I say, Soc? It's glands." Robert stretched his arms over his head. "Hey, we're talking entirely too much about me. Let's look at somebody else. Bell, what are your plans after the trail?"

"Vet'rinary school. At Auburn."

"We know. But has the AT changed how you feel about your future?"

"Yew know, it hayas. Ah always thought Ah might specialize in farm animals. Horses and cows, as opposed to pets. But Ah hayad second thoughts. The largeah animals scared me. Ah wasn't sure Ah could handle 'em."

"You never impressed me as a 'fraidy cat."

"Thass my point. I've changed. We've seen so many bayahs ..."

"How many is it now, love?"

"Eight. No new ones since New Jersey." She returned to Robert. "They taught me how to respect an animal without fearin' it."

"And don't forget the moose we saw. Near Killington."

"One moose and so many bayahs and deer. Ah'm used to these biggah animals now. Ah'm ready to doctah mares. And cows."

"And Socrates." Robert smirked. "He's a large mammal."

"Oh, he's easy. Just an injecshun for distempah every now and then."

"Distemper? Hey, I never ate your panties like that deer," Socrates said.

"You wanted to," Mother Superior retorted. "But you knew she'd chase you into the next county."

"You guys are determined to make me an oral sex freak. For the record, I get salt from peanuts. I don't get off on polyester and lycra."

"Bell, did you learn anything else out here?"

"It's important to undahstand how and why animals act lak they do. And if Ah do undahstand, they'll reciprocate. Animals know when yew want to help them."

"You do have a good stall-side manner."

"Why thank yew, Snaky! Yew know, Ah've discovered one more thing."

"What's that?"

"Ah just enjoy the outdoors so much. Ah could nevah work inside. If Ah wuz a pet vet, Ah'd wind up stuck in an office somewheyah. Thass not for me. Ah need to be out in the fields. And in the barns." She patted War Eagle on the snout. "Nothing personal, boy. I'll always take care of yew." She stroked her dog for several moments. "Is that enuf of my life story?"

"Bell, it sounds like a plan." Robert looked at Socrates. "What about you? You were eager to delve into my future. Let's talk about yours."

"I'm gonna beg off this game."

"Bell and I shared our secrets. Why don't you?"

"I don't have secrets. I have riddles."

"You still don't know?"

"In a word, no. All through college I figured that one day my dream job would crystallize. Then during the months out here, I was sure it would come to me. But not yet."

"I see you as the world's next great microbiologist."

"So do my parents. They want me in graduate school. Already set the drachmas aside. I haven't sent in any applications, and they're pissed. I told them I need time. To make sure I won't be wasting their money."

"What are you doing this fall?"

"There's a job waiting, whenever I want it. Down in Florida, at a botanical garden. A classmate from Duke's been working there since he graduated. They can always use people with my background."

"So from magnolias to bromeliads?"

"I could learn about grafting, cross-pollination. Stuff like that."

"When do you start?"

"Whoa! That's just it. I'm not sure that's what I want to do. I've thought about the Southwest, out in the desert. They have different plant communities, totally unlike anything back east. Saguaro cactus. *Palo verde*."

"Sounds like you have the wanderlust."

"You stole my thunder."

"How's that?"

"When you said you might keep on hiking. A great way to spend the next few years. I'm ready to do the Pacific Crest Trail. Want to join me next spring in Southern California?"

"My knees need at least a year before I go long again. Besides, I start on-the-job training as a grandfather."

"Ah told him to come to Alabamah. Ah'd put him up and everything. Git 'im enrolled at Auburn. But he's like yew, Snaky. Turned his nose up at mah proposal. He thinks he's too good for mah little cow college."

"I never said that."

"Ah can tell from yower body language. Yew squirm ev'ry time I bring it up."

"It's the mosquito bites. They really itch." He bent over and slapped the back of his calf. "Something's nibbling at me right now."

"Maybe it's yore conscience."

The resplendent moon once again asserted its grip on their consciousness. The beams bounced off the sheer face of Franconia Ridge and also into the pool in front of them, lighting the challenge of tomorrow. On the left horizon, a blinking light on a distant aircraft momentarily spoiled the natural panorama. They watched until the blackness swallowed up the intruder.

"Snaky, you're right not to think too far ahead."

"How so?"

"You get caught up in the future, and you'll miss what's happening right now. How many people are sitting inside tonight, worrying about mortgages? Or life insurance, or 401k's? They don't even know this moon is out here."

"Two years ago I was one of those people. But I'll never take the moon for granted again. I'll never drive by a lake like this without stopping. I'm scared I'd miss something."

"Exactly. We live in the present on the AT. It's great. I want to keep doing this. I worry about being at school somewhere. Tucked away in some lab, looking at cross-sections of vascular systems or rhizomes. I might miss an eclipse. Or the aurora borealis. Or an unknown comet waiting to be discovered."

"Just what the world needs," Mother Superior snorted. "The comet Socrates."

"Like Halley's comet, it vould come efery sefenty-six yeers."

"No. Trust me." Southern Bell laughed. "It would come a lot more often that thayat."

"Thanks for the testimonial. I'm guessing at least twice a day."

"You're setting yourself up for cosmic flameout," Mother Superior countered. "You can't shoot your whole wad now without any thoughts of tomorrow. The trick is to learn how to live in the present and live for the future. Both at the same time."

"And how do you do that?"

"It's not easy. I have the opposite problem. I spend too much time worrying about what might happen."

"It's your army training. Be prepared for anything."

"Maybe. But I miss out on a lot of great things."

"Dat's right. I had to push you to come on dis hike."

"That's true. My life was out of balance. I should have taken a sabbatical years ago. I was married to my job. I guarantee I won't wait so long before the next one."

"Three yeers. You promised. Ven my contract is up."

"Sounds like you guys have plans."

"Ve do. Ve vill join MSF."

"What's that?"

"*Medicins sans frontieres.*"

"Czechmate, I only had two years of French in high school."

Mother Superior interceded. "You know it as 'Doctors Without Borders.'"

"Right! They go all over the world to treat poor people."

"*Ja.* Dey help fictims of var, epidemics, disasters. Any area that's medically underserfed."

"Like where?"

"They'fe been in Rvanda. The Sudan. Und Afghanistan."

"It was started by a group of doctors from France thirty years ago. Today it's international. Twenty-five hundred doctors, nurses, and administrators in eighty countries. When her contract's up at St. Catherine's, Czechmate wants to sign on for a few years. Made me think of how much I enjoyed being overseas with the army. We could really help these indigenous populations."

"You going back to the desert?"

"Probably not. But Snakes, this group's like the army. They really have the logistics down. You remember the prepo sets?"

"Yeah. Our unit at Fort Hood had tanks waiting for us in Germany."

"Let's say there's a typhoon somewhere. They have field hospitals already packed up and ready for shipment. Loaded with weeks of medicine, vaccines, dressings. Water treatment equipment. The works. They fly the stuff to the disaster area. The medical personnel meet it on site. They uncase it and they're operating within a day or so."

"Where would you guys go?"

"It vould depend on the need. I am thinking somevere in Africa. Dere iss a chronic shortage of medical care in many countries. Und der AIDS epidemic is joost awful. Millions are dying, und dey leafe small children as orphans."

"From what I hear there's no shortage of bad guys. Rival factions starving each other. Withholding medicine."

"*Ja*. Dat's true."

"You guys need to be careful."

"Dat iss vy I vant Mother dere with me. She konn kick ass!"

"Hon, we're supposed to treat the ravages of war, not add to them."

"You heard about Rvanda? 1994? Dere vas genocide. Hundreds of thousands of people killed. Thousands of women raped. Joost because dey belonged to a different tribe."

"Not a great day for the United States. We stood by and let it happen."

"All the European countries did nothing, too. It vas terrible. But MSF vent dere und has been dere ever since. Surgery, rehabilitation. Improved sanitation und nutrition. Efen counseling for the rape victims." She paused for a moment. "I vould like to be a part of dat."

Robert glanced at Mother Superior. Her expression revealed nothing. He looked back to Czechmate. "Matey, when it comes to plans, you and Mother are at the top of the list. MSF will be a fine effort."

"I haf received much from many good people. Vonce I learn to be a better nurse, it is time to give back."

"Not trying to talk you out of Doctors Without Borders, but do you ever plan to return to Europe?"

"I might vork in Germany. Perhaps in München, vere my aunt lived. But I vill never return to Czech Republic."

He moved on quickly. "Do you want to be a US citizen?"

"*Ja.* I vill do dat before I join MSF."

"Since you're coming to Rob's wedding, can we come to your citizenship ceremony?"

"I will reserfe four seats on the front row."

"Goodie. Can Ah bring War Eagle?"

"Of course. I vill tell the judge he iss there to, how you say, vouchbark for me."

"Wheyah did he go?" The Lab had wandered afield, taking advantage of lunar illumination to rummage through the stones and logs that lined the lakeside. Several yards up the shore, he barked at shadows in the woods and plunged into the trees.

"Shiyut! He's onto a scent. Probly a rabbit."

"Let's hope it's not a skunk." Socrates jumped up and ran along the shore in pursuit. "Call him."

"Come heyah, War Eagle!" She placed two fingers between her lips and emitted a shrill whistle. "Git back here, boy!"

"I always wanted to whistle like that," Robert said with admiration.

War Eagle splashed through the shallow water at lake's edge, returning beside Socrates, who hopped along the rocks on the bank.

"Ah swear, Ah don't know whut Ah'm gonna do with you!" She grabbed the dampened coat behind his ears with both hands to get his undivided attention. "Dawg, what's yower problem? Yew've taken to running off whenevah it suits yew. I want yew to behave, yew hear? Stay close to Momma."

"War Eagle wants to live in the present also," Robert offered. "He knows there are only two more states to explore before he goes home."

"As much as Ah hate to, Ah'm gonna have to use his leash." The despised word sparked concern in the Lab. He nuzzled her arm with his damp nose to get back in her good graces. "Yew gonna behave?" He let out a penitent whimper. She stroked his snout. "Nice try. But I'll rein yew in tomorrah."

"Speaking of tomorrow, I have a proposition for you guys."

"Shoot."

"When I talked to Heather, she said we're only a few miles from Franconia Notch. That's where the Old Man of the Mountain is."

"The Great Stone Face?"

"The same. That guy is like the mascot of New Hampshire."

"Yeah. His profile's on the licence plates. And on the state quarter."

"Let's do some sightseeing. Reward ourselves with a light day. We could go see the Old Man and walk through the Flume."

"What's the Flume?"

"It's this natural granite canyon. Heather says it's about a thousand feet long and fifty feet high, on both sides. There's a trail into the gorge."

"Good idea." Mother Superior concurred. "Not a zero, but close to it. We've been pushing hard the last few days."

"Tell you what we could do," Robert said. "There's a state park in the notch. Why don't we go there, right after you guys finish 'work for stay' in the morning? I bet we can leave our packs at the park office while we play tourists."

"You want to stay the night there?"

"We could. But there's another option."

"Snaky, you been reading the map?"

"While you were bussing tables. There's a campsite three miles up from the notch. And I do mean up. Twenty-five hundred feet straight up on Franconia Ridge. We mess around until about four in the afternoon. Then we load up and attack that sucker."

"That late in the day?"

"We have to do it sometime. Does it really matter when? This way we eat a good dinner afterward and get a good night's sleep on the ridge. The next morning we don't have to mess with that climb. Breaks up the effort."

"Makes sense. Sandwich sightseeing between two short sections of trail. Sounds downright civilized."

"Vorks for me."

"Ah approve. But tell me one thing, sugah. Every time Ah turn around, it's Heathah this and Heathah that. What else did yew and she talk about?"

"Nothing, sweetie. Except she gave me lotion to put on my hands after I washed dishes. They were wrinkled and pruney. Here, feel."

Southern Bell grabbed his hands and squeezed as hard as she could.

"Ouch! What was that for?"

"Tell me these hayands haven't been in any hanky-panky."

Socrates jerked free and held them up to her. "Pure as the driven snow."

"No more Heathah. We can't get out of here soon enough tomorrah."

"Bell's right. It'll be a full day. Let's get some sleep."

The other four started for the hut. Robert lingered. "I'll be along. I need more moon worship."

"Don't moon too long. Remembah that ridge tomorrah."

They left. Robert sat back down on the long, flat rock. He craned his neck to see the white globe, now risen to the top of the heavens. He stared at the bright ball, trying to decode the striations on its surface.

I know you're there. I always said you hung the moon.

The familiar face appeared in the incandescence.

I found you. Instead of the old man.

He fixed her face in his eyes, doting on every detail of her countenance.

It's a brave new world, Angie. Did I sound brave tonight?

The emptiness inside was her answer.

Hon, I have to do those things. But all I really want is you back again.

He tapped into his reservoir of strength and composure, and he accepted the hollow pangs in a way that would have been impossible a few months ago.

I know you're happy. Rob found his love. Like you knew he would. Mandy's baby, our grandchild, will be here soon. Mandy and Rob. The two greatest gifts you ever gave me.

The lunar clarity blurred. He stood up and wiped the corners of his eyes with the back of his hand. He walked back toward the hut. After a few steps he glanced once more at the moon.

I love you.

Chapter 21

A time to break down, and a time to build up.
Ecclesiastes 3:3

The trail from Lonesome Lake dumped them onto the highway in Franconia Notch. Precisely when needed, trail magic appeared. A driver stopped and offered a ride in his pickup. Czechmate and Mother Superior climbed into the cab, and Robert, Southern Bell, Socrates, and War Eagle scrambled into the bed. The angel transported them to the Lafayette Campground, where a park ranger agreed to stash their packs in a back office.

Their incredible string of luck continued. They met a camper from Boston at the park headquarters, who was on his way to buy supplies in the town of Franconia. He also drove a truck, and he offered to drop them at the site for viewing the Old Man. They repeated the pecking order from the first ride.

The truck rolled toward the overlook below Cannon Mountain. Robert relaxed in the warm sun and open air. He was soon lost in reflection.

From Harpers Ferry to Vermont they had racked up an unbroken succession of twenties and near twenties, stopping only to resupply. At one point Robert worried that they had become automatons, marching in a trance to the heart of Maine. But in recent weeks, detours like this had become more common, in sharp contrast to their relentless progress through the Midatlantic.

The first major departure came at Vermont's Stratton Mountain. A shade under four thousand feet, it was the highest peak since Stony Man in the Shenandoah. They renewed the challenge of scaling a prominent mountain. They crested at noon and found a throng of "unhikers" dressed in cotton garments unstained by perspiration. The presence of "the great washed," as Socrates labeled them, was a clear indication of motorized transportation to the summit. A ski lift ran to and from the lodge and restaurant in the valley below. The operator informed them that the round trip on the lift was free for thru-hikers, and that the restaurant served a midday buffet.

The siren song of "all you can eat" was irresistible. They rode down for an appointment with gluttony. Several hours later, they returned to the peak. Their daily goal for high mileage had been buried under several thousand calories. Fortunately the three miles to the shelter at Stratton Pond were downhill. They were pulled to evening camp by the gravitational force on their distended stomachs.

That one breach in discipline quickly led to others. They walked only ten miles the next day, arriving at the highway to Manchester. Robert and Socrates assumed they would take a short break by the roadside and then scale Bromley Mountain. They were unaware that Manchester was home to a large outlet mall. The Manchester blip, however, was prominent on the ladies' radar.

"We're going into town to shop," Mother Superior announced.

Robert was puzzled. "What for? We're okay on food."

"No, silly. Shop. Clothes, shoes, purses. The good stuff. Fifty stores, just waiting for us."

"Jeez, a mall?" Socrates was horrified. "Aren't we out here to get away from crass commercialism? Besides, it makes absolutely no sense. If you buy some shit, what are you going to do? Hump it all the way to Katahdin?"

"Who said anything about buying? We're just shopping."

"Soc, this is something beyond male understanding."

"Right, Snakes. It's a girl thing. Just like deer, we have to browse to stay viable."

"If Ah see something Ah reayully lak, Ah might mail it home to Momma. Besides, her buthday's in two weeks. All Ah did for Mother's Day was a little ol' card. Ah need to find her a nice gift."

"Hon, the last thing I want to do is parade through fifty stores while you look at skirts and tank tops. Why don't the three of you leave your packs here? Snaky and I'll take turns guarding and napping."

"Ah bet there's a Friendly's in Manchestah."

Socrates's demeanor changed instantly. "Why the hell didn't you say that in the first place? I'm dying for a Fribble. And a humongous burger."

"I guess the boys can sacrifice for the good of the group," Robert added. "Besides, that feast at the ski lodge has worn off. Soc, I'll see your shake and raise you one."

The off-trail junket became ingrained. Just beyond Killington, they stopped at the Inn at the Long Trail in Sherburne Pass. The inn served Guiness on tap, and they shared several rounds. For lunch, they ordered Guiness stew, the house specialty. The beef was tantalizingly marinated in the stout. Robert hiked to camp that evening with a buzz and woke the next morning with his first AT hangover.

Three days later, they crossed the Connecticut River into Hanover, New Hampshire. They took a zero and found lodging in one of the Dartmouth student residences. In the morning they wandered through town and across the campus. They lunched at Thayer Hall with the students. In the afternoon, they purchased several trail items at the Dartmouth Co-op. At the insistence of Socrates and Southern Bell, they went to the latest *Star Wars* movie. Robert was not an aficionado, but for two hours he became absorbed in the titanic struggles with the empire and forgot about the demands of the AT. That evening they culminated their indolence with a pilgrimage to Ben and Jerry's, where each devoured a giant cone.

Now they were off the trail again, sightseeing at Franconia Notch. It seemed they were spending more time not hiking than hiking. Robert recalled a caution from one of the guidebooks. It was common practice to slow down when closing in on the end of the trail. Consciously or subconsciously, hikers reduced mileage to stretch out the time. The evening before, they had talked about life after the AT, but no one had stated the obvious: *they did not want this to end.*

Their friendship had been tempered in the AT crucible to endure for a lifetime. But Katahdin meant they would say good-bye and return to the real world. Mother Superior and Czechmate faced a grueling regimen in classrooms and hospitals. Southern Bell would plunge into the rigors of graduate training. Only Socrates would continue the nomadic lifestyle that delighted them now. Robert pondered his own immediate future. He did not relish going home to dismantle the physical ties to his long and happy union with Angie. He did not want this to end.

On a hot night in late August many years ago, he and Angie left Mandy at her freshman dormitory in Florida. As they strolled to the car in the parking lot, he realized that the child-parent relationship of the previous eighteen years had come to an end. Mandy was on her own. Things would never be the same. Similarly, the friendships with the four, intensified by continuous exposure and shared travail, would lose potency when they separated. He vowed to prize their remaining moments.

—⚏—

The five jockeyed with the throng of tourists on the platform at the base of Cannon Mountain, hoping for a line of sight to the granite profile above. The crowd parted and left an unobstructed view. To Robert the chiseled face was the work of a master sculptor. He could not accept that the features were carved by millions of years of wind and water. The head jumped out at him, unlike the subtle visage of the "grandfather" in North Carolina.

"No doubt it's a man," he offered.

Socrates scoffed. "A blinding flash of the obvious."

"What I mean is, for a likeness, it puts Grandfather Mountain to shame."

"You can't move to North Carolina if you trash our landmarks."

"Please forgive me. But it's the truth."

The Old Man stimulated Socrates's competitive juices. "Okay, guys, who does he remind you of? Best answer wins a Coke."

"You're buying?"

"Yep."

"Suddenly this game is worth the effort."

"Matey, you go first."

"Der *Dafid*."

"Der who?"

"Michelangelo's *Dafid*. I saw him in Vlorence."

Mother Superior chimed in. "Hon, *David*'s a full-length statue. The Old Man's just a head. How can you compare the two?"

"It iss der scope. Ve are so small standing heer under it. Dat's how I felt in der museum, looking up at der statue."

"I see your point. But the face is wrong." Mother Superior continued. "The Old Man's chin is more pronounced."

"Who do you think he is?"

"I dunno. With a beard, maybe Abe Lincoln."

Southern Bell gently restrained War Eagle with the leash. "Ah tell yew who he is. "Kirk Douglas. As Spartacus."

"You had to bring the movies into this. If that's Kirk Douglas, where's the dimple in the chin?"

She pouted. "Yower eyes are as weak as yower imagination. Yew can hardly see the dimple from heyah. Ah saw it head on from the truck, when we rode ovah."

"That's not a dimple. It's a pimple. But who do you think, Snaky?"

"I wish I had a nifty classical comparison like Czechmate. But I'm in Hollywood with Bell. It's the chin. He reminds me of Jay Leno."

"No way! The face is not that full."

"Okay. A younger Leno."

"Nah. His cheekbones aren't as prominent as the Old Man's."

"All right, genius. Suppose you tell us who he is?"

"That's easy. Coach K."

Robert groaned. "C'mon. Take off those damn blue blinders."

"Just tweaking you. But actually, there's a resemblance to the Blue Devil, don't you think?"

Robert looked up again at the granite. "It's a stretch. No horns. If you get by that, there's a slight match. But only if you bleed blue and white."

"Soc, that's a crock of shit," Mother Superior retorted. "Snakes may cut you some slack, but I won't."

"And Ah won't either. No Dook allowed. Take anothah gandah and tell us who he really looks lak."

Socrates scanned the mountain for several seconds. "That's it! My bad for not seeing him sooner."

"Who?" Southern Bell demanded.

"Elvis!"

She shoved him so hard he jostled a nearby tourist. "Can't yew evah be serious? Even jus' one time?"

"I'm deadly serious. That's 'The King.' The early Elvis, before he puffed up."

"Soc, you claim to have a fertile mind, but you aren't showing it today. That's just something a smartass college kid would say." Mother Superior smirked. "But that's why we love you."

"Enough to say I win the Coke?"

"No way. Anybody but you. Bell saw the dimple. Give it to her."

Robert turned so that his profile aligned with the Old Man. He inhaled deeply and jutted his chin.

"Snaky, whatcha doing?"

"Just posing." He pointed to the rocks above. "To see if I could look like the Old Man."

Socrates pounced like a cougar. "Guys, the secret of the universe is right under our noses. And we failed to see. The Old Man is Snaky."

Mother Superior leaped aboard. "You're right. The deep creases around the mouth. The circles under the eyes. I see them etched in the granite."

"Und dat cute little vattle drooping near der Adam's apple. I see it also on der mountain. Der *Dafid* nefer had one of those."

Socrates shouted, "And the gray stubble on the chin, trying like hell to be a real beard!"

"Okay! Okay!" Robert capitulated. "Bell, get in your licks. Everybody else has."

"All Ah'm saying is yew left yowerself wide open."

"My only consolation is now I win the Coke."

She rolled her eyes at Socrates. "Ah can still git him to buy me one."

Socrates grinned. "Talk is cheap. And Coke is cheap."

"I think we've finished with the Old Man. And harping on my decrepitude. Let's go to the parking lot and find a ride back to the campground."

Socrates and Southern Bell led the group down the path. They strolled arm in arm and bantered like typical lovers. Socrates whispered something in her ear. She responded with a peck on the cheek. Distracted by his flirtation, she did not see the family exit the car in the parking lot with a comely Labrador bitch. War Eagle immediately acquired the scent. He lunged with sudden force and jerked the leash free of Southern Bell's relaxed grip.

"War Eagle! Come back heyah! Yew hear? Rat now!"

In full stride and full fervor, the Lab did not respond. The others chuckled at his amorous dash. He entered the lot and raced between the parallel lines of parked cars. The loop of the leash bounced behind him on the pavement.

The backup bulbs on a large minivan illuminated.

"War Eagle! Look out!"

Southern Bell hurtled down the path. "Stop! Baby! Please stop!" Socrates ran after her.

Oblivious to approaching danger, the Lab charged in full stride toward his tryst. The driver, seeing no cars, accelerated in reverse. War Eagle swerved but could not stop. His hind legs buckled under one rear tire. The Lab let out an excruciating yelp. The unsuspecting driver braked, but too late.

Southern Bell fell to her knees on the pavement beside War Eagle. "My precious! How are yew?"

He scratched his front paws on the pavement and tried to stand. The rear legs remained motionless. He slumped on his side. His piercing cries subsided into anguished whimpers. She cradled his head and looked into his glazed eyes. "Mah baby! Stay with me now! Stay with me!"

A short, heavy-set man bounded from the car. He approached Southern Bell nervously. "I'm sorry. I never saw your dog. He came out of nowhere." She acknowledged his apology with a nod, but said nothing. He turned to Socrates. "I'm sorry. Can I do anything?"

Socrates also did not reply. He examined the misshapen hindquarters. A piece of bone protruded from the damaged leg. "Bell, his leg's broken. And his hip doesn't look right. We gotta get him to a vet."

"Ah can see his laig is broken. It's worse than thayat. It's crushed. But how will we move him? Ah'm afraid we'll hurt him even mowah."

The circle around Southern Bell and War Eagle expanded to include the family and the other Lab. The youngest daughter, who looked to be six or seven, cried softly. "He's hurt! He's hurt!"

Her mother caressed the daughter's blonde hair. With her other hand she held the leash tightly to restrain the skittish Labrador. The dog barked. "Ginger, shush!" She turned to her husband. "Charles, we need to help."

He squatted next to Socrates. "There's a vet in North Woodstock. I'll be glad to drive your dog over there."

"Thanks," Socrates replied. "We need to get help quick."

"But how we gonna move hiyum?" Frustrated, Southern Bell repeated her plaint. "Ah'm afraid if we lift him, we'll aggravate his injury. Ah wish Ah had mah Thermarest."

"What's a Thermarest?" the young mother asked.

"An inflatable mattress," Robert explained.

"Charles, we have that life raft in the car. The green one the kids use. In the netting in the back." She spoke to Mother Superior. "Maybe you can slide it under his back legs and inflate it."

Charles ran to his SUV and returned with the raft. Mother Superior unrolled it. She adroitly slid one end under the crippled legs. She and Czechmate, pulling alternately, worked it gently under the pelvis. "Snakes. Start inflating."

Robert blew into the raft with measured breaths. After it was partially filled, Mother Superior signaled him to stop. Working in tandem, the nurses slid the mat further under the damaged hip. War Eagle whined.

"Bell, his back end's on the raft," Mother Superior said. "Can you swing his front around?"

Southern Bell gritted her teeth. "Ah'll try."

"Czechmate and I will hold him steady back here. You pivot his front." The nurses cradled the raft under War Eagle. Southern Bell straddled the lab. She squatted and slid her hands under his front legs.

"Baby, Ah'm gonna lift you up for a second." She rotated him onto the mat. He uttered a plaintive cry. She patted his snout. "Sorry, sugah. Ah won't hurt yew again." She turned to the others. "Let's get him in the car."

"I'll bring it right over." Charles ran to his SUV.

"Snakes, more air," Mother Superior demanded. "As tight as you can. Give him more cushion."

The sight of the limp, broken form beside him caused Robert to gag on the plastic plug, but he forced several more breaths into the raft. War Eagle's weight made the task difficult.

Charles backed the car within a few feet of the lab. He, Southern Bell, Socrates, and the two nurses fanned around the mattress and slid their hands underneath. On Southern Bell's command they lifted the raft and quickly placed it in the back of the car. She piled in the back with War Eagle. Charles and Socrates jumped into the front seat.

Robert rushed to the front window. "Soc, we'll get a campsite at Lafayette and wait for you there."

Charles hollered out his window. "Jen, I'll be back as soon as I can." He sped toward the highway. The short man followed in his minivan. The others watched with apprehension as the cars sped to North Woodstock.

The evening drizzle spattered on the rainfly. Robert tossed on his mattress. His options for busywork were exhausted. He had pitched the tent for Socrates and Southern Bell and stowed their gear inside to keep it dry. He cooked and consumed his dinner joylessly, the most unappetizing meal he had eaten on the entire AT. Afterward he spread a layer of Sno-Seal on his boots, even though they did not need it. He disassembled his Whisperlite and cleaned it thoroughly. He asked Czechmate if he could clean hers. When the forced activity ran out, he tried to talk to Mother Superior and Czechmate. They were just as agitated and unable to sustain a conversation. They retired to their respective tents, hoping for the solace of sleep. They could do nothing but wait.

He was in the same fitful place when he heard a voice, weighted with fatigue and sadness. "Snaky. You there?"

He unzipped the tent and the rainfly. Socrates squatted by the tent. Robert slid out and stood up. His friend also rose. His face was totally bereft of vitality.

"You okay, Soc?"

He shook his head woodenly. In their months on the trail, he had never touched Socrates, except for a slap on the back or a high five. Instinctively he extended his arms. Socrates stepped forward to be enclosed. He placed his head on Robert's shoulder and sobbed. He had been what he had to be this day, a source of strength for Southern Bell. Now it was time to lean on someone else.

Behind Socrates, Southern Bell sat on the bench at the picnic table, holding hands with Mother Superior and Czechmate.

"It wuz a compound frackchur of the femah. The pelvic girdle was crushed. The doc said there was no way, absolutely no way, he would evah walk again. And he was sufferin'." Czechmate handed her a tissue, and she blew her nose. "Mah baby was in so much pain. What else could Ah do?"

"You did vat you had to do."

"I called Momma. She loved him almost as much as Ah did." Southern Bell took a deep breath. "We made the decision togethah."

Socrates raised his head and wiped his eyes. He looked at Southern Bell and struggled to compose himself. "The hardest thing I ever did. Just standing there. Not able to do anything. I was worthless."

"You weren't worthless, Soc. You were there for her."

"We stood at the table when the vet gave him the shot. He was sedated by then, so it didn't hurt. He never even yipped. He just closed his eyes and left us. Unbelievable. This whole day has been unbelievable."

"It all happened so fast."

"But when I look back, it's in super slo-mo. I see every detail. Why did I distract her? Why wasn't I holding the leash? I could have reined him in."

"Don't blame yourself. Or Bell. That's the worst thing you can do."

"I'd do anything to bring him back."

"I can tell you not to rehash it like this. You can promise not to. But you will. You'll play it back over and over. In a way, that's good. It helps you get through it. Just don't be self-destructive."

"I keep asking why. He was such a noble animal. He never hurt anybody or anything."

"A victim of his own exuberance. Chasing Labrador tail."

Socrates shot him an excruciating look. Robert was quick to respond. "I'm not making a joke, buddy. All I meant was he did what he was genetically imprinted to do. I don't think we humans realize how difficult we make it for animals to live their lives the way nature intended."

Socrates's stomach growled.

Robert asked, "You and Bell get anything to eat?"

"No," he answered. "Never had time. Besides, I'm not hungry."

"How'd you get here?"

"The guy in the minivan."

"The one who hit him?"

"Yeah. Dave's his name. Nice guy. He followed us to the vet. Waited until the end. He was really concerned. Turns out he knew where the pet crematorium was. He took the body there and brought us here." His stomach growled again.

"You need to eat. I have an extra dinner in my pack. I can fix it for you guys."

"Okay. She might like that."

Robert dug out his stove and pot and took them to the picnic table. Southern Bell, her eyes brimming with tears, stopped conversing with the nurses. He set the utensils on the table and grasped her right hand. A wayward tear slid down his cheek. "Bell, you know we love you."

She nodded. A few tears rolled across her reddened face. He continued, "How 'bout a cup of cider? And dinner? Soc says you haven't eaten."

Mother Superior interjected, "He makes a mean cup of cider, Bell. Take him up on it."

She nodded again. He squeezed her hand and moved to set up his kitchen. Soon the gentle roar of the Whisperlite blotted out the patter of raindrops and the mournful sighs from the table.

"Snaky, you there?"

Robert sat up with a start.

"Snaky, wake up!"

The soft illumination from Socrates's headlamp filtered through the rainfly. The luminous dial on his watch read two thirty. "What?"

"Open up. We need to talk."

He unzipped the rainfly and scrambled outside. The night air, cool with moisture, made him shiver. "About what?"

"Bell says she's quitting. Going back to Alabama."

He dove back into the tent for his fleece and his sandals. Socrates knelt at the door while he dressed. "Soc, it's natural for her to run the gamut of emotions ..."

He cut him off. "No. She's dead serious. She says she's catching the bus or the train to Boston today. After she picks up the ashes."

"You can't talk her out of it?"

"I've been trying for hours. She's got it in her head it's her fault. Worse, it's a sign she shouldn't complete the hike. Like she's not worthy."

"I know how she feels."

"That's why I'm here. Talk to her. Maybe she'll listen to you."

"Sure. But I don't think I can change anything tonight. It takes time."

Socrates grasped his shoulder. "Please try. I can't bear the thought ..."

"Did you tell her that?"

"No."

"Idiot. That's what she needs to hear. I'll talk to her, but you have to tell her how you feel."

They walked to the other tent. The fly and inside flap were unzipped, as Socrates had left them. Robert heard sniffles inside. He bent over and spoke softly. "Bell?"

The whimpers stopped. "Whut?"

"It's Snaky. May I come in?"

She waited several seconds. "If yew want to."

Robert sat on the floor of the tent between the unzipped flaps, facing to the outside. He kicked off his shoes and scooted backward until he rested on top of Socrates's sleeping bag and foam pad.

The circle of his pinchlight revealed a dejected figure. Southern Bell was inside her sleeping bag, but only from the waist down. Her upper body was warmed solely by a T-shirt. Her pallid face seemed to have lost its freckles.

Robert debated how to approach her. In the counseling sessions after Angie's death, his minister had sidestepped nothing. Like her, he went right to the point. "Soc tells me you're thinking of going home. Back to Alabama."

"Yeah. Ah can pick up ..." She paused. "Ah can pick up his ashes this mawnin'. Then Ah'll take him home. There's no reason for me to stay."

"I can think of four good reasons. Mother, Matey, me, and especially Soc. We want you with us. We'll help you through this. We'll get you to Maine."

"Yew've all been great. Ah'm sure yew'll continue to be. But Ah'll feel bettah if Ah go back home."

"Bell, listen to the voice of experience. You're not going to feel better. Doesn't matter if you're in Alabama with your mother or on the trail with us. You'll feel like shit for a long time."

Her lips tried to form a smile. "Ah thought Socks asked yew to come in heyah and cheer me up."

"He asked me to share what I know. I know you've lost someone you dearly love. You hurt. It won't get better for a while. You'll have to live with it until you figure out how to make it better. Your mom can't do that. We can't do that. Only you can. All anybody else can do is help you along. The four of us want to do that."

She looked frustrated. "Yew want me heyah. She wants me theyah. Ah'm not sure wheyah I want me."

"I said there were four reasons for going on. But I can think of two more. The first is you."

"Whut do yew mean?"

"Before today, would you have given any thought to quitting?"

"No, but—"

"I know. It was a whole different world when you had War Eagle. But has that part of you, deep inside, that wanted to hike the AT since last March, since way before then even, has that part of you changed?"

"That part of me will nevah change."

"And it won't change in Soc, in Mother, Czechmate, or me either. Only one and a half states to go. It's getting stronger."

"But he was mah baby. It wuz as much his hike as it wuz mine."

"That's the final reason. It can still be his hike. One other thing I've learned. If you take someone along in your heart, it's almost as good as taking them in person. Not as good. Never as good. But almost as good. It's one way I learned to feel better. I brought Angie with me. So take War Eagle along with you. Let him finish his thru-hike."

Southern Bell sat up on her mattress pad. For the first time, her face showed animation. "Yew've just given me an ideah. Ah could spread his ashes on the mountaintops …"

"Like Mount Washington?"

"Yayah. And the Biggalows."

"Saddleback and Chairback."

"And Katahdin. Ah want mah baby on Katahdin. Thass whut I want."

She grasped his hands between hers. "I'm goin' on. Thank yew, Snaky. I'll call Momma in the morning."

"Good." Robert smiled.

"But lak yew said, it still hurts."

"We'll help you. Just like you guys helped me. You're strong enough to get through the pain."

"Ah hope so."

"Get some sleep. You'll need it when we go up that mountain."

"Ah'll try." She slid her hand behind his neck and pulled him forward. She kissed him on the cheek. "Thank yew."

"Thank you for staying. Now let's get to bed." He found his sandals, put them on, and slid out of the tent. Socrates, waiting at the picnic table, walked over expectantly. Robert gave him a thumbs-up.

"You're too much," he said with relief. "Thanks."

Robert stuck his head back through the flaps. "Bell? Soc has something he wants to say." He flashed a grin at Socrates. "Don't you, buddy?"

Socrates gripped his forearm as he walked by. "Why do I feel like I've been set up?"

"You're a Duke man. Rise to the occasion."

Chapter 22

Won't you look down upon me, Jesus,
You've got to help me make a stand.
James Taylor

A homemade blue sign nailed to a tree greeted them at the state line. "Welcome to Maine—The way life should be." At first Robert dismissed it as chamber of commerce blather. However, the Pine Tree State lived up to its promise. The northern woods were full of beauty, enchantment, and a parade of interesting creatures.

The first entertainer was a Canada jay, splendidly garbed in gray-and-white plumage. It lit at their campsite one evening and began to scavenge for crumbs on the ground. When they momentarily left dinner unattended, it opted for more substantial morsels. Like a thief caught red-handed, the bird looked at them with guileless innocence. Taken in by such feigned artlessness, they forgave the unabashed larceny. Compared to his raucous blue cousin, the Canada jay was a sophisticated gentleman.

The evening call of the loon was another treat, especially for the three southerners. The first time she heard its plaintive wail, Southern Bell woke from mourning. "*On Golden Pond*! The loons! The loons! Now Ah understand whut the fuss wuz all about."

Further into the unbroken beauty of the Maine woods, Robert discovered a new pastime: the search for moose. The trail passed many ponds and streams, prime locations for *Alces americana*. The bulls and cows liked to muck in the water near the shore and feed on pondside foliage. Sometimes they waded deeper to escape the blood-seeking advances of black flies and mosquitoes. He spotted several cows on distant shorelines. When he finally saw one at close range, her size and mobility sobered him. He concluded that moose were best viewed from a safe distance, like rattlesnakes and bears.

The winding path through the Maine backcountry reinforced their newfound predilection to dawdle in the woods rather than charge to the finish line. A southbounder they met in New Hampshire had grumbled about the circuitous route. The AT "went over every mountaintop and by every pond in the whole damn state." His complaint became Robert's expectation. He made fast friends with every summit. Each had a varied array of trees and plants and a unique combination of rugged ridges and escarpments.

The unusual names of the mountains intrigued him. Goose Eye. Old Speck. East Baldpate. Old Blue. Bemis. Saddleback. Sugarloaf. The Crockers. The Bigelows. Without access to a library or the Internet to unearth the origin of the place names, he fabricated his own history for each mountain and passed it off as gospel to his companions. Socrates countered with his own naming stories. The ladies soaked up all the malarkey. They were too enthralled by the natural grandeur to hold them to account.

Moxie Bald was the consensus favorite. The elongated top was covered with fully ripened blueberries. Robert had favorite berry caches in Georgia and North Carolina, but none compared to the succulence found here. They gorged at Moxie for over an hour. When they could eat no more, they painted smiley-faces on each other's cheeks with berry-stained fingers. Before departing, they held a contest to see who could make the most grotesque face. Socrates won when he wiggled his inky tongue and proclaimed, "I'm a leech."

Maine was a repository of blue treasures. The sky was deep and rich, devoid of haze and pollution. It reminded Robert of the pristine Sierra firmament along the John Muir Trail. Against the cerulean background, the cumulus clouds billowed from the horizon to the stratosphere.

There was blue on the ground also. Like other New England states, Maine was carpeted with the bluebead lily. *Clintonia borealis* sent up tall stalks from a cluster of large, oval leaves. The stalks were crowned with inviting indigo berries. However, the fruit was bitter and poisonous. The inedible *Clintonia* became a marker for a different appetite, a constant reminder of Robert's hunger to experience nature in all its abundance.

Like the white blazes on the tree, the bluebead confirmed that he was headed in the right direction.

The lily did not grow alone. It partnered with bunchberry, a low-growing herb Socrates identified as a member of the dogwood family. Its eye-opening clusters of bright red berries attracted a variety of songbirds. Even more plentiful was the common wood sorrel. Its flower sported five tiny white petals streaked with purplish veins, nested in a bed of shamrock leaves. The triad covered the ground in a vivid red, white, and blue blanket. Robert wondered if Betsy Ross had walked here. The floral profusion could have been the inspiration for the colors in Old Glory.

Blue was an accurate descriptor for Southern Bell. Each day brought moments of intense sadness. The first day after the accident, at Mount Lafayette, she had tried to scatter some of War Eagle's ashes from the Ziploc bag. The capricious wind blew the dust back into her face. The fine cinders lumped in the streaks of her tears. Czechmate came to her rescue and gently wiped away the moistened ash.

On Mount Washington, the gale howled at thirty knots. Socrates tried to discourage her from scattering more ashes. When she persisted, he asked to do it for her, but she declined. Having learned her lesson at Lafayette, she stood with the wind at her back. She unclenched her fist, and the fine particles rode the gusts away from her.

The ritual continued into Maine. With each successive scatter, she seemed more at peace. The painful ceremony evolved into a solemn dedication to the memory of her companion. Just as Robert had done, she dealt with her grief one mountain at a time. On Moxie Bald she talked to War Eagle for the first time. "Baby, Ah'm gonna leave yew heyah to enjoy the blueberries, just lak the rest of us." Quiet and reflective, she spoke infrequently. The others respected her silence and supported her with timely hugs and acts of kindness.

The night before crossing the Kennebec River, they stayed at a lean-to on the bank of Pierce Pond. At sunset they were transfixed by the haunting call of another loon, launched from a hidden cove across the water. The dirge, magnified by the forest stillness, cast a somber shroud over their conversation. Wrestling with memories, Southern Bell interrupted the distant lamentation.

"It's singin' for War Eagle."

Mother Superior replied, "A beautiful way to be remembered."

There was another wail. "Hear that, baby? It's cryin' for yew." She stared into the twilight. "Yew know, Ah did the right thing."

"What's that, sweetie?"

"Stayin' on the trail."

Mother Superior responded, "We're glad you feel that way."

"It's such a peaceful place. Ev'ry day it finds a way to put me at rest."

Socrates put his arm around her shoulder. "Bell, you're gonna make it."

"Yew're damn right Ah am. Ah'm going to Katahdin. And so is War Eagle."

―⁂―

The five waved good-bye to the shuttle driver, who returned to the boarding house in Monson. They found the trail, meandering north from the gravel shoulder into a small slit in the fir forest. Pieces of dark gray slate punctuated the pathway. Bottles and cans were scattered among the stones.

Robert registered his disappointment. "Shit!"

"What's the matter with you?"

"It's just so ordinary."

"What?" Socrates growled.

"This is the start of the hundred-mile wilderness. The most fabled section on the whole AT. And what have we got? A nondescript trail littered with beer cans."

"What were you expecting? Dancing girls? Seventy-six trombones?" Socrates marched in a small circle and thrust an imaginary slide to and fro as he hummed the catchy refrain.

"I'm not greedy. Dancing girls would be enough. But that aside, this place does not inspire. Unlike the rest of Maine. Before now it's been magical. Awesome mountains. Sparkling lakes. Fabulous forests."

"You becoming a romantic?"

"Snakes has always been a romantic," Mother Superior interjected.

"He iss right. Maine iss special. Der forest reminds me of Germany. But efen better. It iss so empty." Czechmate spread her arms and whirled in a circle. "Voopee! Vere did der people go?"

"Lemme get this straight," Mother Superior asked. "To begin the wilderness, you want some kind of sendoff?"

Robert gestured at the littered roadside. "Something better than this."

"Girls, come here."

She whispered to Czechmate and Southern Bell. The ladies locked arms behind their backs. Mother Superior began a dance count. On "eight," they stepped left, lifted their right knees high, hopped, and high-kicked. They made a quarter turn right and repeated the sequence with their left legs. After the third repetition, they were hopelessly unsynchronized. Southern Bell kicked when the others kneed, and all three staggered. Unfazed by the lack of polish, Robert and Socrates whooped.

"Rockettes! Radio City Music Hall!"

"No! Vegas showgirls!"

The trio restarted the routine. A car full of young men roared around the curve. The driver braked and sat on his horn. Two riders leaned out the windows and whistled. The ladies took a deep bow, heads to the ground. Howls of machismo poured from the car. The dancers turned around, bowed again, and wiggled their asses seductively. One man bellowed a graphic proposition, and then the car squealed away.

The chorus girls celebrated their newfound calling with a series of high fives. It was the first time Southern Bell had laughed since Franconia Notch.

Mother Superior faced Robert. "Was that what you wanted?"

"Positively smashing. Thank you, Irma La Douce."

"You ready to hike the wilderness now?"

"Right after I bring candy and flowers to your stage door."

—w—

That afternoon, Robert, Socrates, and the "chorus line" stopped for a dip in the chilly waters of Big Wilson Stream. Afterward, they completed a fifteen-mile day from Monson to the lean-to at Long Pond Stream. The shelter rested on top of a steep slope above the gorge, where the creek tumbled from an upstream pond.

Setting up camp was not the most immediate concern. Southern Bell's right knee was tender from the continuous pounding on the slate. She and Socrates backtracked to the gorge for a therapeutic soaking. The nurses stretched out on their Thermarests for some cherished downtime. Robert volunteered to schlepp water, an offer enthusiastically accepted.

Robert shunned the connecting trail back to the AT and bushwhacked to the stream, straight down from the front of the lean-to. His sandals slid on the carpet of needles that covered the precipitous incline. He descended cautiously, careful not to drop his armload of filter, bottles, and bladders.

A small spillway plummeted over one of the boulders and into a small pool. He sat on a nearby rock and filled the collection of reservoirs. The task went quickly. He lingered to soak his feet in the pool. The invigorating water dissipated the aches inflicted by miles of rocks and roots. He marveled at life's simple pleasures. The cold puddle pampered him more than the consummate trappings of the finest five-star hotel. He hoped Southern Bell found similar relief.

The emptiness in his stomach demanded attention. He bowed to the pangs of hunger and slipped his quickened feet back into the sandals. He collected the bottles and bladders and then tackled the ascent up the slope. Traction was elusive, and he inched his way through the roots and rocks. The roof of the lean-to appeared above the top of the bank. In a few more steps, the entire structure was visible. He stopped to catch his breath.

Czechmate sat on the edge of the platform. Her sweaty blonde hair, loosened from the french twist, hung in tangles around her face. Mother Superior stood beside her with the brush. With long, deliberate strokes, she groomed each tangle until Czechmate's hair fell free to her shoulders.

Mother Superior talked as she brushed. Czechmate giggled in response and looked at her partner with trust and fondness. Robert recalled the first night he had met them. It was the same sweet chemistry.

A faint rustle to the right diverted his gaze. A hiker stood on the trail leading from the AT into the lean-to. Robert shuddered involuntarily. The consequence of their last month's dalliance was painfully evident. Preacher had caught up.

Robert wondered what to say to him. The hostile parting in Massachusetts seemingly had closed any avenues of pleasant conversation. He looked at Preacher's face. Beneath the close-cropped hair at his temples, the skin flushed crimson. The pain and anger in his expression on the porch in Dalton continued to seethe. His stare was fixated on the nurses.

Preacher took off his pack and leaned it against a tree. The nurses, unaware of his presence, continued their chat. Preacher retrieved an object from the pack and tugged at it with his right hand. Eyes narrowed, he walked with purpose toward Mother Superior. The late afternoon light bounced off a fully extended blade.

Robert dropped the containers. They clunked as they hit the ground. The women looked up to see Robert running toward them.

"Preacher! Stop!"

Mother Superior and Czechmate turned to face Preacher, who strode toward them. With sandals flopping, Robert rushed to block Preacher's advance.

"Stop! For God's sake, stop!"

Preacher squinted through constricted slits.

"My God, man! What are you doing?"

Preacher stopped. He brandished the knife, his first acknowledgment of Robert's presence.

Robert stood his ground. An eerie calm settled over him. His voice was too tranquil for one staring at a naked blade. "Put the knife down, Preacher."

Preacher erupted. He charged furiously, leading with the knife in his right hand. Robert instinctively reverted to the catcher, facing the runner barreling down on home plate. Lacking a mask and chest protector, he raised his arms for a shield. He stepped uphill at the last possible moment. Keeping one arm high in self-defense, he "tagged" Preacher hard on the shoulder with the other. Preacher's momentum carried him downhill, and he stumbled several yards before regaining his balance.

The force of his charge alarmed Robert. He was no match for Preacher's strength. He felt a sharp sting on his right forearm. An angry red line erupted across the skin two inches below his elbow. It widened into a crimson band.

"Snecks! You're bleeding!"

He did not have time to gauge the severity of the wound. Preacher gathered himself down the hill and charged again. Robert feinted to the left as before. Preacher took the bait. Robert stepped right to avoid the blade and grasped Preacher's right arm near the wrist with both hands. He momentarily immobilized the knife. Preacher countered by attacking Robert's grip with his free hand. With superior strength, he pulled one of Robert's hands away. Robert realized the clinch was about to turn deadly.

He let go of Preacher's wrist and danced backward. Preacher slashed. Robert raised his arms again and at the same time delivered a hard shot with his left foot to Preacher's testicles.

The contact knocked Robert to the ground. Staggered by the low blow, Preacher lurched backward. He bent over at the waist to regain his breath.

Robert felt another sting, this time on his left arm. A gash extended from his watchband to his elbow. Given the flow of blood, it was more serious.

Robert backpedaled on all fours toward the lean-to and waited for the next onslaught. Out of the corner of his eye, he saw the nurses. "Get out of here! Get the hell out of here!"

Mother Superior did not leave. She faced Preacher squarely, pointing the tips of her trekking poles at his face. She hissed like a venomous cobra. "Come and get *me*, you chicken-shit bastard!"

Preacher refocused on his original target. "You lesbian bitch! You'll pay for what you've done!"

She waved the poles menacingly. "And just what will you do to this lesbian bitch?"

Robert felt the lean-to behind him. He grasped the platform with his right hand and pulled himself erect. Old Hickory leaned against the wall, where he had left it. He grabbed the staff. Fixed on a different foe, Preacher no longer paid him close attention.

"C'mon! What are you waiting for?" Mother Superior spit at him. She swung her hiking pole like a saber, and it whistled in its own wind.

Preacher ran at her, knife at the ready. Robert grasped the meat end of Old Hickory and went after him. He swung with all his remaining strength and struck Preacher directly behind the left kneecap. The leg buckled. Caught by surprise, Preacher could not break his fall. His left shoulder crashed into a large, jagged rock. The knife pitched out of his grasp and landed harmlessly at Mother Superior's feet. He rolled over on his back and screamed, grasping at his left shoulder with his right hand.

Mother Superior bent over and retrieved the bloody knife. She approached Preacher cautiously, pointing the tips of her poles in his contorted face. When she was convinced that he was in no condition to continue his attack, she took charge of the carnage, as if it were a triage station in a war zone.

"Preacher, I'll get to you in a minute, after you cool off. In the meantime, rest your left arm on your stomach. Don't move it."

She turned to Czechmate. "Sweetie, get the first-aid bag. Bring me a pair of latex gloves. And get a pair for yourself. Snakes has lost a lot of blood. Put the large gauze pads on those wounds. When you finish with the compresses, use the butterfly closures. They'll have to do until we can get him to a hospital. And check his vitals. He's pale."

Czechmate hurried to her pack for the medical supplies. "Vat about him?" She nodded at Preacher, writhing in pain.

"He'll have to wait. Until he lets us treat him."

"I don't vant to go near him."

"You may have to. You're a nurse." She continued calmly. "Without a hands-on inspection, I'd say he has a middle fracture of the clavicle. Can't tell the degree of displacement or angulation. There may be internal shoulder damage. And possible ligament damage in the left knee." She looked at Robert with admiration. "You know how to swing the bat."

Robert leaned on Old Hickory to keep from falling. "Not really. I'm cursed with warning track power."

"What you just did was tape measure, my friend. Now hobble over to the platform and let Czechmate tend to you. I don't want you passing out on me." She glanced at Preacher. "You're both candidates for shock."

With Czechmate's assistance, Robert sat down on the floor of the lean-to. He was breathing rapidly. He was unsure if it was symptomatic of his trauma, or of the adrenaline rushing through his system. In Tennessee his reaction to fear had been a violent spasm of nausea. Now, to his surprise, he did not feel sick or debilitated, but uniquely exhilarated. For a year the specter of death had shadowed him. Many times he thought he had learned to live with the fear and sorrow it had thrust upon him. It was a bogus accommodation. He did not understand until now. The bell that tolled for Angie was set to ring for him. Death had come straight at him in a headlong rush, and he had eluded it.

The liberation lifted him. Fear was replaced by the limitless possibilities in the seconds, minutes, hours, days, weeks, months, and years of his future. His light-headedness was not from loss of blood. He was giddy with victory.

Thank you for a second chance.

Czechmate tended his wounds. She stanched the bleeding quickly and expertly with gauze compresses held in place with Ace bandages. After the flow stopped, she removed the bandages and applied antibiotic ointment to the open cuts. She affixed several butterfly stitches to close the gape of his wounds. "He vill need many sutures in each arm," she reported to Mother Superior. "Particularly der left."

"But you stopped the bleeding?"

"Ja."

"Good. He's ambulatory. We can get him to help."

"He looks a little spacy." Czechmate eyed Robert with concern. "Snecks, iss dere anything I can do for you?"

In his postcombative flightiness, he remembered a night in Virginia. "Yeah. Play our favorite game."

"Vat game?"

"You know, where you pretend you're Angie, and you comfort me?"

Czechmate was taken aback. Robert snickered. When she realized she'd been had, she did not protest. Instead, she reached over and stroked his cheek enticingly. The seductive touch stopped his laughter. She bent over and kissed him sensuously on the lips. A long strand of her hair tickled the cavity behind his clavicle. It was his turn for consternation, but he could not ruin the moment by asking what she was doing. She pulled back from the embrace and gazed alluringly into his eyes. "Snecks, I'd luff to play our little game. But you haf lost too much blood. You vill not be able to get it up!"

Mother Superior cackled. "You go, girl!" She turned to Robert with a scowl. "For Christ's sake, Snakes, chill out and rest. We may not get you out of here before tomorrow."

"What the shit is going on?" Socrates and Southern Bell rushed in on the same trail where Preacher had entered. "We heard all kinds of shouting." He saw Preacher on the ground. "Where did he come from?"

"Don't know," Mother Superior responded. "He just showed up."

"What the hell happened to him?"

"He came in here with this." She held up the bloody knife. "To slice and dice me." She nodded toward Robert. "Snakes took him down."

Robert credited her contribution. "It was a tag team."

Socrates saw Robert's bandaged arms and the scarlet stains on his T-shirt. "My God, man! Are you okay?"

"You wouldn't have any Ben and Jerry's in your pack, would you?"

Socrates turned to Mother Superior. "Is he okay?"

"We think he's all right, except for loss of blood. He has two beautiful gashes on his arms that need to be sewn up." She paused. "He also has an unusual posttraumatic reaction. You'd think he'd be depressed, but it's the opposite. He's elated."

"Snaky, Ah don't have ice creayum, but Ah have one of those big ole Snickers bars. Would yew lak it?"

"Bless you!"

"Soc, I'm glad you're here." Mother Superior was businesslike. "Preacher needs medical attention. I've been reluctant to help him because he might come at me again. I need you to restrain him if he acts up."

Socrates became cautious. "Did you check to see if he has another knife? Or a gun?"

"If he had a gun, genius, he'd have blown me away by now. Unless it's in his pack."

Robert piped up. "Mother, get that pair of handcuffs out of your pack! You know, the ones in your dominatrix kit."

Mother Superior shot him another look of disgust. "Good idea! They're right next to my nightstick. I'll get it out and whack your ass until you stop raving. Sweetie, take some adhesive and tape his damn mouth shut." She looked down at Preacher. "Can you hear me?"

He nodded.

"I think you have a broken collarbone. And possible shoulder and knee injuries. I won't know how serious until I examine you. You need a doctor, but the odds are we can't get you to a hospital before tomorrow. Until then, you're my patient. Do you understand?"

He nodded again.

"Will you let me treat you? Without trying to attack me?"

"Yes." His expression was a mixture of pain and disconsolation.

"While I'm working with that bone and with your knee, I may cause pain. It won't be on purpose. I'm trying to diagnose."

He motioned to Soc. "Cell phone. In my pack. Outside pocket."

Socrates glanced at Mother Superior.

"It's worth a try," she said.

Socrates retrieved the pack from the tree where Preacher had left it. He set it down inside the lean-to and found the phone.

"Bring his jacket over here," Mother Superior ordered. "We need to keep him warm."

Socrates took the phone to the clearing in front of the shelter. He turned it on and looked at the dial. "No signal. It figures. We're in the middle of a wilderness."

Preacher was visibly disappointed. "Try again."

Socrates dialed once more, with the same result. "Out of coverage."

"Okay, Soc. Put it down and come over here. Let's get to work."

Southern Bell sat next to Robert, hand-feeding him bites from the Snickers bar. She had a sudden flash. "Socks, whut about those two guys fishing at the streayum? Reckon they're still down theyah?"

"The father and son! Bell, you're cooking! The dad said his truck was nearby, where they were camping."

"That's the break we're looking for," Mother Superior replied. "That's what, less than a mile away?"

"All the rest of yew guys have a job. Let me go find them."

Robert was disappointed. "You don't consider feeding me a job?"

Southern Bell commiserated with Czechmate. "Ah may have to walk a ways to find them, but Ah swear, my job's easier than yowers."

"Ve all haf our cross to bear."

"Hon, the batteries in mah headlamp are weak. Can Ah take yours?"

"Sure. And take your jacket and cap. It's getting cool."

Southern Bell stuffed two candy bars in the pocket of her jacket and grabbed a water bottle from the pile down the hill. "Wish me luck."

Socrates kissed her. "Be careful, dear." She walked away, and he knelt by Preacher.

Mother Superior dropped to her knees. She took a pair of scissors from the kit and deftly cut through the neckband of Preacher's T-shirt, opening the seam all the way to the shoulder. "Keep your left hand pressed over your navel and hold your arm still." She folded back the front portion of the shirt. A pointed lump pressed up against the skin. She touched it gently. Preacher flinched.

"Sorry, but I can confirm you have a broken collarbone." She probed downward along the pectoral muscle. Preacher did not react. "I don't think you sustained lung damage. Are you having trouble breathing?"

Preacher shook his head. "No. Just pain where you touched me. And my knee."

"Let's take a look." Mother Superior walked on her knees down to his leg. "We'll raise your leg so I can look at the back of your knee. Keep that left arm immobile. Soc, come around me. When I say to, lift his left leg about a foot in the air. Ready? Now."

Mother Superior examined the soft tissue behind the knee. "Just as I thought. Swollen and discolored. Lots of blood and fluid. You have ruptured bursae. It needs to be iced to hold down the swelling, but that'll have to wait till we get to civilization."

She motioned for Socrates to move. "Okay. I'm checking for ligament damage." She held the leg firmly and tested the motion of the knee from side to side. Preacher grimaced. "Function seems normal. The joint is tight. The pain's from the swelling. You have one helluva bruise." She placed his leg on the ground.

"I think we can move you. But I need a sling to keep your arm stationary." She looked at Czechmate. "Can you think of anything?"

Czechmate pondered for a few moments. "Vat about that rope Snecks uses for a clothesline?"

"That'll work. Loop it four or five times and tape the strands together."

Czechmate turned to Robert, lying across the floorboards of the lean-to. "Snecks, vere iss your rope?"

"In the top pocket. But be careful. The deer might eat your panties again."

Czechmate rolled her eyes in exasperation. She opened his pack and found the rope. She fashioned several loops and bound them into one thick strand with pieces of duct tape.

Mother Superior took the sling. "Good. Now get his mattress ready." She slid one end of the sling over Preacher's head and gently cradled his left wrist in the other end of the loop.

"We're ready to move you. Remember. Hold your arm still. Can you sit up on your own?"

Preacher pushed off on his right elbow into a sitting position.

Mother continued. "Soc, kneel to his right. Preacher, put your right arm on his shoulder. Yeah. Like that. Now bring your right leg up under you. I'll try to steady you on the left. Okay. Push up!"

Preacher wobbled into a crouch. With additional effort he reached a standing position. She draped his jacket across his shoulders. The three made their way slowly to the platform, and Preacher collapsed onto his Thermarest.

"Soc, go police up those bottles and bladders," Mother Superior ordered. "We'll put one under his knee. It may be cool enough to retard swelling. We also need to get water down Snakes. He's lost beaucoup fluids. And then you can start dinner."

Chapter 23

*I've been tryin' to get down to the heart of the matter ...
But I think it's about forgiveness.*
Don Henley

The glare from the overhead fluorescent bulbs ricocheted off the antiseptic ceiling. Robert squinted. His drowsy eyes acquired a darkened television mounted on a metal frame bolted to the wall. The murky screen resembled the blackened portal on the rear door of the ambulance. He vaguely recalled a jostling ride on a gurney through miles of Maine wilderness.

He refocused his gaze onto a slender chrome tower. A transparent plastic bag, suspended from the pole, dripped a clear solution into a tube anchored in his bandaged forearm.

He heard a whoosh. A pair of blackout curtains parted. Warm yellow sunshine streamed through a bank of windows, supplanting the cool blue of the fixtures. Robert moaned.

"There you are! I thought you'd sleep the whole day through." The daylight outlined an attractive silhouette advancing toward him. She picked up a thermometer from a bedside tray and inserted it under his tongue. After a few seconds, she exclaimed, "Dammit! That's the rectal bulb."

Robert tried to spit out the thermometer. She gently restrained him. "I'm kidding! I'm kidding!" She felt for his pulse. "Just testing your reactions."

He slumped onto the pillow while she checked his vitals. Her ash-blonde hair was pinned behind her head, much the same as Czechmate's. She appeared to be in her midforties. Her face was softly creased around the corners of her eyes and mouth. The lines were the benign result of countless sparkling glances and beautiful smiles, both now on display. A small plastic tag pinned on her uniform read "Suzanne." She wore no rings.

"Your pulse is normal. Much better than when the EMTs first clocked you. It's amazing what two units of O positive and a good night's sleep can do." She chided him. "You boys need to realize something about Maine. When you rumble in the jungle, it takes a while to bring you in. Lucky for you there were nurses around." She eyed him coquettishly. "If it weren't for us angels of mercy, you'd be in a helluva mess."

Robert mumbled around the thermometer. "Do I hap to lithen to thith bullthit?"

"Your nurse friends said you'd be feisty." She reeled him in again with another photogenic smile. "It's a good sign." She took the thermometer. He admired the deep blue of her eyes as she read the gauge. "Ninety-eight even. Another good sign. We don't need you running a fever." She recorded the readings on his chart.

"Suzanne?"

"Yes, Robert?"

"Do you wear contacts?"

"No. Why?"

"You have very pretty eyes."

"Thank you." The fetching grin danced across her face again.

"What are you doing tonight?"

"Slow down, big boy. You're not going anywhere that soon."

"Tomorrow night then? Dinner and a movie?"

"You're a piece of work. Tell you what. I'll give you a rain check. For later, when you're back on your feet."

"Okay. Day after tomorrow."

Robert's stomach let out a long, loud growl.

"Wow! I bet you want breakfast."

"A dozen blueberry pancakes with butter and maple syrup. And bacon, eggs, and orange juice."

"You hikers do have the appetite. The nutritionist says corn flakes, but I'll see what I can do."

"If you spill syrup on your arm, I may try to eat it."

She pulled her hand back in mock horror. "I'll get you some food as quick as I can." She pointed to a glass and pitcher on the bedside tray. "Drink plenty of water. Restore your fluids." She walked to the door.

Robert made a final attempt. "You never said 'no,' so it's a 'yes'?"

She pointed toward the sunshine and winked. "It's bound to stop raining one of these days."

Robert lay back on the pillow. He liked her looks and her spirit. He was certain the attraction flowed both ways. The immediacy of his advances surprised him. He had never been that forward before, but it felt good to say what was on his mind. It felt good to take a chance.

Across the room, the bathroom door was ajar. The toilet prompted him that he needed to pee. He tossed the sheet and cotton blanket to the foot of the bed. He recoiled in disgust at the sight of his skimpy gown. Half the hospital, including Suzanne, had probably seen him in his glory. He pivoted his naked legs over the side of the bed. The dull pain in his right hip reminded him of yesterday's fall. The tether in his arm posed a challenge, but the IV drip stand was on wheels. He stood up slowly and made sure of his balance. He pushed the stand to the toilet and sat down.

His pack rested on a shelf behind the bathroom door, with his boots underneath. Old Hickory leaned against the wall.

A rash of questions, held at bay by the distraction of waking up in the hospital, surged to the fore. Is all my gear here? My wallet? My watch? Where are my friends? I need to talk to Mandy and Rob. When can I hike? How's Preacher? Why did he do this?

He stood up, determined to find answers. Light-headed, he grasped the doorknob. He breathed deeply and waited for his head to clear. He flushed the toilet and limped slowly back to the bed, clutching the IV apparatus. The door from the hallway opened behind him.

"Look. Snaky traded Old Hickory for a new walking stick."

"Ayund traded his shorts for newfangled hiking duds. Ah pahticularly lak that revealin' slit down the backside."

"Nice cheeks, buddy."

"Snecks, did der deer eat your shorts?"

Robert sat on the edge of the bed. He pivoted his legs onto the mattress and tugged at the hem of his gown, like a self-conscious woman in a miniskirt. He pulled up the sheet. "That's it. No more cheap thrills." He looked at Mother Superior and Czechmate. "Why are you wearing nurse pajamas?"

"More on that in a minute. The nurse says your blood pressure has improved." Mother Superior eyed him suspiciously. "She had this funny look. Said your vitals weren't what worried her. What did you say to her?"

"I asked her out."

"Good for you, man. She's hot." Socrates looked cautiously at Southern Bell. "For someone her age."

She did not deploy her elbow, her usual response to his provocative declarations. "Ah agree. She's an attractive woman."

"Yeah. Attractive. That's the word."

"I also talked to the doctor. They want to keep you three or four days." Mother Superior elaborated. "You lost a lot of blood. You need to regain your strength. And make sure you don't have an infection. It might have been longer had I not convinced them you'd receive first-rate care back on the trail."

Robert brightened. "You guys'll wait for me? I thought you were short on time."

"Relax. We worked it out this morning. This hospital has a temporary nursing shortage. Czechmate and I will fill in for three days, for free room and board. I told St. Catherine's it would help us to observe medical procedures in rural areas. I gave them this big spiel on how much we learned watching them pull you out of the wilderness."

"You're a great bullshit artist."

"Hey! They okayed the delay. I won't miss any classes. Just the preliminaries."

"Ah got a job, too. With the local vet. From Greenville, Alabamah, to Greenville, Maine. Yew remembah Sam, yower ambulance driver?"

Robert shook his head. "'Fraid not."

"He's her brother. Hooked us up this mawning. One of her assistants is on vacation. She let me and Socks tent behind her house, near the kennel."

"And you, Soc?"

"I'm lecturing at the Greenville Geographic Society's evening symposium. On the biota of the Appalachian ecosystem."

"In other words, you're raising a glass at a local establishment."

"Something like that."

"And helpin' me feed the animals and clean the kennel."

Socrates squirmed. "There's a pool hall here. I can hone my nine-ball game."

"Dream on, stud. Lak Ah'm gonna sit all night and watch you git hustled by the local shark. We can see a movie when we finish workin'. Ah'm so far behind, it's pathetic."

"So, everybody's set up in Greenville." Mother Superior continued. "We found our angels. We'll wait for you to get better. Then we'll all tackle the last one hundred miles to the big K."

"I'll tell you something. He could have cut my arms off and I'd still hike that last hundred. Nothing'll keep me from finishing."

"That's the spirit. Oh, I almost forgot." She reached in her pocket and handed Robert his wallet and his watch. "They gave me these last night."

"Thanks. I wondered where they were."

"I took some liberties. I found Mandy's phone number and called her."

"Thanks again. I thought about that a few minutes ago."

"She was really upset. I told her you'd be all right, but she's got to hear it from you."

"Did you call Rob?"

"She said she would."

"Good. I'll call her after breakfast." Robert turned serious. "What happened to Preacher?"

"He's four doors down the hall. His knee swelled up like a melon. Bruises and strained ligaments. He won't be walking for a while. His shoulder's in a sling, immobilized. The sheriff'll come by to get your story. He's already questioned us. They're talking about charging him with assault with a deadly weapon."

"Sounds like his hike is done."

"For sure. And so's his Vermont campaign." She turned to Czechmate. "You have the clipping?"

"*Ja.*" She retrieved a neatly folded square of newsprint from her pocket and passed it to Mother Superior.

"This may explain." Mother Superior unfolded the article and handed it to Robert. "Czechmate found it in the Portland paper, in the waiting room."

"Oklahoma Senator in Alleged Same-Sex Relationship," Robert read. "Reliable sources in Oklahoma City report today that Senator Rosemary Fairchild, a staunch supporter of the family-values agenda of the religious right, has been sexually involved for the last two years with a former legislative aide. The revelation comes as a surprise to national and state political leaders. Throughout her career, Senator Fairchild has been a champion of conservative causes, including legislation defining marriage as a union between a man and a woman. She currently serves as honorary chair of Christians for a Better America, a religious lobbying group.

"The alleged partner, Jeannette Thomas of Tulsa, divulged her story to Robin Smith, senior political reporter of *The Oklahoman*. The relationship is said to have ended several months ago. Ms. Thomas gave no reason why she disclosed the information at this time. The paper has verified the accuracy of her story.

"A spokesperson for the senator neither confirmed nor denied the report. Senator Fairchild will hold a press conference at her Oklahoma City office tomorrow at 10 a.m."

Robert looked at Mother Superior. "Wow!"

"She let him down. Big time. That article is three days old. Her news conference was yesterday. She didn't deny it."

"He needed a target for his anger and frustration."

"Me. Classic transference. We've been sparring for months. Do you remember what he said? Right before you caned him?"

"I don't recall."

"He said he would make me pay for what I'd done. I didn't understand at the time. It's still speculation, but it answers some questions. When I talked to the sheriff's deputy this morning, I showed him the article and shared my theories."

"It certainly gets at a motive."

"He thought so, too. They're talking to Preacher right now."

The door opened. Suzanne entered, followed by an orderly with a large tray. He set it on the bedside table and removed the cover. One plate held several strips of bacon and a heaping pile of scrambled eggs. The other contained a stack of pancakes, covered in blueberry compote.

Robert grabbed the fork and shoveled in a large bite of eggs. "Suzanne, I could kiss you for this." He picked up a stick of bacon between his fingers and bit off half with a satisfied purr.

"Ten minutes ago you didn't need an excuse to kiss me."

Socrates guffawed. "He's been hitting on you?"

"He's an operator." Suzanne watched as Robert devoured a wedge of pancake. "I thought he cared, but he was using me to get food."

Robert inhaled another giant portion. He smeared blueberry on his cheek, but didn't stop to wipe it off.

Suzanne added, "It's such a shame. He's so sexy in that gown."

Robert cringed at the dig. "That reminds me. Where are my clothes?"

"The police took what you had on. Evidence." Suzanne added, "Your other stuff smelled so bad it went to the laundry to be fumigated."

"They couldn't have been that bad. I only wore them one day." He asked her politely, "Can you get me a robe? I need to make a visit."

"We usually have something in lost and found. Just where are you going? The supermarket?"

Robert stopped eating. "I need to talk to Preacher."

Mother Superior exploded. "Are you crazy? That bastard tried to kill you!"

He crunched another slice of bacon. "This may sound weird, but I need to find out what made him come at me with a knife. I thought we were friends. Not close, mind you. But at least we tolerated each other."

"Snakes, I don't think this is a good idea. The police have guarded him since he got here. They may not let you in."

Robert drained the orange juice and attacked the eggs again. Suzanne shook her head in amazement. "I never thought I'd pay to watch somebody eat, but you're worth the price of admission."

He swallowed the mouthful of eggs. "There's another reason I want to see him. I think he's lonely."

Socrates was incredulous. "Are you out of your gourd? If he is, he brought it on himself. Let him stew in his own juice."

"Why should yew cayah?"

"Guys, think about it. He's by himself, all banged up in a strange hospital. No family. No friends. I have all you guys. The only visitors he has are the police, and they're about to put him in jail." He looked at Suzanne. "Is he your patient?"

"No. That's Jaynie's section."

"See?" Robert grinned. "He didn't even get the good-looking nurse." Suzanne blushed.

"What do you hope to achieve by this?" Mother Superior asked.

"I'm not sure. But I have to try." He sucked down another bite. "Baseball lady, do you remember John Rocker?"

"That racist dork! I've been trying to forget him ever since he shot off his stupid mouth about New Yorkers."

"I know. He pitched for the Braves, but most Atlantans wanted to run him off, right after he popped his cork."

Socrates intervened. "Snaky, for the last five months I've tried to understand how you think. But I'm clueless. What does that loudmouthed prick have to do with you and Preacher?"

"You remember our conversation in North Carolina? You said that regardless of size or limitations, all living things are still in the game."

"I was talking about plants. Not assholes or maniacs."

"When everybody was screaming for Rocker's head, two people tried to talk sense into him. Andrew Young and Henry Aaron."

"Andrew Young of the United Nations?"

"Yup. And Hammerin' Hank of the Hall of Fame. Rather than isolate him, they tried to bring him back into the community. Back into the game."

"It didn't work."

"The important thing, Soc, is they gave enough of a damn to try. They didn't write him off."

"You think you can convince Preacher of the error of his ways?"

"I have no illusions. But I want to give it a shot."

Mother Superior shook her head. "You've been out of character ever since he attacked. Totally unpredictable."

"Except for breakfast. Dat vass totally predictable."

"I watched Angie die. In spite of that, I never really thought it would happen to me. Until yesterday. I came face-to-face with my own mortality. My life's assumed a special clarity. And urgency. It's a cliché, but today's the first day of the rest of my life. And the first day of the rest of Preacher's life, too."

A man in uniform appeared at the door. "Come on in, Sheriff."

The others turned to face the officer. "Hello again," Mother Superior said. "We warmed him up. He's waiting for you." She looked at Robert. "We need to go to work. Take care of your business. But make sure the guard's there when you talk to him."

Robert knocked on the door. The deputy opened it and motioned for him to enter. The space, spotless and well lit, mirrored his room down the hall. No longer tethered to the IV, he shuffled to a bedside chair. Preacher's damaged shoulder rested on several pillows. A second stack supported his swollen knee. In spite of the cushions, he looked uncomfortable.

"Morning, Preacher."

He stared indifferently. "What do you want?"

"I'd like to talk. If it's okay." Preacher did not acknowledge his request. Robert sat down. He fingered the belt on his borrowed cotton robe. "How are you?"

Preacher shrugged. The movement pained his shoulder, and he gritted his teeth. With another visible twinge, he repositioned his throbbing knee.

"Preach, I didn't want to hurt you. But you were so strong. So, so ... possessed. I couldn't stop you any other way. And I had to stop you."

Preacher's eyes, full of fire during the battle, were now vacant. "Is that what you came here to say?"

"No. I need to know something. I need to know why you, a God-fearing Christian, would try to kill somebody. Break the sixth commandment. Why?"

Preacher winced at the words. Rather than look at Robert, he stared out the window. He responded meekly, "I don't know. I really don't." He shook his head. "In my whole life I've never been taken over like that. Voices were screaming inside my head. 'Go get her! Go get her! Make it right!'"

Robert pursued the opening. "This has something to do with Senator Fairchild, doesn't it?"

At the sound of her name, Preacher moaned in disgust. "That bitch!" The familiar red hue reappeared across his cheeks and temples. "I was psyched about that Vermont campaign. Then she cuts me off at the knees."

"The Senator's not God. She's human, like you and me. Perhaps your expectations of her were too high."

"Maybe my expectations of God were too high."

"You don't mean that, Preach. God doesn't fail us. We fail ourselves." Robert hesitated. "But maybe they were the wrong expectations."

Preacher almost smiled. "Ever since we met you've said I have the wrong ideas."

"You are always so dead certain about everything. All I've tried to do is suggest alternatives."

"Well, I'm not dead certain about anything anymore. You happy now?" With his good hand he reached for the glass by the bed and sucked a big mouthful of water through the straw.

"Can I make another suggestion?"

"I don't see you shutting up on your own," he muttered. "And I can't get out of this bed to make you."

"You ought to get selfish."

Preacher was caught off guard. "What do you mean?"

"It's time to take care of yourself. For several years you've listened to other people. Followed their directions. And you've concentrated on saving other people's souls."

"That's my ministry."

"Forget about them. Concentrate on your own soul. Periodically you have to reexamine yourself. And your relationship with God. I found that out the hard way. Believe me, my balloon burst as loud as yours. As far as I was concerned, He didn't give a shit about me."

"I've never said that."

"But you have doubts. Or lower expectations. If you feel that way, should you be out evangelizing? 'The Lord my God is a half-assed God.' How many converts will that get you?"

This time he smiled. "You have a point."

"Then straighten it out. You've been standing behind a stained-glass curtain. Come out into the brutal sunlight."

"Do you still feel that God doesn't give a shit?"

"It takes time. The path I've walked for years and years isn't where He wants me anymore."

"So you changed."

"Actually, I'm just beginning to change. It's not easy. Half the time I kick and scream. But the good thing about fighting is I stay in contact. I don't walk away."

"How? How did you stay in contact?"

"I pray. I read the Bible. I force myself to do it. It's hard to be reverent and attentive when you're pissed off. Or disillusioned. But you have to stay engaged."

"I made a profession of faith years ago. I gave Him my soul. I thought that sealed the deal."

"Preach, He gave you your soul. It's always been His. When you give it back, you don't do it all at once. You give a little each day."

"Is this some of your dollar-store theology?"

"Not theology. Just common sense. Life's a work in progress. Like a thru-hike. Your profession of faith comes on Springer Mountain. Not on Katahdin. As you move north you get wiser. When you hiked on the AT in Georgia, you made mistakes you've never repeated since. And you understand stuff now in Maine you couldn't even fathom back in North Carolina. Life's the same, just a longer journey. You grow and learn until you reach the big Katahdin in the sky."

Preacher looked at the deputy. "You can talk about Katahdin. I'm going to jail. I won't take any journeys for a long time."

"I just talked to the sheriff. I told him I don't want to press charges."

Preacher looked at him incredulously. "Why?"

"I'm oriented on the future. I want to get on with my life. I want you to get on with yours. There are no scores to settle."

Preacher pointed to Robert's bandaged arm. "You're not even mad?"

"Being mad requires energy. I'm saving mine for the last hundred miles. And for life after the trail. You know, this whole situation reminds me of a sign I saw in front of a church in Georgia."

"What did it say?"

"Every saint has a past, and every sinner has a future."

"That's good. But even if you drop charges, they won't let me walk."

"No. You're not off the hook. The DA will prosecute. But he might seek a lesser charge than assault with a deadly weapon. You got a lawyer?"

"My dad lined one up. He's supposed to see me today."

"I'm guessing if you show remorse and agree to some form of rehab, you get a suspended sentence. You don't have any prior felonies, do you?"

Preacher managed a weak laugh. "Just two speeding tickets. But I still can't believe you went to bat for me. What's the catch?"

"Only that you get selfish, like I asked. Do some real self-evaluation. You still want to be a preacher?"

"I think so. Yes."

"Well, most preachers don't go around wielding a lethal weapon. Their business is saving lives, not taking them. You have a deep reservoir of anger inside. Before you can preach, you need to drain it.

Remember, Paul spoke of being consumed by passions. You need to address those."

"You sound like my mom. She lectured me over the phone. Said I can't go through life as an avenging angel. Like Saul of Tarsus, I have to find another role." He repositioned his leg. "She's right. You're right. I'll start working on it when I get out of here."

"You should always listen to your mom. And I think she would tell you not to wait. Start now."

"Start how?"

Robert stood up and toddled to a small chest near the bed. He opened the top drawer. "Just as I thought. The Gideons." He placed the Bible in Preacher's good hand. "Not the first time we've done this."

Preacher propped the Bible on his abdomen and opened it with his right hand. The bold type in the top right-hand corner of the page read EXODUS.

"Don't read from the Old Testament."

"Why not? You said concentrate on God. He's in here."

"Concentrate on the God who is flesh and lives among us. Read the Gospels. Matthew, Mark, Luke, and John. That's where He is." He helped Preacher flip to the New Testament.

Preacher lapsed into defensiveness. "Are you going to tell me how to read the Bible? That I can't believe what it says to me?"

"No. But I will suggest the Konnarock interpretation."

"What's that supposed to mean?" Preacher remained wary. "Nobody on that crew read Bibles. Except for me."

"Reading the Bible is like building trail."

"The Gospel according to Sidehill!" Preacher scoffed. "You've invented a new apostle!"

"When you read a passage the first time, you encounter some duff."

"Give me a break." Preacher held up the Bible. "This is the tenth chapter of Mark. There are no decayed leaves stuck to the pages."

"It's the Word of God expressed in the words of man. Because a man wrote it down, it's got extraneous stuff in it. Duff. And if you don't clean out all that insubstantial matter, if you build your life on it, it can wash away. Your faith will slip down the mountain."

"How can you presume to pass judgment on the words of God? To toss them away like duff?"

"It's not easy. Getting rid of duff is hard work. Makes my back ache just thinking about it. But duff on the trail is not up to AT standards. Likewise, the standard for reading the Bible is the life of Jesus. Everything needs to be interpreted through His witness. He helps you separate the duff from the soil. And believe me, it takes more work to figure that out than it does to toss duff down the hill."

"I don't like your analogy. There are too many stumbling blocks."

"Stumbling blocks? Now you're talking rocks and roots."

"Rocks and roots?"

"Yeah. If you don't get those out of your life path, you'll trip all over them." Robert bent over the Bible. "Like here, in Mark 10. The story of the rich young man. Jesus told him to sell all he had and give it to the poor. He couldn't do it. He stumbled. Tell me, when you made your profession of faith, did you give away everything you owned?"

"No."

"Let me guess. You kept your DVD and your cell phone."

"Be serious, Snakes."

"So you're really not saved then?"

"I can't earn my salvation. Christ did that for me."

"Exactly. But in gratitude you give all your stuff away. That's what He said to the rich young man."

"Did you give all your money to the poor?"

"No. I stumbled all over that root. But that's my point. The story of the rich young man is an impediment to our smug little march toward heaven. Just like rocks and roots. We have to take our Pulaskis and chop and dig until we figure out what God is saying."

"And what is that?"

"In this case He's saying all the things that are important to us, like status, position, and wealth, are insignificant when compared to His purpose. Remember the disciples arguing over who would have the place of honor in the kingdom?"

"They missed the point."

"And we do too. We haven't grubbed enough in those rocks and roots."

"That's all we have to look forward to? A lifetime digging in the dirt?"

"You ever hear of Sisyphus?"

"No. Wait. Is he the guy condemned to roll the stone up the hill?"

"He's the one. Every time he got close to the top, it rolled back down. He started all over again. There was no hope for him."

"But there's hope for us?"

"Yes. Because after we dig through the duff and grub out the rocks and roots, God leads us to the mineral soil. And on that foundation we can build a life that will last."

"The foundation is the life of Jesus Christ."

"That's why I said start with the Gospels. Find what Jesus would do. Find the mineral soil."

"So you don't read the Old Testament anymore?"

"Preacher, I read it all the time. But I read it in the light of what's in those four gospels." Robert felt unsteady, and he slumped awkwardly back into the chair. "I'm tired. I need to get back to my room."

"When will they release you?"

"Three days. When I get stronger."

Preacher took a deep breath. "Dancing Snakes, I'm sorry I did this to you."

"It's okay. We're all gonna be okay."

"Do you forgive me?"

Robert was taken aback. "Yeah. Sure. I forgive you. But you really need to ask forgiveness from God."

"I have. And I will again."

Robert stood up. He waited for his head to clear. "I'm going back to my room for a nap."

"Thanks for coming. I always enjoy talking to you."

Robert extended his palm. Preacher grasped it firmly with his one good hand.

"By the way, Preach, there's mineral soil in the Old Testament also."

"Oh really? Where?"

"Micah 6:8."

"I'll check it out."

Robert walked slowly to the door. The guard opened it for him. He turned around. Preacher was flipping pages in the Bible.

"Preach, keep going north."

Chapter 24

i thank You God for most this amazing day
for the leaping greenly spirits of trees
and a blue true dream of sky, and for everything
which is natural which is infinite which is yes
e.e. cumming

"Hi, Mandy."

"Dad! How are you?"

"The hospital just released me."

"A day early! You sure you're okay?"

"Actually, they kicked me out. I wore out my welcome."

"My father? Pushy? Never! So what's next? You'll take it easy, I hope."

"We hike tomorrow."

"Nnnnngh!" Her grumble rattled his eardrum.

"I'm glad you approve." Robert changed the subject. "How's the baby?"

"Kicking me, several times a day. Just like its grandfather."

"Sweetheart, relax. I have two first-rate nurses with me every step of the way. Socrates volunteered to carry my food. I'm Tom Sawyer. They're gonna paint my fence all the way to Katahdin."

"Promise me you won't overdo it."

"I promise. But it's only a hundred miles. One or two big mountains, and then nothing major until Katahdin. And that'll be a slack-pack. Besides, I want to finish with my friends."

"When will I see you?"

"One of the reasons I called. After I summit, I come back to Greenville. For the doctor's final checkup. I plan to rent a car and spend a few days sightseeing."

"You're having a hard time giving this up, aren't you?"

"Maine's a beautiful place, Mandy. It grows on you. You and Steven and the baby need to come up here."

"How long will you stay?"

"I don't know. I promised my nurse I'd take her to dinner."

"Dad! Is this a date?"

"Yes."

"Good for you."

"You really mean that?"

"Well, it's been almost a year. I can see where you'd want to get back in circulation."

"Your mom will always be the love of my life."

"I know that."

"But I'm ready to explore other possibilities."

"Is she pretty?"

"I think so. Soc says she's 'hot.'"

"Wow! What's her name?"

"Suzanne. I'm guessing she's at least ten years younger than I am."

"You cradle robber!"

"I'm compensating. Your mom gave me grief about being younger than she was."

"You will let me know how your date goes."

"I'll be just as communicative as your brother. By the way, I just talked to Rob."

"He's okay?"

"As usual, he didn't say much. Except the wedding is December 1."

"Good. They set the date. Now we can make reservations."

"All three of you are going?"

"That's the plan. And speaking of plans, when are you coming to see us?"

"The week after Labor Day. You still want me?"

"Not if you bring a new wife."

"What about a girlfriend?"

"Dad!"

"Just kidding."

Mandy grew serious. "What about Preacher?"

"He walked yesterday, on crutches. And his parents are here."

"What about the charges?"

"His lawyer is bargaining with the DA. He sees the judge next week."

"Dad, I know you believe you did the right thing. But for my sake, and for your grandchild, please stay away from him."

"I'll probably never see him again. But if I do, he won't hurt me. We reached an understanding."

She sighed through the phone. "Dad, this is embarrassing. I absolutely have to go to the bathroom."

"Pregnant women and dirty old men have something in common! Just one more favor and I'll let you go. I called Warren the other day."

"How's Grandpa?"

"Got the recording. He and Elizabeth apparently are on vacation. Can you call him for me?"

"Sure."

"Tell them what happened. And tell him that stick saved my life. The next time I see them I'm taking them out for a fancy dinner."

"Okay. But I really need to go."

"I love you, Tinklebell. I'll call you from Millinocket. Bye-bye."

—◊—

The trail to the lean-to ventured to the left through rocks, roots, and needles. Puffing heavily, Robert stopped at the junction.

"What's the matter?" Mother Superior inquired.

"Breathing hard, that's all. More adrenaline than anything else. I'd like to go back there. I never signed the register."

"You should do that."

They walked the short distance to the Long Pond Stream Lean-to. Robert wondered what his reaction would be when he viewed the battleground. The conflict remained a surreal blur, and he did not wish to revive its irrational intensity. He hoped instead to enjoy the beauty of the spot, as if the incident never occurred. As they closed in, he heard voices. Two hikers were loading packs on the shelter platform. They flashed twin masses of red hair, an instantly familiar adornment.

"I'll be damned. Raggedy Anton and Andy!"

"It's the Snaky One!"

"Last I saw you two was what, back in the Smokies?"

"Are you all right? The word is somebody sliced you up. The register over there is full of stories about you. And your stick. Old Hickory, right?" Andy eyed the pole. "Can I have its autograph?"

Raggedy Anton noticed his arms. "My God! Look at those candy stripes!"

"Aren't they pretty? Had to spend a few days at the hospital in Greenville. But I'm on the trail again. Headed for the big 'K.' Say, do you know these folks?"

"Don't think so."

"Okay. Guys, this is Raggedy Anton and Andy. We spent a cold, wet morning way back on Blood Mountain. Got out of the weather at the store in Neel Gap." He pointed in order to each of his friends. "This is Mother Superior, Czechmate, Southern Bell, and Socrates. You met him briefly going up Cheoah and at Mountain Mama's. We've been more or less together since the Roan Highlands."

They exchanged greetings. Raggedy Anton approached Robert. "We figured you were finished with the AT. And back home. Then we got here last night and read about the War of the Worlds." He looked at Robert's arms again. "Nasty. Don't those sutures bother you?"

"They itch, but they're healing nicely. I can't complain. I've received more magic than anyone who ever hiked in Maine." He pointed to Mother Superior and Czechmate. "My nurses take super care of me."

Andy piped in. "This is your first day back?"

"Yeah. We got a ride from Greenville into Long Pond Stream this morning. I came here to sign the register."

"By all means! We need to capture this part of history." He pointed behind him. "It's over there in the corner."

Robert set Old Hickory and his pack against the wall. He sat on the edge of the platform and pivoted his legs up and onto the floor. He rose to his knees and then stood up, careful not to put weight on either arm. He retrieved the spiral notebook and sat down on the edge with his feet dangling over the side. He thumbed through the pages for the first clean sheet and pulled the pen out of the sheath of metal spirals. He clicked the button to expose the point.

This is the day that the Lord has made. Let us rejoice and be glad in it. I'm a thru-hiker. Today I want to go from Long Pond Stream to Chairback Gap Lean-to. Please give me wisdom, patience, and perseverance. Thank You for letting me walk in Your world.

He swung his foot back and forth. The reciprocating motion recalled a hundred other shelters on a hundred other days. He glanced at his friends. The four talked and laughed with the two, as if they had known each other for years. Socrates admired Andy's new trekking poles. Behind them, Czechmate examined a bruise on Raggedy Anton's arm. Mother Superior rummaged through her first-aid supplies. Their instant cameraderie reminded him why he was out here.

Thank you for my family. For Angie, Mandy, and Rob. Thank you for all the strangers on the AT who have become my friends and my new family. Thank you for the magic.
Dances with Snakes.

He stood up, put the book down on the floor, and reshouldered his pack. "Okay. I'm done." He walked over to Andy. "Where you guys going tonight?"
"Chairback."
"We're headed there too."
"Before we leave, can I get a picture? In front of the lean-to, with your stick."
"Why don't I stand there with Old Hickory and all my friends? Hey, guys. You too, Raggedy Ass. Get over here."
After Andy took the group pictures, Mother Superior led the seven down the lean-to trail to the AT. Over her shoulder she hollered at Robert. "You ready for the wilderness?"
"I'm a thru-hiker. This is what I do. And this time I don't need dancing girls."

—⚡—

Mother Superior pointed to a brown rectangular marker. "That's it!"
"Der sign?"

Stained-Glass Curtain

"Right over there!" The sign, mounted on a sawhorse, was anchored in the high point of the rocky ridge. Against the deep blue sky, the silhouette seemed out of place.

Robert recalled the Indian legend of the wrathful god, Pamola, who resided on Katahdin. He was so angered when humans violated the sanctity of his mountain that he destroyed them. The goal Robert had pursued through years of dreams and months of toil was within his grasp, but he felt like an intruder, a candidate for divine retribution.

"C'mon! Hurry up!" Mother Superior's exhortation spurred him to overcome his misgivings.

They had labored mightily to scale four thousand feet of countless rocks and boulders, but the sight of the summit opened a reserve of untapped energy. They quickened their pace and surrounded the marker. The quintet stood reverently at the shrine. The white letters on the brown boards spelled out what each had hiked over two thousand miles to read: "Katahdin. Baxter Peak, elevation 5,267 ft. Northern Terminus of the Appalachian Trail."

"Ah really don't know what to say. Except we are finally heyah."

Socrates leaned to the sign and planted a kiss on the letter K. He turned to the others. "A final high five?"

"No. This deserfs something bigger. Ve should do a high-ten."

They extended ten arms skyward and joined fifty fingers at the top of the pyramid. Mother Superior, the shortest, strained on tiptoes to amalgamate. After a few moments of silence, Socrates let out a loud whoop. The others echoed his ecstasy. They locked arms in a circle and hopped up and down. Robert wondered if Pamola would interfere with the celebration. He hoped he would accept their ritual as a form of tribute. The stomping continued until they were out of breath.

Robert found himself next to Mother Superior. In the joy of the moment, she grasped his hands. "Snakes, I have to say this. You're the nicest man I have ever known."

Robert broke into a wide grin. "And so are you."

She inhaled as if terribly offended and retaliated with a playful roundhouse. He dodged the blow and encircled her in a bear hug. He lifted her off the ground and swung her to and fro. "Careful!" she warned. "You'll pop a stitch."

Robert ignored her admonition. He looked her straight in the eye and kissed her fully on the lips. She was startled at first, but then returned the caress. The others roared in approval. Laughing, he set her down on the ground.

"Iss my turn!" It was all he could do to stand up straight before Czechmate leaped on him. Intertwined, they shared an enthusiastic kiss. He set her down gently and pushed a wispy strand of blonde hair out of her eyes. "Why did we wait so long to do that again?"

She stepped back, laughing. "I vas here! Vere were you?"

Her caprice jump-started his wishful thinking, but only for a moment. He recognized the tease. "Damn! I was never good at these games."

"On the contrary, you are fery goot at dem."

"Thanks. You and Katahdin have made my day." He looked at Southern Bell. "I'm on a roll. Can I have a kiss?"

Socrates stepped between them. "Not until I have mine first." He sounded more serious than celebratory. He pulled her gently toward him and tenderly stroked the side of her cheek. "We did it, sweetheart."

"Yes we diyud. We hiked the whole damn thing."

"I love you."

Southern Bell gasped. "Say that again."

"I love you."

"Yew nevah said that befowah!"

"I'm saying it now."

She kissed him before he could make another move. They embraced for a long time. The other three applauded. Robert managed a passable whistle. Mother Superior cheered, "You go, girl!"

Finally they parted. Southern Bell grasped his shoulder. "Theyah's one thing. Reach in mah pack and git that bag with the last of his ashes."

Socrates unzipped the pocket on her day pack and pulled out the Ziploc. Only a small amount remained inside. He handed it to her. She gave it back. "No, yew do it."

"Sweetheart, he was yours."

"No. He was ours. You do it."

Socrates pointed to the marker. "Around the signpost?"

"That'ull be fine."

Socrates scattered the ashes at the base of the marker. The others watched silently. The gentle eddies spread the dust in wider concentric circles. She waited until the powder settled before she spoke. "Ah promised Ah'd bring yew to Katahdin." A tear rolled down her cheek. "And here yew are. Rest in peace, baby."

"Rest in peace, War Eagle." Socrates gave her a reassuring squeeze.

They snapped pictures for several minutes. First came shots of each, alone at the sign. Next came the various combinations: the couples, then the girls, then the boys, then Robert between the nurses, Robert with Socrates and Southern Bell. Pierre and Gabrielle, a couple from Montreal out on a day hike, arrived at the summit. They took several photos of the Fab Five together around the sign.

When the shoot was over, they admired the panorama. Fortunately, it was a "Class I" day. Only a few high clouds, blown about by a light breeze, marred the blue. The view was astonishing. The unspoiled Maine landscape spread in all directions. The dark green blanket of forest was broken here and there by the clear waters of small ponds and large lakes. The sunlight shimmered off the placid surfaces and bounced a blinding reflection back to the high mountain. To the east, the jagged profile of the Knife Edge sliced through the blue sky, a narrow, serrated septum stretching from Katahdin to the basin below.

For the first time in his life, Robert could not assimilate a view. Images rushed at him, too fast and too numerous to be absorbed. The guidebook boasted that on a clear day one could see from Canada in the north to the Atlantic in the south. Robert swore that he saw the entire world, extending in a gentle curvature at the base of the horizon. He wanted to stay on Katahdin forever, to examine every facet on the thousands of gemstones yet to be discovered on the earth below.

He felt pangs of sorrow. When he walked down the mountain, his friends would depart for their distant piece of the expanse below, leaving him alone. He wished, like Joshua, to halt the heavenly bodies and freeze this moment for all time.

Whatcha thinking, Snaky?" Socrates put his arm on his shoulder.

"Good news and bad news."

"Bad news on a day like today? How's that possible?"

"I'm gonna miss you guys."

"Maybe not. Auburn's not that far down the road from Atlanta."

Southern Bell stared at him, dumbfounded. "Whut did yew just say?"

Pretending not to notice her, Socrates continued. "We'll be busy, what with Bell in vet school and me in biology. But we'll make time for a good friend who comes to visit."

"Are yew serious?"

"What, baby?"

"What yew just said?"

"I want an advanced degree, too. Doh, why don't we do this together?"

"At Auburn?"

"Well, that's where you'll be, right?"

"Yayah."

"Then that's where I am."

She embraced him joyfully, wrapping both her arms and legs around his wiry frame. "Ah love you, baby! Ah do! Ah do!"

Socrates made a face and coughed. "Air! Please, air!"

She released her constrictive hold and slid to the ground. "Ah'm sorry! Ah didn't mean to choke yew."

Socrates breathed in and out for several seconds. "Don't make me turn blue. At least not until after I meet your mother."

Southern Bell squealed and leaped on him again. "Ah don't know whut's gotten in to you, but don't stop. Pulleeze, don't stop."

He placed her back on the ground and resumed his conversation with Robert. "Really, I mean it. You'll have to come over and watch us kick Crimson Tide ass."

Bemused, Robert replied, "Whatever happened to Tarhole ass?"

"Down in Auburn, we kick Bulldog ass, Tiger ass, Razorback ass, Gator ass, Vol ass, Rebel ass. And of course the aforementioned Crimson Tide ass. Always kick Tide ass."

Southern Bell was radiant. "The leppurd has changed his spots!"

Socrates continued with Robert. "So don't say it's bad news, man. You can come see us anytime."

"Well, it still is. Mother and Matey are leaving tomorrow."

Southern Bell turned to them. "That soon?"

"Ve have to go to vork," Czechmate pouted.

Mother Superior continued. "Snakes is driving us to the airport in Bangor. That is, if he can rent a car in Millinocket. Otherwise, we are on the bus. Then we fly back to Baltimore." She looked at her watch. "I hate to say this, but it's time to head down the mountain."

"Bummer," Socrates replied. "But you're right. Let's load up."

They put on the small day packs and gathered once more at the sign. Robert patted the word "Katahdin" with his hand. "I think we should all give it a good-bye kiss."

"I already kissed the K," Socrates reminded him. "So this time, I'll kiss the D, for Duke." He leaned over and bussed the D.

Robert jabbed him on the shoulder. "Things have returned to normal. I knew you couldn't forsake your roots."

Socrates smiled. "No way, Coach K."

Southern Bell poked him from the other side. "Kick Tide ayuss. Ah shoulda known bettah than believe you."

"Love, I made some serious accommodations today. But you need to understand. I bleed blue and white forever."

"Crazies everywhere can breathe again. Now, where were we?" Robert grasped the ends of the sign with both hands and placed a gentle caress on the second A. "This is for you, Angie."

"Ah'll kiss the I, for inspeerashun. That's whut this hike has been for me. And whut yew all have been."

"You guys are taking all the good letters," Mother Superior complained. She pondered and then bent to kiss the H. "For health. I'm thankful we had good health on the hike. I hope we all keep it."

Czechmate bent over and pecked the N. "Iss for all the nurses. Eferywhere." She smiled at Robert. "Including your friend in Greenville."

Robert thought for a moment. "We didn't kiss one A and the T. But it's okay. The AT will always be here for us."

"You got that right."

Socrates took the first steps down the mountain. The others followed. They walked for a few moments before he stopped. "Snaky, I almost forgot. What's the good news?"

"Right out there in front of you." Robert waved his hand at the earth below. "Look at all that space. Somewhere in that big world, there's a place for me. And a place for everybody else, too."